2018

The stories of "bluff, leathery, riotous realities" in this book are riveting.
Maybe they'll move us into our own acts of compassion.
– **Luci Shaw,** Writer in Residence, Regent College

I treasure books that make me laugh and books that make me cry.
This novel by Tim Stafford did both. It offers unsentimental hope:
the true craziness of the gospel.
– **John Wilson,** Editor, *Books & Culture* (1995-2016)

The thing I love most about these characters is that they seem real. They are ordinary,
everyday people, with the same flaws I observe all around me--and in myself.
And now these characters are in my mind, and I can't quit thinking about them.
– **Joyce Denham,** Author, *Dragon Slayers* and *Secrets of the Ancient Manual Revealed*

An emotional roller-coaster ride that is a must-read for anyone concerned about the
growing problem of homelessness in America – and the challenges, spiritual and
otherwise, that face those trying to do something about it."
– **Paul Gullixson,** Editorial Director, *The Press Democrat*

Many of us, walking down a city street, try to avoid the eyes of the homeless.
Those Who Hope *allows us to look in the eyes of these men and see lives with humor,*
dignity, sorrow, and even joy.
– **Dean Anderson,** Author, Bill the Warthog Mysteries

Tim Stafford's beautifully layered story will keep you reading, but long after you finish, it
will keep you thinking."
– **Scott Bolinder,** Executive Director, Institute For Bible Reading

I find my thoughts returning, as the days pass, to all the novel's characters. Here are
characters real enough to be lost and, in good time, found.
– **Peter Lundstrom,** Author, *God: The Short Version*

The descriptions in scene after scene just grabbed me. A sharp-eyed view from a master
storyteller into a world of addiction, loneliness and hope.
– **Robert Digitale,** Author, *Horse Stalker* and *Blaze and Sky-fire*

Those Who Hope

A Novel

by Tim Stafford

Also by Tim Stafford

FICTION

A Thorn in the Heart

The Stamp of Glory

Sisters

The Law of Love

Birmingham

NON-FICTION

Love, Sex and the Whole Person

The Friendship Gap

The Student Bible

Knowing the Face of God

As Our Years Increase

That's Not What I Meant

Never Mind the Joneses

Shaking the System

Surprised by Jesus

Personal God

Miracles

The Adam Quest

Those Who Hope

A Novel

by Tim Stafford

Franklin Park Press

The characters, names and events as well as all places, incidents, organizations and dialog in this novel are either the products of the writer's imagination or are used fictitiously.

ISBN 1977574904

Visit the author's website at timstafford.wordpress.com

Cover and book design:

Mario Zelaya, Zelaya Designs, Santa Rosa CA

for Michael Navin

Lord, the LORD Almighty, may those who hope in you not be disgraced because of me.

— Psalm 69:6

1

The Drug Test

✧

Jake Dorner's boss, Kent Spires, had paused in the clear morning chill to greet four men clustered near the Sonoma Gospel Mission's main door. Jake joined him, shaking hands. Reflexively he tried to assess all four, his eyes scrutinizing faces and postures and clothes. Gerald and Damien he knew; they had left the program in the last year. Gerald had come court-ordered, and left after 30 days when the charges were dropped. He was a meth user—smoked it. From the looks of him, he still did. His eyes had tiny folds of skin all around the eye sockets, and he wouldn't quite look Jake in the eye, though he was friendly enough.

Damien, Jake remembered, had joined the program in a cold, biting rainstorm, the kind of miserable weather that often inspired the desire to change. Was that December last year? Damien was 45 or 50 years old and liked to talk, on and on and on about his two sons, who were successful, apparently—had jobs and paid their own rent. Damien was proud of them. He never really bought the program but he stayed in the house, laboring through the process, all the way to the third phase. By then summer had come and the weather was warm. Damien discovered that he wasn't an alcoholic, he just liked to drink. Apparently he still did: a discernible whiff of alcohol came off him.

The other two men did not offer names. One was short and jumpy, like a terrier, and he wore layers of clothes: at least one sweater, a Dodgers jacket, and an ancient overcoat, open and flapping in the morning air. He was almost certainly sleeping rough but that didn't necessarily mean he was an addict. The other was an African-American with smooth, dark skin and a lovely, sleepy face. He might just be down on his luck. He might just be passing by and saying hello to a friend. Hard to tell.

Jake automatically thought of people on the street as candidates for the ten-month drug and alcohol rehab program he oversaw at the mission. If they were addicts, he wanted to invite them in. He wished with all his heart that someone had done that for him.

"You guys know, any time you want help, you can come inside. We're there for you."

"Why would we need help?" Damien asked, and winked broadly.

"Well, for example, suppose you wanted to quit drinking, Damien. That's what we're here for."

"All right, I'll keep that in mind," Damien said with a smile.

Jake could invite, but there was never any serious discussion of the program out here. Nearly everybody knew nearly everybody, at least to nod, and they all understood that there is no changing anybody else's mind for them. That was the creed of the street, if there was any: each one to their own way. The mission was part of the landscape of the street, and Jake and Kent were part of the mission, just as these men with their layered clothes and weathered faces were part of the street. They had their parts to play, and no hard feelings.

The weather in Sonoma County is good more days than not, and this May day the morning fog had disappeared early from the sky, leaving a blue expanse so brilliant it seemed to shimmer, like the pearling inside an abalone shell. What a beautiful day, Jake thought. He was trying to remember to give thanks for everything, even the expected. It did not come naturally to him. Growing up, his family had never taught him any notion of gratefulness. It was simply not in their vocabulary, and at any rate he always found himself surprised that he had anything to be grateful for.

The mission stood on 6th Ave., a gray stucco expanse with its first-floor windows covered up and painted over. It was an ugly brute of a building, its only décor the neon "Jesus Saves" sign jutting out near the second-story roofline.

Jake and Kent were standing on the street because they had just escorted Buddy Grace, a real estate developer, from Jake's upstairs office. Grace had wanted to talk to them about plans to develop the neighborhood. He had intimated—as though he were announcing a lottery winner—that he wanted to buy the mission property for an excellent price, or build them a newer, better place in another location. He had seemed to grow larger and more energized as he spoke about it.

It surprised them both, the idea that a developer had this building in his thoughts. It made you look at it as though you had never seen it. Back in Jake's office, Kent took a seat and asked softly what Jake thought of Grace's offer.

"He didn't mention a price," Jake said.

"I think he was just getting a feel for us."

"Then I'd say a new building sounds good. With a roof that doesn't leak."

"The roof is leaking?" Kent said. "Again?"

"Not again. It never stopped. We can't find where it's coming from."

"We need a new roof."

"Exactly. With a new building under it."

Like Jake, Kent had a full beard, but he was smaller and softer in body and manner. Jake looked like a lumberjack, and his bluntness fit in naturally with homeless people. He had been one of them not so long ago. Kent's way was subtler. He had nothing large or brassy about him, he fumbled and stuttered and seemed embarrassed by his own skin. That was entirely deceptive, as Jake knew as well as anyone. Kent had run the rehab program at one time; now he had moved up, to work in the main office on Berger Avenue a mile away.

Kent smiled softly and shook his head, as though in wonder. "This old place."

"You don't deal with it like I deal with it." The response contained a hint of resentment. Jake would tell anyone that he owed Kent his life. When Jake had been completely stuck in addiction and loss, Kent had helped him get on the right path and, for that matter, had hired him for this job. But Kent forgot what the place was like, and the problems that came with it.

Kent's normal response to a challenge was subdued and humble. "No, that's true. Not any more. Still."

"You don't want to move? Why not?"

Kent hesitated a moment before saying, "You know, I had your job for a long time."

"I know."

"So I understand where you are coming from. But I don't feel right about leaving this corner. I have this feeling that we don't have permission to leave. It could make sense financially, but...."

Jake nodded and tried to dismiss the subject from his mind. He was a practical man, and he knew that the building was outside his purview. He ran the program. He took responsibility for 30 addicts and alcoholics who lived in the building as part of the drug and alcohol rehab program, plus the 50 or 60 homeless guests who ate and slept here on a temporary basis every day. That was quite enough to worry about. He wouldn't take on real estate.

"Want to stay around?" he asked Kent as a way to change the subject. "We are drug testing today." He wouldn't argue about the building, but he would like Kent to experience the program again—to feel the stress and the failure. It had been years since Kent had witnessed a drug test. He raised money and handled PR, which were crucial to their survival, but Jake felt that Kent had left him behind in order to do them.

"Do you need help?" Kent asked. He would come if he were really needed.

"No, we have it covered. I thought you might be interested in seeing what goes down."

"I've seen it."

"Not for a long, long time," Jake said.

"I haven't forgotten," Kent said. "It's always a moment of truth."

The mission had loudspeakers throughout the building, which Jake used to call all program members to the chapel. This was a high-ceilinged room with banks of fluorescent lights suspended on chains. The only decoration came from two maroon felt banners that hung above the platform like twin bruises—Scripture verses spelled out with fat white letters. Green plastic chairs were arranged along the perimeter of the room; the stained carpet might have come out of an old movie theater. It was as plain and ugly as a room could be, but Jake felt a certain reverence toward it. Many of the hard things and the great things happened in it.

The men filing in were mostly young, in their 20s or 30s. They swaggered to their seats wearing jeans or Bermuda shorts, cowboy shirts with bright metal buttons or other effusions of style. The program did not allow T-shirts or sleeveless vests; otherwise they were free to wear what they liked, and they did. They found their clothes at the mission thrift store, and took great interest in them. Jake stood in the middle of the room watching as they jostled one another and slapped hands, as loose as a pack of dogs. There was nothing melancholy about this group.

It had felt different when he joined the program years before. He had hated the mission then, finding it dirty, depressing and hopeless. As he remembered it, the men had been miserably embattled, and himself more than anyone. Knowing that it was his last hope didn't make him despise it any less. Nowadays he didn't like to return to that time in his thoughts. His past could still leap out of the shadows and grab him, if he looked at it too much.

Whatever the past, the program belonged to him now.

"Most of you know what this is about," Jake said in a deep, rough voice that demanded notice. "For those of you who are new, understand that we do testing for everybody's good. The last thing any of you need is to be around somebody who is using.

"It's just a test. Everybody is treated the same. Nobody is pointing fingers or snitching. If you aren't using substances you have absolutely nothing to worry about. If you are, I hope for your sake that the test detects that. It's always best to deal with the truth. Your enemy is not the test and it's not the men administering the test. Your enemy is addiction.

"This program exists for you. We are here for you. There's no other reason for me to show up in the morning, except to help you. If you get caught we don't hold anything against you. There's no blaming. But as you know, if you use, you choose to leave the program. We are not choosing to dismiss you. In fact we don't want any of you to leave. You choose to leave by your decision to use. You can come back in 72 hours, and if you pass the drug test, you can make a fresh start. That's always the offer. I hope none of you has to do that, but if you do, be aware that we are still here for you.

"We'll call you out of class, one or two at a time. Nobody leaves the building until we are done. Does anybody have a question?"

Jake and his assistant Knox Johnson set up in two staff offices on the corridor behind the front desk, meeting the men as they were summoned in pairs. Knox was a lanky, loose-jointed jet-black man who had come to the mission two years before, completely wasted on alcohol. At first Jake thought he was brain damaged—he couldn't talk in a straight sentence—but his mind came back as he went through the program. He had been named Assistant Program Director six months ago.

They took the samples in a bathroom just down the hall. The men acted lighthearted as they went off with their little cups, making jokes about their aim. Under the surface there were nerves.

At one time Jake had been prone to predictions. After his own conversion he had felt tremendous confidence in the program and projected every man's triumphs in a straight line upward. He had learned better. He had learned that addiction is persistent, a parasite that seems to disappear but then comes back at you out of the dark. Kent had called the test a moment of truth, but the truth could be cruel. The results came back positive far too often, sometimes with men he was sure were clean. Every time Knox appeared to tell him what had happened, Jake looked at him with apprehension. Failure was always on the threshold here. These men could break your heart.

That was the reason Jake never let up on the men in the program. He told them, "You've spent your whole life taking it easy, and look where it got you."

The first six cruised through the test without incident, and Jake felt his face begin to relax. Maybe, for once, they would all pass. He looked around Knox's office while the next pair was fetched, saw afresh the clutter and the Far Side cartoons taped clumsily to the wall, and the dust like a thin felt on the bookshelves. He would be glad to be done with this. He wanted to talk about his feelings with Knox, but he didn't trust himself to keep it positive. Knox had only been sober for a year. He was an alcoholic with a wife and three teenage kids at home. Jake didn't want to bring him down with his worries.

Daniel sat at the front desk, a proud spot because of its power. People from the street lined up to see him, asking to use the bathroom, to get a sandwich, to leave a message for somebody in the program. The volunteers all walked past him, nodding at him. Today, since they were drug testing, he could keep an eye on the men as they came back and forth with their samples. He would know who passed and who failed sooner than almost anybody.

Daniel was a bit of a peacock. He was on the short side, and self-conscious about it, but he made up for it by dressing well. His style was all his own: silk shirts buttoned to the top button; loose dress slacks, preferably in a check pattern; red tennis shoes. Since he was in phase 3 of the program he got first crack at clothes that came in as donations—and truthfully, not many of the men were interested in the clothes he wanted. He liked the attention he got when people commented on his style. One of the volunteers might say, "You are certainly looking sharp today," and he would say, "Of course."

From his swivel chair behind the glass partition Daniel could not only see the line in the mission anteroom, he got a partial view of the street. He kept track of the riff-raff, and when somebody came to the desk asking after so-and-so, he took a certain pride in being able to say if and when they had passed by. Today was busy. The sunshine brought people out of their holes, and they tended to be more sociable when they were really dry. It looked like a party on the sidewalk.

Whenever more people thronged the sidewalk, more came to the front desk. He now had a line of six people, almost out the door. He knew most of them, and knew what they wanted before they said anything. Except Kasha. She was a familiar figure at the mission, but he didn't remember her standing in line.

You couldn't miss her: she wore a brilliant pink jogging suit, made from some shiny material, and her dirty-blond hair was piled on top of her head. Kasha was quite short, and broad, and she was always talking. She was talking now, though as far as Daniel could see nobody was listening to her.

He kept an eye on her until she made it to the front of the line. "I want an application," she said.

"For what?"

"To be a counselor."

"What?"

"To be a counselor."

"I don't have any application for that," Daniel said.

"Well get one," Kasha said, belligerently.

"Kasha, there ain't no such thing. We don't even have counselors any more."

"You have to have counselors. You can't be a rehab center if you don't have counselors."

Daniel shrugged.

"I want an application," Kasha said. "You're discriminating. That's complete crap."

Daniel frowned and blew air out of his mouth. "Kasha, you are holding other people up. You have to move along. I don't have any application, not for counselor, not for anything."

"Then I want to talk to Jake."

"You can't talk to Jake right now, we are drug testing."

"Why should I care that you are fucking drug testing? You're not testing me. Give me an application, or go get Jake."

"I can't do that. You have to come back tomorrow if you want to talk to Jake. And it's not going to do you any good anyway. He doesn't have an application either."

Jake heard violent shouting coming from the front desk. Poking his head out of the office he saw a crowd in the reception anteroom beyond the glass window; the door to the street was open and more people were trying to get in. At the center of a crowd stood Kasha Gold, dressed in brilliant pink warm-up clothes, cursing Daniel at the front desk. He was yelling back at her through the glass window.

Jake knew Kasha. She posed as a homeless activist but he thought she was mentally ill.

He put a hand on Daniel's shoulder to get him to stop shouting, then put his face close to the glass and made his voice like steel pellets. "Kasha, you can't abuse people here. If you want to tell me calmly what you want, I'll listen to you, but you can't keep yelling like that."

She turned her tongue on him. She was saying something about an application, but she made no sense. Jake shrugged her off and addressed the knot of people crowding around her. He had a buzz saw voice and he managed to talk over Kasha's abuse. "Look, everybody, you're not helping the situation. We want you to leave, now. We can't help you under these conditions. Leave and come back later."

"I just want to use the bathroom," someone yelled, and others laughed.

"The bathroom is closed. The kitchen is not giving out sandwiches. Come back later." He turned his eyes to Kasha, whose curses had turned into an eerie scream, deafening them all.

"You go girl!" one of the men shouted in a high-pitched voice.

She had her hands levered under the glass, in the space where documents or money could be passed. She was pulling on it, apparently trying to break it. Jake turned to Knox, who was just behind him. "Call the police," he said quietly, and then turned back to Kasha.

"Give it up, Kasha. If you don't leave we'll have you arrested."

She seemed to see him for the first time. "You do that. I will bring charges against you, Jake."

"For what, Kasha?"

"Sexual assault."

"The only person assaulting anybody is you. Now shut up and leave."

Jake made an impressive figure when he was angry, his thickness and his impassivity conjuring an immovable force, a lava flow. He got Kasha's attention, purely through the power of his mouth. She looked daggers at him, then turned slowly and left, shouting threats and curses as she went. Jake ushered out the remaining spectators, then went back to drug testing. Little cups. Test strips. All in a day's work.

The police came strolling into Knox's office as though the whole thing was a joke. They knew Kasha, of course; everybody did. She had made a name suing the Salvation Army thrift store, where she had worked for a time. She claimed she had been denied promotion because of gender discrimination and then publicly slandered; the store settled out of court, nobody knew for how much but Jake heard $50,000.

The police left without promising anything, but Jake did not remain in peace for long. Kasha must have been just around the corner—why couldn't the cops find her?—for her voice came from the front desk again. She had found a stick—a medical cane, it appeared—that she was using to beat on the glass. She held the cane like a spear, aiming the point right at Daniel's head, ramming it into the glass.

"What do you want, Kasha? What on earth do you want from us?"

She did not even lift her eyes, but kept hammering on the glass. Jake wondered if she could break it.

"Kasha! What Do You Want?!"

"I want an application."

Jake was temporarily flummoxed. "For what?"

"A job, you fucking jerk-off."

"For what job?"

"Counselor. I'm experienced and fully qualified."

"Kasha, we don't have counselors. We have coaches, and they are all volunteers. Get out of here!"

"I don't care, I want a fucking application."

"You can apply to be a volunteer online. That's the only application we have. Now go, Kasha."

She continued hacking at the glass with her aluminum stick, until the window splintered with a loud noise. Daniel jumped as a foot-long piece fell in his lap. Kasha stopped hammering. "My God," she said. "The window broke. That's scary."

Jake had walked into the anteroom, and he threw his arms around her in a bear hug. The slippery polyester crackled as he grabbed her; she was soft and hard to grip. Kasha was a big woman but he was bigger; he turned her around and walked her out the door, then released her with a little nudge forward. She walked off down the sidewalk, shouting at him.

"What's she saying?" The question came from Sam Callahan, a small, pale house member, the youngest person in the program. He had come outside at the commotion, like everybody else. His eyes were wide; he looked terrified.

"She says she is unhappy with us. Everybody, get back into the house. We still have testing to do. Sam, you go back in. Nobody is going to hurt anybody."

Sam Callahan was hiding in the corridor, terrified not at the commotion Kasha made, but at his proximity to drug testing. He didn't know when his turn would come. He had never been tested before, and did not know what to expect; and he was too timid to ask any of the other men for details.

He was clean, he knew that, and he told himself that therefore he had nothing to fear. Tobacco, though? Sam had smoked a cigarette yesterday, something he never did, and he was worried sick about it. He thought he remembered hearing that tobacco was on the list of substances that would get you dismissed from the program. Somebody would know, if he could ask, but he couldn't bear to do so. To ask would be as much as to say that he was guilty.

Not that Sam loved the program so much; but he had nowhere to go. His father had sent him here and told him not to come home. He didn't know how to live on the streets. He listened carefully to the other men in the program as they talked over dinner or in the chapel before services, and he heard a lot about violence and thieves. Sam was terrified of being beaten up. You needed a dog, they said, a pit bull, to keep them off. But with a pit bull you couldn't go anywhere, not into the library or the mission or certainly into the mall.

Sam had grown up victimized; on his pale and delicate skin he had a pigmentation ailment, something he was born with that mottled his skin with spots and streaks as white as a fish belly. When the ailment was bad he looked like he had been dropped into a pool of acid. Since kindergarten, kids teased him about it, and teasing led to picking, and picking led to slaps and pinches and trips and other forms of physical harassment. Sam had no idea how to counteract that. Nothing like it had happened in the mission so far. In fact he felt the other men liked him. But he couldn't go out on the street, to sleep under bridges and encounter thieves and vagrants. The thought of it caused his mind to freeze in place.

The same police officers came again, shaking their heads when they saw the glass. "Can't you guys handle her?" one of them said to Daniel. "Look, she's a girl."

Daniel asked them whether they had ever tried to handle a demon. The police laughed.

The exchange annoyed Jake. He asked whether they had different laws for women than men. The officer immediately went cold on him. "You're welcome to press charges."

"Fine, then I want to press them."

"Go to the station. They'll give you the papers to fill out."

"Why should I go to the station? You're right here. And I asked you, do you have different laws for Kasha than everybody else? Because I think if I smashed up the front of a business you wouldn't treat it like a joke."

The second officer intervened and told Jake they would arrest Kasha if they caught her in the act.

"Yeah, that's a big help."

"Do you have a problem?"

Jake hesitated. He had a habit of going too far, which his boss Kent had warned him about more than once. You never want to get the police mad at you. He spoke more deliberately and softly. "Yeah, my window is broken. I have to get it fixed." He turned away and stared at the wall.

Funny how Kasha got his goat. He saw messed-up people every day, and fights were common, but the people causing the trouble didn't ordinarily see themselves as saints and social workers. He had first met Kasha at a county meeting for homeless providers. How Kasha got in he never knew, but he supposed that she gave a cock-and-bull story about her role as an advocate for the poor. She practically dominated the meeting, acting as though she were a spokesperson for the homeless; and she went out of her way to target him, though they had never before met. She insinuated that the mission patronized the poor. He, Jake, was the one who needed to change, not the addicts and waffle-brains who came looking for food and a bathroom. She was willing to offer a training program for him and all his staff. She, Kasha, would help him to understand the people he served. His resistance was a problem. He needed to acknowledge that. Nobody could help him until he did.

Jake hadn't given an inch, he had shot right back, but everybody else at the meeting just listened. They usually acted friendly to the mission—how could they do otherwise, knowing the services it provided the homeless?—but of course the mission's Christian base set it apart. Jake wasn't sure how the other providers would respond if they had to choose between supporting the mission and believing Kasha.

Since then, he saw Kasha regularly, as she often came by the mission for the evening meal. They usually sparred verbally. She displayed an insinuating chumminess at times. "Hey, how is my little brother?" she would ask, and nudge at him. At other times she reminded him and anyone listening how offensively he had behaved in front of all the other providers. "I'm trying to forgive you," she said in front of a crowd. "The wounds go deep when you've been treated that way."

"Whatever," he told her.

There was nothing to do but go back to drug testing. Knox went to fetch the next pair. One went off to the bathroom with Knox as his monitor. Sam Callahan was left behind, the smallest and tenderest of all the men in the program. Sam had started cocaine in middle school and graduated to opiates in high school. His skin was pale like the pelt on a bird and his frame small. He was 19. He mumbled and had a slight stutter. The guys in the program, rough and rude with each other, were instinctively protective of Sam. According to what people said, Sam had passed out and nearly died lying in a field in the dark; they said that one of his friends came back to find him and called an ambulance, which saved his life. He spent a week in intensive care and now the hospital was trying to collect the bill. Sam's parents told him he couldn't be at home any longer, apparently because they thought they would be liable for his medical bills. They put him on a bus to Santa Rosa, where an uncle met him and brought him down to the program.

Sam seemed to hover in the room like a moth, delicate and shabby. Jake knew that testing was bound to be hard for Sam and that he probably needed all his concentration just to keep breathing. Trying to talk to Sam under these circumstances would be cruel.

Knox came back with a thumbs up and then led Sam away. When he returned ten minutes later he made no gesture but looked stricken.

"Tobacco," he said.

The test identified ten substances, including nicotine; tobacco was not allowed in the program.

Jake showed nothing on his face. "All right, bring him in."

For just a flash, he thought of letting Sam off. He was by no means sure that Sam could survive outside these walls. And it was only tobacco. He had a tender spot in his heart for Sam, which he knew was not necessarily helpful to Sam.

Sam was trembling like a bird. He knew.

"Sam," Jake said in a voice that was imitation velvet, "when did you smoke?"

Sam turned an even deadlier shade of pale, like a woodland fungus. "S-s-smoke?"

"You've got nicotine in your urine, Sam. How did it get there?"

Sam looked almost absent-minded, as though he really had to switch on his brain to remember. As though he had not been thinking about it the entire time since the testing was announced.

"When did you smoke, Sam?"

"Yesterday. J-j-just a few puffs with one of the guests. I caught him smoking in the pantry, and he offered me his cigarette."

"Did you smoke the whole thing?"

"Yes."

"So not just a few puffs, Sam. It's better just to be straight. Don't add lying. Sam, it kills me to say this, but you know I have to. You have chosen to leave the program. Just like I said in the chapel. You did know the requirements, didn't you?"

Sam had the look of a man whose brain was being eaten by the larva of a tropical wasp. Jake did not want to berate him or prolong his agony with a lecture. Sam was not hearing anything.

"Knox will take you upstairs to get your things. Are we keeping anything for you? A phone?"

"No. Yes. I had a phone."

"I'll get it. You want to make a phone call?"

Sam's words came with a tape delay. He really was not processing. Was it possible he was also using, and that the tests had not picked it up?

"I could call my mother."

"Then do, right now. I hope she can help." Though he had his doubts. Nobody, neither family nor friends, had visited Sam since he joined the program.

Jake had the phone in a zip-lock bag when Sam came back down with a paper sack of clothes. "Did you get hold of your mom?"

"She said my uncle will come. He lives in Cloverdale."

"Good. Sam, it's not over. This is a bad moment, but it doesn't have to be the end. Don't forget what you've learned here. Don't forget God. He is good all the time. You are welcome to come back in 72 hours."

"But I have to start all over." He sounded as though he was on the edge of tears.

"That's true. You need to. You know why? Because you are an addict and you haven't yet learned how to live clean and sober. You know what, Sam? I'm glad you got caught. Now you have to think about why you did what you did. If you messed up while you're in the program, what would you do outside? Something has to change or you'll keep repeating the same mistakes that almost killed you, Sam. I don't want that, brother. That is the last thing I want. You know I love you, Sam."

When he released Sam out the door, he gave him a long bear hug. Sam hugged back, like a bat clinging to its perch.

Jake realized he could not think straight, not even to make small talk. Sam had undone him. He told Knox to hold off bringing more guys in.

As he sat staring at the wall he could hear Daniel and somebody else at the front desk passing the time. The beautiful day was going by outside the windowless wall. He wondered what would happen to Sam. He hoped he would come back but there were no guarantees.

He heard Daniel cursing loudly. He was amazed; he had never heard Daniel say an ugly word. Cursing was not acceptable at the mission, but Jake hesitated before rising slowly out of his chair. He did not even think of Kasha until he put his head in the door and saw her pink-suited form slamming her aluminum cane at Daniel through the open space where the window had been. Daniel let out a yelp and jumped back, holding his forearm. Kasha was leaning toward him with her cane held high like a spear when Jake grabbed her and twisted her arm behind her back. She cried out in pain, but he slapped his other hand across her mouth and said, "You're not leaving this time. You're waiting for the police."

She struggled. She tried to kick him, and she did step hard on his instep, but he hung on. Then she went limp, slumping in his arms. He let her down slowly, draping her on the floor. "You're getting yourself dirty, Kasha," he said. "That floor must be filthy."

She had begun sobbing, a disconcerting sound. He hated it. His wife was a stoic, but on the few times when she broke into tears it upset his equilibrium completely. "Kasha, shut up! Stop that!" he said, but she paid no mind. Occasionally she would flail at him as he stood over her. Wordlessly he shooed out the gawkers, then locked the street door. Daniel was watching from the hallway, along with half the house. Jake saw that Daniel was nursing his arm, and asked him how he felt.

"It's broken," he whimpered. "Hurts like hell."

"Broken? Really?" He reached out to examine it, but Daniel pulled back with a warning not to touch. Jake sent two of the house members around through the back door to wait on the sidewalk for the police. "Somebody did call the police, didn't you?" he asked the circle of faces crowding around.

Then he turned back to Kasha, who was sitting on the floor, sprawled awkwardly. "Why do you keep coming back? What is it you're looking for, Kasha?"

She looked at him viciously. Many people had given him the evil eye over the years, but this mad stare was the top.

The police came and took statements, then cuffed Kasha—who acted subdued, surprisingly—and took her away. The drug testing went on. Thankfully, no one else failed. Kasha's arrest was the subject of much conversation at dinner and chapel. Sam's demise was little remarked, and by the next morning it was all but forgotten.

2

Jake and Krystle

✧

Reggie's Hot Wheels tricycle was on the sidewalk where it was not supposed to be. Jake grabbed one handle and carried the plastic toy up to the porch of the small house they rented near the junior college. The porch was concrete, painted a dark red which flaked off like sunburned skin to show a coat of white and then cement gray underneath. Pots of pink impatiens lined the edge. The flowers were Krystle's. They were pretty, Jake could see, though he would never have thought of planting them. In his upbringing there was no place for flowers. Krystle stood at odds with his past, a fact that squeezed his heart with astonished love for her, and with grieving for all he had lost and suffered.

Jake had been raised in chaos, his father long gone, his mother a vacancy, his home invaded by uncles who did drugs and sold drugs. Krystle had grown up in a pastor's home, in a small town on the Eel River, with four brothers who were all still alive and employed and who loved to meet at holidays and play board games. When Krystle was home with them, she was happiest and most at peace.

Jake found her on the sofa, reading a story to Reggie. She looked up with a smile. Seeing her, Jake felt his whole self let down and his stomach fill with peace. Reggie squirmed out of her grasp and ran to Jake, who scooped him up and flew him around the room. Reggie never cried out but the tightness in his body told his happiness. In appearance Reggie was a smaller Jake, but he was quiet like his mother.

Krystle rose to kiss him. She was naturally graceful, like a dancer. "How was your day?"

He had to ponder the thicket of activity that had filled it. "Oh, we had an arrest. This woman Kasha... have I told you about her? No? She came to the desk three times screaming and cursing and hitting. I think she is mental. The third time she hit Daniel so hard she broke his arm. The police came to arrest her. Actually they came all three times, but they wouldn't do anything until she broke Daniel's arm."

Krystle's dark eyes were round as marbles. "She didn't hurt you?"

He shook his head, smiling. "I had to restrain her, though. I haven't told you about Kasha, huh? She is a piece of work. The police are no help; they just laugh at her. She broke the glass at the front desk, too."

To Jake, Krystle looked like a girl in an old black and white movie, with an enchanting rosebud smile. She was more complex than that image suggested, he had learned, stubborn in her own ways, and slow to forgive when someone had hurt her. Jake had to be selective about what he told her about the mission, where hurts and offenses punctuated every day.

"How did you restrain her?" she asked.

"I threw a bear hug on her."

Krystle lowered her chin, so that her eyes looked out from under her eyebrows. "You are careful, aren't you, Jake?"

"You bet. Very careful. Kasha is about your size." Which was not the whole truth: Kasha was about her height, but she probably weighed twice what Krystle did.

He had not been afraid, not in the least. Being big had its advantages. Something in the altercation had disturbed him, though, even as he spoke of it lightly. Perhaps it was that Daniel had been hurt. He was supposed to create a safe environment, and perhaps if he had dealt with Kasha more effectively, if he had put a stop to her earlier, he would have. He would need to think that through.

He looked at Krystle's elfin shape and regretted he could not talk to her about it. She became afraid for him. Perhaps that was a matter of size, too: Krystle was tiny, and physically very shy. When she visited the mission, the roughness of the men unsettled her. Which was odd, because, as Jake told her, he had been as rough as any of them, and she loved him abundantly. Krystle treasured his testimony of a transformed life, and the changes he witnessed in other men. But the actual business, the bluff, leathery, riotous realities of the men he served, was to Krystle a very foreign country, and one that could disturb her.

To change the subject he asked what she and Reggie had been doing. Then before she could respond he remembered Sam, and told her about his failing the drug test.

"Have I met Sam?" she asked.

"I don't know. He's the youngest guy in the program. And the smallest, too."

"So it hurt."

Invariably Krystle went to the place he avoided. Failure was so undisguised in drug rehab, and loss so common. Jake put his arms around her.

"It always hurts. I'm not tough enough."

"You're not tough enough?" She scoffed at that.

Reggie came and inserted himself between them. Both of them put hands on him, wrapping him into their huddle.

"It was for tobacco," Jake said. "Just stupid. One cigarette. I could have shot him." He shook his head.

For a few moments, they stood together, comforting each other. Jake remembered something else, an insignificant element of a full day.

"We had a guy come by wanting to buy the mission. A developer who is working on Railroad Square."

"Where would you go?" Krystle asked almost sleepily.

"He suggested Sebastopol Road. He would build us a new building. Kent doesn't want to move, though."

"What do you think?"

"It's up to Kent, not me. I would love to get out of that old building, though."

She looked at him with surprise. "But Jake, that old building is where you found the Lord."

"Yeah," he said. "I'd give that up for better plumbing."

In high school, Jake had been a state finalist in the discus. His teammates called him Big Man, or just Big. Thanks to sports—track, football and basketball—he stayed away from trouble, keeping a distance from his uncles. The quiet of the gym, the open, wordless spaces of the track and the ball field, offered him tranquility the way some people find it in church. Jake was single-minded and lived at the weight room—he only slept at home—and in his senior year of high school won a partial track scholarship to Fresno State. In August Jake left Taft, his small valley town, without a shred of regret. He was not angry at anyone, but he was intent on a new life far away. He was never coming back to Taft.

In his first college track season he strained a triceps. It was a minor injury, causing minimal pain, but plucking at his follow-through whenever he tried to throw. He thought nothing of it. He did not tell his coach. When his arm continued to hurt he worked harder, lifting weights and throwing through the pain. He ended up doing himself serious damage. His arm became so weak he could not lift weights heavier than a baby. Jake had never before been injured, and he felt completely disoriented. All he could think was to get back what he had lost.

At the gym he got talking to a man named Martin who knew all about what he had done in high school and seemed friendly with the coaches. Martin convinced him to try a supplement, a powder that dissolved in milk. Within a week Jake could see that it made his muscles grow. Unfortunately it did not heal his triceps. Even so Jake found something mesmerizing in the promise of a quantity of powder to affect his body. It intrigued him, like a scientific discovery. Martin offered a bottle of large white pills that he said might be more effective, and Jake took them. He thought he felt some healing. As soon as he started exercising again, though, the pain reasserted itself. Desperate, he went from supplements to pills to injectables, and from there it was only a short hop to other drugs. He wanted to feel good again, and the belief that some chemical would make the difference, that it was strictly a question of finding the right ingredients, came to dominate his thinking.

With or without drugs, he had no life without track and its regulated schedule. Ten times a day he reminded himself it was time to go to the gym, and then stopped short when he remembered his condition. He quit going to classes. He couldn't see the point. You went to class in order to get grades that enabled you to do sports. Utterly at loose ends, he stayed in his apartment and ate pizza. He watched his body swell like a white fungus.

By August he had run out of money. He could have gone home to Taft, but that didn't seem possible to him; he had told all his friends he was never coming back. In September he was evicted from his apartment. He lived in a homeless camp by the river, in a tent he borrowed from his former track coach. For a time he managed by being of a fearsome size. He took other people's food and sometimes their drugs without even needing to threaten them. Then he learned to steal from houses, usually by entering in broad daylight through a poorly secured sliding glass door. It was too easy. He often found drugs in the medicine cabinet. He sold some to buy food, and used the rest. He stayed high all the time.

These memories were now a blur. He was not even entirely sure how he got to Santa Rosa. Somebody had given him a ride in a truck, but he could not say who. All his memories from that period seemed to be a mild colorless mush of tents and mildewed sleeping bags, smoky fires, weed, and loopy, anonymous, occasionally hostile exchanges with a rainbow nation of losers. He remembered names, especially colorful ones like Fruit Loops and Mountain Midget, but he could not put them with faces; and vice versa.

The beginning of the end of this phase came when he broke into a house and a guy sleeping in a back bedroom came out with a baseball bat just as Jake entered the den. Jake would always remember how the man looked: his sleep-filled eyes barely open, his hair black and shiny. He had on only boxers, and he dialed his phone with one hand while holding on to the bat with the other and keeping his eyes fixed on Jake. Dialing so clumsily, he got wrong numbers twice before reaching 911. Jake started to laugh at his ineptitude, which terrified the guy. Jake put up his hands and told him to relax. He felt almost relieved to be caught.

A short time after reaching his jail cell, the drugs—opioids and ecstasy, mainly—began to exit his body, turning his skin into hairy caterpillars. He had not realized until then the extent to which his body, once a finely burnished organism, had been poisoned. For three days he lay on the cell floor itching and burning and aching. Termites chewed through his bones. By the time a court-appointed attorney got to him he had passed through the worst of it, and could actually pay attention. The lawyer asked him what he wanted to do. Jake asked what he meant.

"You want to do time? Or do you want to go to rehab?"

The first court-ordered rehab was 30 days, a complete joke. You couldn't get clean in that amount of time, and nobody in the program was under any serious delusion that they would. Guys were doing drugs in the bathrooms; they kept their stashes under their pillows. Jake sat in class while an intern—a skinny guy just out of psychology school, the kind of kid Jake could scare to death on the street—tried to get them to examine their inner lives.

The guys in the program, sitting in a circle on plastic chairs, took off on weird shaggy dog stories. One older guy with a gray pony tail and a fringed leather jacket went on and on about his motorcycle trip in the desert, drug hits followed by police encounters followed by weird campfire music followed by women followed to motel rooms... stories so tantalizing you kept waiting for a punch line that never came, until you realized it would never come because there was no punch line.

Other guys made jokes that nobody else understood, and laughed at them, and looked around at the rest of them as though to say, don't you get it? Jake did none of that. He behaved himself, keeping quiet, until the 30 days were up. When his head was straight he could see that the drugs were doing him no favors. He wanted to get sober.

It was not so easy, he found. When he completed the program he had no money; with shoulder-length hair and a jagged front tooth broken in a fight he had tried to break up, he looked like what he was, an addict with a record for breaking and entering. Nobody wanted to give that guy a job. For the first time it occurred to Jake that change might not come so easily. Once again he found himself camping out under oak trees along the creek, smoking or injecting if somebody offered stuff; and then stealing to get more. It was some time before he got caught, but when he did, he spent more days in jail and more time in court-ordered rehab. He had never been violent, so the judges gave him every chance.

Most of the programs were out in the country, back off the road in a cluster of ranch-style houses. Some were small; some were large. Professional counselors ran some, but those were expensive and tended to be over in a few weeks. Others were religious and made you sit through revival meetings, which made no sense to Jake. Some programs ran like a boot camp, with a lot of shouting and pushups. In those you had to walk on eggshells to keep all the rules, or else get sent back to jail.

Each time he began a program, Jake felt optimistic that it would work and he would stay clean. At AA and NA meetings he heard men talk of reaching the point of being sick and tired of being sick and tired, men whose sobriety had lasted 15 years, or 22, or any number. This religion of recovery appealed to him with a purity reminiscent of track and field. He knew he could achieve it, if he could only get his thoughts right. It seemed to him, listening carefully, that there was a delicate balance, as sensitive as a shade of light at dusk, which he had to find and stick to. Sometimes he felt that he had grasped it, but it always flew away.

Through the worst, Jake never lost that aura of determination that had fueled him as an athlete. People noticed it and treated him better than he deserved. He seemed to have his feet on the ground. He actually believed in himself, on his good days. Likewise the many would-be helpers he encountered in various court settings and rehab programs often believed in him. Because they liked him, they wanted to believe that he could get well with just a little more of their help. Jake could never complain that nobody cared. Lots of people had cared. It just wasn't enough.

After he had been through several programs, however, the judges stopped offering rehab that cost money. Jake went to the Salvation Army farm—that was free—and found that he liked it better than the professionalized programs. Some of his rehab counselors had talked through the 12 steps as though they were a mind game, therapeutic make-believe. It seemed cleaner to talk about a Higher Power that you actually believed existed outside your brain. The Salvation Army staff spoke of Jesus Christ as a real person to talk to, and a power you could feel.

He failed to get it, though. After nine months he left the farm and stayed sober all of a week. By that time meth had become his drug of choice, but he used anything and everything: opiates, ecstasy, weed, coke, and some drugs that he didn't know a name for. For the first time he didn't care about consequences. He would do anything to obliterate himself.

He was sitting stoned in a friend's car in the Mendocino Avenue Taco Bell parking lot, mesmerized by the gleaming lights reflected in the wet pavement, when a cop approached from behind. Jake and his friend were both beyond noticing until the officer was at the window with his flashlight spotlighting the pills they had in a baggy on the seat. He cuffed them both and put them in the back seat of his car.

Jake's friend was cursing and snarling, but it was all right with Jake. He was too stoned to care. Let life carry him wherever it will.

On the way to the station the cop turned on the radio, tuning it to KLOVE. He noticed that Jake was singing along under his breath.

"Sounds like you have been to church once or twice in your life," he said.

"Not really," Jake replied. "I did rehab up in Healdsburg with the Salvation Army. They sing all those songs."

"Did you ever try the Sonoma Gospel Mission?"

"No."

"You should give that a look. Those are good people down there."

"That's downtown, isn't it? That's nasty down there. I like to be out in the country."

"It's not a resort, you know. You're supposed to be getting sober."

"Yeah, but that's no reason you shouldn't do it in a nice place."

Without knowing why he did it, however, Jake asked the judge to send him to the mission. He wondered what he had done when he first entered its dingy hallways. The Salvation Army was hardly deluxe accommodations, but this was ghetto.

At his interview he told Kent, who ran the program, that he was ready to change. He said he was a Christian who had accepted Christ. He knew the words they expected you to say in the Christian programs. Sometimes he actually thought he meant it. But from the beginning he was on the watch for loopholes in the system.

In any rehab program, you could count on finding at least a few guys just playing a game. If you followed their lead, you would learn how to have it both ways: getting the benefits of the program while still retaining your corner on life. Jake noticed two Mexicans talking very privately in a corner of the mission dining room, their necks bent in toward each other. It was a noisy place, with plates clattering and men milling through the buffet line while happily yelling to each other. Most people would overlook the Mexicans, but if you were looking for it you saw that something was up. He asked them what the secret was. They laughed while keeping their eyes on their plates.

Intrigued, he sat down next to them in chapel. They moved to seats across the aisle.

He next cornered them at dinner. "You think I'm a narc?" he asked. He showed them the lines running up his arms. "Do narcs look like that?" he asked.

They were getting pills from the guests who came in for dinner and a bed. Lying awake listening to the slow breathing of his bunkmates he thought of that. Within a few days he had convinced the Mexicans to cut him in.

He used for a week before a surprise inspection. The Mexicans were quick enough to hide their stuff, but Jake was caught with a vial of five pills in his cubby. When Kent called Jake into his office his shoulders sagged like bags of grain; his eyes seemed like reservoirs ripe and ready to fill. He shook his head. "I'll be honest with you, Jake," he said. "I thought you were on the road to sobriety. You seemed to be doing so well. I don't understand why you are choosing this. Who is it for? It's not for you. This is killing you. You are in the process of dying."

On his own again, Jake walked as far as he could out into the country and set up camp in a field shielded from the road by an old cypress. That same night it rained. In the dark he had to gather his sopping sleeping bag and go searching for a space under the eaves of a building. Who is it for? he asked himself as he lay in the wet bag trying to get warm. Later that day, he was hiding in an alleyway listening to a homeowner who had heard him breaking in the back door and came out calling for somebody named Dave. Again he asked himself, Who is it for? He wasn't helping himself, and he wasn't helping anybody else, so what made sense of this? He still believed that sobriety lay just a paper's width away, a mere matter of making up his mind to put his mind to it.

So he went back to the mission, telling Kent that he had seen the wisdom of his words. He would put himself into the hands of God to seek sobriety. Kent told him he had to be clean, and he had to be out of the program at least 72 hours. Jake slept—or didn't sleep—in doorways two more nights, then presented himself for drug testing.

Detox was nothing this time. He had not been out long enough to graft the chemicals into his nervous system. Nevertheless, life at the mission that second time was agony. He had done it all before, and now he saw it starkly, hideously. Starting over at the bottom, as a candidate, he slept in the 12-man room, stuffy and stinky; and he attended classes with men dumb as posts, who acted like eighth graders giving the substitute teacher a hard time. The place was rancid with complaining. The classes were in Bible knowledge, life skills, and recovery. Jake had no objection to learning these subjects, but he couldn't concentrate to listen, and the classes were constantly disrupted by men who asked stupid questions or talked out of turn.

Candidates—men in their first month—were not allowed to leave the mission except for church. They worked in the kitchen, the laundry, at the thrift store, or cleaning the house. The dinginess of the rooms, the stained walls and floors, the smells of cooked cabbage and grease that seeped through the walls gave Jake claustrophobia. Besides, the question continued to reverberate through his thoughts. He was as miserable inside as outside, and who was it for?

He had lost any vision of a good future. The present agony ran on like a winding road that had no destination. Ten months, the length of the program, might as well be an eternity in hell. Every morning when his alarm sounded at 5:30 he wanted to give up and leave, and he would have if the street were any better. Every morning he set off on the road to hell again, unable to see beyond the next curve, unable to see the sky above, hemmed in.

He finished his month-long candidacy. At Phase and Praise he recited the Bible verses candidates were required to memorize, and read an essay—required—that he had felt proud of as he wrote. As the words came out of his mouth they became as heavy as turds, and as meaningless. At the conclusion of the meeting many of his peers bustled around him offering to slap hands or to hug, but he felt deflated, and showed it to the extent that some of the men asked him what was wrong, or got offended that he wouldn't smile at them. He told them to get lost, leave him alone, and some didn't take that well.

After candidacy he was allowed to leave the building for AA meetings and to take a walk with an approved accountability partner, but that very limited freedom only accentuated his wretchedness. AA was just posing and speechifying; most of the people there were looking for connections to get drugs or sex. On his walks he passed stores that were pointless to him, because he had no money, and he looked at women whom he was not allowed to talk to. Life was off limits, and being permitted now to walk among it offered only more frustration. He felt that he made zero progress in seizing sobriety. The Bible verses he learned made no sense to him, and when he talked the 12 steps he was just parroting words.

Jake never made friends of the other men. They were simply an irritant to him: their smells, their noise, their immaturity. None of them was finding sobriety, he was sure. They were all just trudging through this nausea for three meals a day and a roof over their heads.

Of everything he did, he hated morning devotions the most vehemently. He was required to attend at 6:30 every morning, always short on sleep from lying awake with the snoring and the fug of man-smell in the bedroom. He entered the chapel filled with exhaustion and loathing. Somebody always tried to ramp up emotions with pleas for passion and sincerity and deeper commitment. These revivalist orations reminded him of locker room pep talks. He wanted to shout at them, and tell them to shut up.

At the same time, at his very nadir of disgust he still wanted to be sober. He had little hope, but remained desperate to quit this endless and meaningless round of intoxication and homelessness. Through songs and prayers and speeches the morning devotions sketched out another life, a triumphant life that he continued to find plausible though utterly beyond his reach. What Kent Spires had said was true: he was dying. Mandatory devotions rubbed his face in it.

What exactly made the difference on the particular Wednesday when his life was changed, he could never say. It was perhaps true that he had reached the very bottom. He was certainly excruciatingly miserable that day, so much so that he entered chapel, took a chair, immediately lowered his head onto his knees, and did not move it again. He could not bear to speak or to be spoken to.

They sang a song he had never heard, "Grace greater than all my sins." He barely noticed it, being deep in his suffering, until somewhere well into the verses, the word "grace" appeared to shimmer. He could see it, picked out in silver. The tones of the word acquired a tactile quality; they were golden, like honey, flowing and mellifluous; they soothed his ears. Did anyone else hear and see the song like that? He thought they must, and peeked, but no one else seemed affected.

Grace was greater. Than all.

He fell off his chair, onto his knees, and began to sob. The sounds flopped around in his chest, like a dolphin trying to swim and breathe inside him. He went all the way onto the floor, smelling the faint sour blend of throw-up and carpet cleaner, which would ever after retain a halo effect. Jake felt hands on him now, and heard the labor of sighs and prayers. He was not alone after all. His sobs continued, great gusting exhausts that emptied him like a balloon, and not just once but a dozen times. "Get it all out. Get it ALL out," somebody encouraged him, so he let it drain him, let his chest seize and spasm as though it must belong to somebody else.

Then he was empty. His nose was in the carpet but he was calm. He knew where he was but he could not move.

Kent Spires was the one whose head was nearest. Jake could hear his gentle voice clearly over all the rest. "Do you want to ask Jesus in?" This made perfect sense. Empty as a coffin, he could be filled. Bereft of all confidence, he needed to borrow hope that belonged to someone else. From Jesus. Ask Jesus in. Grace. Greater than all.

"Yes," Jake grunted.

"Then say it. Speak to Jesus."

He tried but no words came. He was left hanging in mid-air, mouth open but wordless.

"Dear Lord Jesus," Kent prompted him. Jake repeated the words, and as soon as he said them, he felt as though he had swallowed a light bulb. His insides were filled up by something warm and light as a feather, yet still and dense. He began to repeat himself: "Dear Lord Jesus." It came out of him like a song. It was all he could say. The words themselves seemed to have a taste, like sesame. "Dear Lord Jesus." That was all he could say, so he said it again and again, like music.

Krystle was gently reproving. "You never would have said such a thing," she said.

"What?"

"That you'd give up the mission for better plumbing."

"No, I didn't say that. I'd give up the old building. The mission will go on, whether it's there or someplace else."

"Is that really true?" she asked.

He moved toward her, and placed his hands on her tiny birdlike shoulders. He loved her. She was sweet beyond words. He could not believe she was his. "You think it's the building?" he asked. "Not the people? Not the program? Not the Spirit of God?"

She offered a hint of a smile and looked confused. "It's all those things," she said. "But sometimes, you know, a place is part of it too. Like your home is part of your family. Like a summer campground where you went when you were little. Aren't there places like that?"

"Maybe," he said. "I never had them."

3

The Development Money

✧

Buddy Grace leaned over the iPad, following along as his partner Stephen Ames walked through the funding phases of their Railroad Square development. They were on the second floor of a glassy Fourth Street office building, in an underfurnished room with floor-to-ceiling views of Taylor Mountain. The floors were some blond tropical wood, and the steel-and-leather chairs and tables were scattered about the wide space as though the movers had dropped them there and were coming back with more. Buddy doubted that anybody actually worked here. It was far too empty and far too quiet, like a really overpriced art gallery. This was a statement room, and the statement was: you are in way over your head.

He and Stephen were talking to two executives from Wine Country Savings, an institution they had done business with before. One was Jason Pridie, a young loan officer at pains to demonstrate how relaxed he was, slouching against the table and laughing at every opportunity. The other was Howard Zenikov, an old timer who knew everything and everybody in Santa Rosa; he was now some kind of officer at the bank.

This was not their office, it was somebody's idea of what their office should be. These guys were local. Buddy was fairly sure that their personal ideas about luxury started with a La-Z-Boy. However, if they were pretenders so were he and Stephen: this was a much more difficult deal than any they had attempted, not just an office complex, but a neighborhood. There were many moving parts, including state and federal regulations, and the numbers were certainly bigger than any Buddy had dealt with. That was why Stephen kept going over them. He was the finance guy and naturally assumed that the only reason not to do a project was the numbers.

Buddy, who favored intuition over math, had decided ten minutes earlier that the numbers were a sideshow. The unstated sticking point, Buddy thought, was subtler and harder to dislodge: a fundamental skepticism that Railroad Square could ever be anything more than a funky one-street district for six or seven restaurants and antique stores.

Even at its heyday, in the Depression years, it had been on the rougher side of town, mostly Italian. The railroad had quit in the 1950s, and in the 60s the freeway cut the town in half and left the square on the unwanted side. At the time Railroad Square had been totally dilapidated. Since then a few restaurants and a small theater had gentrified one street, giving it a slightly Bohemian feel.

Stephen, slim and neat with jet-black oiled hair and a tight navy blazer, kept emphasizing that the money was spread over six years. Year by year it was not a huge risk.

"Sure, in Windsor," said Pridie, who was the youngest of them all and didn't wear a tie. "But Railroad Square? Luxury housing in Railroad Square?"

Buddy pounced on that before Stephen could drag them back to the numbers. "I think that's the key question, Jason. You put your finger on it. Here's what you might be forgetting. A lot of retired people are moving into Sonoma County. They have the money, and they like it here. But they are not the same retired people we are used to. Used to be they wanted to live by the golf course in Oakmont, or if they were really adventurous, maybe Bennett Valley in their own little ranchette. But the new ones are baby boomers; they grew up listening to Janis Joplin. They don't necessarily want to live in Oakmont."

Jason gave him a pained look. "What worries seniors the most, Buddy? All seniors."

Buddy smiled. "How far is the bathroom?" He laughed as though he thought it was genuinely funny, and the others smiled.

"No," Jason said. "Security! They want to feel safe. And Railroad Square doesn't."

"No, you're right, it has an urban look and feel," Buddy said. "But urban isn't scary to this generation. It's hip. Wine is hip. Sonoma Wine Country is hip. Urban is hip. No, not every retired couple wants that, but there are a lot who do. Who don't even like golf."

It came out of his mouth spontaneously, and he immediately wished to take it back. He had momentarily forgotten that Jason more than loved golf. For Jason it was a moral test: golf equaled the right kind of people.

Stephen jumped back into the argument then, but they were talking numbers again, and Buddy didn't need to listen to that. He loved Stephen, and he needed him for a partner, but sometimes his cluelessness stuck out like a bad haircut.

Buddy thought he knew what really bothered Jason: homeless people. Jason couldn't imagine an upscale development in the home of the homeless.

Buddy didn't bring it up—couldn't, he thought. It was an impolite subject that, once drawn to the surface, would poison the conversation. Everybody has a story about homelessness, and wants to tell it as though it is the only truth. Buddy wasn't sure that once they started circling that drain they could ever escape its vortex. They would feel guilty for their prejudice and their heartlessness, and all the more they would say no. No. He couldn't let them get to no.

The fourth man in the room, Howard Zenikov, brought it up without Buddy's help. Howard was sitting on a sofa far from the table where the iPad and the drawings were laid out; he had on his straw-colored suit with no memory of a pleat, the jacket flopped open; his long gray greased hair combed straight back. Howard was a local legend at eighty years old, having built half the homes in the city as well as a local shopping center, and having thumbed his nose at city hall so many times. He had sat through the whole discussion saying hardly a word, but now he asked Buddy if he was going to be serious.

"Absolutely, Howard. I'm dead serious."

"C'mon, Buddy. Railroad Square. The days of winos and Rosa never ended down there. You can't do this kind of development unless you can control the property. You want to gentrify Railroad Square? What are you going to do about the bums?"

Buddy pulled a chair away from the conference table, carried it over to Zenikov's sofa. He placed it down facing him. He took the seat and leaned forward, uncomfortably close to Zenikov. "There's a reason the homeless congregation stays down there," he said. "You know what it is?"

Zenikov looked as though he wanted to abort this conversation, but his curiosity got him. "No, I don't, but I have a feeling you're going to tell me."

"The mission. The Sonoma Gospel Mission. They feed them. They give them beds. Everybody on the street knows the mission. It has been there for fifty years. You with me, Howard?"

Buddy saw that he had his attention.

"I was talking to the leaders of the mission just before I came here, Howard. I'm close to them. I understand them. My church supports their work. I made them an offer. We're going to get them to move out of there and over to Sebastopol Road. You take the mission away from Railroad Square, and do you still have a homeless problem? I don't think you do. There's no place for them to eat. Not a single fast food place in the neighborhood. There's no place for them to sit. No park. No grass. No benches, either. Without the mission, most of them will move on. You don't see them in Healdsburg, do you, hanging out around all those fancy restaurants and tasting rooms? It's not because the police move them out. They aren't there because they don't feel comfortable there. There's no mission. The Salvation Army is way out at Lytton Springs. That's how it will be in Railroad Square, too. I know it's hard to imagine, but that's because you can't imagine the mission gone."

Howard was a Jew and his network of contacts didn't extend to a Christian mission. He wasn't completely sure that Buddy's observation was right. But he didn't deny it either.

"Did you get an agreement?" he asked.

"It's too early for that. But it makes sense for them. We can put up a new building for them and the numbers still work. They'll be out of that rat trap."

Howard gave a short laugh that sounded almost like a hiccup. "All right," he said. "You get them to move."

4

Sam's Choice

✧

When he woke up Sam Callahan remembered instantly that he was in his cousin Lil's bedroom. It made him feel ashamed. His aunt had given him Lil's bed, putting her to sleep on a cushion in the master bedroom. Lil was a little girl. Her bedside lamp had a shade trimmed in pink lace; there were two skinny dolls on the bookshelf and a Disneyland poster on the wall. Sam could not feel right displacing a little girl. He didn't deserve a bed.

The floor would be fine. All he wanted was the safety of four walls. Thinking of what was being done for him made Sam want to stay under the covers forever, or better, simply cease to exist.

He buried his head in the pillow and remembered feeling similar anguish waking up in the Modesto hospital. Then, he had not known where he was. He no memory then or now of the drugs he had ingested or even of his companions the night before. His father told him that his high school friend Fred Craven had found him unconscious in a soft plowed field 20 yards off the bike path that ran along Putah Creek. Sam still could not understand how he got to Putah Creek, since that was not a place he usually visited. He sometimes used with Fred, but never at Putah Creek. His father said he would have died, except that Fred came back to find him after everyone had run away. What were they running from? Cops? He could ask Fred who the others were and what had happened, if he ever got the chance, but Fred had not come to see him in the hospital.

His uncle, also named Sam, knocked on the bedroom door and without opening it told him to come and have breakfast. The kitchen was empty when he got there; they had put out Cheerios and milk. The room was decorated country style, with ruffles on the curtains and a blue-and-white checked fabric on the chair cushions. A ceramic Palomino horse, rearing up, stood on the counter by the microwave, and overseeing the eating nook was a painting of an Indian. This was his aunt Susan's decor. The whole house was done up that way. It made him feel uncomfortable and out of place. He understood that the look was supposed to be homey, but he preferred the bare-bones, no-pretense style of the mission, which to him was more like a real home.

Halfway through the Cheerios his uncle came in and sat with him, saying nothing. Sam was caught between wanting to be left alone—indeed, to die—and the slight current of comfort he derived from human company.

"We're going to church this morning," his uncle said. "We'd like you to come."

Sam replied so softly his uncle could not hear, so Sam had to repeat that he didn't have dress-up clothes.

"That's okay. Our church is cool. And we're going to your cousin's wedding this afternoon. You can wear the same clothes."

"Which cousin?"

"Reese, Matt's boy. He's marrying a girl from Novato."

"Am I invited?"

"I'm sure you'll be welcome."

It was an outdoor wedding with white-tablecloth tables under a white tent. People were dressed up but not too dressed up; a lot of the men wore jeans, he noticed. The place was an events venue that had been a farm. Over a fence was a vineyard. The wedding party dressed in a house that had probably been where the farmer lived—maybe he still did—and they set folding chairs for the ceremony on a spreading lawn. The dance floor was between that and the white tent. Sam sat at a family table in the white tent, mainly alone. Most people had gone to the bar or the dance floor; at only one other table were some old people still sitting.

From time to time people came by to speak with Sam. Some he thought he recognized, but when they introduced themselves he could not remember hearing of their names, and he didn't want to ask for clarification about where they sat on the family tree. He said as little as possible, and after making a few polite sentences and tapping his shoulder as though out of fondness they went off.

One claimed she was his aunt. Aunt Cleta, she said, or something like that. He didn't ever remember hearing such a name. Cleta had that white skin that turns to freckles, and she was showing quite a lot of it with her strapless dress. Maybe she had been drinking, because her speech seemed mushy. "Why don't you come meet everybody, Sam? There are a lot of people your age."

Previously Sam would have gone with her. He didn't mind drinking beer with people. You didn't need to say much. He was trying to hold on to not drinking, though. He thought he could do it if he stayed at the table, but if he went with Aunt Cleta and stood around with people who were into their second or third beer, he knew his resolve would break up. Servers came and offered him wine from the two bottles on the table, one white and one red. That was not so hard to resist: he didn't like wine.

He would have had fun at this wedding a few months ago, drinking and dancing. You didn't have to talk. The DJ was trying to get everybody on the dance floor, and one of his girl cousins, or maybe his aunts, came to try to drag him out. He wouldn't go, though she kept at him for at least a minute.

She was pretty. Just a small thing, with coffee skin and a little Latin face, and she must have been in the wedding party because she had on one of the lavender dresses they all were wearing. He didn't remember seeing her before.

"Where are you from?" she asked, sitting down in the chair next to his. She wore those big glasses that made her look super-smart.

When he didn't answer she repeated the question, with a smile. "Come on now, I didn't ask for your Social Security number or anything. Somebody said you're Reese's cousin, but I don't think you're from around here. I would remember you if you were."

She wouldn't stop, so he told her he didn't really know where he was from.

"Well, where are you staying right this minute?"

"I'm staying with my uncle Sam, but I don't think I'll be there more than a day or two."

"So where are you going?"

"I don't know. Maybe back into rehab."

He had not meant that to scare her, but maybe it did. Later he saw her with some guy on the dance floor. She seemed nice. The mission had a rule that you could not fraternize with the opposite sex, and though he didn't really understand why, he thought it was a good rule, for him. Girls had always seemed dangerous to him, and never more than now. He felt that he was up against a wall of water held back by a leaky dam. The slightest mistake could break open that wall and flood him away. No matter how much he wanted to, he could not go touching that wall.

His uncle Sam came over and sat with him for a bit. Sam was not a talker either. He had a blond handlebar mustache that seemed bigger than his head, making him look like an old-timey character in a western movie. He was very serious, as though he were at a funeral instead of a wedding.

"You're not drinking?" he asked, and Sam shook his head no.

After a few minutes of silence his uncle said, "I can't believe that mission kicked you out for a cigarette. You don't even smoke, do you?"

"No. Not usually. I do a little."

"You were in there for heroin, and they kick you out for a cigarette. I told that guy Jake that they really fucked you over."

Sam didn't feel the need to answer this, but his uncle went on for a while about how stupid that was, until the subject ran dry.

"So where you going to go, Sam? Do you have a plan?"

"Not really."

Sam was more grateful than he could say for his uncle taking him in, but he didn't feel comfortable in his house and didn't want to stay any longer than he had to. He had a feeling that was mutual. This was confirmed. His uncle said, "You know you can't stay with us. Lil needs her own room. It's not fair to her."

Sam nodded yes, but he didn't know where else he could go. When his father put him on the bus he had told him not to think about coming back. His parents didn't want him influencing his brothers.

"I think your dad would take you back, if you asked," his uncle said. "But you'd have to stop using. He's not going to put up with that shit. I don't know why he's so high and mighty about it, he did a lot of it himself in his day."

Sam knew his father was still using. That was one more reason not to go back there.

"I can't ask him," he said.

His uncle shrugged. "Well, you know better than I do. You got a friend you can stay with?"

To say "friend" reminded Sam of Danny Donovan, his friend throughout grade school. They had shot blackbirds with Danny's BB gun. They had raised pigeons together. Then Sam had been held back in sixth grade and Danny went ahead. He'd passed him in the hall a year later but never said hi.

He had never again had a friend like Danny. Fred might be a friend. He had come back to find him, and saved his life. But maybe Fred came back just because he worried what the law would do to him if

Sam died. Maybe he was not a real friend. Fred hadn't come to see him in the hospital.

"I might go back to the mission."

His uncle raised his eyebrows and frowned. "After what they did to you?"

Sam made a short animal noise, a sound of subdued pain. He nodded to himself. "I signed up for the program, and I knew I wasn't allowed to smoke."

His uncle shrugged. "If you think so, I'm not going to stand in your way. When do you want to go?"

"I can go back after 72 hours."

5

Buddy and the Sonoma Gospel

✧

Buddy Grace carefully parked his gleaming black Mercedes on Fourth Street, in front of the Santa Rosa Support Guild thrift store. He was three blocks from the Sonoma Gospel Mission, but he thought his car was least likely to be damaged if he parked here. He didn't mind a walk through the neighborhood.

Buddy had made good money in development, as he was happy to tell. What he wouldn't say aloud, because it made him look like a bleeding heart, was that he believed in development for the common good. He had an idealistic streak and saw his work as nearly charitable, creating beautiful and useful buildings, upgrading the run-down, making society hum. He was morally impatient with whatever held back his projects.

He certainly perceived Railroad Square through the lens of uplift. As he walked from his car to McKinley Street he mused over the neighborhood. He could count five or six decent restaurants, two coffee houses with character, a dry cleaner, an antique store, a skateboard shop, a third-generation furniture and appliance store, and a vintage clothing store featuring dresses from the 1950s. Also a tiny spice shop, a Persian carpet store with rugs perennially half-price, and, miraculously, an old-fashioned butcher. Railroad Square had great potential. The train was coming back, and who doesn't like trains? The whole district could explode. He had envisaged that transformation and, for Buddy, that was next to making it real. When he imagined it, his spirits lifted and he believed he was doing what God had created him to do.

To make it really successful demanded a patina of hip. Classy buildings and upscale apartments would mix with the random and eclectic to turn grunge into avant-garde. It was a question of style. Applying that style skillfully would make the neighborhood a place anybody might live in, not just the young and the economically challenged. It would also make Buddy rich.

Buddy was well dressed, in a slate gray sports coat over a silky black turtleneck, with dress slacks and tassel loafers. He was keyed up, too, because he hoped to make a sale. As he strolled down McKinley and drew close to the mission, the necessary transformation appeared to display itself in reverse. The closer he got the more he disapproved of: litter, ugliness, dilapidation, and most of all, people. They loitered, or leaned against buildings. He passed a man with greasy hair and a bulldog pup sitting in a doorway, talking to himself. The streets adjacent to the mission were like a low spot in a field where all the rank water collected. These people were not going anywhere.

Such negativity made Buddy uneasy. He was naturally optimistic, and he liked to think well of people. All the same, he knew that for the good of the neighborhood, for the good of everybody, the low-life had to go.

And that meant the mission. He didn't really believe it would be a loss for anybody. If the mission's programs worked as they were supposed to you wouldn't see homelessness like this. He suspected that the mission actually encouraged it, by taking in men who had burned their bridges and lived from bottle to bottle or pill to pill. If the mission were gone, some of those men might be forced to get sober and go to work.

He would never put this view so bluntly to anyone, unless perhaps it was to someone he knew would agree, and then only after they had a few drinks. Buddy not only wanted to seem charitable, he really was. He could be remarkably generous. Life, however, had forced him to live by the law of the jungle, and he took some pride in his survival. Since he had risen above his beginnings, he thought anybody could.

Half a dozen men clustered by the mission's front door, dressed in what-have-you, hair unruly, rings in their ears and their faces. They made way for Buddy, sliding aside without looking at him. Physically a big man, he was not fearful. He had grown up in the shadow of down-and-out, and found it not frightening but distasteful. As he was about to go inside, he paused to peruse the mission's blue-gray stucco and featureless windows. His thought was that this building demanded to be torn down. Such ugliness should be replaced by something graceful and modern.

Behind glass in a dim anteroom, a man with bright tattoos up both arms was talking on the phone. He put up a finger to Buddy, telling him to hold on.

"CJ, get off the phone." That came from a man leaning against the wall. It was dark enough that Buddy had not even seen him when he came in.

"That's okay," Buddy said.

"He's been on there for twenty minutes," said the man, who had a small goat-like face and black-framed glasses. "C'mon, CJ, this man is here on business."

CJ carried on talking, unperturbed. He appeared to be enjoying his use of the phone, with no intention of ending the conversation any time soon.

"You bring something to donate?" the goat-man asked Buddy. "I could get some guys from the kitchen if you need help unloading it."

"No, I'm here to see one of the staff."

"Who? You want to see Knox?"

"No, I don't think I know Knox. Jake Dorner."

In a few minutes CJ got off the phone and called Jake, who appeared shortly thereafter and led Buddy into the heart of the building. This was his second visit and he looked around him more carefully than before. Turning down a dim corridor and then up a flight of stairs, Buddy caught glimpses of a kitchen, a laundry room, a room stuffed with bunk beds. The place seemed sanitary enough—worn, with horrible carpet, but not dirty. It smelled of cleaning solution. It was the plainness Buddy couldn't stand, the cheap and undesigned minimalism bought by poverty. He wanted to shake it off like a dog coming out of the water.

Jake had a chest like a cement mixer and the beard of a Viking. He led the way into the same upstairs office where Buddy had first presented the idea of buying the mission. This time he intended to get a commitment.

The office was surprisingly neat—a few books on a shelf alongside a gold plastic trophy for basketball. On the wall was a San Francisco Giants poster. Kent, a smaller bearded man, was already there. He stood and shook hands. He was the one with the power to decide, Buddy knew, but he didn't tend to say much. He reminded Buddy of some of the characters he had known growing up in small town Oklahoma, cordial with a handshake but easily lapsing into silence. You could underestimate people like that.

Both Kent and Jake were dressed in what looked like burgundy bowling shirts, loose untucked garments with black panels down the sides, monogrammed with SGM—for Sonoma Gospel Mission. "Hey, how do I get one of those shirts?" Buddy asked with a grin, and the two men laughed. Buddy made small talk. He reminded Kent that his pastor had once introduced them at a mission fair at First Presbyterian Church. Kent said he had known Pastor Smith since they served on a youth commission, twenty years before.

This was all good. Buddy had grown up in church, like anybody in Oklahoma, and he still attended occasionally, though it wasn't a big part of his life as an adult. Most of Buddy's business was done in offices, restaurants or golf courses. The mission was a very different kind of place, like church raised to the fifth power. Buddy sought common ground, and was glad he had a church connection to fall back on.

He moved toward business. "Gentlemen," he said. "Thank you so much for taking time for me. I have good news. I've talked to our finance people, and they are quite enthusiastic. It's a clear go. In ten years you won't recognize this neighborhood.

"We believe that everything west of the freeway will be transformed—not just a narrow corridor along Fourth, but everything up and down McKinley as well. The new train is going to be the catalyst."

He went directly into describing his plans, the retail shops and restaurants on Fourth Street, the four-story condominiums flanking them, an anchor hotel. He did not mention the Sonoma Wine Country Center next to the hotel; he thought that might be delicate, given the mission's work with alcoholics.

Buddy brought tremendous physical energy to something he believed in. All the same, while he talked he was observing carefully. The two men were listening, but their eyes had the beady wariness of small birds'. Because they were doubtful? Because they did not understand how development worked? Buddy wasn't sure, but he kept filling the office with a picture of urban prosperity. Soon he had a tricky turn to make: getting them to see that it would be best for the mission to leave.

"There's no question, given what we're planning, that your property will be affected. The whole street will be affected."

"Sixth Street? Or McKinley?" Jake asked.

"Both. On McKinley you'll see retail, some very upscale retail. Too shi-shi for me, but it's coming. On Sixth, I expect housing."

"There's housing now."

"Yes, but I mean new housing designed for urban densities. Condominiums, townhouses, upscale apartments. Probably six- to eight-story buildings. People will want to be walking distance from the train. It's a little too soon to be sure exactly what the mix will be, but it's coming. We are looking to acquire properties in this area now, before any of this happens. And we are prepared to pay based on their future value. Right now none of these properties would go for much, if you could even sell them. Would you agree? But we see a different future, and we are willing to pay for it. You are in a great location, and we are ready to reward you for it."

He let that sit for a moment. He still could not read the men's expressions—they looked so sober they might be waiting to take a math test—but his confidence rested in the belief that money talks.

"Or, what might be even better for you, we could do a land swap. With the value of this property, based on our evaluation of its future, we could trade for a parcel twice the size on Sebastopol Road and build to your specifications. There could be some significant tax advantages in that."

Again, he let it rest. Give them time to take the hook. Buddy loved this part of the pitch. Let other people manufacture the numbers. He knew how people thought; he knew what it took to draw them in.

He asked them: could they see some advantages in a move?

"You're offering to buy this building, is that right?" Jake asked.

"Or swap. Whatever makes more sense. We would offer you considerably better terms than you could get on the market today. That's all for discussion."

He waited again. They were certainly not falling over themselves. Silence made Buddy anxious.

He finally asked. "What information do you need to help you make that call?"

Jake started to open his mouth to speak, but then backed off and looked toward Kent, the smaller man.

Kent seemed to be a gentle soul. He had a quick, soft smile on his face. "We appreciate your interest in coming to talk to us," he said, "but we aren't really anxious to move. The men who use our services usually don't have cars. They can walk here."

"Wouldn't that be the same on Sebastopol Road?"

Kent hesitated a beat. "I don't know. We'd have to look at that. This is a pretty good location for the men. It's very central."

"Don't you have trouble with the neighbors?" Buddy knew that they did; it had been written about in the newspaper.

"Sometimes." Kent said. "Most of the time we are on pretty good terms. We try to convince them that we're a good influence." He gave a twinkle of smile.

"I'm sure you are," Buddy said. "But remember that big changes are coming. Imagine how your new neighbors will think about the mission. If they've invested millions to remake the neighborhood, how do you think they will feel about it?"

He knew it was a strong argument. With gentrification came people who wanted everything their way.

They didn't argue with him, but they didn't really respond, either. Jake kept glancing at Kent. Kent kept saying that the mission had a long history on McKinley Street, and it wouldn't be easy to move. Eventually he just stopped talking. Buddy couldn't budge him; he was like a plant with a deep taproot.

Buddy kept it positive; he suggested Kent think over what he had said and call him with any further questions. After shaking hands and leaving his card, he found his own way out.

6

More on Jake

✧

Frustrations roiled Jake's mind as he walked from the mission toward the downtown mall. Krystle had asked him to meet her and Reggie after work, to shop and to see the new flooring. Apparently the mall had embedded seashells in the walkways, an ornamentation that intrigued Krystle and held no interest whatsoever for Jake. He wanted to please Krystle, however. He had no hobbies; the mall was as good as anything else he might do.

His mind had not really left the mission, however. With rising irritation Jake thought of Kent's response to Buddy. Kent had never even pretended to show an interest in Jake's perspective.

But Jake lived with problems that were mere shadows to Kent. Bedbugs, for example. They had spent thousands on fumigators, but the bugs persisted, and the men in the program had angry red marks up and down their arms and legs and in their scrotums. Kent acted like he knew all about it; he said they could never get rid of the bedbugs because the homeless guests brought in new ones every night. The pest control people, however, said the bugs were in the walls. They wanted to tent the whole building, which would cost thousands of dollars the mission didn't have.

Bedbugs were only the most outstanding reason Jake was interested in a new building. Rainy season was far off, but when it came, as it surely would, the leaky roof would go from being a nuisance to a trial. Also, the heating system would turn some rooms into a sauna and leave others as refrigerators. The men in the New Life program deserved better.

Jake thought that seeking "permission" might be Kent's way of putting off doing anything.

At one time Jake Dorner had wanted nothing more than to be like Kent Spires. He watched Kent closely and tried to imitate his gentleness and humility. Those traits never seemed to come to Jake naturally, however. In frustration he once asked his pastor, Raymond Dull, what he could do about it. Dull replied with a bemused kindness that God had made Jake his own unique self, and Jake would need to find his own way of living that. Jake accepted the advice, but he still felt thwarted. Sometimes he thought he was very good at what he did at the mission. He had a natural understanding of how to communicate with the men in the program, because he was like them. But he always felt clumsy and brash, graceless.

Jake's attitudes toward Kent had changed over the years. He still admired him, but he now saw that while Kent was gentle, he was also stubborn. When Jake proposed changes Kent always listened, but he rarely modified his approach. He always worried about the money. That seemed to be the all-purpose obstacle to everything.

As he approached the mall's windowless brick façade and then entered the bright, hard interior, Jake felt a growing eagerness. Talking to Krystle was always a relief.

The place appeared almost deserted. It was, after all, a Tuesday. Two or three Latina mothers herded coveys of children along, and one elderly Anglo couple steered twin walkers down the esplanade, getting their exercise. Merchandise spilled out of broad doorways: shoes and clothing, toys and video games. Jake always took a jolt from the shiny surfaces, so different from the atmosphere of the mission. It seemed designed to repel the drunks and the homeless. You could do nothing here without money.

Jake found Krystle in the food court, talking on the phone. Reggie was tugging on his mother's arm, and she was fending him off. When Jake was still at a distance, Reggie saw him and began jumping and pulling on his mother to get free. Krystle held on to his wrist, without looking up to see what had caught his attention. When she finally did, she wrinkled her face in a smile and kept talking, letting Reggie run to him. Jake lifted Reggie in the air, turned him upside down, and gave him a belly burp. The softness of Reggie's skin, the feeling of pliable delight tightening Reggie's torso, the bubbling laughter, all gave Jake a moment of relief. He held on to Reggie and sat down in one of the little connected-table-and-chairs sets that the food court offered.

He could hear that Krystle was talking to her mother. Jake maintained a wary coexistence with Krystle's mother. He knew absolutely that Krystle depended on her, seeking daily conversation on the phone. He conceded that Krystle's happiness and well-being seemed to depend on those conversations, so he never questioned them. However, he wished very much that Krystle could turn her attention to him when he arrived. She had all day to talk to her mom.

While the conversation continued, he took Reggie by the hand and walked around the food court. The choices were all familiar; none of the fast-food restaurants had changed or upgraded. Their employees looked bored; the shops' bouncy signage looked stuck together with Superglue. Jake found the effect annoying and tiresome: he preferred the dilapidated dining room at the mission. Krystle, however, loved to eat here. Something about the atmosphere made her happy, which was enough for Jake. He didn't really care what he ate, as long as there was enough.

Reggie declared in a small voice that he wanted Chinese food from the Panda House. Jake told him they would see what his mother said. Krystle was all authority in matters of raising Reggie. She was timid in many other things, but not regarding what Reggie should eat.

They toddled back in her direction, holding hands, and took a seat again. Krystle was describing Reggie's weight gain to her mother in exacting detail. He was in the 75th percentile for his age, she said, and cooked carrots were the only vegetables he would eat. "I know," she said to something her mother offered, "those little ones that come in a bag. He won't touch them unless they are cooked. He will go hungry. I know, I've tried. If you try to force him he screams."

Jake grew increasingly nettled as he listened in. There was nothing urgent in what they were talking about; they could continue this subject any time, tomorrow or next week or next year, probably. Yet she showed no interest in ending the conversation. Reggie was writhing out of his grip, restless, bored. They went for another tour of the restaurants, but this time Reggie was not so easily distracted. He began to whine that he wanted to go home.

"We will, but mom and I have some shopping to do first, and we're going to eat." Reggie's complaining picked up in volume. Jake glanced over at Krystle, but she was leaning forward into her conversation, as though trying to ingest the phone. Jake wondered why she was so oblivious to him, and then felt ashamed of his own annoyance. He was beginning to feel thoroughly unhappy, and he was hungry too.

"What kind of Chinese food do you want?" he asked Reggie. He held him up before the buffet; Reggie pointed at the dishes he wanted ladled onto the Styrofoam plate. Reggie would not eat all of it; Jake would finish off whatever he left. He knew Reggie could not drink soda; Jake asked for water and was given a small paper cup he could fill by the soda machine.

They had it all on a plastic tray, adding paper napkins and plastic forks. Jake grabbed three or four plastic pouches of soy sauce, plus two packets of pepper flakes. When they sat down he made Reggie tuck a napkin into his shirt, even knowing that Reggie would cover himself with sweet and sour sauce.

They were just beginning to eat when Krystle appeared by their side and put a hand on the tray, shielding it from Reggie as though it were a dangerous animal. "Reggie!" she said vehemently. "No!"

Jake stared at her in surprise. "What's the matter?"

"That food is the worst!" she said. "It's loaded with MSG. What were you thinking?"

"Reggie said that's what he wanted."

"He doesn't even know what it is!"

Jake blinked. "I think he does. He said he wanted Chinese food from the Panda House."

"He has never eaten that, never!"

"Then how did he know he wanted it? I don't think he read the signs."

"He must have heard about it from somewhere."

"Well, not from me! I was just trying to keep the peace while you talked on the phone."

"I'm not on the phone."

"Well, you were, for a long time. I had no idea when you were going to get off. You didn't seem to know that Reggie and I existed."

She stared at him with her deep, black eyes, and turned instantly from an angry mother to a hurt girl child. Slumping into a chair near their table, carefully laying the tray of Chinese food aside, she appealed to Jake with tears in her eyes. "I was talking to my mother, Jake. Don't be harsh with me!"

He did not know what to do when she spoke to him that way. He was angry at the way she had reprimanded him, but he felt helpless before her helplessness. Jake reached out a hand to her. "I'm not being harsh. I know you love your mother, but when you're talking to her it's like Reggie and I aren't there. He was getting restless and upset, and we were both hungry. So I got him some food. I had no idea you would be so against it."

By this time Reggie had picked up the tension between them—his round head swiveled back and forth, trying to make sense of them—and he began to whimper. He got out of his chair and tried to climb into his mother's lap, which wasn't really possible in the small space between the chair and its table. Jake found it amusing and began to laugh. "Look, you hold him, and I'll get something to eat. What do you recommend?"

She recommended a salad from the Western Grill, with dressing on the side. Jake got his with beef slices, and Krystle's with tofu. When he set them down before Krystle, he looked longingly at the tray of Chinese food—orange beef and sweet and sour pork, with fried rice—which still sat on the adjacent table, congealing into a soft mud. He would have eaten it happily himself, but he judged it was a bad idea. They ate in relative silence. Krystle did her best to feed forkfuls of salad to Reggie, and met resistance.

"I want the Panda," he whined in a high-pitched voice.

"That's not good for you," Krystle said with kindly firmness. "This salad has lots of vitamins. It will make you strong." She stuck another forkful at him, and he turned his head away.

"He watches you," she said to Jake.

"I'm eating it," he replied. "Look."

"If you showed more enthusiasm for nutrition he would too."

Jake had no answer to that, so he said nothing. He was still smarting from their spat, and that continued throughout the meal. He asked Krystle what she wanted to shop for, but she had drawn inward, like a snail shrinking into itself. She said never mind, it could wait. They finished the meal in silence and Jake looked once again at the foam plate of Chinese food.

"Go ahead, eat it," Krystle said. "We shouldn't waste it."

As they walked together through the mall, on their way to the exit, Jake took note of the polished tan flooring, with starfish and seahorses and scallops apparently floating in water under their feet, ripples of sand beneath. He wanted to stop and show them to Reggie, but one look at Krystle eliminated that thought. She had her eyes lowered and her face seemed dark and lifeless.

He hated himself then. Part of him protested that he had done nothing wrong, but all the same he wondered why they found it hard to get along. He loved Krystle helplessly. He never doubted, fundamentally, that she loved him too. But right now, life was strained.

They got in the car and drove home without a word. The streets were gloomy with the fading sunshine. Shreds of fog were blowing in from the sea, and the sky above the hills had turned the palest bone-blue. Already in this late spring those hills were the color of straw. They would see no more rain for months.

The car, Jake noticed, was lugging. He was considering whether to ask Krystle whether she had noticed it when she volunteered. "I couldn't get the car started today. It quit about ten times."

"It started up for me," Jake said.

"Well, it's warm now. I'm just telling you. Don't you think it sounds funny?"

He only grunted. He had little mechanical knowledge, and he did not like to display it. Krystle's brothers knew all about motors, and Krystle had at first assumed that he did too, like all men. Her brothers talked about their new trucks whenever the family was together, and Jake had nothing to say. He had never had a nice car or truck, and never cared. But being with men who felt such an affinity for them made him ashamed of his ignorance.

Sometimes Jake wished he had never taken this life. If he had a job in construction he would not come home full of stress and disappointment. The pressure of making ends meet would dissipate.

Krystle's mother wished for that. She said nothing to his face, but he knew she was critical of his money-earning prowess. He felt called by God to the mission, and he never doubted it when he was at the mission. But whenever he was with Krystle's family he felt confused. The whole family vacationed together every summer at a mountain resort, which the brothers paid for. They insisted, and he accepted, because he and Krystle could not have afforded the place. Her brothers all made good money, and the cost made no big difference to them, but Jake felt their mother's critical eye. She too depended on her sons' generosity, but that was a different case: she was their mother.

He helped Krystle put Reggie to bed. She washed him in the tub and got him into his pajamas; Jake sat in his comfortable chair and read aloud from the Bible storybook while Reggie sprawled in his lap. Krystle nestled at his feet, and he laid a hand on her shoulder. For a few minutes the tensions of the day were put aside. They were family. Reggie fell asleep and Jake carried him carefully to his bed. Holding his sleeping form, warm and alive and utterly limp, worked to heal his sense of anxiety.

Krystle made two cups of herbal tea and they sat across from each other at the kitchen table. When Krystle told about her day with Reggie it was endlessly detailed. Jake did not listen closely to whom they had seen at the park, or what Reggie had eaten for lunch, but he found it restful to listen to Krystle's low, animated voice. She was happy and vigilant as a mom, and this filled a gap in Jake, who had never really experienced family.

He told her about Buddy's visit, and Kent's refusal to entertain the idea of a new building. She puckered her lips. "I don't see why you are so anxious to move."

"I'm not so anxious to move. I just wish that Kent would listen to me. He didn't even ask my opinion."

"Maybe that's because he knows your opinion already."

He did not like it when she disagreed with him. It triggered something fearfully close to rage in him, which he felt as dangerous. For Krystle, marriage came as a matter of course. She had always had family. But for him it was a precious commodity that might slip out of his grasp; he knew it could be smashed through his carelessness, and he feared that it would be.

"I just want him to listen to me. Like I want you to listen to me."

"I listen to you."

He had nothing to say to that. It did not feel like truth at the moment. It was almost unbearable to him, to feel such a longing for the security of his family, and to find himself incapable of living in it and preserving it. He felt he was a smasher, who wrecked things. He would have told that to Krystle, but he did not want to alarm her. She believed in him, and he knew too much about himself to share the same belief.

He stood up from his chair, feeling suddenly claustrophobic, as though he was being crushed. "I'm going out," he said on impulse, having no idea where he would go.

She looked at him with alarm, suddenly crestfallen. "Where are you going?" Jake felt a sudden and terrible surge of sympathy for her, but at the same moment he knew he might explode. The pressure seemed unbearable.

He could not look at her lovely, tender face. "I'm just going out for a bike ride," he said. "I need some air." And without further explanation he went out the back door, unlocked his bicycle from where it was chained to the porch, and set off on the dark streets. He should have a light. He should have a helmet. But the feeling of nearly exploding dissipated as he rode. The streets were empty, and he was invisible. No one could talk to him or tell him what he should do.

For half an hour he sped around the back streets, feeling the chilly night air brush back his hair and cool his face. He tried not to think too much, but his thoughts went where he did not want to go. In his mind he complained that Kent treated him like a minimum-wage day laborer; and his wife talked to him like a little boy who needed a lecture; and anyway he was a drug addict. He knew, even as he talked to himself, that it was this last matter that was at the heart of his frustration. He lived in the shadow of his past, and while everyone else might only see the triumph of a new life, he saw his past as a canyon he might stumble into, since he walked along its edge every day.

When he returned to the house, Krystle rushed out the back door, crying, as he locked up the bike. He thought something terrible had happened; his first thought was of Reggie.

"Where did you go?" Krystle asked with a voice filled with terror.

"Nowhere," he said. "I just rode around. I needed some air."

"You need to tell me where you are going!"

"Why? I told you I didn't go anywhere." He did not like to say where he was going; he did not want to be kept on a leash.

"Because it frightens me! And it frightens Reggie."

"Reggie was asleep."

"He woke up, and he was frightened."

"He woke up because you made so much noise."

Reggie had followed his mother out onto the porch. Jake looked up to see him standing in the shadow of the door, watching, listening. Rather than his usual robust self he looked like a waif, slight and somber.

"Look at that," Jake said with disgust, and went to pick him up. Reggie began to cry when he did, and he was inconsolable. Krystle tried to take him from Jake's arms, but Jake turned away from her, wanting to hold Reggie and prove that he could comfort as well as she. But he proved the opposite. Reggie kept wailing until the sound split his ears. He finally turned him over to his mother, who took him into his bedroom. Jake could hear her consoling him, but he did not join them. Instead, in a flash, he punched the living room wall. He felt the plasterboard yield to his knuckles, and his hand bloomed with pain. He jerked his hand back and hit the wall again, this time plunging his whole fist through the hole that opened up.

Krystle came out of Reggie's room. "What are you doing?" she cried. "What are you doing? Are you crazy?"

7

Phase and Praise

✧

The men of the program stood shoulder to shoulder in the middle of the chapel floor. The noise of their singing was primitive: a deep male register, shouted tunelessly but with gusto, the sound of brotherhood. It was the same week by week, never failing to bring tears to Jake's eyes. He stood directly before the band, facing the plywood cross, his hands lifted high in the air. In this very place, seven years ago, he had surrendered his life to God. He remembered it every Friday at Phase and Praise. He always marveled that it had happened here, between the same plasterboard walls with the taped joints showing—that nothing in this shabby physical world had changed while for him, everything had changed.

He was still recovering from his fight with Krystle. She said everything was fine, but he was still emotionally bruised, and he was not sure about the truth of how Krystle was. This Phase and Praise worship was what he needed, to remind him of his new life.

The mission's rehab program lasted 10 months—a one month trial followed by three, three-month phases. Most Fridays two or three guys moved up from one phase to another, and sometimes as many as six. Today there were just two.

Jordie led the band, his yellow hair falling below his shoulders and his stringy arms covered with tattoos. Jordie played keyboard and sang with extreme intensity, not always quite on pitch. Nor were the other instruments—guitars, bass, drums—always in tune. But they spoke with a passionate voice, and the men in the program responded as they were meant to respond, with the deepest sincerity.

Some did, at least: Jake could see that some men new to the program stuck to observing. It was no doubt strange for them to see, a roomful of addicts high on God. Jake could remember the cynical view he had held before he was changed. The program always had people who pretended to be fully engaged, aping the sincerity of the true believers. A few also openly kept their distance, plainly distrustful of the reckless faith on display. Jake respected them, because he had been one of them not so long ago. That was one reason he was good at his job: he understood everybody, the addicts, the skeptics, the true believers.

Jake lifted up on his toes while he put his hands high above his head and raised his soul to the heavens. For the moment he experienced no responsibility, no need for self-preservation, just a tide of joyfulness washing through him as he sang his heart out.

When he had been saved, this feeling had caught him by surprise. He had no idea that any such frame of mind existed. He had been in his fifth rehab and his second go-round with the mission; he did the program because it was court-ordered and because he wanted, sometimes strongly, to be clean and sober. He tried hard, but he had not surrendered. The very essence of his existence was self-preservation, and he had always been smarter than most, except that for all his smarts he got caught falling down the same chute time and again.

Then God so overpowering, so immense, had made him look up. He had stopped entirely and surrendered to the great God.

You can't really explain it, Jake thought. It's God, it's not something you can order up. Though once he had discovered that state of mind, he found he could find it again.

And this became the order of his life: to bring it to others. The truth was so obvious, when you once had surrendered; you wanted to grab the men and shake them and tell them how different their lives could be. At first he had done just that, and felt amply justified, though he learned that it was God's business and you couldn't force it on anybody.

The third song came to a shuddering, tuneless end, the drums banging a hellacious noise. The men retreated like sheep to their chairs. Jake stood at the front of the room and introduced their first Phase-Up, Elvis Sebastiano, going from first to second phase. Elvis had huge guns and wore an Aussie-style outback hat with the side of the brim rolled up. He was a meth user; his partner of twelve years had called up the mission one day and said she had had all she could take, please come get him. Knox had gone to collect him. He had come like a lamb.

Jake enjoyed Elvis, as most people did. Elvis was funny, with the gift of gab, but he suffered from terrible anxiety and resorted to his fists when he became frustrated. Not that he had done so in his five months at the mission—violence or the threat of violence led to immediate dismissal—but he had a reputation on the street. Sometimes guests who saw him in the dining room backed out of the room, visibly disturbed. The guys in the program thought that was funny but Elvis didn't.

Elvis had taken an extra month to complete Phase 1. His 13-year-old daughter would call him crying on the phone, begging for him to take her home from her uncle's house. As a consequence Elvis got agitated, lost focus and skipped going to church, which was a requirement. He missed a number of AA meetings as well. Jake had talked to him to straighten that out, and laid down the penalty of the extra month.

Jake would not have been surprised if Elvis left the program at that point. Addicts could be hypersensitive to criticism; their egos were fragile and they reacted emotionally. But Elvis surprised everybody by taking it well. He told all the guys in the house that he was going to make it to graduation, if it took him 20 months or 20 years. With his outspoken enthusiasm he made a great leading example in the house. Still, Jake had no doubt Elvis might lose focus again on any day and be gone. He kept a close eye on him.

With just a little prompting, Elvis got through reciting his Bible verses. That was a requirement for Phase-Up: you had to memorize three passages of Scripture, and then read an essay you had written. Elvis grinned a lopsided smile as he pulled a wad of white paper out of the back pocket of his jeans. " I hope that I don't lose you guys with any big words," he said. "You know I got quite an education. Teachers always liked me and wanted me to sit right near them, at the front of the class." He grinned again, peeking up to see whether he got a laugh, then gave a deep breath. "Okay, enough of that, here goes," and he began to read from the paper, looking up occasionally to see his audience, and losing his place every time.

"I was ten years old when they came in the nighttime to tell my mom that my dad wasn't coming back from his boat. Mom was missing in action for the next ten years, and when she finally came to I was already in prison. Before that I graduated high school but most of what I learned, I learned outside of class. It went okay for a while and then I came to the point where I had lost my health, I had lost all my friendships, I had lost my daughter Amber, and I was just about to lose Angel who is the love of my life. She is the one who called Knox and said to come get me.

"So I came here, and I saw right away this is a different deal. I thought, wow, these people are serious. Nice of them to want to help me out but I'm not sure I can do this. I grew up believing in God but I never really paid him much attention. So when I came here I just tried to keep my head down and go along." Elvis was already freelancing from his written essay, and now he looked up from the paper to say, "Some of you new guys, I know that's exactly what you're doing. It's okay. Nobody is going to force you to do anything here. But for this program to do you any good, you have to get beyond that."

Elvis went back to the paper. It took him a minute to find the right line, and he stopped and started two or three times before he located it. The men in the program were smiling and nodding at each other; they expected something funny from Elvis. Elvis, however, was dead earnest. "The biggest change I've seen in the last three months—no, make that four months—is taking the whole thing seriously with God. And I'm learning not to isolate myself when I get worried about something. I appreciate all the guys in the program, and I thank my coach and my mentor who have been really supportive. I appreciate them giving their time, and I am learning to turn to them in times of difficulty, to pray for me and encourage me. I'm not used to it, but I am learning how to depend on other people. I am thankful for my church and I really love going there, even if I sometimes forget that I am not only encouraged to go but I am required to go." He looked up from his paper with a class-clown smirk and drew a few guffaws.

"I want to thank the Lord Jesus Christ, my God and Savior, for bringing me to this day when I have genuine hope for a clean and sober life. I am grateful to the mission and all you guys for walking with me on this journey. I have a daughter who I love very much, a brother who has chosen a better path than I have and is taking care of my daughter, and a lady named Angel who cared enough for me to get me here. I want to keep learning and growing through this program so I can take care of my daughter, and be a trustworthy person for her the rest of my life. I appreciate everybody's prayers and support, and I hope I can be an encouraging brother to you all."

Jake listened intently, trying to gauge Elvis's sincerity. He was a restless soul, and restlessness was sure to rise again; Phase 2 usually brought it out with its greater freedom. Men tended to think they had made it through the hard part when they reached this far, while in reality this was where they often drifted off course. They got cocky and thought they had it down.

The truth was, he had no idea whether Elvis would make it.

When people at church talked to him about the program, they wanted to know its success rate. It was a question that he resisted. He didn't actually know the success rate, but it wasn't high, he knew that. He was tempted to ask people: what do you think is the success rate of your church? People don't change easily; they don't shed addictions like a snake's skin. And they all remain vulnerable. He was vulnerable himself; he knew that for a certainty. Somebody might have a great story to tell today but find himself down at the bottom of the canyon tomorrow. Or even dead.

The struggle of Phase 2 was a good thing. He often told this to the men when they were fighting to survive. Life is difficult, he told them. This is life. After his own change he had floated like a soap bubble for at least two months. Everything was amazing and wonderful. But then it had all got him down. Funny how the dirt had bothered him; he hadn't been raised in a pristine environment. His mother had quit cleaning before he was born, and he and the rest of the kids didn't know any difference. But something about his addiction made him feel different about the dirt, the gray smear around the doorknobs, the mottled hyena pattern on the chapel carpet. It repulsed him.

The worst had been the other men. So emotional. So reactive. Guys sulked. Guys gossiped. There were in-groups and out-groups, and they mattered as much as they had in middle school. Each incident they made into a Judge Judy. That had ridden into him like somebody dumping dust down the back of his pants, until everything itched and scratched and he hated every instant he had to live with these men. He spilled it all to his mentor one day, who said simply: you're living with 30 addicts. What did you expect? And don't you think you affect people the same way?

Those trials would come to Elvis. And it would be especially hard for Elvis, who was naturally emotional. Who took out his emotions by hurting people.

Elvis's mentor came forward with the pin. Each man got one to attach to his name badge at phase-up: this one a gold cross. The mentor was an older man with clipped gray hair. He made a little speech, and they applauded Elvis. He made a circuit of the room, hugging every man, one by one.

Then Jake introduced DJ, who had just finished the candidate phase. Usually men entering the first phase were only beginning to make their personalities felt, but this was DJ's fourth time in the program. Most of the guys knew DJ. So after DJ recited his scriptures and read his essay, the comments that came were quite personal.

One by one they slipped up their hands until Jake called on them. Several of them told DJ they were inspired by his willingness to keep trying; they believed he could stick in the program this time.

Jake often reminded himself: they weren't here by choice. They were here by desperation. You could easily forget the abyss they teetered on. They had failed so often. Most of them had burned their family and friends so many times there was nobody left, just this last-chance ghetto with the stained carpet.

Jake had been in that precise place. When he had phased up, as Elvis had today, he had no more idea what direction his life would go than he knew how to do algebra. Now he had a loving wife and a beautiful son. He was a respectable member of society. Anybody could be. Though sometimes when he thought of all he had gained it seemed as weak as a spider's web. You could wipe it clean with a swipe of your hand.

8

THE LORD'S PERMISSION

✧

Buddy kept his manner offhand when Kent came on the phone. He said he had the impression Kent wasn't anxious to move the mission to Sebastopol Avenue, but he had some new information that he wanted to share. "I've been talking to the banks," he said. "You know how conservative banks are. It's hard for them to grasp the idea of renovating the Railroad Square neighborhood. I've really had to sell it to them, and that includes a future in which the Sonoma Gospel Mission continues to serve the poor right there on McKinley Street. I believe that's possible, and I've told them so. I believe it could be beautiful.

"The good news is that I've just about convinced them of the overall plan. The bad news is, they just don't see how it can work with the mission in its present location. I can't get that across to them. God knows I've tried. They see conflict with the neighbors. They see a culture clash between the homeless and a new generation of young professionals who have been spoiled rotten since the day they were born. Kent, I've tried my best to help them see that everybody can get along, which I really believe. But the sad truth is, I've reached my limits with them. They have a lot of years of experience, and they feel they know what is best."

He paused to let that sink in, and then, after a long sigh, went on. "So here's what I've done. I've told them that we need more money to make this a win-win. I know we haven't talked about any dollar amounts, but I think I told you in general what I was thinking—that we could pay you for the property based on what we believe it will be worth in a decade. I know you're attached to that property, so I told the banks we have to do better than that. We have to double that. We have to provide you enough to make your work grow in a way that you could never even dream of otherwise. Kent, does that sound like something you could talk about?"

After a long gap, Kent said that of course they could talk about it. "Buddy, I thought we had discussed some kind of swap, where you would build us a new building on Sebastopol Road."

"Absolutely. There can be some tax advantages to a swap. What I'm saying, Kent, is that we do that, plus we provide you the same amount in cash as a charitable contribution. With that money you can expand your programs. You can build another building twice the size if you want. Think what you can do with that money."

By the tone of his voice Kent seemed clearly interested. He asked how many dollars Buddy thought they would get. Buddy tried to dance around that—almost inevitably, imagination is better than facts—but Kent patiently insisted and eventually got him to name a figure. It did not sound that large to Buddy but Kent seemed positively impressed.

"What do you think the timing would be?" Kent asked.

"For what?" Buddy wanted to know.

"For when you would begin. When the money would be released, when the building could begin, when we could move out of the old building."

"Wow, that's really hard to say. Banks move so slowly, and there's the city permits and all that. My hope would be to get the money in six months and begin to build within a year. But I wouldn't want to put anything in writing."

All Buddy could offer were guesses and generalities, but in the midst of those hypotheticals he felt that he had done it again, what he always tried to do: he had made everybody happy. He was relieved for a second time. They seemed to have exhausted the questions, and were settling into the state of agreement.

"So Kent, do we have a deal?" Buddy asked, because he knew from his high school days selling pots and pans door to door that you want a verbal commitment.

Until that moment he had no hint of resistance. But there it was. "I don't want you to think I'm ungrateful," Kent said in that sweet, halting voice that reminded Buddy of Baptist deacons he had known growing up. "I know you have our best at heart. I appreciate that. It probably all makes sense from a dollars and cents point of view. But I guess the best I can tell you is that I need more time."

Buddy was aware of his heart beating hard into the silence. It beat hard enough to slightly shake the core of his body.

"Can you explain, Kent? Because I've tried my level best to set out a generous deal for you."

"I recognize that, Buddy. From a worldly standpoint, what you are saying makes such great sense. But I don't yet feel I have permission to move out of that old building."

"Are you talking about your board? Because I'd be happy to make a presentation to them."

"No, not the board." Kent's voice grew softer, as though he was embarrassed.

Kent's words mystified Buddy, leaving him no idea where to grab on. Under his mystification he felt a sense of doom. He absolutely had to make this work, but a lightning strike creased through his mind: he began to feel that it was impossible, for unknowable reasons.

"I'm sorry, I'm lost," Buddy said. "I need more help to understand whose permission we are talking about."

Kent was silent for at least ten seconds. "Buddy, it goes back a long way," he volunteered. "Some of the old board members could tell you. When we got the building, back in the 50s, there was a miracle. I wasn't here then but they say it was clearly God speaking. I guess they were thinking of another building and they had it all settled when God just told them to wait. And he delivered the McKinley Street building. The old men still talk about it with awe.

"So you see, I don't want to go against that. I would need permission."

It was now Buddy's turn to be silent. He went to church, but not that kind of church. He would quite gladly have pretended not to have heard what Kent said, except that he couldn't let this deal collapse. So he went on. He ventured cautiously forward.

"You're saying you would need permission from God."

"Yes."

"What would that permission look like?" he asked. "How would you know that God wanted you to move?"

"I don't know," Kent said. "I realize this probably sounds strange to you, but I'm listening. I'm hopeful I'll get the right message when the time comes."

"So you think it will come?"

Buddy could almost hear the shrug over the phone. "It could."

"Do you think something will happen? Like a magical sign?" For Buddy, merely to ask such a question was excruciatingly weird.

"That's one possibility."

"What other possibilities are there?"

Kent's voice signaled that he was reluctant to speculate. "Well, something might make it impossible to stay on McKinley Street."

"Why isn't it a sign that I've come to you with an opportunity to get a new building and have money to expand your work?"

Kent sounded apologetic again. "Buddy, I appreciate that you are doing all you can for us, and don't take this wrong, but it's just money. I can't tell you how many times we've had to pass up an offer of money. We've had people come to us offering literally millions of dollars if we would just change our program. We've been told of government grants that could provide all our needs, if we would just eliminate the God-talk."

"But I'm not asking you to change anything. What I'm offering would help you do what you already do."

A sigh. "That's true. But you asked me why your offer isn't a sign. To give up a building that God gave us and that God has used, we have to see something more than money. I don't know what that would be, but I believe we will recognize it when we see it."

"It could be something pushing you out?"

Another long and reluctant pause. "It could be. If an earthquake leveled the building, I would take that as an indication. But I don't want to try to predict what God might do."

9

Code Violations

✧

For some time after the phone call, Buddy sat at his desk, practicing relaxation techniques: letting his eyelids grow heavy, permitting his hands to slip into dead weight. Despite the efforts, anger welled up in his upper chest and he found it hard to breathe. He was being deprived of something he felt was his right. After going to such lengths to create a win for everybody, and develop the neighborhood in a way that would prove to be a tremendous bonus to the mission, he was told that he must wait for "permission," something Kent could not describe.

Buddy was so agitated he could not sit still. He could not possibly talk to anyone. Buddy did something he had not done for years: he went for a walk. He even left his phone on his desk, though he had not reached the stairs before insecurity gripped him and he went back to get it.

From the parking lot he made his way to Bennett Valley Road, and then hesitated, perplexed. There was a sidewalk built into the wood chip and shrub landscaping of a Carmen's Burgers, but it ended in thirty yards, where the Oil Stop property began. Buddy set off nonetheless, threading himself along a faint pathway in the grasses by Oil Stop, stepping over a broken bottle and several smashed cans of Coors. Then he encountered a chain link fence protecting a U-Rent, which forced him onto the edge of the road, with cars zooming past his elbow. He looked across the street to see a section of sidewalk there, in front of the Catholic cemetery, but looking ahead he could see that it ended too, at the edge of the property, so he persevered walking in traffic.

Beyond the U-Rent was a dentist's office, set well back from the road. He was able to get off the road, walking on the manicured lawn. At the corner light he pushed a button and then waited interminably. He stared at a small swale of cardboard debris and charcoal-colored grit that had built up in a Bermuda triangle of the intersection, where cars cut the corner.

He was traversing a landscape designed for cars; people on foot were hardly an afterthought. Soon Buddy's mind was engaged in thinking about the place of pedestrians in development, the question of why they had been so neglected, and whether they would make a comeback in new urban projects like Railroad Square. He could add that to his pitch, he realized. It would go down well with the environmentalists.

His anger slipped away. He did, after all, sympathize with the mission's work helping the homeless. Like many people who have risen from poverty, Buddy placed great faith in inspiration and motivation, which he believed was at the core of the mission's religious principles. He had always had plenty of motivation in himself—he came out of the womb kicking—but he knew it was common for other people to find it in God.

By this time he had found his way past the fairgrounds and onto regular residential streets, with sidewalks. It was much easier to walk here, and he found himself enjoying the small boxy houses and the flowerbeds, so similar to the homes he had known as a boy.

What stuck in his craw was the fact that he was offering the mission so much. He wasn't stealing from them, he was helping them. They obviously needed the money. Yet they were ready to turn him down, for lack of something they called permission.

As he thought of this his resentment rekindled, but so did the memory that he had no deal, and that without a deal he had no money, and that without money he didn't know what he would do.

Buddy had grown up in small-town Oklahoma, middle class in a world barely aware that class existed: only that some few were rich because of success at business; some few were poor because they drank or were black; and almost everybody else had about the same as he: a bedroom to share with two brothers, a TV in the living room, a bicycle, and a wardrobe of jeans and T-shirts. In the summer they swam in the community swimming pool and watched the girls out of the corners of their eyes. In the fall they played football, in winter basketball, and in spring, baseball. Buddy's family could be portrayed as poor—at the end of the month money was always scarce—but he never felt poor.

What he felt was the desire to rise. When he learned the Bible story of Joseph and his brothers, he identified: he expected that the rest of the world would eventually bow to him.

His mother shared this ambition for him. She wanted Buddy to become a preacher, and he had no objection. Preachers were respected and educated, and (unlike bankers and oilmen) anybody could rise to be one. It took talent and hard work, nothing more. When he was little he preached sermons to his little brothers for pretend church.

In fifth grade he followed some sixth grade boys to the creek, where they huddled around a boy flipping a knife into two frogs he had caught mating. Buddy caught only a glimpse of the blood and guts but that was plenty. He escaped the ring of boys and ran away wiping tears. His father, when he heard about it, told him he needed to toughen up. His mother, however, took note. She described him as the compassionate one in the family so many times that he adopted the identity. He made a point to protect helpless kids from bullies or to encourage children who failed a test. He noticed others' pain. This wasn't an especially admired trait in small town Oklahoma, but it did seem to point him out as a preacher.

His mother was proud, and she scrimped so that he could go to Bible college. He never told her that his career aspirations changed in high school; she wouldn't have sent him. He wanted a college education, and that was the only way he knew to get one. Lots of people in Oklahoma went to Bible college without intending anything sacred.

These days he never mentioned Bible college. If he said anything, he said he attended Steerforth University, which was true. He didn't have to mention that it had been Steerforth Bible College when he attended. That would seem too strange for the average Californian.

He met Charlotte there. She came from Oklahoma City, a world of sophistication and privilege compared to his home town. She went to Steerforth because it was the only way her mother would let her get away from home.

She was nothing like a beauty, but she was interesting to look at; she had style. Charlotte loved the movies, which students at Steerforth were not allowed to attend, but which she contrived to see nonetheless on the sly. Movies were more than a source of entertainment to her; they were inspiration. She watched them to learn how to live.

She must have sensed a kindred spirit in Buddy, because she quite brazenly invited him to go to the movies with her. When he asked her how they would do that, she suggested that they say that they were going to a Navigators training meeting. They would buy tickets separately and meet in the theater lobby. Forbidden fruit soon became part of Buddy's regular diet. His interest in his classes rapidly waned in comparison to his interest in getting his hands inside Charlotte's bra.

One thing led to another until in the spring term the dean called him in. Buddy remembered precisely the solitary walk across campus to the dean's office. The come-up was no surprise. He had failed several classes. He knew he would be sent home, and he had no one to blame but himself. "I've done everything wrong," he said to himself. "I'm finished." Absurdly, he could hear the birds singing with abandon, as though they were celebrating his departure. He was nineteen years old and he dreaded facing his mother. Wild ideas swam through his brain: he would not go home, he would go to work on the oil fields.

As soon as he reached the dean's office he blurted out a plea. He claimed no excuse; he begged forgiveness. He had no hope of staying at the school, and that was not in his mind. He wanted to be absolved, so he could feel whole again. He had a sensitive conscience, and sometimes a lively sense of guilt, both triggered by failure.

The dean was a bony, balding man they called Mole, because he had a large black mole under his left eye. He did not bother to dress down Buddy; he urged him to go home and think it over and come back when he was ready to be serious. "We won't hold it against you, Buddy, but you know as well as I do that right now you are wasting your parents' money."

Buddy was relieved to escape the dean's office without facing white-hot wrath, but neither did he feel absolved. He still had to face his mother. In the meantime, he had to pack and say good-bye to Charlotte.

He waited for her in the library, in a corner of the stacks that stunk of old books and mold. It had often been their private place of meeting. When Charlotte appeared she looked askew, her hair tossed, her face rosy. No matter: he began to tell her his news. Before he got anywhere, she stopped him, grabbed both his hands in hers, and said that she was pregnant.

Buddy had a difficult time understanding her words, and when he did, it seemed to him as though he would have to die. He began to weep.

"What are you doing?" Charlotte demanded.

"I'm so sorry. It's my fault," he said. "I've done everything wrong."

"What's the matter, you don't like children?"

It might not be said that Charlotte was happy to be expecting a child, but she was not unhappy, either. Charlotte was unashamed. To her it was a fact of life, and a challenge to be met. To Buddy's wonder she suggested they get married immediately by a justice of the peace and move to Texas, where she had a cousin who would take them in until they got settled. She taught Buddy the most fundamental lesson of his life, which was to believe that every circumstance is for good if you only press forward.

At that point in his life, Buddy knew nothing about money. His father worked in a potato chip factory, and never thought of anything better than his two paychecks a month. Charlotte expanded Buddy's horizons. In Fort Worth he got a job on a car lot, first cleaning cars and soon selling them, a job for which it turned out he was sublimely suited. He had the gift of gab. He genuinely enjoyed meeting people, and he never lost sight of the sale. Consequently he made good money, which he and Charlotte saved. Charlotte was always on the lookout for a chance, and she saw an opportunity to buy out the owner of the duplex they lived in. They would be collecting rent instead of paying it. This led to ownership of an apartment complex and then, via an inspired act of chutzpah, building an apartment complex from scratch.

Buddy's father had not been a fix-it man, and neither was Buddy, but—as he would come to believe—that saved him from a disastrous life as a carpenter-plumber-handyman. He had to hire people to do the construction and therefore learned how to make money by multiplication instead of addition, just as he had learned how to make money selling cars he did not own.

As a builder and a landlord he had a flexible schedule, which enabled him to begin taking college classes again. He didn't need to; he was already making plenty of money. But Buddy never lost his mother's faith in education. He noticed that while plenty of rich people didn't have much of it, the people he admired most had college degrees. So he stuck at it, going to local schools until he had one too.

He also attended church. Charlotte never had time for it, but Buddy retained a belief that children needed the influence of Sunday school. He took their children and, while they were at class, attended services himself. It wasn't difficult for him; he had grown up doing it. Buddy got asked occasionally to serve on a committee or maybe to help with the annual barbecue. He usually begged off.

He was getting rich. He had three young children and a Corvette. He learned to play golf and launched a wine collection.

Then one day Charlotte approached him with a strange look on her face. She had a drink in her hand and he wondered whether she had drunk several already. They always kissed when they met, and they did so now. Charlotte drew back and, without taking her eyes off him, said, "Buddy, I don't know how to get into this so let me just say it now while I can. You know Ken?"

He nodded, and immediately he knew. A tremor ran through him. He had suspected nothing. Ken was in the oil business, supplying equipment to wildcatters. He had done extremely well. They met at the golf club, and Buddy sometimes played in a foursome with him.

"Well, Ken and I have been seeing each other. There's quite an attraction. I like him a lot, and he likes me. We are good for each other."

Buddy's face turned red but he stayed calm. He was shocked beyond all measure. "How far has it gone?" he asked.

"It's gone pretty far," she said. "Like I said, there's quite an attraction."

"Damn," he said. "Shit." Buddy was not one to use language, and that was as violent as he ever got. He was going to be upset, he could feel that, but he never wavered in his love for Charlotte. "I don't know what to say," he said. "I know we can get through this. I'm glad you told me now, before it went any farther." He took a deep suck of air. "Charlotte, it's going to be hard but I forgive you. I might need some time but I love you, and I'm going to forgive you."

A little smile came on her lips, the kind of look she gave him when he said something stupid and naïve. "That's great, Buddy. But I'm not really asking for forgiveness. I'm asking for a divorce."

It took him some time to take that in. When he did, it made a kind of sense. She was moving up. She didn't say it that way but Buddy figured it out. They were both ambitious people and she had found a way to jump ahead. She didn't need him.

Divorce induced in Buddy his first real crisis, which caught him completely by surprise. It was not like he had never encountered divorce. Other friends had divorced and he had offered words of condolence without feeling that it was a terrible tragedy. He had thought of divorce as sad, on the level with getting laid off from your job or being turned down for a loan.

His emotions, however, were as raw as hamburger. Charlotte was the only woman he had known. She was his mentor in courage. He relied on her judgment in knowing what to do and how things should look. He could tell her anything, and he did: they had together dreamed their way and calculated their way through every business deal he ever made.

In the first shock he couldn't stop talking about it, asking friends to talk to Charlotte, asking what he had done wrong. He felt horribly guilty but he didn't know for what. In desperation he went to his pastor and poured out his feelings. The pastor told him to pray, but that wasn't workable for Buddy. His prayers sounded stupid to him. He tried repeatedly to reach Charlotte but she systematically cut him off: trading for a different car, changing her phone number, refusing to talk when he did finally locate her.

Exhausted from the emotion, he finally gave up trying to get her back. For months he lived a zombie life: dead but still moving. One day he got in the car and drove from Texas to California, leaving all his properties in Charlotte's hands. He believed she would not cheat him, but whether she did or not was all the same. None of it meant anything to him any more. In Huntington Beach he parked his car near the water and walked on the sand. Days went by and he made a routine of it: walk in the morning, eat lunch at a seaside café, then walk in the afternoon and evening. He regained his high school weight, and needed new clothes.

He met Diana in the café. She waited on him and once, when he lingered over a glass of wine, sat down with him. Only six months had passed since Charlotte had made her announcement, but for Buddy it seemed like he had been stuck on an endless trip through purgatory, trudging toward Hades. Now Diana flicked his life back on. She was an artist doing large abstracts in oil. He felt inadequate to such a sophisticated woman, but the challenge she represented made him feel alive. Buddy got Charlotte to sell a property in Dallas; he put up the money to open a gallery in Redondo Beach. Diana moved in with him. Only a short blip had interrupted his plans, all for the good.

He never married Diana. Her paintings didn't sell and the two of them drifted apart, with only one calamitous argument weeks after their relationship was over in substance, even while they still shared an apartment. He closed the art gallery and moved to Pasadena, far from the beach, and then east to the Inland Empire. In the high desert you could build anything if you moved quickly. He made stacks of money in housing subdivisions—nice ones, with amenities. He married Edith, who played tennis and enjoyed spending stacks of money. It was during this period of his life that Buddy began to buy paintings, as though an embryonic affinity had been planted during his time with Diana, and only now began to flourish. Edith liked interior decorating, and she required paintings. Buddy found he enjoyed going out to purchase them; he had good taste. He bought art books and learned the language of the art world. He drank chardonnay at art gallery openings as far as Santa Barbara.

He and Edith were together for almost four years, and when she divorced Buddy she managed to get a lot of what he had earned during those years. No matter: there was more where that came from. Buddy moved north, dabbling at construction in the East Bay. He did one housing subdivision but mostly strip malls. Then he plunged on an office building near the BART line.

He was, unfortunately, highly leveraged when the 2008 crash demolished his holdings. Moving to Santa Rosa was an economy move. As Charlotte had taught him, he kept smiling and moving forward. Lately, though, he caught a scent in the air that he did not remember. The property business remained depressed. He had begun to suspect that he could not catch every fall.

But this Railroad Square development had come to him like a dream. He saw in it all he had wanted for himself. He could catch the wave at just the right time, and transform a neighborhood. It would be a new model for the North Bay. Everybody would benefit, and if all went well, he might make so much money he would never need to work again.

Buddy wandered toward downtown and into the Sonoma County Administrative Center. Both city and county shared the complex of would-be-Bauhaus concrete structures that could pass for tornado shelters. Its low buildings sprawled over five acres in no discernible pattern. You could sometimes find an inexperienced citizen wandering its pathways searching for an office. All the signs, when there were any at all, used a tiny modernist script that you had to stoop down to read. The architect must have hated people.

Nor were the staff helpful, Buddy thought. Somebody in the bureaucracy had injected a dose of surliness into the system early on, and it had caught like a virus. Maybe they gave Buddy grief because he was a developer, though why people whose salaries depended on the fees they charged developers should hold a grudge against them was beyond Buddy's imagination. Sometimes he was tempted to ask. He didn't; it wasn't wise to get on the wrong side. Better to smile and move forward.

As he wandered through the complex it occurred to him that he could visit some of this rudeness on the mission. They were waiting for some sign. Kent had said that it could be something pushing them out. Maybe he could give them that little push.

He had never been inside the county health department. It had the unwelcoming aspect of many government agencies: a counter that served as a wall to keep the public at bay, bare beige walls, serviceable metal desks and filing cabinets that staff had cluttered with photos and clippings. Buddy talked to the woman who met him at the counter—Sally, he read on the nameplate. She was a stylish fiftyish, a graying blonde, chewing gum. Not bad looking, he noted, considering her age.

"If somebody suspected that an eating establishment had rats in their kitchen," Buddy began, "but he didn't want the word to get back that he had made a complaint, what could he do?"

She looked at him deadpan, taking so long to respond that he was about to repeat his question when her lips moved. "Talking about a restaurant?"

"Uh, sort of. A kind of cafeteria."

"Like a school? A nursing home? What are we talking about?"

"A homeless shelter." He had not wanted to come out and say that.

"Which one?"

"Do I have to say that?"

"If you got a complaint and you want us to do something about it, it helps if we know which one it is." Her tone was impatient.

"The Sonoma Gospel Mission. On Sixth Street."

Again she stared at him, as though her computer were searching the Internet on a slow connection. "You know which one that is?" Buddy asked.

"Can't stand those people," she said. "They put on that free meal at the fairgrounds every Thanksgiving, and before you get a turkey wing to eat, you have to stand in line and listen to a sermon. You're saying they have rats?"

"I don't know that they have rats. I was wondering what could happen if I was worried about rats. I don't want it to get back to them."

"How could it get back to them? I don't know who the hell you are."

"Right," Buddy responded. "That's the way I want it to be. Could you send an inspector to check?"

"Sixth Street, right?" she said, and disappeared behind a partition in the back of the room. Buddy could hear her opening and slamming file drawers. Finally she came out with a dark green hanging file stuffed with paper. "The place is a mess," she said to herself as she leafed through it. "Look at this."

"Have you had problems there before?" he asked sympathetically.

"The place is a mess," she said again, flipping through papers. "I hate this." She then looked up at Buddy. "No."

"No what?"

"No what did you ask? No we haven't had problems. They've never been cited."

"There's a first time for everything," he said drily.

"You can always find something," she said, for the first time seeming to brighten in her aspect. "There's not a dining establishment in the city you can't find something. Thanks for the tip, Mr...."

"No need to thank me," he said.

Pleased with himself, feeling new hope and energy, he proceeded to the planning department. This was his territory; like any developer he had managed many projects through its bureaucracy. Knowing the stickiness of the permit process, he thought he could find something to trip up the mission.

There had been code violations at the mission, he learned, mostly having to do with plumbing and in particular the upstairs showers. But the problems were three years old and seemed to have been straightened out.

"I bet you have to keep an eye on those people," he said to an inspector he knew by sight, if not by name.

"What do you mean?"

"In an old building, there's always the tendency to cut corners."

The inspector shrugged. "You know anybody who doesn't have that tendency? But those guys are pretty good. These old things"—he riffled through the paperwork—"I remember the problems they had with the showers. There are so many state codes for health and public accommodation and you name it, half the time we don't know what they are supposed to do. They had to help us figure it out by calling some of the other rescue missions they know."

On a roll, Buddy visited the police department. A friend there let him look at police logs. He was searching randomly for arrests in the area around the mission when he came on Kasha's. She had been charged, and then made her own complaints, which were duly received. Then all the charges were dropped. The whole thing was written in staccato sentences laced with code numbers, which Buddy found difficult to make sense of.

"Why would the charges get dropped?" he asked his friend. "Supposedly she broke the man's arm."

He studied the papers and then shrugged. "Maybe the only witness skipped town. Hard to say."

Buddy copied down Kasha's information. He wasn't sure what he could do with it.

10

Easy Money

✧

Elvis Sebastiano learned of his daughter Amber's birth long after the fact. He had been in prison for robbing Big O Tires' petty cash, a crime hardly worth the trouble to report except that he had hit one of the technicians, an annoying kid he remembered from middle school. For that he got burglary and aggravated assault.

He hardly knew Amber's mother, named Lilly Baines. Drugs and sex were their only points in common. Somebody in prison told him she was pregnant and claiming that the baby was his, but that hardly registered. He had other things to think about in prison, like survival.

When he got out, he went back to Fort Bragg and immediately found his dealer, who lived in an old redwood-sided cabin in the woods north of the river, off the road to Willits. Ted had somehow ended up with five old farm tractors, which were strewn about the property. He tried to get Elvis to take one off his hands. That led to other topics and Elvis asked about Lilly. Ted said that she was gone, he didn't know where, somebody said Las Vegas.

"She told somebody I was the father," Elvis commented.

"Everybody," Ted said. "She told everybody that."

"If that was so, why did she leave without telling me where?"

Ted's sudden stillness and his small, amused smile caused Elvis to stop. "What?" he said.

"She left you a message. I guess you didn't get it. It's more than a message. She left you a baby."

Lilly had told anyone and everyone that she had done all the work of birthing Amber, and now Elvis should raise her. It was her concept of shared parenting. She had left the baby with his aunt Allie, a vegan who taught yoga classes down in Mendocino. He went to see her that same day. When he held the squalling infant Elvis was touched. He swore on the spot that he would take care of her; he didn't know whether she was really his but he would take her for his own, if Allie would do the honors of actually raising her. Allie, who wore long, flowing hippie dresses and had hair to her waist, was okay with that arrangement. She had never married or had children, and she liked the thought of a little girl to dress up and care for.

Elvis mostly forgot about Amber. He was in and out of prison, and whenever he came out he went right back on meth, so he wasn't good for anybody, let alone a little girl. He rarely remembered Amber's birthday and was usually somewhere else at Christmas. From time to time she came to his mind and he went to see her, usually carrying a large and age-inappropriate gift such as the hulking red lizard that he presented to her when she was two. He still had a picture of that, somewhere. She was an occasional diversion for him. She made him feel good when he remembered that he was a parent.

In the past year, though, she had mysteriously worked her way into his heart. It made no sense, but it was unquestionably true. She even appeared in his dreams. Perhaps it was simply because she had become a teenager, a complaining, sarcastic, bleak-sighted adolescent who looked something like his pictures when he was a kid and at the least was recognizably a human being and not a play doll.

In the year before his lady Angel reached her limit and delivered Elvis to the mission, Amber came to stay with them in Santa Rosa over school vacations. She was 12 then and already acting like a punk. She had her ear buds on before breakfast and got annoyed if she couldn't hear you over the blast of her music. Her language was foul. It was typical of Elvis that Amber interested him only when she stopped being cute and instead became difficult.

Recently she was staying with his older brother, an ex-professional football player who had retired at 28 and lived on the headlands south of Fort Bragg. Allie had cancer and Tom took Amber in while Allie was in treatment, which was generous of him considering he and Elvis had never gotten along. Tom believed in discipline and kept strict rules, and Amber hated him. She was failing three classes at school and was always grounded. Elvis called her from the mission most nights and often she was crying. He could do nothing to help her. "Amber, I have to stick to this program. I'm no good to you or anybody unless I'm clean."

She said she understood, but how could she, really? She was 13.

Angel was also involved with Amber, even though Elvis urged her to stay out of it. A couple of weeks ago she had said she couldn't stand another minute of what she was hearing, so she drove to Fort Bragg and collected Amber, without bothering to work it through with Tom first.

When Elvis heard what his brother had been doing he would have liked to punch his brother's teeth in. Tom didn't believe in meds, so he had thrown away the prescriptions that dealt with Amber's ADD. It made Elvis sick to think of what his daughter had endured. But he didn't say anything about it when he talked to Tom. He gritted his teeth and kept quiet.

His brothers at the mission congratulated him for that; the Bible says to be slow to anger and slow to speak. Elvis talked that line too, but self-restraint was totally alien to his nature. He wanted to walk out of the mission, go beat up his brother, and then build a new life with Angel and Amber. He knew he could do it. He would go back to his old job running a landscaping crew. The boss said he was welcome any time, working off-book.

What held him back, however, was a memory of the last time he had been free, how he had located his drug-dealing neighbor the very first day—spying on him from the window, observing him as he washed his car. Elvis had never met the man, and had no idea of his name, but something about the way he looked around him, as though sniffing the air, told Elvis he would open the flow of drugs.

Elvis remembered that he was an addict. This program was his last chance to change, or he might lose his daughter forever. He would lose Angel, too.

He had to stay, and hope that Amber would be all right without him.

Sam's uncle brought him back to the mission, hardly speaking during the 45-minute drive through camel-colored hills and the flashing geometry of vineyards. He took it as a personal affront that he had to return his nephew to a place that had kicked him out for smoking. This did not help Sam's mood. He came back to the mission in a horrible funk. A haze seemed to hang around his eyes and ears as he handed over his cell phone, peed in a cup and took a bunk in the 12-man room. He had made it in time for lunch, and he entered the dining room at the end of a line of men. The smell of stew revolted him. He had been gone just three days but everything seemed alien. The backs of the men in front of him in line seemed huge, hulking and monsterish. The dining room not only didn't have ruffles on the curtains, half the chairs were coming apart. He couldn't speak.

Yet when he got his plate and looked for a seat the guys saw him and stood up to shake hands and welcome him back. He remembered that he had been sad to leave. They put him on laundry, which meant hours of uneventful monotony, folding sheets and towels to the clunk and surge of washing machines and dryers. It was a simple existence and a secure one. Within a day he had fallen into familiar routines.

So he was back in the program. Even so, in those few days outside he had acquired a different attitude toward the mission, which had shown a cold heart in kicking him out for a single infraction, as his uncle said. He felt less sure that the program was his only way ahead. He had no alternative right now—nowhere to go except to sleep by the creek, which terrified him. Nevertheless, being outside for three days had made him aware of how small and constricted the mission was. He was standing on the perimeter of the program now, watching. What he was watching for, he did not know.

You were not supposed to be in Knox's office unless you had business with Knox, but the hallway outside was a collection point for guys running errands for guest services. It was a noisy, interesting place. There were always a few people hanging around, and Knox was too softhearted to make them leave. Just about everybody on the street came to the front desk wanting something, sooner or later. So when he was not doing laundry, Sam hung around the hallway, looking out at the front desk, watching for something, he did not know what.

Knox had a stack of magazines inside his door, and Sam picked up one just as he had seen others do. It was a National Geographic with a cover photograph of a horse running over a brilliant green field. He flipped through until he came to an article on North Dakota discussing something called fracking. The word caught his attention: it sounded like a drug. He looked carefully at the pictures and read their captions, but could not really understand the subject. Fracking was compared to a gold rush, and it seemed to have created a crisis. People had crowded into North Dakota because of fracking and there was no place for them to live. One of the pictures showed a mother and five children like a family in the Oklahoma Dust Bowl, pained and desperate.

When Knox came back to his office Sam showed him the article and asked what it was about. Knox said that they had a new way of drilling for oil and gas. "I guess it's blowing up so fast they can't even get enough workers. And the ones they got, they don't have a place to put them. Everybody is making money, and none of them can even rent a room.

"It's cold up there, too," Knox said. "You can't sleep out of doors."

At dinner Sam gathered his courage and asked cautiously if anybody at the table knew about fracking. Some of them had heard of it. Louis claimed he had a cousin who said you could make $10,000 a month on a construction crew. But considering the fortune to be made, Louis seemed only mildly curious. Elvis Sebastiano was the only one at the table who apparently found the subject as fascinating as Sam did.

The two of them knew each other slightly. You could not live pressed together in the program without encountering everybody. Both of them had been so preoccupied with their own troubles, however, that they saw each other as though viewing small figures at the bottom of a cliff.

Now that they discovered something in common, though, they felt some mutual attraction. Elvis thought he saw himself in Sam. That is, he thought he saw the young and innocent boy he once had been, whose father had died. It brought out something tender in his heart.

To Sam, Elvis seemed much older, more experienced, more confident than he. He could never imagine someone like Elvis wanting to talk to him. Yet quite suddenly, Elvis did. He was of the opinion that they ought to go up to North Dakota and make some serious money. With a little effort he thought a guy could save enough to buy a nice car and still have some left. They began to discuss what kind of car to buy, and how long it would take to save that much. That discussion actually interested the other guys at the table. Some said six months, others a year, and Louis thought you could do it in three months.

But Louis quickly tired of the subject. "What the hell, you can't get there, so why think about it?"

"Why can't you get there?"

"You haven't got a car. And no money for gas. It would cost you $100 just to pay for gas. Maybe $150."

"You could take the Greyhound."

"That costs money too. And what would you do when you got there? Walk? People in that state drive twenty miles for a pack of cigarettes."

The guys in the program spent much of their time talking about life outside, where they could not go: the women they knew, the places they liked to eat, music concerts, sports. They argued over which seats were the best in AT&T Park and talked about games they had apparently attended, even though it was doubtful that any of them had the money to buy a ticket. Sam took it in unclouded by doubt. His experience in Modesto had never been like that, but then, he just got out of high school a year ago. Therefore he accepted the common judgment: fracking was impossible.

That night when Sam was reading his Bible in bed, Elvis surprised him by coming in to talk. Elvis had on his Aussie outback hat and a faux fur vest, open on his bare chest. There was nowhere to sit in the room, which had a row of six bunk beds stacked like library shelves. So Elvis sat on the floor with his back against the wall. He still had fracking on his mind.

He began by saying how they should go there and get jobs when they finished the program. "How long until you are done, Sam?"

Sam blushed and stuttered out that he had ten months. Elvis looked at him. "Oh yeah, I forgot. You went and came back so quick."

"How long for you, Elvis?"

"I just phased up. Six months to go."

Guys wandered in and out. Some added to the conversation. Richard, a two-week-old candidate, said they should talk to Santiago Gomez, who had $9,000 waiting for him in the mission safe.

"Where did he get that money?" Elvis wanted to know. "Somebody die?"

"I heard that he got it from insurance. He was in some kind of accident a long time ago and they finally settled it. You ever notice his teeth? I think his teeth got busted out in the accident and they had to pay for new ones."

You weren't allowed to hold on to funds while you were in the program; the mission held them for you until you graduated. For most of them this was inconsequential. They might have fifteen dollars in their pocket when they joined. Nine thousand dollars was unbelievable.

"I'm going to go talk to him," Elvis said, jumping to his feet.

He found Santiago in the yard, doing reps with the free weights. The mission had put up a single fluorescent shop light over the weight area. The rest of the yard was dark, though enough light filtered from streetlights and windows to show dimly a cluttered space used for storage, for barbecue, for storing and repairing bicycles, and for lifting. There were a few benches where, on a sweet day, you might find one of the men stretched out with his face to the sun.

Santiago had a sleepy flat face and a rounded middle. He wore nothing but athletic shorts and a pair of running shoes. His skin shone with sweat. Santiago never smiled, because his teeth were bad. He looked lazy and harmless unless you noticed his arms and legs, which appeared to be molded from oak branches.

Elvis grabbed two dumbbells and began lifting alongside Santiago, at first silently and then throwing out a few cursory comments on the day. He knew Santiago was no talker. He had lifted with him before.

Elvis didn't mention the money, feeling that would be in bad taste. He began talking about North Dakota, saying he and Sam had been discussing it. Did Santiago know about fracking? Santiago grunted, a sound that could be no or yes.

"Knox says they are paying big bucks for anybody who has two working arms and at least one leg. They are pulling oil out of the ground so fast they just need bodies, more than they can get. To do anything. Drivers. Cooks. Even janitors are pulling gold-plated checks with all kinds of bennies—health, dental, pension, whatever you want. It's unbelievable."

Santiago did not even grunt, which Elvis interpreted as a sign of interest.

"Yeah, Sam and I were talking that we ought to just get up there."

As he said it, he caught himself. He couldn't help Amber from up there. For an instant a gap opened and his mind was flooded with light. He came within a breath of dropping the dumbbells and walking back inside. And yet he felt a fever driving him forward. It was like when he watched his dope-dealing neighbor. He had the obsession to procure something, the frenzy to see what he could get. He glimpsed the similarity and pushed forward anyway.

"We are thinking that we could go as a group, so we had accountability to stay sober. Almost like taking the program on the road. We'd get a good car and drive up there together. Takes about two days to do it."

"I know a guy we could get a car from," Santiago said, speaking so softly that Elvis could barely make out the words. In fact, Elvis was not sure he heard correctly.

"Yeah, we need a car. That's the big hang-up. Who's your friend?"

"Oh, he's not a friend, he's just a guy who sells cars. He gets them from the state auction. I hear they are good cars, he's reliable."

"You want to come and talk to Sam?" Elvis hung out the possibility like a flag.

Santiago grunted, and this time he clearly meant yes.

Jake's Challenges

Sam knocked timidly on Jake's office door, little pecks that might have come from a bird. Jake yelled, "Come" from his desk, but Sam did not enter until Jake walked to the door and opened it himself. He knew it was Sam; who else in the house would be afraid to knock? Jake felt a deep tenderness for Sam, because he seemed so helpless.

"You wanted to see me," Sam stuttered.

"Yeah. Sit down." He waved Sam into a chair and fell heavily into his own. "I wanted to make sure that you are doing all right. Are you settling back in? Do you need anything?"

Sam blinked at him, as though he were examining the questions for hooks. "No. I'm fine." He said it as though he was not sure it was the right answer.

"It can be hard, starting over," Jake said. "Sometimes it's hard to get your head back into the same place."

Sam was a hiding creature, and he said nothing. How did Jake divine what went on in his head? Sam half expected him to ask about the fracking business, even though they had all sworn secrecy.

Jake never noticed Sam's failure to respond, for he was remembering his own journey back into the house. He would never forget traversing the passageway to Kent's office. His feet had not cooperated—he tripped twice on the stairs—and he kept his eyes lowered for fear of seeing someone who knew him, who could mock him, who would think it was funny that he had returned. For the first week he had moved like a man in a suit of armor.

"You've got to put yourself into it with all your heart, and ignore what anybody else thinks," Jake said to Sam. "You find out that other people are so tied up in worrying about their own problems they don't really notice you. You might think they are thinking about you, but not really. Did anybody say anything?"

"No," Sam said. "Everybody was pretty great."

"They hardly had time to notice you were gone, and you were back again." Jake was still thinking of his own experience. "But it probably seemed like forever to you. You were at your uncle's?"

Sam nodded. He would have stopped there but he saw that Jake waited for more, so he edged carefully into telling about his cousin's wedding. "Used to be at something like that I would drink myself silly, and dance, and talk to everybody. This time I really didn't know how to act." He flushed slightly at the thought, which genuinely embarrassed him.

Sam was so delicately constructed it was hard to think of him as 19. Jake felt toward him the way he felt toward his son Reggie. You want so much to provide what you yourself never received.

Jake had never met his father, at least not to his memory. His mother gave out no information, and as a boy he had believed that she kept his location a secret for obscure adult reasons. After his mother was dead it occurred to Jake that quite possibly his mother had no idea where his father was or what he did. Maybe she didn't even know who his father was. He had gone to clean out her house. Hoping to find a clue about his father, he had searched her things but found nothing but meaningless paper: old Visa bills, parking tickets, his own painting masterpieces from the third grade, a church bulletin. (When had she gone to church? Never with him.) No secret love notes, no will, no good-bye letter to him or anybody.

"Did you ever talk to your father?" Jake asked Sam.

Sam hesitated and nodded yes. His father had called him at his uncle's house.

"How did that go?"

Sam shrugged.

As much as Jake cared for the father he had never met, he knew that relationships with flesh-and-blood fathers could be difficult. The men at the mission told lots of stories about their fathers.

"He's happy that you came back?"

Sam shrugged again. "I guess so. He said not to come home."

"Until you finish the program."

"Uh, I don't know. He just said not to come home."

Jake was about to offer his thoughts when a knock came and CJ poked his head in. "There's a lady downstairs says she is from the county health department. She wants to see the kitchen. Should we let her?"

"I'll come down." Before leaving the office, he told Sam thanks for talking; he was glad he had come back and that everything was going well.

She was a short woman wearing short black trousers and a loose black blouse with frills down the front. Her face was broad and flat and light brown: she might be Taiwanese or Filipino or even Latin American. Jake was never good at ethnicity. He asked her if he could see some identification, which she offered with some suggestion of annoyance.

"What seems to be the trouble?" he asked.

"No trouble," she said curtly. "I'm here for an inspection."

"But we've never been inspected before." Like anyone who has been in repeated trouble with the authorities, Jake found his body tightening and his breathing constricted. The mission was made up of men habitually at odds with the authorities, and the electricity running through the house at this moment might have stunned a guinea pig.

"Yes you have. Everybody gets inspected."

"But not since I've been here. Five years."

She just stared at him, and he felt his anger rise.

"You want to see the kitchen?" he asked.

"That's the idea."

She took her time, waddling through the walk-in freezer, the refrigerator, the food pantry. She looked carefully at the dishwasher and ran a finger over the inside wall. For the serving line she took a small piece of white cloth out of her pocket and ran it along the edge. She got down on her knees to look under the tables, and came out with a sponge held between her thumb and index finger.

"I'll take that," Jake said, and threw it into the trash.

"Where do you keep your sponges?" she wanted to know. Where did they cut meat? Where did they prepare salads? Except for the sponge, she didn't seem to find anything out of the ordinary.

She took a chair and sat down at one of the serving tables, going through a series of forms. There were boxes to check—dozens of them, it seemed. Jake stood a yard from her elbow, trying to see what she was writing. Four or five kitchen staff in their white and black coats ranged around the kitchen, watching silently, while house members crowded together in the corridor leading from the front offices, and in the dining room entrance from the chapel. The woman—she had given her name, hadn't she?—was it Barbara?—appeared oblivious. She took her time, flipping through pages and scribbling, sometimes pausing to read. Standing behind her, Jake couldn't make out anything. Finally she stopped, sighed, and went back through everything she had written, tapping on the pages with her pen. She reached the last page again, screwed up her mouth, straightened the papers and stood.

"I'm closing the kitchen," she said, tearing off a carbon duplicate and handing it to Jake.

His face went stiff and he swelled upward and outward to tower over her. "What?"

She didn't answer.

"You're closing the kitchen? What am I supposed to do for dinner?"

She gave a just-visible shrug.

He grew even larger. "I have a hundred people coming for dinner. What am I supposed to do with them?"

"They aren't coming here. I just closed your kitchen."

"What on earth are you talking about? What's wrong with our kitchen?"

"Rats," she said. "You've got rats."

Jake was momentarily speechless. "We don't have rats. Show me a rat!"

"Rats come out at night. I found rat evidence. You can't have rats in your kitchen."

"How am I supposed to get rid of rats that you can't even find?"

"That's up to you. Some people would call an exterminator. But I can't tell you what to do. That's not my department."

He tried to keep his cool. "What is your department, then? You just shut people down?"

She wagged her head as though she were thinking about it. "My department is to protect the Sonoma County public from health hazards."

She took another copy from her clipboard, found a tape dispenser in a satchel she had strapped around her neck, and taped the form to the wall. It was a faded blue, but the large black letters were perfectly legible: "CLOSED by order of the Sonoma County Health Department." She had dated and signed it.

She nodded at him and began to walk toward the exit. He put a hand on her and stopped her. She shrugged his hand off.

"You talk about a health hazard, you want 100 homeless people to go hungry tonight? Or you want them to cook for themselves? In their camps by the creek? Why don't you inspect their kitchens?" With each question his voice grew louder.

Barbara, if that was her name, looked him in the eye and said, "This kitchen is closed. When you've done something about the rats, I'll talk to you again."

"What do I have to do?" he shouted as she went out into the corridor toward the street. "You want the rats delivered to your office?"

Then, pursuing her partway to the door, "Who put you up to this? Who sent you here?"

12

The Frackers

✧

Two days after the health department closed the kitchen, Elvis, Sam, Santiago and CJ left the mission for San Francisco. They would have gone sooner but Jake and Knox were too busy with the food situation to get Santiago his check.

The *Press Democrat* ran a story about the kitchen's closing, quoting Kent Spires to the effect that they had been surprised by the findings and were working to correct them as soon as possible. Kent was never one to make waves, but some of the people on the street told the reporter that if the city was concerned with health, they should be helping the mission, not shutting it down. The next day two different TV crews showed up and interviewed anybody on the sidewalk who looked homeless. One of the local restaurants handed out free take-out meals, with Tri-tip sandwiches, coleslaw and cans of soda. Afterwards the street was littered with paper wrappers and Styrofoam clamshells, which an overnight breeze blew all down 6th street, to the neighbors' distress. Some of them called the mission to complain, and in response all the men in guest services, ordinarily dedicated to assisting homeless guests, trooped up and down with black trash bags and plastic gloves, picking up on behalf of the mission, even though they were not the ones who had littered.

Cars kept arriving at the front door with food donations, all of which the mission had to turn away because of the health department. Rat exterminators in blue uniforms with gold piping spent hours poking into corners and sealing holes; then the health department was called back to certify the result. On the second day the house was provided with take-out burritos from a Mexican restaurant, along with Mexican Coke, a great treat for some of the men who swore they could taste the difference.

The four frackers, as they were dubbed by their peers, could hardly leave in the midst of such an interesting hubbub, even if they had Santiago's $9,000, which they didn't. Their delayed departure provided all the more time for chatter and controversy over their move, with some men champing to come along and others predicting disaster. Between the frackers and the health department, the mission had rarely had such lively conversation.

Santiago finally got his money in the form of a cashier's check and $500 cash, as he had requested. When Jake handed it over, he shook their hands and wished them all the best. He said the house would pray for them to be successful. This demonstrated great restraint on his part. Inside he was seething over both the kitchen shutdown and their ridiculous departure.

He fully expected it to end in disaster. He told Krystle that they were headed for a relapse, and he told Kent Spires the same, but he refrained from telling the frackers directly. He reminded himself that when people have made up their minds you have to let them go.

But then, looking at their dumb, eager faces, he couldn't help himself. He told them they were making a mistake, and he questioned whether they were listening to God. A glance at Sam had set him off. The other three were old enough to choke on their own vomit, but they shouldn't drag Sam in.

"When did you become the only one who can hear God's voice?" CJ answered back, and that set Jake off. Had they talked about it with their pastors? Had they consulted with anybody? They were acting like addicts, going by their feelings, and it could only lead one direction. Jake's voice rose louder, and he couldn't stop lecturing them. Nor could CJ keep himself from answering back with smart cracks that, as far as Jake was concerned, only confirmed how far off base they were.

The other three frackers just listened, Elvis because he thought it was funny, Sam because he was always intimidated by a ruckus, and

Santiago because he had the gift of silence, feeling no need to say a thing, no matter what happened. Finally Elvis said, "Well, Jake, thanks but we gotta go. We have a bus to catch."

The four set off on foot to catch the 140X for San Francisco. It was not far to the transit mall: under the freeway, through the brick shopping mall, and a couple of blocks south on B Street. They carried all their clothes and toiletries in backpacks, chattering like boys going off camping. Even Sam was smiling. They went a block out of their way to change a twenty in the Donut Shoppe, since the bus took exact fares. The man behind the counter said they had to buy something to get change, so Santiago bought half a dozen donuts. Then they had to run to catch the bus; it was already loading. They were giggling and sweating by the time they threw themselves into their seats.

It was a heady moment, and for the first 15 minutes of the ride they talked all at once, one on top of the others, while making the donuts disappear. They felt that they were on the adventure of their lives, and that the golden apple had fallen in their laps. You think we'll stay in motels? I'm gonna get a job driving truck. What do you want to eat with your first paycheck? Inevitably the chatter died down, because it was all imagination. They didn't know each other well. They had been pressed together in the mission's close quarter, which gave some sense of brotherhood, but they were brothers who had not grown up together.

Sam pressed his face against the bus window. South of Rohnert Park, cities were separated by wide bands of open country: pasturelands sprinkled with black cows, distant gray hills. At intervals, a low furze of city lay well back from the road. For months Sam's life had been limited to the narrow and crowded dinginess of the mission, with occasional walks through the neighborhood on his way to 12-step meetings or Sunday morning church. The wideness of the hills, the spaciousness of the skies, mesmerized them all. Soon the only sound was the surge of the bus's engine and the hum of its tires on the highway.

The bus was not crowded and each one of them had his own window seat. Elvis left his and came to sit next to Sam. He had on a goofy outfit: orange sweat pants tucked into red cowboy boots, and a faux sheepskin vest over a deep blue t-shirt. A leather thong around his neck dangled a black arrowhead. He still wore his Australian outback hat. He was twice the size of Sam.

"It's too quiet," Elvis said. "You want to talk?"

"Sure," Sam said, surprised that Elvis had picked him. "What about?"

"It don't matter. Let's talk about sobriety. You think you're going to be okay if you're not in the program?"

"I think I'll be okay if I can go to 12-step meetings," Sam said. He was worried about that. He was trusting Elvis to steer him straight, but he knew that he needed support to stay sober.

"There's bound to be plenty of meetings we can go to in North Dakota."

Sam gave a barely-visible shrug. "I hope so."

"I'll help you if you help me," Elvis said, with a lopsided smile. "I don't really know why I'm on this trip. You think we are really going to get to North Dakota with these guys?"

Taken aback, Sam said, "I thought you wanted to go."

"Yeah, but I get into some things I shouldn't. You know, when somebody talks about it, it sounds cool and I'm kinda impulsive. I've been jumping into stuff since I was in third grade."

Sam looked up to Elvis as a much stronger person than himself, and therefore it came as a puzzle to him that Elvis was in a situation he hadn't planned on. Sam was not impulsive. He was more a drifter. He didn't know how to say no.

Elvis began telling about the trouble he had found with his impulsivity. About stealing the cement truck from the job site, for no reason other than that he could—he walked by and there it was, running and unoccupied. He told about growing a marijuana patch in the hills above the river, until a Salvadoran gang came along with assault rifles and encouraged him to leave.

From Novato the freeway widened. Shopping malls and frontage-road stores coasted past them, with the hills above no longer pastureland but forested suburbia. High above on their right was Mt. Tamalpais. To the left, glimpses of the bay. The bus roared as it climbed a hill toward the Golden Gate, where trees and bushes were sculpted like a woman's haircut by the perennial wind. They passed through the rainbow tunnel and the wide spread of the bay sprang forward, dotted with boats. A river of fog transected the bridge, coming from the dark, shrouded ocean on their right and visibly dissipating over the bay to their left, white floss floating in the light-bearing sky.

"What is that?" Sam asked, with awe in his voice.

"What do you mean what is that? You've never seen that before?"

"No."

"You have to have seen that. Haven't you been to San Francisco?"

Sam shook his head, and then cringed, expecting a barrage of mockery. But Elvis seized Sam's shoulder with both hands and put his mouth close to his ear. "That's the Golden Gate Bridge, man. And that's San Francisco. This is the Bay, man. You gotta know these places."

Sam remembered seeing pictures of it, now that Elvis told him. It did not look the same in life. The river of fog, cutting and blotting out the roadway, seemed like a living creature. He had never seen that in a picture.

The bus let them off on Market Street, where they stood on its wide sidewalk temporarily stuck without a plan. Sam's neck craned in all directions. He had never seen such big buildings, such frenetic activity. A tide of anxiety crept into his stomach. Elvis and CJ felt they had to defer to Santiago, since he had the money. But Santiago was not an easy person to push toward a decision. His soft face, without any corners or wrinkles, looked at each of them with interest, listening to what they said, but never giving a definite answer in response. He agreed that he needed to call his friend. He had a phone, reactivated in the days before he left the mission. But he was worried that he would use up his minutes. He did not see how he could call, given that possibility.

Elvis came up with the bright, impractical idea that if they checked into a hotel Santiago would be able to use the room telephone and save his minutes. Santiago seemed happy with that. The next obstacle was finding a hotel, any hotel. They spent several minutes trying to decide which direction to walk. Santiago finally settled it by saying they should go to Fisherman's Wharf, because he remembered hotels there.

They set off in the direction of the Ferry Building, walking single file with their backpacks. Sam brought up the rear, feeling his nerves. He had drifted into a situation he had never intended. He didn't even have bus fare back to the mission, and anyway he had cut his ties there. He knew he couldn't call his uncle again.

Elvis was marching ahead of him, his feet kicking outward with each step. Sam said his name. He found it amazing that he could do that—just speak up and talk to Elvis. Elvis half-turned to let him catch up and walk alongside. The sidewalk was crowded and he had to dodge in and out to stay with Elvis, but almost instantly he felt less anxious.

"Whassa matter, Bub?"

"I'm okay," Sam answered, though he was not sure he was.

Elvis purposely bumped into him, his face laughing. "Hey, life is full of surprises. You think maybe nobody is in charge here?" He lifted a hand and pushed off Sam's shoulder. "Don't worry, we'll be okay. Life wouldn't be any fun if everything was predictable." He poked his face closer to Sam's. "You believe that?"

"Sometimes."

"Well, you better believe it now. Cause we are headed for North Dakota!" He pushed on Sam's shoulder again.

That was a bright vision. He and Elvis talked about it some more as they walked: how much money they would make, the kind of car they could buy. Elvis said, "Guy as handsome as you, with a pocket full of money, you'll have the girls falling off you. Think about that!"

They reached the Ferry Building and walked north along the Embarcadero, a brilliant sun making silhouettes of the shaggy heads of palm trees above them. They shared the wide sidewalk with ladies walking their little white dogs, with tourists in golf shirts, with homeless men pushing shopping carts. The sun glinted off the bay, throwing up sparkles. CJ was complaining that it was a long way to walk; he kept stopping to look around, searching for a hotel. Elvis turned and yelled at him to catch up. Soon the four of them were strung out over 50 yards or more.

Santiago, in the lead, kept walking purposefully, oblivious to those behind him. At the right moment he peeled off inland, going directly to a Sheraton hotel. The building was a tourist confection, painted a coral color, with actual parking spaces surrounding it, as though the whole had been dropped into place from a Southern California beach community. Santiago walked straight into the office without waiting for the rest of them. They felt shy of following him in, so stood in the parking lot watching a tourist family unpack their minivan in their shorts and brand-new San Francisco t-shirts. Santiago seemed to take forever, but CJ refused to let Elvis go in to see what kept him. "Elvis, one look at you and they might say no rooms available."

When Santiago emerged they crowded around him. "Did you get it? Did you get a room?" His smooth face showed no emotion, and he didn't say a word, but he walked purposefully to a stairway and led them all to a third floor room. The lock clicked open when he ran the room key through the card reader, and they flooded through the door. Once inside, their jubilation exploded. CJ jumped vigorously on the bed, Elvis flicked through channels on the television, Sam smiled from ear to ear and drank a glass of water from the tap. As CJ jumped he shouted, in time with his jumps, "Good-bye, mission! Hello, hotel! We are living in luxury!"

Santiago called his friend. He huddled over the phone, speaking in Spanish, which none of the rest of them knew. The conversation carried on for a long time. Elvis had made himself comfortable on the bed, leaning back against a pillow, his legs splayed. "Santiago!" he called. "Stop asking about his mother!" Santiago responded with a hint of a smile.

Finally Santiago hung up the phone and said that his friend was coming to pick him up.

"What did he say about cars?" CJ's small face was full of eagerness, like a kid asking about the score in a game his team had won.

Very slowly Santiago said, "Yeah, he said he has a car for me."

Sam gave Elvis a high five.

"What kind?"

Once again a shadow of a smile crossed Santiago's lips. "He didn't tell me that."

They sprawled on the beds and watched television while they waited. The mission permitted no TVs, and as a result they were more than usually sensitive to its hypnotic jabber. They located Judge Judy and stared, fascinated, at the wrangling and the lying. Judge Judy's weary ability to puncture the baloney struck them as wonderful; who would not wish to rule your family or your society with the same authority? Who would not wish for—and fear—such a penetrating judge? When the knock came at the door it startled them all.

Santiago's friend was a tall, skinny white man with short black hair. Santiago did not introduce him. They said a few words in Spanish. "Okay," Santiago said as he put his hand on the doorknob. "I'll be back."

"Ask him what kind of cars he has," CJ said, but Santiago had already left.

13

Kasha

Kasha's neighborhood was west of the freeway, in an island of county land without curbs or sidewalks. Houses were sited on big lots, often with outbuildings, if not travel trailers and broken down vehicles. Expecting something squalid, Buddy was surprised to find Kasha's address in a neat cul-de-sac, an in-fill project of six units that he might have designed himself. The redwood siding had been painted a neutral beige, and the stairs to the second level were floating concrete lozenges suspended almost invisibly on a steel support. Facing the street was a small garden with neat redwood raised beds; vegetables were sprouting toward summer.

He was prepared to leave a note if she was not at home. Indeed, he was reaching into his breast pocket for one of his cards when the door slowly opened.

Kasha was short, with a tangle of blondish hair flopping on her head like a mop. Buddy introduced himself and without hesitation she invited him in, walking with a pronounced limp, and swishing loudly as her bright green polyester pant legs rubbed together. She offered him a seat in the living room, which was tidy and largely unadorned, except in one corner where a shrine had been created, with a small iconic Buddha and three candles. There were no pictures on the walls, and no family photographs. The furniture was Scandinavian, wood frames and fabric cushions. Like the rest of the apartment, they were neat but unprepossessing.

"I couldn't help noticing you are walking with a limp," Buddy said. "Did that come from your problems at the Sonoma Gospel Mission?"

She looked blank for a moment and then asked what he knew about the SGM.

"I read the police report," he said. "It's a public document." He raised his hands in self-defense. "This is nothing official. I'm just a private citizen with some concerns about the Sonoma Gospel Mission, and I wanted to learn whatever I could from your experiences. Have you had a lot of interaction with them?"

"With who?"

"With the mission."

"Mr. Grace, I've been serving as an advocate for the poor for 18 years in Santa Rosa. I know all the agencies very well. I can give you an evaluation, if you want that. I have written a 35-page report. I know the poor and the homeless in Santa Rosa. I know them as an advocate, and I know them as one of their community. I have been homeless myself. I lived out of my car for more than a year. I have my own evaluation of the situation, but more importantly I have the homeless people's evaluation. They talk to me about what they experience. They are very open with me, because they recognize someone who is willing to listen and to truly understand."

"That must be very interesting," Buddy said.

"I think so, but apparently the agencies don't agree. They don't listen. They don't really want to hear from the people they claim to be serving. I'm trying to be a bridge, to help foster understanding, but that is easier said than done."

She lowered her voice to a confidential tone. "I was trying to help the mission when I was assaulted. Of all the groups in Santa Rosa they probably have the most contact day-to-day with the neediest people, but unfortunately they are the last to want to hear. I keep trying. I'll try again, if they will let me."

"You said assaulted?" Buddy said. "I saw that in the police report but it was hard to believe. It's really shocking."

She did not immediately respond, but looked off into the corner. She was not an ugly woman, Buddy noted; possibly if she did something with her hair and lost some weight and wore different clothes she might be moderately attractive. He wondered how she would come off in court, if she were to testify.

"I'm glad to hear you were shocked, Mr. Grace. That encourages me, that someone still possesses feeling."

"Buddy."

"Buddy. There has been no response. The police have apparently decided to cover it up. There's nothing I can do. I can't be preoccupied with something they did to me, when other people are abused in much worse ways and have nobody to advocate for them. You know, we don't have any police ombudsman or other governing authority over these agencies."

Buddy shook his head. "Doesn't seem right. But the police did drop charges against you, didn't they?"

Kasha rolled her eyes and didn't answer.

"Ms. Gold?"

"Call me Kasha, please."

"Kasha, I'll be honest with you. I'm very concerned about what happened, but I don't want to be publicly involved. I have some financial interests in that part of town, and I don't want to have those entangled. But I am really concerned. And I wonder if there is any way that I can be of help."

She just looked at him, waiting. She is good, he thought. She may be crazy, but she's good at it.

Buddy had no choice but to keep on talking. "Have you thought of bringing suit against the mission? I don't know whether your limp came as a result of these events, but you certainly experienced pain and suffering."

"I certainly did. More than anybody can know."

"And if the police and the district attorney don't want to acknowledge what you have been through, the civil courts do provide some remedy. Have you ever been in a civil court case?"

She actually simpered, the memory of it crossing her face with pleasure. "Yes, I have, Buddy, I have been involved in litigation. Successfully."

"So you know what I am talking about. It's possible that some of my friends in the legal world could be helpful to you. I'd be happy to make the right introductions, if that seems like the right thing to do. But tell me a little more about what happened, Kasha. The police report was sort of bare bones."

"Oh, there is a lot to tell. Do you have time?"

"I have some time." He smiled encouragingly.

She leaned back, looked toward the ceiling. "There are some parts that are quite hard to talk about."

"I'm sure."

"But to me, the worst part is not the physical assault, it's the discrimination. I went in to ask for a job application. I'm so concerned about their program, and I want to help them. I'm not concerned with the money, but unless they can acknowledge their need for help, there's no possibility of improvement. I went to their window three times, and each time they refused to give me what I asked for. They gave me no reason, they simply refused. That's blatant discrimination. They are all men there, you know; they don't have a single woman on their staff. I don't take no for an answer, Mr. Grace. I was determined. It's a crime, what they are doing with contributions that people willingly give to help the poor."

"So then what happened?" Buddy asked. He had a deep-seated aversion toward hysterical women, and he was beginning to see what made people avoid Kasha. Something unreal radiated from her, and he felt pulled toward its gravity field.

"They seized me. Assaulted me, I would say. Threw me on the ground. Touched me sexually. It was awful. I have nightmares. I'll probably have nightmares the rest of my life."

"PTSD?"

"Exactly. I never dreamed that people calling themselves Christians could treat a woman in that way. Now it will be a nightmare for me the rest of my life."

"And other people saw all this?"

"Of course. I had an audience. It happened right at their front desk. They don't care. They enjoyed it. But yes, plenty of people saw what happened, and I could introduce you to them, if you wanted more evidence."

"That might be important," he said. "Not for me. Your word is plenty for me. But if a case were to go to court, you would want somebody to back you up. You think that's possible?"

She shrugged, as though the world was against her. "They saw it. They were there. I can't speak for them."

"But you could find them."

"They're homeless people, Mr. Grace."

"Buddy." He patiently drilled the point home. "But you could find them, if you had to."

Buddy had heard enough by now to doubt that Kasha was an entirely reliable source of information, and he watched her carefully on this point. It would be important to bring witnesses.

"Some of them, Buddy. Some of them, certainly. They are flesh and blood. They don't disappear." She was looking at her lap and she seemed to muse over the point.

Then she looked up and smiled. "I'm sorry, Buddy, I haven't offered you anything. Would you like a cup of tea? I have a tisane that I make myself. It's very good."

He said he should be going. "This is my card, if you need to contact me. And this is a friend of mine who is a lawyer. Adam McLeod. A very good guy, I think you'll find. I'm going to tell him about your situation and encourage him to help you. From what you describe, you should get a day in court. Adam can help you sort it out."

She made a prim face. "Buddy, I don't have money for a lawyer."

"Oh, don't worry," he said. "Pro bono. I'll make sure it doesn't cost you a thing."

As he was going out the door he asked again. "But you definitely can find people who saw what went on at the SGM?"

"The homeless are a tight-knit community," she assured him. "We all stand up for each other."

14

Homelessness

✧

The frackers whom Santiago left behind at the Fisherman's Wharf Sheraton Hotel had no way to tell the time—no one had a phone except Sam, and his battery was dead—but hunger had begun to nip at them. Santiago had left the hotel room in early afternoon. Dinner at the mission began at 5:00, and they had eaten only a donut since breakfast.

"Are you sure you don't have any money?" CJ asked. He was running his fingers over the tattoos that blanketed his arms, as though he were looking for a blank spot where he could add more.

Elvis had taken control of the remote, switching between a period drama set in some ancient time of knights and princesses, and a black-and-white movie with Humphrey Bogart and Lauren Bacall. Whenever a commercial came on one channel, he changed to the other. Absorbed in TV, he had not immediately realized how much they depended on Santiago's return. No one knew Santiago's number. Nobody had any money to buy food.

"He could call us," Elvis pointed out. "He knows the room number."

The knights-and-princesses movie ended, and Elvis announced that he was going out.

"For what?" Sam asked.

"Just to look around."

"Don't go far," CJ said. "When Santiago comes we might want to go out and get some food. We're not going to go looking for you."

Outside a cold wind had kicked up, and clots of low, fast-moving cloud obscured the sun. Elvis had a jacket inside, but decided against going back to get it. He walked the two blocks to the bay. The sidewalk that had been crowded when they arrived was now deserted. A couple of street merchants were folding up their tables to go; the rest had already vanished.

"Hey," Elvis asked, "you guys know if there is a soup kitchen around here?" One of the vendors pursed his lips and shook his head; the other did not even bother to look up.

Elvis saw whitecaps far out on the water; nearer to shore the water looked like ink. He sat on a bench, leaning back and looking up at the light. The dimming sky was still beautiful, iridescent with silvery rays puncturing the fast-moving fog. Elvis tried to sort out his own agitation. He felt like a Mexican jumping bean. He had put himself into this, a stupid trip with people he didn't really know. How was this going to help Amber?

He thought about his impulsivity and his irritability. Without warning the desire for meth ran through his body. It took his breath away.

He had not felt that for at least a month. He had thought those impulses were gone, but there it was. He wondered: would he always have it? Could he never lose it?

The cold wind began to chill him. He got up and walked back to the hotel.

CJ had discovered the mini-bar. "Look," he said, holding up a bag of mini-pretzels. "Snacks! They come with the room!"

Sam had his nose buried in the little fridge under the television, his limbs curled in front of him like a squirrel. There were snacks—chocolate chip cookies, more pretzels, a bag of potato chips—but mainly there were drinks. Sam pulled them out and stacked them on the dresser. Two Heinekens, eight tiny bottles of liquor, one Coke and one Sprite. Then he found the price list. "No, wait," he said. "CJ, those pretzels cost five dollars. All this stuff. The Coke is six dollars." He was already feeling great alarm from seeing the beer and the liquor.

Sam wasn't a drinker but exposure to alcoholics had primed him to see the drinks as a bomb with a timer set to explode. On top of that, the prices triggered something close to panic.

"It's okay," CJ said. "Santiago has money."

"But these prices are a total rip-off!"

"We'll pay him back," Elvis said. "It's okay, Sam."

The snacks did not go far, the containers being as tiny as the liquor bottles. They drank the sodas, and then Sam carefully returned the beer and liquor to the mini-fridge, out of sight and out of mind, he hoped. They were still hungry, and bored by watching television, and increasingly prone to ask what could be taking Santiago so long.

"What were we thinking?" CJ asked, addressing no one. His small fox face had turned sour. He was looking over his tattoos again.

On TV came a burst of laughter as a very young man with skinny legs came bouncing on-set with a flourish.

"What do you mean?" Sam asked.

"We didn't ask Santiago anything. Didn't get any money. Didn't say, when will you be back. Didn't get his number."

"Forget about it, CJ," Elvis growled.

"Why should I? We messed up."

"It's water under the bridge. If you can't do anything about it, don't talk about it."

Despite that good advice, their fretfulness grew. The covers on the two beds were pulled and twisted, the pillows strangled into tortured shapes, and the three of them lay tossing, distracted less and less by the TV. Now it was news programs, which did not interest them at all. They ended up staring at the shopping channel.

"Where is he?" CJ wanted to know.

"He'll come," Sam said. "He's a good guy."

"Can't do anything about it," Elvis said. "Better sleep. Tomorrow might be a long day."

Elvis did ultimately go off, snoring loudly, and CJ grew quiet, but Sam, while exhausted by all his expended nervous energy, came nowhere close to sleep. He lay on his back, listening to street sounds coming from outside the hotel, ready to leap to his feet at the least sign that Santiago had returned. He wished he could make Elvis stop snoring. He thought about drift, how a boat will seem perfectly still on the water and yet silently, immeasurably make its way across distances, thanks to wind and current. Then he fell asleep.

In the morning he was the last to wake. Tangled in the bedclothes he opened his eyes to the dim light, and heard conversation between low, familiar voices. "Santiago!" he cried out. "When did you get back?" He felt a surge of happiness: he had been sure Santiago would come.

He sat up. The only light came from the bathroom, and a rim of light around the heavily curtained window. Two shadowy figures were sitting on the other bed; their conversation had stopped.

"Santiago?" Sam said.

After a short silence Elvis said, "Sorry, Bub, no Santiago."

Still in the backdrift of sleep, Sam asked several times where Santiago had gone, until the news penetrated that Santiago had never come back.

CJ discovered the envelope, slipped under the door while they were asleep. "What is this?" he asked. "Somebody put a bill under our door."

Elvis looked over his shoulder, studying the paper. "It's a bill for the room," he said.

"But Santiago paid for it."

"Yeah, see right here, $265, $265 paid. But there's all this other crap. Telephone calls. And mini-bar. We owe them $32.85."

"How can we owe for the mini-bar? Nobody has been in here to see what we took."

"They have a scale inside." Sam said that in a low voice. "I read it on the price list. They charge you automatically."

"The hell with that," CJ said, flinging the piece of paper into the air, where it floated and flounced its way to the floor. "We don't have any money, so we can't pay it."

Elvis started laughing. "Santiago!" he cried out. "What have you done to us!?"

Sam flopped down on the bed again, wishing for the oblivion of sleep. Then he popped up again. "What are we going to do? This is crazy!"

Elvis was still laughing. "Oh, Sammy boy, it's going to be all right. Take it easy! What can they do to us? Arrest us for stealing potato chips? Chill, Sammy boy. We need to find out where Santiago is."

They called the mission, asking for Oscar, who was Santiago's Spanish-speaking friend. Oscar gave Elvis Santiago's number. "I don't know why I didn't think of that last night," Elvis said.

He punched Santiago's number and they waited. "Pick up, pick up," CJ urged.

It seemed impossible that he would, but he did. "Santiago," Elvis said. "It's Elvis. Where are you?"

CJ and Sam listened intently to the silence.

"What happened to the car?"

...

"Well, you can't just leave us here, man. We're stranded."

...

"We don't have a quarter between us. They are making us pay for the phone calls, and they're going to call the police if we don't ante up. You've got to at least come and help us out."

...

"Santiago."

...

"Santiago."

Elvis put the phone down. "He hung up."

Elvis explained that Santiago was with a girl. He didn't want to go to North Dakota after all.

"What about his friend?" CJ asked. "What happened to him?"

Elvis shrugged. "Dunno."

CJ seized the phone and redialed the number. All three of them listened closely, in seemingly infinite time, before CJ slammed the phone down. "He's not answering," he said.

15

Going Home

✧

CJ thought they should tough it out. He said the manager would yell at them and then let them go. Elvis wasn't sure. He knew of cases where they prosecuted, and with his record he didn't want to test that. "It's safer just to leave. We can walk away. They don't have our names."

Elvis got his way and they fled the hotel, one at a time.

Elvis said they should wander out as though they were going for a cup of coffee. And they should leave behind their backpacks. There was nothing in them they couldn't replace in any thrift store.

CJ went first; his plan was to reach the parking lot and head left. Elvis made him put on a long sleeve shirt to cover his tattoos. That way, he would be harder to identify.

A minute after he went out the door—at the count of one thousand and sixty—Sam followed. He headed right, the opposite direction, trying to look as casual as he could, not hurrying too much, just as Elvis had said.

His life as an addict had never included stealing; he had always got money from his parents or a part-time job. The escape was terrifying for him, not thrilling. He kept his eyes down, noticing the rough asphalt, with its paste of dirty cream paint smeared on the surface to mark parking spaces. He couldn't stop breathing in short, puffy spurts. He did not look up but kept focused on his pathway. Sam expected a hand on his shoulder any minute.

But nobody stopped him. The morning was misty and still, and there were only a few people out. On the edge of the parking lot an elderly Chinese man did a slow pantomime, brushing through the muted air as though painting a scene. A few feet away a teenage girl in white shorts and turquoise halter-top jabbed moodily at her cell phone, trying to make it behave.

After he had gone three blocks Sam took courage to stop and look around. Peeking backwards on the fog-cloaked street he saw nobody. The city had gleamed yesterday when they came, but in this gloom everything looked dead: paper trash in the gutter, signs cluttering the windows of stores that had yet to open, a paperback book with its cover torn off, propped on a window ledge.

He was starving, which he had not realized until now. His stomach had a hard, rusty metal disk in it. He had escaped the hotel, but in doing so had been ejected into airless space. Where was Elvis? Where was CJ? They had not formed a plan to meet. A great avenue of woe opened in his chest.

Sam pondered whether to stay put—he had learned in Cub Scouts that if you got lost in the woods you should wait to be found—or to circulate, hoping to bump into them. He decided he could not bear to stay still. There was nowhere to rest here; he had to keep moving. Both CJ and Elvis were presumably looking for him, too, somewhere in an undefined cloud around the hotel.

He set out in the direction of the bay, glancing down every alleyway and cross street, scanning for his companions. Several times his eye saw someone that he took momentarily for CJ.

This was his life in a nutshell: stay in motion, look for the comfort of a familiar face. Contrariwise the mission insisted that he think. He was regularly asked to write about resentments, fears and insecurities, to take stock of the injuries he had done others. You couldn't truly work the steps without thinking, which was so taxing.

On the Embarcadero, street vendors were setting out their jewelry and photography. The sun was beginning to drive through holes in the clouds. He spotted Elvis, stretched out on a patch of grass. Fearful of drawing attention by shouting, he walked up and stood close enough for his shadow to fall on Elvis.

Elvis looked up, shaded his eyes, and then smiled. "Well there you are. Whatcha doing?"

Sam flopped down alongside him. The grass was wet; he got up again and sat on his haunches. "I'm glad I found you." Then suddenly his hunger came back, grabbing his gut. "I'm hungry, Elvis."

"Yeah, me too. Should we go find something to eat?"

"We don't have any money."

"That's no problem. We'll find something."

They began to walk down the Embarcadero, back toward Market. "What about CJ?" Sam asked. "Should we look for him?"

"Don't worry about CJ. He's been around."

After they had walked for a few blocks Elvis asked Sam how hungry he was.

"I'm pretty hungry."

"Can you wait an hour? Or is this a life and death deal? Cause if it is we can just go steal stuff."

He laughed when he saw Sam's expression. "Whatsa matter, you never did any shoplifting?"

"I can wait," Sam said.

"That's good. I don't want to get caught. I got a record about as long as a Nevada freight train. But if it's life and death!" He laughed again.

The sun was out in full now, reflected in a million mirrors of the sparkling bay. A breeze had picked up, stiff and cold. "What do you want to do with yourself today, Sam? I mean after we eat. You want to see the city? This is your chance. We could tour around and see the sights."

It was an almost psychotic question for Sam, who was hanging on minute for minute, trying to calm himself. Elvis saw how it was and nudged him. "Don't worry, Sammy, this city is like a luxury resort for homeless people. If you try to go hungry in San Francisco you'll have a social worker on your case, trying to spoon feed you. We don't have a thing to worry about, we're in San Francisco."

As if to prove it, Elvis spotted a police car parked just off the Embarcadero, in a restricted parking zone. He went over and tapped on the window. Sam kept a respectful distance but was close enough to hear Elvis. "Officer, we're a couple of homeless guys. Could you direct us where to go to find a meal?" He listened, made directional signals with his hands, then repeated directions. He came back to Sam with a smile. "I was hoping they would give us a ride," he said.

Elvis had grown up with many cousins in his age range, but nobody like Sam. Sam seemed younger than Elvis could ever remember being himself. He was genuinely curious what conditions produced so much worry and sensitivity. As they strolled, Elvis began to ask Sam what life had been like when he was a kid.

"It was just ordinary," Sam said. "My dad is a plumber. He was usually gone when I got up, but I saw him after school."

"Were you good at school?"

"Not really. I guess my mind wandered a lot."

"To what? What did your mind wander to?"

Sam had to think about that. "Race cars. Superman." And then, as if explaining, "My parents fought a lot."

In high school he had smoked marijuana a lot, and done a couple of lines of cocaine. He was just wasting time, looking for something to do; he didn't think the drugs had their hooks in him. He tried heroin right before he graduated. That was different altogether. For the first time in his life he wasn't worried. For the first time he knew everything would be all right. Heroin was like velvet, smooth and comforting, so soft you wanted to lay your cheek against it. Heroin was like that fog belt moving over the Golden Gate Bridge: strong, silent, dark. He felt such great inner confidence.

It became an obsession. He thought about little else. The only thing holding back his habit was lack of cash. Sooner or later, he supposed, he would have begun to steal.

It was a new thought. He would have become a thief. He would maybe have spent his life in prison. Or been shot and killed.

"So that affected you?" Elvis asked.

Sam had drifted so far into his own thoughts he could not understand the question. "What?"

"You said your parents fought. Man, I think everybody's parents fought. My dad died when I was just a little guy, but I remember them fighting before then. I think my mother missed it after he was gone. She was so used to it. I don't think the fighting bothered me. What bothered me was my dad dead and my mother MIA. I just grew up wild."

"Is that how you got addicted? You did crank, didn't you?"

"Yeah. I guess that was it, if you want to find something to blame. Everybody I grew up with was messing with drugs. Some of those guys are dead. A lot of them are in prison. To tell you the truth, Trouble R Us was the name of my neighborhood. I never remember making a choice to do drugs. It just happened."

"But don't you think there were other people who didn't do drugs?" Sam hoped that Elvis, being older, might help him to understand himself. "I don't remember making a choice either, but I do remember that there were kids who didn't use. I don't even know their names, they didn't hang out with me. I wonder sometimes why I didn't hang out with them. That's why I say about my parents' fighting. It was like I didn't deserve anything better."

Elvis didn't remember feeling crappy about what he deserved. "That's not it for me. I just get so nervous. Stuff bothers me, and I don't know how to handle it." It was funny: he did drugs because he couldn't handle it, and the more he did drugs the less he could handle it. It was a self-defeating line, but he never really faced into it until Angel told him he didn't have any choice. He remembered that furious deadpan expression on her face. She met him at the kitchen door, as he was coming in from wherever he had been. Probably scoring some drugs, but maybe work. He didn't remember. Angel had that deep leather tan combined with sweet red-gold hair. When she flashed that smile, it grabbed into him. But she had not smiled that day. She told him that he was not making it. He wasn't doing her any good and he wasn't doing Amber any good and furthermore he wasn't doing himself any good. She had already called the mission and they were sending a man to get him.

So he went.

"You think," Elvis asked, "that anybody really changes?"

Sam was so confused by the question he could not make an answer.

"I mean," Elvis continued, "I look at the people at meetings, and they say they've been sober for so many years, but you can kinda read into them that they are the same people they have always been."

"They're addicts," Sam said. "They're just not using."

"Yeah, that's it."

"But it's good they aren't using."

"True," Elvis said. "I just wish that I could really be different. I don't look forward to a lifetime of holding off the Apaches, you know what I mean? It would be nice to just feel natural about it. Just say no, you know? You know that slogan? It's like, oh, just say no. Like it's simple."

That sank Sam into deep silence. He had little hope that he could survive a lifetime of resisting temptation, not if he could still remember the confidence that heroin would bring.

South of Market the streets were wider and grittier: warehouses and parking lots and muscular buildings without faces. After zigzagging through long, featureless blocks they arrived at a newish brick building. You could tell it was a homeless magnet by the number of people in heavily layered clothes who stood on the narrow sidewalk, smoking. There were girls with metal studs in their faces and their hair metallic blue. There were stooped old leathery men, dressed in army jackets with the stuffing coming out. Elvis asked a very young kid in leather pants and ripped t-shirt where they could get some food, and he pointed them in the front door. As soon as they pushed it open they could smell the eggs. Sam was ravenous again. They had entered a shiny metallic lobby, with another set of steel doors opening further inward. When they pushed through these they found a cafeteria. Nobody even looked at them as they grabbed plates and trays and made their way through the line. The woman who put eggs on their plates apologized for being out of sausage. "It goes fast, honey, every morning. I don't know why we can't get more." She was almost too cheerful. Elvis said no to kale but Sam took some. They were pointed to a conveyer belt where slices of bread could be placed, to be carried inside a large tin machine and come out toasted.

"This is like a nice restaurant," Sam said in wonder. A moderate murmur of conversation filled the room, which had a high ceiling with skylights. About a third of the seats were taken. The tables were black rectangles; around them were chairs with molded wood seats and backs on thin metal frames. It was simple but attractive, despite the paper plates and plastic forks.

"I told you, didn't I? San Francisco is Mecca for homeless people."

Sam wished he could be like Elvis, cheerful in the midst of chaos. Sam needed to know where he was going. At least, where he was going to sleep.

"You think we can eat dinner here?" he asked. Already he had swallowed enough food to ease his hunger.

"I don't see why not."

But as he pondered the afternoon and evening, Sam could feel his anxiety rising again. "What did Santiago say?" he asked Elvis. "Did he have some excuse for leaving us?"

"He wasn't making a lot of sense," Elvis said. "He was loaded. I think he was drunk as a skunk. I couldn't see trying to talk him into changing his mind. I don't think he had a mind at that point."

"You think he had been up all night?"

"Day is night, night is day. He was loaded. That's why I was asking, does anybody really change? Santiago, that dude had it together. I really think he did. He was on the path. All it took was an hour with his former friends, and he was caught like an alligator in a swimming pool."

It not only explained what had gone wrong with their plans, it also raised questions about any other plans.

"Do you feel you could go off like that?" Sam asked. "Just like that?"

"Yes, absolutely, I know I could. I've done it too many times to think. But I'm not going to. This is my chance and I'm not going to blow it. I've got a lady and I've got a daughter and they let me know that I don't get another chance."

"I don't have anybody like that in my life. It's just me." To say it was excruciating.

"Yeah, well, that's tough, man. You have to do it for yourself. Or for God. The higher power. Jesus. You have to get in touch with him."

"I shouldn't have left the mission."

"You can go back."

Sam had been slumping lower ever since they began this conversation, and he felt as though he could barely lift his head. "You think I can? The second time in a week? They don't have to take you back, you know. Especially after we went parading around, telling the guys how cool it was going to be, how we'd be making big money and driving nice rides."

"Hey, that might give them a reason to have you around again. You'd be a great lesson. Don't do this, you see how it turns out?"

A woman approached their table and asked whether she could sit down. You could tell at a glance that she wasn't homeless. She was young enough, probably in her twenties, and she had a plain kitchen face without makeup; her hair was cut in a pixie, more practical than stylish. Something in her eyes said that a compass oriented her. She introduced herself as Rebecca and asked their names, then asked whether they had ever been in the Sister Evangeline Center before.

"The what?" Elvis said.

"I take it that's a no," she said, with an impish smile. "Sister Evangeline Center. That's what we call this place."

"You work here?"

"I do."

"You a cook?"

"No. I'm a social worker. Besides serving meals, we provide other kinds of help to people in the community. I was wondering whether there's anything that we can do for you."

"Maybe," Elvis said. "We aren't part of the community, though. We just got here today."

"Where did you come from?"

"Santa Rosa, yesterday. Fort Bragg before that, for me. Sam comes from Modesto, I think." Sam nodded.

"So if you just arrived I'm guessing that you might need a place to stay."

"Bingo."

"I think we can help you with that. But tell me more about what brought you here, if you don't mind."

Elvis told her a short version, leaving out the hotel and most of the double cross. It made Sam nervous to listen to him, because the story sounded like it was made up out of toilet paper and silly string, and would fall apart with just the slightest poke. Rebecca didn't poke, though, she just nodded pleasantly and asked where they wanted to end up. Did they want to stay in San Francisco, or go somewhere else? And did they have any plans that somebody could help them with?

Elvis said he wanted to get back north. "It's too much city here for me," he said. That was a surprise to Sam, who had understood that San Francisco was Mecca.

Rebecca asked whether he had a way to get there. "I can always hitchhike," he said. "I'm not in any hurry. Especially if you can give us a place to sleep tonight."

"Depending on how far you're going, we do have some bus passes that could help. Golden Gate Transit takes you to Santa Rosa, if that's where you are thinking." She turned to Sam. "What about you? The same?"

"No," he said. "I can't go back there." That was unpremeditated; he knew it as he spoke it. "My family is in Modesto, and I think that's where I want to go, if they'll take me."

Her eyes were a deep brown. She seemed gentle enough to Sam but those eyes cut right inside him. "Do you have a way to find out? I don't know if I can get you to Modesto. You might need to see if there's somebody in your family who can help make it happen."

He blushed. "I can't ask them to drive up here."

"They can get your ticket on Greyhound. You want to call them and see? I can let you use my phone."

He hesitated.

"Want to do it in my office, so you'll have some privacy?"

Sam nodded.

16

The Law

✧

Adam McLeod left a message with Buddy's redheaded receptionist: "Your girlfriend called." When Buddy returned the call Adam said, "You know this woman Kasha? She wouldn't tell me anything over the phone. It had to be in person. Buddy, you got something cooking with this babe? At your age? I thought you had outgrown that."

Adam had first met Buddy at Rotary, not long after he moved to Sonoma County. Adam's humor was sardonic and quirky. His favorite form of friendly behavior was the insult. Considerably older than Buddy, near an age for retirement, he seemed unmoved by ambition, but he was impressively thorough. If he read a document, he did it meticulously. If you needed to know exactly what your insurance policy would cover, he could tell you. Buddy used Adam for routine real estate transactions, because he was confident that Adam would do it right.

Buddy did not know whether Adam would be willing to do what he wanted done. He felt confident, however, that Adam would not be shocked. Buddy couldn't stand working with somebody who was silently disapproving.

Buddy felt uncomfortable himself. When talking to Kasha he had grown aware of an eerie disjuncture between her self-presentation and reality; and he couldn't pretend to himself that he really thought she had been assaulted. Of course, he wasn't there that day so he didn't know, but he felt uneasy about promoting her into a lawsuit. He didn't hate the mission.

He had half-hoped that Kasha would never call Adam. She had, however, and Buddy's basic philosophy of life came into play: smile and move forward. Believe that it will all work out.

"I want you to help Kasha file suit," Buddy said.

"For what?"

"That's what I want you to figure out. Sexual assault? Sex discrimination? Age discrimination? Negligence? You know better than I do what will work. By which I mean, scare the pants off somebody."

"That's the legal term," Adam said. "In laymen's language we don't say 'pants.' Do you have a rival for her affections, then? Somebody you want to go away?"

"Yes and no," Buddy said. "Can I come by and tell you about it?"

Adam had his offices in a nondescript building on Mendocino Avenue, sharing a hallway with a dentist and two tax accountants. The nameplate on the door said, "McLeod and Sons." Buddy let himself into the waiting room, which was decorated like his grandmother's house: comfortable, slightly worn fabric-covered chairs, a leather ottoman, and a low coffee table with a brass rail around its perimeter. There was no receptionist; Adam heard the door and came out to meet him.

"I didn't know your sons were part of the firm," Buddy said.

"They're not. I don't have any sons." Adam coughed out a dry laugh. "I thought that sounded more impressive."

Adam had a neat goatee, perfectly white. He wore a gray suit coat and a white shirt, open at the collar, like a man who has had a long day and has stripped off his tie. Buddy followed him into his office, which was decorated with framed diplomas and one large acrylic painting of city lights reflected on water, the sort of picture you would find in a Holiday Inn. Neat stacks of paper covered most of his very expansive desk. Sitting down almost primly in his office chair, he said, "So what's the big secret between you and Kasha?"

Against his usual instincts, Buddy thought that he should tell all, or at least most. Adam would find out sooner or later. Better sooner.

You could make the case he was really doing the mission a favor. They might never thank him—he hoped, actually, that they would never know what they had to thank him for—but he was showing them a way out, which would be to their benefit. As things stood, they were doomed to conflict with their neighbors and with the city.

"Adam, I'm trying to do a real estate deal involving Railroad Square. It's the biggest thing I've ever done. It's very complicated, and it involves a lot of money over a lot of years. The bank, I'll just tell you, is skeptical. They have doubts about the kind of neighborhood we're working in, especially as long as Sonoma Gospel Mission is right in the middle of it. I've told the bankers I'll get the mission to move. I've offered the mission a very good deal to move and swap buildings, but they don't want to budge.

"It's really in their interest. That neighborhood is going to gentrify when the train comes and they are going to be more and more at odds with the neighbors. I mean, nobody likes to live next door to a homeless shelter. But they don't see it. I'm trying to help them see it."

"Thus the health department."

Buddy looked surprised. His surprise turned into a smile. "You're good. You must have had a rotten youth."

"No, just a career in law. You're not the first person ever to think of the health department." Adam was smiling like a satisfied cat. He liked to be on the inside of the joke.

Buddy was happy to include him there. Involving Adam made Buddy feel less anxious about his moral peril.

He didn't really mind that Adam knew about the health department, which had done exactly what he had hoped. Unfortunately the ploy had backfired. When the TV cameras came out, and the local restaurants handed out free meals, the mission got the best publicity it had had in ages.

He realized now that he had made a mistake pitting a soup kitchen against a government bureaucracy. In the court of public opinion, the soup kitchen is bound to win. It all came of acting on impulse.

"The health department was a nudge," he said. "It's going to take something more like a shove."

"And Kasha is the one to shove?" Adam asked, his eyebrows raised.

Buddy raised and lowered his shoulders, as though gathering himself for the onslaught. "Kasha is a homeless activist. She says she was sexually assaulted, in front of witnesses, at the mission. She says she asked for a job application and three times they refused to give her one."

"I hear she was arrested," Adam said.

Impressed that Adam was still a beat ahead of him, Buddy smiled as though Adam were the star pupil. "And all charges were dropped."

"And so were her charges against the mission."

"Let's say," Buddy interjected, "that Kasha has a reputation. Let's say everybody knows Kasha. Not everybody likes Kasha. But does that mean she can be assaulted? Discriminated against? Does that mean she doesn't get the protection of the law?"

One of Buddy's gifts was to believe what he was saying while he said it.

"The law is blind," Adam said.

"Yes."

Despite his sincerity, for a fraction of a second Buddy wondered again whether he should be doing this. He glimpsed himself as a man who was careless with other people's lives, and that momentary vision frightened him. He did not see himself that way, and he hated to think that others might.

In a moment the fear passed over him, and he came back to his bustling and energetic self. In an odd way such vistas were comforting, for they proved to him he had a conscience. Buddy wouldn't like to think of himself as lacking scruples.

"I'd like to make it possible for Kasha to have her day in court," Buddy said.

"Her day in court," Adam said.

"You meet with her and see what you can do. Send me the bill."

"You actually think she'll get to court?"

"No. I suspect she is—what do you legal beagles call it?—an unreliable witness. But I'm thinking that when you decide on the suit you can call a press conference. My goal is to turn up the heat."

"As hot as it will go?" Adam asked, smiling as he raised his eyebrows.

"Absolutely," Buddy said. "If we're going to do this thing."

17

Home Again

Some time before he went into the New Life program Elvis Sebastiano had rented a place just off Third Street, half a mile from the mission. Angel remained there after he left, and now his daughter Amber had joined her. When Elvis got off the bus from San Francisco, he walked straight there, found the hidden key in the toolbox in the garage, and let himself in the back door. The first thing he did was to take a shower. Then he found clean clothes and made himself a cup of coffee, French press. He sat in the living room sipping and savoring and considering the state of his life as he looked out the front window.

A strong breeze was lifting the arms of the trees all down the street, blowing white shreds of blossom across the front yard. The sight of that loveliness accentuated his comfort: clean, warm, stretched out in his own chair. It occurred to him that he might be crowded into a Motel 6 in North Dakota with three other losers. That made him laugh. Lucky that Santiago met a girl.

The house was a dinky two bedroom, built in the Thirties but well made and well kept. Angel's stuff was spread all over—sweaters on the backs of chairs, women's magazines on their seats—and so was Amber's, mostly school papers. Examining their junk brought the happiest feelings to Elvis, mixed with trepidation. He loved Angel but didn't know what she would say when she saw him. She, after all, had told Knox to come get him. She was judge and jury for his recovery.

Thinking about her approval made him want to be busy and helpful. Angel believed in good food but she was not much of a cook, and so he thought of cooking dinner, to make an offering of appeasement.

He went through the kitchen seeing what was available. Frozen pork chops. One artichoke, its thorned tips dried out. A plastic bag of fresh spinach. A bag of potatoes, growing greenish sprouts. He rooted further in the pantry and found a can of diced tomatoes, an onion, and some peanut oil. He had learned to cook after his father died, when his mother went AWOL, as a necessity for survival. He came to enjoy it. He always felt calmest and most in control when he had something cooking.

Before he got started, though, Amber came in. She didn't see him as she made her way through the door, and he kept quiet to watch. She threw her backpack into the corner and flopped onto the sofa. He had not seen her in several weeks, and—was it his imagination?—she seemed to have changed. Her face appeared firmer, more defined, with the force of a woman, not a girl. He was glad she had not gone for any punk stuff. She looked good without makeup, without hair color. She had a strong, almost angry look. You wouldn't cross her.

"Amber," he said.

She turned and her first expression was fury. This flowed over her face in a moment, then slid away, and she came toward him with her arms tilted out wide. She hung on him like a limpet.

"Dontcha wanna know why I'm here?" he said. "I quit the program."

She still hung on. She wasn't crying or squeezing; she just held him. "How long are you going to stay?" she asked.

"Dunno, but I'm sure glad to see you. How's school?"

Her arms went limp and fell to her side. "I hate it. Angel makes me go but it's not going to do any good. I'm stupid. And people are so mean! They just laugh at me."

"Are you talking about the teachers, or the other kids?"

"The kids! Dummy!"

"I'm not a dummy any more than you are. C'mon Amber. Why don't you help me cook some dinner?"

She stood around while he cut up the onion and fried it. He tried to get her to talk but she wasn't forthcoming. He had to remind himself that she was 13. What had he been like at 13? He had hated school too. Even all these years later he found it painful to remember. When he had to read aloud in class his mind went slack, his mouth went mute, and he couldn't manage it. The other kids would snigger, and that was why he slapped them in the bathroom when he caught them. God, he liked to scare them. He had only graduated because of sports, and that was a joke. The coaches got him tutors who did his homework for him; it was easier for everybody.

He noticed that Amber didn't go anywhere.

Angel must have smelled the onions when she walked in. She had a leather satchel over her shoulder, and a sackful of groceries in her arms, which she threw down before hugging him. "What in the?" she said.

"I quit the program," he said.

She stepped back to look at him. "What did you do that for?"

He didn't want to tell her about the fracking. He figured that would come out eventually but he didn't feel like explaining it right now.

He said as much, and she let it go. She looked wonderful, he thought: tan and rosy, her hair the color of a dark sunrise. She got busy putting away her groceries. He asked her about what she had been doing. "We'll talk," she said. "Later. You'll tell me about you, and I'll tell you about me." From the way she said it, he could tell she was mad. The voice was stiff, and so was her face.

He thought, better not say anything. He was like a possum trapped in a cage with a couple of tigers. He proceeded to slice the potatoes and fry them, then the pork chops, then the spinach. When they all sat down to dinner he said, "Mind if I pray?" He was still awkward about it, but nevertheless had a good feeling in bowing his head and saying a thank you for the food and for being home again. He realized in doing so that he remained tied in to the mission, the only place he had ever been where men would pray and hug and cry.

Angel decided that she would talk. While they ate she opened up about her father, who lived in Petaluma in bad health and was probably dying. She went to see him every day and spent hours on the phone with his health insurance and his doctors. She worked as a dispatcher for Clover Cement, and she was trying to take care of Amber and get her in to see a psychiatrist who could check her medications. It was all too much; she was overwhelmed. She and his brother Tom had exchanged words about her care of Amber and Angel said she never wanted to see that asshole again.

She could get fiercely angry and she was extremely loyal. She and Elvis had been together for 12 years and she had seen him at his best and his worst. Once she began talking she went on and on. At some point he thought: she is beginning to fray.

He watched her carefully, observing the tightness in her jaw. She talked like someone nailing down a board after bending the nail—banging it repeatedly, harder, faster. When she got to his grandmother, he said whoa.

"She's 94 years old, for God's sake," he said.

"Then she's old enough to know better."

His grandmother was frail, light as dandelion fluff. She lived with Tom, in whose house she had been following Amber from room to room bothering her about school and her hair and anything else. That was another reason Angel had gone to get her.

"She's bored," Elvis said. "Think about it. She's stuck in that house, she can't drive, she's too deaf to hear the TV. The only person home is Amber."

"But Dad," Amber said. "She wouldn't let me alone. Even in my own room, she would follow me in there."

"Yeah, I know," he said, feeling suddenly deflated.

He tried to be good, not talking much and helping out wherever possible. Angel was not giving him much credit, but she didn't tell him to get out, either. He felt that he was balancing on the edge of a cliff. One mis-step, and he would go plunging down. He needed a plan, but where do you find a direction for your life? They don't sell them at Wal-Mart. Trying to connect with Amber proved futile; she was in that moody teenage girl place, where she hated everything but didn't want to talk about it. He could see that she was spiraling down but he couldn't grab on to her and get her to stop.

He felt a little desperate about Angel, as though she was the one holding the end of his rope at the top of the cliff, and he wasn't sure whether she would let go. The third day he was home he borrowed money for groceries and bought a ton of frozen shrimp; he made a Thai curry, which he knew Angel loved. Then they watched a movie he had rented, Winged Migration, which was so boring for Amber that she went to her room. Then they watched Dirty Dancing for the twentieth time—he could do most of the dialogue in different voices, Humphrey Bogart and a squeaky mouse, which Angel laughed at despite herself. Halfway through Elvis froze the movie.

"What are you doing?" she asked.

"I don't want to miss anything while I kiss you," he said.

In the end they didn't watch any more, they kissed and wriggled together and he carried her into the bedroom, her shushing him and complaining while he swung her around like a baby. They acted like kids. It felt wonderful to fit together again.

But that didn't answer any questions. In the morning Angel rushed off to work and he took Amber to school, and the celebration of the previous night seemed to have been swallowed up without leaving any memory. In the evening Angel asked in a pointed way if he planned to go back to work, and he said yes, but he didn't do anything about it. He felt that he was waiting for something. He didn't know what.

His neighbor Nick, a little gray-haired man with a big stomach, had a black and white dog, part pit bull. Elvis began to walk it every day. He liked the dog, and he liked having an excuse to get out. He felt useless, but walking a dog was just about the only thing he felt up to. For some reason, he didn't want to go back to being foreman on a landscaping crew. His boss Priscilla had told him he was welcome back at any time, but he didn't call her. It was too familiar, he decided. It represented an old way of life.

He had unfinished business at the mission, he knew, but he couldn't go back there either. When he took Turk for his walk he didn't go near the place. If he met some of the guys in the program, they would ask about what happened to fracking. They probably knew anyway. He wondered whether CJ had gone back to the mission, or whether he was in Santa Rosa. Sam he knew had gone to Modesto; his father had sent him a ticket on the bus. He wondered how Sam was doing, living with his family.

He took Turk on the walking path along the creek. It was peaceful out there, with the trees and wild grasses. Most everything was drying up for the summer, but clumps of yellowing green grass survived among the oak trees. Turk was happy, and so was Elvis, to a degree. As long as he kept walking, his pointlessness didn't stare at him. Wednesdays he went to the farmers' market and bought vegetables. He cooked every night, which Angel seemed to appreciate. She still hadn't asked him why he had left the program. Sometimes he tried to think what he could say when she did ask. Or what he could say if she asked him again why he wasn't working.

One afternoon he took the path all the way to Olive Street. There was a mini-mart there, which survived by selling liquor and frozen yogurt and lottery tickets. Parked in front of it was a red Corvette with an elaborate painting on its hood. He stopped to admire it. It depicted a voluptuous woman in profile with fishnet stockings and a low-cut, clinging outfit that showed her nipples. Around her head were arrayed twin cocktail glasses, a pair of dice, a pack of cigarettes, and a syringe.

Turk was more interested in the tires; he was spraying one of them when a man came out of the store and yelled at him to get his fucking dog the fuck out of there. Elvis was pulling on the leash when he realized the voice was familiar. He looked up and saw that it came from an old acquaintance, James. As soon as they recognized each other it was friendly; they shook hands with multiple grips and greeted and asked each other what was up.

"Is this your car?" Elvis asked. "I was admiring the artwork. Seems like you covered all the major vices."

"Oh yeah," James said. "Are you still in that scene? I heard you quit and got religion."

"Well, yeah, I did. I was at the mission."

"The mission?"

"You know, down on Sixth Street. I was in the program there. I'm done with that now."

"Hey, man, that's great. I bet that was a good thing." James passed over it quickly. "Look, you ever hang out any more?"

"Not really. I've been in that program. It's a good place. Good people."

"So, you're sober?"

"I am. I believe you could say that. One day at a time."

"Well look, I need to go, but let me give you my number. Call me if you want to hang out. You got your phone?"

"No, I don't have a phone. Just a landline. Write down your number. You got a piece of paper?"

James slapped his pockets and said he didn't. Elvis found a grocery receipt in his wallet, but then they didn't have a pen to write with.

"Just tell it to me," Elvis said. "I'll write it down when I get home."

The number had flown out of his memory by the time he got to the house. He sat in the living room, put his feet up, and pondered his encounter with James. "God didn't want me in contact with him," he thought. "First no paper. Then no pen. That was God. I really don't need to get in touch with James."

Nevertheless he thought about him and wondered how he could contact him. It made him very jumpy.

18

Modesto

✧

It was already hot, the sun glaring and the heat affronting like a car left out with the windows closed, even though it was only the middle of June, the season was technically still spring and much hotter days were due, come July. Sam worked on fixing a sewer line near where it joined the main; you could tell it had been leaking by the deep green grass spreading in a blotchy circle from the sidewalk.

Sam was trying but he felt useless. His dad said no work, no eat, but Sam could do nothing right. His dad quickly grew impatient and cursed at him and then took over. Sam stood and watched and wished he could get out of the sun, for there was no shade on this job.

Sam and his father were both short men, but his father was stumpy and strong, a bulldog, whereas from somewhere in the family Sam had inherited a slight physique. He looked younger than he was—he could pass for 16—and he lacked physical confidence. This weakness, more than anything, aggravated his father, who was perpetually pissed at something. He had sent the bus ticket to bring Sam home, yes, but he seemed determined to make Sam pay the price.

When they arrived home after work each day, his dad went immediately to his room, where (Sam knew—the smell was obvious) he smoked dope. Sam's mother did not come home until much later—she worked the late shift at Sears. Though she was always kind to Sam, she was very tired. Her frame was skinny, almost gaunt, and she constantly wanted to hug him. Sam tried not to let her get too close. She loved him, but it was money she had given him that he used on drugs.

His brothers were usually out, playing baseball or staying over at friends. He generally had the house to himself. He rattled around.

His own company left him aware of the echoing space inside, the sour self that never left him alone. He tried watching TV or playing his brothers' video games, but they failed to distract him for long. When he watched or played he would end up with his chest tight. Sometimes he shouted at himself in agony.

There was nowhere to go in Modesto, certainly not on foot, but he borrowed his brother Rafe's BMX bike, and found himself haunting the locations where he and his drug friends had used. The field behind the middle school had been their normal rendezvous. He was surprised to find the weeds and hardpan deserted and seemingly abandoned. Some kind of vine had grown up on the broken chain-link fence at the back of the lot. Sam spent part of one afternoon stripping it away, seizing the long tendrils and pulling them through his fingers so the leaves came clean and only a long, leathery stem was left. He did it for no reason at all.

Sam knew what he was looking for, but he pretended not to know. If he had been completely honest he would have gone directly to the house of one of his former drug friends. Instead he visited Putah Creek, where he had overdosed and nearly died a few months ago.

He hadn't been able to place Putah Creek in his memory, and even now it seemed unfamiliar. In this hot late spring the wild grass on the banks was straw-blond and mowed flat. He could hop over the channelized creek, a muddy trickle. Sam walked up to the field on the other side—soft and newly plowed when it served as his bed, he understood, but now sprouting rows of beans. A four-inch irrigation line ran out a hundred yards to his left, spraying the field with the rhythmic punch of machine gun sprinklers. You felt isolated here, as though you were far out in the country. You couldn't hear the traffic on Putah Road. It was a wonder that Fred had found him in the dark.

What if Fred had not? What if his brain had completely blinked off while he lay here, his heart slowing to a stop, his blood sluggishly quitting its cyclical journey, his eyes going blind? What if his dreams had been erased and he had been left in the dark to die? Sam could not think of that as such a bad thing. He wanted nothing so much as to resign.

In the parking lot of the local Safeway, Sam bumped into Lester. It was a cautious reunion. "I thought you'd died, man," Lester said. He was a tall, skinny goofball with black-rimmed glasses. He asked Sam if he was all right; last he had heard he was in a coma, in the hospital, and maybe not going to make it.

"Well I did," Sam said. "But that's okay. Lots of people thought the same thing. My dad said they almost pulled the plug on me."

"You remember any of that?"

"All I remember is waking up and wondering what year it was."

Lester said he was working at Taco Time. He was driving a battered blue Tercel; they talked standing next to it, with a dry, hot wind blowing their hair. "You want to hang out sometime? I get off at nine. You know where that is? It's on Main and Nectarine."

The next day, Sam and his dad were doing a repair job on a house off Fig Avenue. It required wriggling under the house, where a sewage leak had created foul mud in the crawl space. They rolled a tarp over it, but it still smelled, and you could feel the mud shaping itself to you through the plastic. His father wanted Sam to go under the house instead of him, so Sam spent the morning squirming in and out and then trying to find the leak while it dripped sewage down his hand and sometimes into his face. He knew he was going to be sick.

"You didn't like working in the sun," his father said. "So I got you a job in the shade."

By lunchtime Sam was so physically exhausted he could barely raise his sandwich to his mouth. They took lunch in the truck with the engine idling and the AC going full blast. Sam's dad pushed his seat back so he could lie prone, with a big red handkerchief over his eyes. Occasionally he would give Sam some advice. He wanted Sam to stay away from his brothers. In his opinion Sam had always been soft, a mama's boy, coddled and protected, and he had brought dishonor on the family. If Sam's brothers had to be around him, then Sam should keep his mouth shut. "If you want to blow your brains out on heroin, be my guest, but do it somewhere else, okay? And leave your brothers alone."

Late that afternoon Sam had to go to the bathroom. Nobody was home, but his dad had a key to the back door. "Don't touch anything," he said, letting Sam in. It was eerie to walk into somebody's house, with all the evidence of living but no life. In the kitchen a box of Wheat Chex was on the table, and bowls and spoons cluttered the counter by the sink. In the dim hallway he could make out a gallery of family photos. He passed a closed door and one open into a bedroom with an unmade bed, then another closed door. Which one was the bathroom? He knocked on the second closed door, feeling foolish to be knocking with nobody home. Sam slowly poked it open. The wallpaper had pink roses in bands running up and down. The toilet seat was covered in pink plush; the vanity was pink Corian. It was fussy and feminine in a way he had never seen growing up in a home with three boys.

Sam liked to poke into things, to see their insides. More than once his curiosity had made trouble for him. As he did his business, his eyes were searching up and down, and afterwards he began to open cabinets and drawers. It was mostly women's stuff: small bottles, shiny devices, mysterious tubes and packets.

In a drawer, in the back, he found medicine bottles and knew their contents without examining the labels. His hand trembling, he opened one and shook out five small pinkish-brown pills with a neat "20" inscribed on each one. His mind seemed to do tricks, magnifying this handful as though his eyes were a zoom lens. Sam quickly shook them back into the bottle, turned the lid tight, placed the bottle carefully back in the drawer, closed the drawer, and walked out of the bathroom.

He desperately wanted to tell someone. Knowing that he teetered on the edge of ruin, he wanted to solidify his escape by putting it into words. If he could only call Elvis at the mission, or even Jake, the program director. But where, and when? He had no phone.

So he went back under the house with his mind focused on his narrow escape. He did not feel triumphant; on the contrary he felt like the boy in the scary movie who eludes one vampire but knows another is stalking him. The impulse to go back into the house kept returning to plague him, though he fought it off.

That night in bed he remembered the soft comfort the pills would bring into his wretchedness, the visceral relaxation and confidence, the smoothing satisfaction. He tossed in his bed, unable to sleep, with his heart thudding. Sam began to pray. Until now it had not occurred to him to pray, but since he felt so desperate, he tried. He prayed the Lord's Prayer, and attempted to compose some appropriate words for his situation. Really his prayer amounted to a single word: Help. Or not a word, a cry.

He must surely have slept sometime, for the hours did pass. In the morning the pale gray light spooned some calmness into him, but he did not feel any penetrating relief. He knew where he was headed.

At work that day his dad still seemed to suffer from his perpetual headache, but this time had little to say. If he had said a word, even to berate Sam, Sam might have fought back, he was so avid to get some human response, to open up his entrails to human observation. He felt that he could not live with himself as he was.

Yet he did live with himself, or survived anyhow, while the hours went by with excruciating slowness. They were digging out the sewer line they had inspected the day before yesterday. It was hot, filthy work, and they had to trench out a good 20 feet, most of it mud, before they found a crushed joint in the old clay pipe, almost disintegrated and surrounded by a mass of tree roots. The leak must have been there for years, to attract those roots from such a distance, for the nearest tree was the next-door neighbor's. By the time they found the tangle, Sam's upper body was trembling with weakness and he could no longer lift the pick-axe over his head without fearing that it would hit him on the way down. He thought the worst was over, and stood panting on the edge of the trench, but in fact he still faced harder work clearing the pipe and installing a new one.

When they reached home at the end of the day, he took a shower, standing under the deluge and letting it purge him. He turned it as hot as he could stand it, then as cold as he could stand it, then hot again until the hot water ran out. Finally he dried himself, dressed, and went out on his brother's bicycle, heading for Taco Time.

19

The Suit

✧

Buddy Grace had imagined a press conference to announce the lawsuit, but he was living pre-Internet, when there were multiple local news sources. Now there was only one paper in town and not a single local-news TV or radio show. Adam McLeod assured him he would call the Bohemian, the Petaluma Argus-Courier, and the other small-town weeklies, though he doubted any of them would cover the story. The *Press Democrat* was all that really mattered. He would touch base with Kathy Bayliss, the city editor, to make sure she gave it the proper attention. "Then we'll just have to wait and see."

They filed on a Tuesday morning. The Wednesday, June 15 headline read, HOMELESS SHELTER SUED FOR SEXUAL ASSAULT. The story started on B1 above the fold, and jumped to B4.

Buddy knew the reporter, Julie Kassebaum. "Nice girl," he said. "Very fair." Julie had managed to contact Kasha and learn that she claimed to be "humiliated, abused, and physically harmed." Kasha told the paper she needed mental health counseling for depression and PTSD but that she had not been able to afford the help she was desperate for. The Sonoma Gospel Mission, she said, had stonewalled her and offered no assistance. She was suing for $4 million in damages so that the mission "would never treat anyone else in the way she had experienced." The story said that Kasha claimed to have been physically assaulted, thrown to the ground and touched in a sexually humiliating way while standing in line to ask a question at the Sonoma Gospel Mission; she accused the mission's program director, Jake Dorner, of being the leading offender, although she said it was possible that others had taken part. Kasha also claimed that the mission had practiced gender discrimination against her, although that was not mentioned in the legal suit.

The Sonoma Gospel Mission, the story said, had not returned calls seeking comment.

"That practically guarantees there will be a follow-up story," Adam told Buddy with unsuppressed jubilation.

They sat in Adam's office savoring the news. Buddy regretted that the place was so ordinary, with its hotel-room art and Perry Mason furniture. Such an outcome, so artful, so dramatic, should be celebrated in a proper environment.

Adam said that he would contact the mission in a few days to see whether they were interested in a settlement. If the situation was right, he might hint that the suit could disappear if they were willing to sell their property and move out of the neighborhood. For obvious reasons, that had to be handled with great delicacy.

"Great delicacy," Buddy agreed. He had not told even Stephen, his partner, what he was doing. "I don't want that getting back to me."

Adam's cat-like pleasure spilled all over his face. He leaned back in his black leather lawyer's chair. "The thing is, if I don't spell it out, it might take time for them to get it. They have to understand that there are wheels within wheels."

"No hurry. Let them feel the heat."

Adam had a bright idea. "What if Kasha were to follow up with an op-ed on the experience of a homeless woman with gender discrimination and sexual violence? I'm sure our friend Paul would publish that. He's always looking for local voices."

"You mention it to her," Buddy said. "She could probably write it herself. She's quite bright, you know." Buddy was feeling positively light-hearted. "I notice that the paper didn't mention her arrest."

"I don't think they had a chance to get to that," Adam said. "When they do, that will be another follow-up story."

Adam rose from his desk and turned to stare at the painting of city lights on the water. When he looked toward Buddy, his face was luminous. "The brilliant thing is, we don't have to win the case. All we have to do is create doubt, and then string it out long enough. Until they fold."

"And for however long that takes, you get to add up the billable hours," Buddy said.

"You are a wise man," Adam answered.

No newspapers or other outside literature were allowed at the mission, so Jake Dorner first heard about the lawsuit from one of the volunteer coaches. Jake went across the street to Aroma Roasters and borrowed a newspaper to read the story for himself. Nestled in the dark interior, he found himself unsure how he should feel. He was tempted to laugh. It sounded exactly like Kasha. She was probably perfectly sincere.

The reporter, Julie Kassebaum, reached him at about 10:00 that morning. He took the call in his office, and tried to explain about Kasha. Kassebaum did not seem to get the picture; she acted deadly serious and a little offended by his lightness. "Mr. Dorner, what makes you think she is mentally disturbed?"

"I don't mean she's necessarily been diagnosed," he said. "I just mean, there are people on the street you know aren't all there. Kasha is one of those. You can ask anybody."

"That's a very serious charge. Can you give me some references who could back you up on that?"

"Like I said, ask anybody. We all know what Kasha is like."

"So for example if I call Catholic Social Services, they'll tell me that Kasha is a nut-case."

His voice grew slightly edgy. "I don't know if Kasha goes to Catholic Social Services or not. If she does, and they aren't scared of their shadow, yeah, they'll tell you she has a screw loose."

"But you don't know whether she goes there. Even though she's a homeless activist and they are the largest provider of services in the county."

"She's not a homeless activist. That's total nonsense. Find me a single person who regards her as helping them. She's a crazy busybody. And no, I have no idea where she goes."

"But you said I could ask anybody and they would say she is crazy."

"All right, not just anybody. Somebody who knows Kasha."

"Are there some others that you could suggest, if not Catholic Social Services?"

"Sure, anybody that comes to our program. About thirty of them saw her break Daniel's arm."

"She did what?"

"Broke Daniel's arm."

"You're accusing her of breaking the arm of one of your staff?"

"He's one of our house members. And I'm not accusing her. It's a fact. You can check his medical records. That's why she got arrested."

"When are we talking about, exactly?"

"The same day she claims she was assaulted. She assaulted Daniel, and then had the nerve to accuse me of it."

He thought a note of coolness came into the reporter's voice. "Let's get back to her accusation, if you don't mind. You say that thirty people witnessed it. Any of them professionals?"

"I doubt it. Not too many professional street people."

"Any of them you can put me in contact with?"

"If I happen to see them, sure. They're here a lot, but they come and go. Of course there were some of our program members."

"Who work for you."

"Well, no, not really. It's a self-governing house. It's their service, part of their recovery."

"Then what do you do?"

"I'm the program manager."

"You're the manager, but they don't work for you?"

"No, not technically. I coordinate their work."

She did not seem impressed by the distinction, but she didn't pursue it. She said she wanted to hear him describe exactly what happened, but when he started at the beginning she cut him off and said please just describe the physical altercation.

"So you don't want to know what led to the physical altercation."

"Mr. Dorner, I want to get at her accusation. She says you physically and sexually assaulted her. I'm trying to hear your side."

Jake explained as best he could that he wrapped his arms around her to stop her beating people and breaking windows with her stick. Then she slid down on the ground and stayed there until the police came.

"The police came?"

"Yes, and arrested her."

"Not you?"

"Of course not me. She broke Daniel's arm and damaged our property."

"Mr. Dorner, you said she slid down on the ground. Are you sure you didn't throw her?"

"Of course not. I was just trying to restrain her. Did you hear what I said? She broke Daniel's arm. She broke our window."

"But you are much bigger and stronger than she is."

"Sure. I couldn't restrain her if I weren't."

"So you could have thrown her down."

"Probably I could. But I didn't."

"And while you were holding her, did you touch her in any sexually sensitive places?"

"No!"

"You wrapped your arms around her and restrained her, but you didn't touch her on her genitals or breasts."

He paused before answering. "If I did it was by accident. You seen Kasha?" He snorted.

"What do you mean by that?"

"By what?"

"By, 'you seen Kasha?'"

"I mean, she's a big girl. It would be hard to restrain her without accidentally touching her breasts."

"So you did touch her breasts."

"Probably. I really don't know."

It was the first time Jake had ever been interviewed, and he did not like the way it went on and on, without any apparent point. He didn't like that the reporter kept her own counsel about whatever beliefs she had; he had to answer questions without knowing what she was driving at. It was a kind of guessing game in which she knew the answer and he was not allowed to ask any questions. Oddly, he was the one who knew what had really happened, yet he felt like the person in the dark.

Nevertheless, he believed he had acquitted himself well. The facts were the facts.

At noon Kent Spires called, wanting to know exactly what had gone on with Kasha. He had, of course, read the news story. His voice was gentle, as always, but to Jake's ear he sounded agitated. His questions about the incident mirrored the reporter's. Could he think of any reason why Kasha would claim she was sexually assaulted? Exactly how and where had he touched Kasha?

Jake hesitated to bring the reporter into it, but from the way Kent was asking questions he knew he would want to know. When he told Kent about the interview and exactly what he had said, there was a long silence on the other end of the phone line.

"You told her that you touched Kasha's breasts."

"I said I probably did, by accident, just grabbing her and putting my arms around her."

"Jake. Why couldn't you just keep your mouth shut? And what were you doing, talking to a reporter, anyway?"

He was stung. "She called. I didn't see any harm in it."

Another pause, and Kent's voice grew softer. "Let's hope there isn't. In the meantime, I think it would be a good idea to refer all questions to me. We're being sued so we are advised to limit our public comments. That's what you tell anybody who asks."

"Kent, I don't see the point of that. I'm the only one who knows what happened. You certainly don't."

"It's more complicated than that, Jake."

"What's complicated? You act like I have something to hide."

"I'm sure you have nothing to hide. But you haven't had any experience talking to the press."

"So I shouldn't talk to this reporter, Julie Kassebaum."

"Or anybody else. No. Send her to me. I hope she's all right."

"What do you mean, all right? Is there a problem?"

"A problem? Yes, being accused of sexual assault on the front page of the paper is a problem for a Christian ministry. Do you have any idea how many calls I've had already?"

This angle had not occurred to Jake. He could understand a kerfuffle getting at the truth. An unbalanced woman had accused him and he expected to be cleared. The question of publicity was different, and less tractable. He found it confusing. Why wasn't the truth enough?

Jake wanted to tell Kent that he should trust God more. The sovereign God could be relied on. But Kent was his boss, and his older brother. He kept his mouth shut.

Jake got a clearer idea of Kent 's problems after spending the afternoon with people looking at him sideways, or asking in a sympathetic way whether he was all right. The way they danced around the subject enraged him, but he couldn't figure out what to do about it. Volunteer teachers came in for their afternoon classes, delicately assuring him how much they appreciated him, as though that should be in doubt. By their tone they might be inquiring of somebody at the hospital about their desperately sick child. Jake very soon got tired of trying to answer questions that were not quite asked. Coaches and mentors and people dropping off food took the same sidewinding approach: they mentioned the incident in an oddly abstracted way, as though they had seen news about some foreign disaster that involved nobody they knew.

Chapel services began at 6:00 every day. People sometimes complained that the mission wouldn't help you until they had preached at you, but that wasn't really true. It was true that the line for dinner led through the chapel. If you attended chapel, you were automatically at the front of the line. But if you didn't want to go to chapel, you would get fed and you would get a bed.

Chapel wasn't an obstacle for most people on the street, who were happy enough to sit in a warm, dry place, hear some music, and listen to a spiritual talk. A few griped, mostly about music they didn't like. By 5:30 an assortment of people had gathered on the sidewalk: men with long beards and trench coats, tattooed women, dark Central Americans with broad, smooth faces, fat, blond Anglos in shorts and high striped socks—you name it, the fellowship of the street. Jake was always glad to see them. They were his people, and he knew he could help them. He unlocked the yard for them to deposit their backpacks and shopping carts and plastic bags of clothes; what looked like garbage was often closely guarded. Jake circulated up and down the block, shaking hands and sharing words of encouragement. None of the people in line seemed to have read the newspaper. At least, they showed no special curiosity about Jake.

Inside the chapel, a group from the Freestone Bible Church was setting up their instruments and PowerPoint. The church's youth pastor, Cleve, was a rotund young man whose clothes ran to cargo shorts and t-shirts; he had a head as round as Charlie Brown's. When he saw Jake he rushed to him and asked urgently how he was doing.

"I'm okay," Jake said. "How are you doing?"

"Oh, man, we are praying for you. We are praying for God to do a power number."

Jake noticed that the members of the band had stopped assembling their instruments and instead were watching him, like friends of friends at the Emergency Room.

Jake shrugged. "God is good. Life goes on. I'm sure it's going to work out."

"Of course, it has to. You're right, God is good. Good word. We will definitely pray for you."

Jake stood in the back during the service. Freestone's worship leader, tall and cadaverous as Abraham Lincoln, with a thick shock of black hair, urged the assembly to put their hearts into the singing. At first he was gently impatient, but at one point he abruptly waved his hands to stop the song and gave a talking-to on how important it was to sing with your whole heart. The guests looked at him blankly.

Jake had tried many times to communicate to the volunteers that lecturing just put off the guests. They hadn't come to get fixed. A lot of them didn't think they needed fixing.

The sermon was long and the service went overtime, which meant the guests got restless and hungry. Jake restrained himself from giving the cut sign to the worship leader, who was asking for an emotional response to the final chorus that he wasn't going to get. Finally the guests filed into the cafeteria (tuna rice casserole, broccoli, fresh fruit, and lots of bread and peanut butter). Jake moved toward the worship leader to thank him for coming. The man wrapped his arms around Jake's middle and would not let go for some time. "Jake, oh Jake," he kept saying under his breath.

One part of Krystle's daily routine—and she was a woman of routines—was a morning visit to the pocket park near their house. The distance was perfect for Reggie—two short blocks of hopping and running ahead and pulling on his mother's arm. Other mothers and grandmothers of small children congregated to let their charges amuse themselves on the asphalted play area with its slide and jungle gym. Krystle liked to watch from a worn wooden park bench, shaded by messy acacia trees. The other adults tended to stand on the scruffy verge of the asphalt, talking to each other while occasionally shouting at their children.

Krystle knew the other women by sight but not necessarily by name. Sometimes she joined them standing alongside the playground, but she tended to remain silent. They complained about their husbands' pornography and boy toys, and she could not relate. Nor was she able to join in discussing TV shows, since she and Jake had agreed not to pay for cable. Even holiday plans could be difficult: the others' extravagant gifts and parties left Krystle feeling ashamed of her poverty.

Despite these and other limitations, she relied on mornings at the park, because she was almost desperate for company.

She had always wanted to be a wife and mother but found the reality isolating and depressing. Reggie had reached the age where he did not want to be cuddled. He was boisterous and wanted to run with other boys at the park. That left Krystle feeling left out, which she knew was silly, but there it was.

There were times when she wondered whether she should have married Jake. The thought came despite her efforts to shut it out. Her mother, with whom she talked nearly every day, certainly encouraged such doubts.

Krystle took a seat on her usual park bench. Holly joined her, as she often did. Her son Zephyr was the same age as Reggie. The two boys liked to play, which naturally drew their mothers together. Holly had a headful of blond curls and usually dressed in clingy pajama-like garments. She was a talker, who would start up on whatever subject was on her mind. She often had something to say about politics, a subject that interested Krystle not one bit. But Krystle liked to have someone to talk with. She didn't like being left alone.

Today Holly looked at her and said, "I didn't think I'd see you here today."

"Why?"

"Well, I read the paper. Oh, my God." Krystle said nothing—she could say nothing because she had no idea what Holly was talking about.

Holly went on. "I didn't think you'd come out of the house after that."

'I'm sorry," Krystle said, "I don't know what you're talking about."

"Did you see the paper?"

"No."

"Well, it's on the front page that your husband is being sued for sexual assault. There aren't any details but apparently he tried to rape a woman. I'm sure you know all about that."

Tears sprang into Krystle's eyes. "That's not true," she said. "It's a filthy rumor."

"Then how did it get on the front page of the paper?"

Holly stood up and walked ten steps ahead, to the edge of the playground, where the other mothers and grandmothers stood. Krystle was left alone, stunned, groping with the incredible. She thought frantically through her recent conversations with Jake, trying to remember whether he had ever mentioned something that might have been twisted into such an accusation. She felt glued to the bench, unable to think or move. It must be a misunderstanding. She had no idea what could have caused it.

If it were true, the earth would surely be shaking, the other mothers would be giving her dirty looks or cursing her. Instead, the day was utterly ordinary, with the morning fog beginning to tear apart and streaks of yellow light finding their way into the tops of the trees. If Krystle stayed still, it seemed, the misunderstanding would vanish like the morning fog.

Krystle heard her son crying. He rarely cried, and the sound bashed her senses like a siren. He was already running to her. She caught him in her arms, and he burrowed deep. "You're all right," she reassured him, holding him. He seemed very upset. "What's wrong?"

"Zephyr said Papa is a rapist!"

Krystle held him tighter. "Zephyr is just calling names. You shouldn't pay any attention to that."

"He wouldn't stop saying it! I want him to stop!"

Krystle took Reggie by the hand and led him to Holly, who was standing with one shoulder tipped toward the sky, pointedly not looking her way. Tapping Holly, Krystle repeated what Reggie had told her.

Holly turned majestically toward her. "Well, I feel very sorry for Reggie. And for you, too."

"I want him to apologize to Reggie."

It was rare for Krystle to speak so directly. Her voice sounded unusually loud to her, audible to all. Though none of the other mothers turned to look, she felt that they listened intently, and that other conversations had stopped.

Holly gave a pitying smile, a turning of the lips and a crinkling of the eyes that Krystle would remember forever. "I can't make him apologize for the truth."

"It's not the truth. It's an absolute lie."

Again, the smile played over Holly's lips. "The newspaper says different. Who am I supposed to believe?"

Jake felt pure relief to leave the mission for home. He preferred walking to and from the house, though it was more than a mile. That way Krystle wasn't stranded without a car.

Once past downtown he was under the light, fresh green of tall trees, watching squirrels, observing kids on their bikes and senior citizens walking dogs. Nature was astonishingly oblivious to his problems. He had felt unhinged all day, but the walk calmed him. He was walking home to his wife and son. Ten years ago he would never have believed such a wonderful thing was possible. It was still a dream to him.

When he went in the front door, the house was strangely quiet. Reggie did not rush out to him, as he usually did. Toys were scattered on the floor, as though play had been suddenly interrupted. Jake looked in the kitchen but nobody was home. When he swung open the door to his bedroom he saw Krystle lying on the bed, the covers over her, and Reggie sleeping beside her.

Jake went to sit on the bed beside her. Reggie's milky smell permeated the room; the sheets were rumpled over Krystle's legs like kindergarten mountains. "Darling?" he said, and she lifted her head to look at him. Her eyes were puffy. "What's wrong?" he asked.

She put a finger to her lips and slipped out of bed. She was fully clothed, in clinging jeans and a white shirt that accentuated her olive skin and deep eyes. For him, now quite alarmed, she seemed heartbreakingly beautiful. She led him out of the room and closed the door behind, then proceeded into the kitchen. It was an old-style room with linoleum on the floor and a hippy table surfaced with heavy orange tiles.

"His friend Zephyr called you a rapist," she said. "At the park."

"He's just a little kid," Jake said. "He doesn't know what that means."

"That's what I said. But his mother said it's in the newspaper."

She could not even cry now. She just stared at him.

Jake felt self-righteous rage rising, but he restrained it. "How did Reggie react? Did he understand?"

"He was extremely upset."

"I don't think he knows what rapist means."

"No, or sexual assault. But Jake, I can't even go out there if I am going to be hearing that." She touched his hand, lightly, and then pulled her fingers away. "What happened? Tell me what happened. That story is terrible. Just terrible."

Then she began to cry, and couldn't stop. He held her and explained to her about Kasha, reminding her that she had heard it before. "You know I wouldn't do anything like that, don't you?"

Reggie appeared in the doorway, his eyes full of sleep. He hurried to come to them, attaching himself like a snail to their legs. He too started crying, and Jake was unable to comfort him, even when he flew him around the room, even when he offered to read him a story. He and Krystle could not talk; she did not want Reggie to hear. He suggested they order a pizza but Krystle demurred. "I don't want anyone looking at us," she said. "Not even at the door." So he watched while she concocted a dinner, touching her hand when he could, and getting Reggie to wrap himself around his legs rather than his mother's. Eventually Reggie, at his suggestion, got out his box of cars and rolled them around the kitchen making engine noises. He would not leave to play in the living room, however.

Dinner was necessarily quiet. What they needed to discuss, they could not say in front of Reggie. Under the circumstances, any other words seemed useless and profane. After they had cleaned up they sat together on the sofa reading to Reggie. Reggie fell asleep, his limp, precious body a heavy lump on them both. After Krystle undressed him and put him to bed, she came back to Jake. Her eyes were jet black, as though they opened into a hole in the universe. He had never seen her like this: so serious, as though she had seen death.

"I've thought about it," she said, looking down at the floor. "I need to go over to Vallejo." Vallejo was where her mother lived. "Can you do without the car? I'll take the bus if you can't."

"No, I can do without," he said, though his heart was screaming against it. "You're leaving me?"

He expected her to disavow that wording, but she didn't. Instead she tried to explain. "Can you understand? It's just too hard for me," she said. "Even if people weren't looking at me I would think they were. And after what Holly said at the park, they will be looking at me. The things they must be thinking."

"Like what?" he asked.

Her face now had the look of a frightened civet cat. "Like how can she live with such a man? How can she let her little boy live there?"

"I didn't do anything. You know that." He was angry; he wanted to hit something. He realized with blazing clarity that he should not let her go, even though he had said that she could.

She began sobbing uncontrollably, and her body doubled up as though she wanted to vomit. She would not let him touch her, either. "I know that. I know that," she said. "But I can't stay here."

20

The Neighborhood Activist

✧

Raquel Raise went out every day between 6:00 and 7:00 in the evening, hoping to cover just one block. As a volunteer with Ecology Action she was assigned to canvas the area around Railroad Square, to learn what residents wanted to see happen when the train resumed service. Ecology Action described itself as a grass-roots community organizing platform. The idea of Raquel's canvas was to assess people's opinions before new development began, so as to be more politically proactive and less reactive to developers' plans.

Raquel was new to Ecology Action, and relatively new to Sonoma County. A few years before she had retired from a government job in Washington D.C. Her career had been as an economist, and she liked working in the background.

Her auburn hair was Raquel's most notable feature: thick and alive like a single organism, a brush that settled onto her shoulders. When you looked at her face you noticed the greenish Celtic eyes, though in fact her mother had been Hungarian by birth and her father Spanish. She was trim and nimble even in late middle age. What kept her from being devastatingly attractive was her utter lack of seductiveness. She looked at people as engineers look at a bridge: all materials and function. At least, that is the matter-of-fact sense she gave off, and no one could really tell because she kept her own counsel.

Raquel carried a leather satchel over one shoulder, and she had a clipboard in hand. Each housing unit she recorded on a separate sheet, which she then stashed in her satchel. She had blown-up maps of the neighborhood on which she marked where she had been and where she needed to return for follow-up. Some people were not at home. More disappointingly, a great many people showed no interest in talking to her; indeed, many were hostile, gesturing at her through the window to go away, or shutting the door in her face before she had time to explain that she was not selling anything.

She sympathized, to some extent. She disliked visits from strangers who went through their sales pitch without taking a breath, or who asked intrusive questions such as how much you are spending each month on electricity. In the process of canvassing, however, she had something of a revelation: a pervasive distrust of strangers had the effect of undermining the possibility of community. She, after all, though a stranger, was also a neighbor; and she was not trying to manipulate or to sell but to gain understanding that would potentially be of value to everyone.

She had bought a home in the neighborhood because she was attracted to its shabby and eclectic appearance. It was a survival from a time eighty years before, when Santa Rosa was a small town serving farmers who came into the county seat to shop or interact with county government. Most of its residents had been people of modest means, working in small warehouses and shops. The neighborhood still held some of those stores and warehouses, though the stores now sold mostly beer and smokes and frozen pizzas, and the warehouses were dilapidated and all but vacant. Raquel did not visit the commercial establishments, but went systematically to the small redwood-sided houses, two bedrooms and a bath unless another room had been added on. Many had low front porches with wind chimes, potted succulents and, sometimes, prayer flags. The small front gardens varied from intensely cultivated vegetable gardens to neglected plots of weeds and bare dirt and woody geraniums.

When the residents were willing to talk with her, she found them full of opinions. In the big picture, they mostly were glad for the new train, and felt a certain amount of pride in the recognition it brought to the Railroad Square neighborhood. But they wanted to be left in peace, holding no wish that the neighborhood—their block especially—would change.

Fairly typical was an elderly Czech man she encountered sitting on his front porch, which was lined with potted geraniums. When he realized that she was not selling anything he stopped being grumpy and instead proudly showed her each of his flowers. He said he had lived on the street for fifty years, and knew every one of his neighbors. "Used to be 100% Eye-talian," he said. "Most of these people now are Latino. To me, I can't tell them apart."

When she asked him if he worried about anything with the railroad coming back, he launched into memories of the bums who rode the rails when he was a boy. "They would come right up to our house and ask for food. We thought they had the house marked, though we never figured out how. My mother always gave them food, and they expected it."

Raquel tried several times to lead him back to the question, only for the old man to start over telling about the bums and his mother. Raquel finally said she had better be going. He seemed disappointed, and struggled to his feet out of politeness when she said good-bye.

She felt a weight of sadness as she walked on from there. The old man, she realized, had reminded her somehow of her developmentally delayed sister Cece.

Her own social cautiousness, she thought, came from growing up with such a sister. Raquel had no specific memory of her parents' warning her, but she had always been anxious that others would tease Cece or humiliate her.

After her parents died, Cece's care had fallen to Raquel. Only after Cece herself died at the age of 54 had Raquel felt free to leave the East for the green winters of Sonoma County.

She missed Cece, she realized. There was no one else who took her for just what she was, and no one else who was always glad to see her. Conversation with Cece, while sometimes comical, had focused on practical concerns. They could communicate about food, about preferences in toilet paper, about warm clothes. They went for walks in season, they watched television together, they collaborated at making cookies. Now Raquel had no one. Volunteering with Ecology Action was unlikely to fill that gap.

Raquel's next house was a Salvadoran family that invited her in and sat her down to share their dinner. She apologized for interrupting them and suggested that she could come back another time, but they insisted she join them. One of the women put a plate of food in front of her before Raquel could protest. Raquel was embarrassed, but knew better than to refuse. She picked at the meal while asking questions. There were four adults around the table, and at least six children, ranging from toddlers in diapers to teenagers in flip-flops and blue jeans. The adults spoke some English but there were obvious gaps in communication until a teenage girl, all arms and legs and a scowling face, began to translate.

Even then, when Raquel's questions were passed on in Spanish, the adults seemed hesitant and confused. There was some conversation between Lupe, the translator, and the adults. Finally Lupe turned to Raquel and said, "They don't really know about the train. They just hope our rent doesn't go up."

Raquel recorded that response, whereupon there was more Spanish conversation and Lupe asked, "They want to know, will the rents be going up?"

Later Raquel pondered the possibility of grass-roots organizing with the kind of people she was encountering. There was, perhaps, a little leverage to be had if you wanted to oppose a developer's plans. You could probably get people to sign a petition, she thought, or attend a block party. But getting them to a meeting or a march, she judged, was all but inconceivable. Raquel was willing to admit that she was inexperienced, and that better organizers might pull off a trick she could not imagine. She doubted it, though.

On her journeys through the neighborhood, Raquel was very aware of the presence of the Sonoma Gospel Mission. She passed by it often enough, and was always sure to nod to the people standing outside.

She was not frightened by homeless people, but she felt distaste for the mission. The neon Jesus Saves sign high over the sidewalk told her all she wanted to know. It wasn't religion per se she detested, but proselytizing.

As time went on she completed her first sweep of the residences, and began to add neighborhood businesses to her canvass. They were generally more difficult to interview. The owners might or might not be present, and if they were, they might be too busy to talk. She tried making appointments, but most of them weren't appointment people—you had to catch them when you could. Slowly she reached them, one by one, discovering that they had far more particularized opinions. They showed very little sentimental interest in the neighborhood, even if they lived in it. They were intensely interested in law and order. And they were focused on sales. They wanted to know whether their customers would be more likely to come as a result of any changes, or not.

So that was it: there were homeowners, there were renters, and there were business people. The neighborhood had very few other kinds of establishments: no office buildings for bookkeepers and therapists, no government agencies, no social-service organizations to speak of. A Boys Club was a prominent exception, and she allowed a small anomaly in her neighborhood boundaries in order to include the Peace and Justice Center on Eighth Street. She admitted to herself that she was avoiding the mission. Eventually that got to her conscience. They, too, were part of the neighborhood.

Raquel did not take a newspaper—she hated the clutter of yellowing newsprint piling up—and so had no way to know that she arrived at the mission doorway five days after Kasha filed her lawsuit. At the recently repaired window, Raquel asked to speak to someone in charge. The receptionist was a broad, cheerful man with long black hair in a ponytail down his back. He asked her what it was about and then made a call. Raquel hardly paid attention to his exchange with whoever was on the line; she was too busy taking in her environment. She could not immediately put her finger on what struck her as odd. The small room was plain and unadorned, without a chair to sit in or a bulletin board to read; the receptionist was little different from what she might expect to find at a county office or a car repair shop. Yet something struck her as unusual.

"Jake says he isn't giving interviews," the receptionist said to her.

"I don't understand," Raquel said. "Why not?"

"He didn't say. I guess he doesn't want his name in the paper any more."

The follow-up story had appeared in the newspaper on Saturday, telling of the altercation between Kasha and the police, and quoting Jake to the effect that he had touched her breasts when he accosted her. Since then, camera crews from all the major Bay Area television stations had appeared. One of them had interviewed Kasha on the sidewalk in front of the mission.

"I'm not a reporter," Raquel said. "I'm just collecting people's opinions about the neighborhood now that the train is coming. I'm talking to all the residents, to find out how they would like to see the neighborhood change, and how they don't want it to change."

"You wouldn't quote him?"

"No. That's not the point. I don't understand what you're concerned with."

"You would if you had been around here the last few days," the receptionist said with a smirk. "Okay, let me see if he'll talk to you."

A minute later he told Raquel that Jake was coming. He then leaned sideways, looking past her to ask a woman next in line how he could help her. Raquel stepped aside and watched as several people asked to use the bathroom, to get food, or to talk with one of the residents.

It came to Raquel what was odd about the place. She had expected it to resemble the Catholic churches she had visited with friends as a child. There were no statues, no scent of incense, and no holy music. It was stripped of religion, profane in the best sense of the word. She wasn't sure whether or not she liked the difference. Was it right for them to cover up their religiosity? To disguise their nature? But then, there was the "Jesus Saves" sign outside. You couldn't say that they were pretending.

Jake arrived, a very large man with short, bristling brown hair, a full beard, and a hunted look in his eye. He wore blue jeans and a loose black and maroon shirt with a Sonoma Gospel Mission logo. Raquel explained what she was doing, though Jake seemed distracted and kept looking past her to the doorway, as though he expected something or someone to come through it.

"You aren't a reporter?" he asked.

"No," she said. "I don't even know what this is about."

"How do I know you're telling the truth?"

He was gruff and quite intimidating, but Raquel was imperturbable. She gave him the brochure and explained about Ecology Action. He didn't seem to listen but he evidently decided her explanation was good enough. He led her upstairs to his office, past bulletin boards that posted lists and charts, past a laundry, past a kitchen where men in white coats chopped vegetables. The office did not even display a cross; there was a sports poster and, on a neat desk, a photo of a dark-haired woman and a small child.

Jake barely listened as she explained about the survey. For such a big man, with such a big blond beard, he seemed furtive. He reminded her of a feral dog she had encountered on one of her hikes: wary, watchful. Only unlike the dog, he was big.

They were interrupted several times by men who knocked and asked a question. Once Jake got up from his desk and was gone for several minutes.

"Sorry about that," he said the fourth or fifth time it happened.

"Is something the matter?" she asked.

For just a moment his frown broke open and he laughed. "Something is always the matter around here." Raquel must have looked at him questioningly, because he dropped the smile and explained. "You know we're running a drug and alcohol rehabilitation program," he said. "Thirty men. They serve the guests. That's the service part of their recovery. They wash the sheets and towels every night, they give out clothes, they clean the toilets and the showers, they cook the meals, they wash the dishes. If you think that's simple, you don't know addicts. There are a lot of issues. Every. Single. Day."

Jake gave this little speech as though he saw some powerful message in it. He didn't look at Raquel while he gave it, and afterwards he glared down at his desk.

"Thank you for explaining," she said. "I appreciate that you're giving me your time."

He waved that away, as though it were a fly annoying him. He showed no interest in what she was about; he answered her questions only because she had asked him to.

"Who are the guests?" she asked.

Jake looked up, puzzled by her question.

"You said that the men in the program serve the guests. I'm not clear on who the guests are."

"Oh," Jake said. "The guests can be anybody. They come for a meal and a bed."

"Homeless men," Raquel said.

"Sure," Jake said. "We call them our guests. We try to treat them that way."

He was polite, but there was a limit. When she finished her purely informational questions she began asking what the mission hoped for as the neighborhood changed. He stopped her and interjected a question. "Why are you asking?"

She explained that Ecology Action wanted a baseline of the neighborhood opinion so that they could help mobilize action when plans were offered. "What happens, often, is that the people making the plans are thinking way ahead, and by the time the neighborhood catches on, it's too late."

He pushed his lips together. "Seems like you're late already."

"What do you mean?"

"It's already happening, isn't it?"

"I don't know," she said. "You must know something that I don't."

"What does this have to do with Buddy Grace?" he asked.

"Nothing that I know of. I don't know who Buddy Grace is."

He shuffled through a small stack of business cards on his desk, found one, and handed it to her. It named Buddy Grace as CEO of Grace and Ames, Commercial Development.

"I don't know him."

"Or his company?" Jake lowered his chin and looked through the tops of his eyes, as though he doubted her honesty.

"No."

He told her about Buddy's visit and the offer he had made. It was her first indication that the information she was accumulating was not ammunition for a purely theoretical situation.

He told her more about what Buddy had said—what kind of changes he was contemplating. She still had the impression that only half his mind was with her, however. She felt that something was poking hard on a painful part of him. She was not the kind of woman who would ask him about it. By nature she did not pry.

Jake finally raised his eyes to look at her, with a gaze that was frank and piercing. "Okay," he said. "I've answered your questions, how about you answer one or two of mine?"

Raquel said she would be glad to.

"What's your agenda?" he asked.

It was a stark question that caught her unprepared. She stuttered that she didn't have any agenda, except to help the neighborhood.

He looked at her warily.

"Our agenda is the community," she added. "We think the people who live in the neighborhood should have a say in what the neighborhood becomes."

"Do you think we need to move out of here?" he asked.

"Who?" she asked, confused.

"The mission."

"No," she said, unsettled. "Unless you want to."

He turned that over. "I don't know," he said. "I'd like a new building, but my boss isn't ready for that. He told Buddy Grace no. I don't think Grace was happy."

Jake seemed to brood on that. Raquel found herself very curious about him. He dipped in and out of conversation, wary yet offering hints of wanting to open up. He spoke in fragments that she did not understand. Something had bruised him, and she wondered what it could be.

Another knock came at the door, a man in suspenders and a western shirt protecting a large, round belly. Jake stood and said rather brusquely that he really needed to go. Had he answered her questions? Raquel said that he had and extended her hand.

"If you feel pressured at all to move out of the neighborhood," she said, "and you want support, you can call me." She had given him an Ecology Action brochure earlier, and written her phone number on it.

Something crossed his face, like the shadow of a bird flying lickety-split across the sun. For a moment she thought he would spill something. But he gathered himself, and did not. "It's not really my department," he said. "My boss makes those decisions. With the board, of course."

He walked her all the way down the stairs and to the street. She shook his hand again, and he apologized for taking her for a reporter.

"That's all right," she said. "What was that about? Has there been some trouble?"

She saw that she had touched on something. He really had a very expressive face. "We've had some bad publicity," he said. "I've had some bad publicity."

"I'm so sorry," Raquel said. It would have been natural to ask for more detail—he left it open to that, certainly—but she did not. She walked home to greet her cat and make herself a cup of chamomile tea, then opened her laptop to google Sonoma Gospel Mission.

21

Back at the Mission

✧

Elvis lasted three weeks and one day at home, until Angel threw a fit and told him to leave. He didn't blame her. In fact, her words came as a relief, because he knew he was on the verge of relapse. Ever since stumbling across James at the neighborhood grocery, he had been plotting surreptitiously how to get in touch with him. He walked the dog back to the market on Olive, hoping to run into James again. He asked acquaintances, casually, whether they had seen James. He searched the Internet for him and then deleted the history before Angel came home.

Nevertheless he failed to cover all his tracks. Angel found a piece of paper on which he had written phone numbers. If he had thought quickly he could have told her they were numbers he called looking for a job. Instead he acted offended that she was doubting him, which made her suspect they were phone numbers for girls.

She started raging, walking back and forth and picking up pillows and magazines to throw at the wall. He straightened her out by saying he was trying to get in touch with an old friend, not a girl. She became very quiet and asked him, point blank, Are you using? He said no, but the way he said it must have given away that something was up, because she stayed on him like a cat going after a cricket. She remembered how he had been with his dealer, protecting that lifeline. Elvis felt so guilty, so detected, that he couldn't fight back. "I haven't done anything," he told Angel. "I'm completely clean." That was true. She sensed, however, that he was planning something, and she knew that planning to get drugs, for an addict, is the same as getting drugs, even if they have to steal or lie or hurt somebody to do it. She told him to stop wasting her time, and get out.

After all she had endured with him, it seemed bizarre that she reached that point just on the basis of a suspicion. He tried to joke with her but his silly words fell flat. She just looked at him. She wasn't kidding. Elvis could see the hurt deep in her eyes, and he had to remember what he had done to her.

"I mean it," she said. "I'm done. Go back to the mission, and stay this time."

Stunned by how quickly it had turned, he went out the door and walked straight there, taking not one thing but the clothes he was wearing. On the way he debated with himself. He could go back and beg Angel. She would probably relent and give him another chance. He thought of her sunburned pelt and her frazzled hair and almost turned around.

But then he thought: I'm going to relapse if I keep on this way. And if that happened, he would lose everything, including Angel and his daughter Amber. He had just glimpsed a future he couldn't joke through or fight through. It scared him.

The guys at the front desk acted happy to see Elvis but he knew they enjoyed his humiliation. They were smirking behind his back, he felt sure. His hands were itching to hurt them, but he stymied that impulse. He dawdled in the dining room, exchanging small talk with the men in white coats doing food prep, until Jake Dorner called him up to his office.

Two of the men in Phase 3, members of the Advisory Council, joined Jake for an interview. They wanted to know what was different this time. That stumped Elvis. Wasn't it enough that he had come back? He made up something about wanting to be a good father for Amber, and they swallowed it. Or perhaps they did not swallow it, but simply let him in with the hope that somehow he would get a clue. At any rate they let him in. They all hugged. Hugging was becoming normal at the mission.

The first night, sleeping on an upper bunk bed in the 12-man room, he dreamed that James found him and they were shooting up together in James' car. The dream frightened Elvis, even when he woke up. In a perverse way, it communicated a message. He needed to take his addiction seriously.

Two mornings later Damien, a young, thoroughly green heroin addict, usually the most peppy member of the house, sat in morning devotions with his eyes drooping. He got to his feet to share and Elvis could see that some powerful feelings were bidding to come out. Damien began to speak, stammered, and then had to stop, his jaw gyrating but no sound emerging. When eventually he got control he said that at church on Sunday he had bumped into his sponsor's brother. He hadn't seen his sponsor in two weeks, so he asked about him. His brother said that Friday Brandon had died of an overdose.

Again Damien's jaw worked as he tried to speak. "Brandon was an awesome brother," he managed to say, his voice crackling and wavering. "Brandon, your life is not in vain. You have reminded me that this is life and death."

Of course Elvis knew that it happens. Two of his friends from high school had died, one by an OD, one shot dead by his dealer. For some reason, though, the death of a man he didn't even know caught his attention. He was unexpectedly moved, and that swayed him toward hope. He thought that maybe his emotions were moving like the tide, swinging over in favor of sobriety.

Undoubtedly deeper forces moved his addictions: hopes and fears from childhood, wounds never healed. His father's death, he knew, was still on him. Life for Elvis was like balancing on top of a ball, and the ball floating on a fast-moving stream. You would feel pretty good and then, without any warning, the ball would hit a subterranean snag and you would be grasping for anything to hold on to. All along you knew those deeper forces were there. The hope was that somehow, through the twelve steps, through the prayers, through all the efforts the mission was throwing at him, other forces equally deep would begin to operate on his side. He wanted to be clean, but he knew he needed some kind of deeper help. He had failed too many times to doubt it.

Elvis slid back into the routines of the house easily enough. Assigned to guest services, he enjoyed hanging out and helping whoever came along. If somebody wandered into the yard looking down and out, Elvis went right up to him and found out what he needed. People who hadn't been around the mission didn't understand how to get a shower, or a sandwich, or what to do with their backpack during meals.

In his spare time he went back into lifting weights. It always felt good. Even if his shoulders were killing him, he liked the burn and the sense that he was pushing himself. Lifting was one thing he did well.

Elvis was lifting in the yard when he noticed Jeff sitting on the bench under the tree, reading, but also watching. "You want to do this?" Elvis called out to him, without reason or premeditation. Elvis was like that.

Jeff flinched like a kid who expected to be bullied.

"Yeah, you," Elvis said. "What's your name? Do you want to lift? I can help you if you want to do it."

And Elvis added, "You should. You look weak." He gave a big smile.

When Jeff still hesitated Elvis took it on as a challenge. "What are you reading?" he asked. Jeff showed him the cover of the book, which was *The Message of John*. "What's it about?" Elvis asked, and Jeff told him that it was about the book of John, in the Bible.

"Cool," Elvis said. "You know the Bible?"

"Yeah. Some."

"Okay, let's make a deal. I'll teach you how to lift, and you teach me the Bible. Cause I don't know the Bible from jack."

It was a spontaneous offer, but it sprang from a genuine sense of need. Everyone in the New Life program attended Bible classes in the afternoon. They were supposed to look things up but Elvis had no idea where to look; he tried to sneak peeks from his neighbors. Much of the time he just stared at some random page, pretending to read what everybody else did. He was not about to tell the teacher that he was totally lost.

Jeff had dark skin and black hair, like a Mexican, but his name was Digitale, which he said was Italian. He was even softer than he looked. He had the squishy torso of an overweight cat. The morning after his first day of lifting he couldn't get his hands above his ears. Elvis made a point of poking him in the shoulder, just to watch him wince. It seemed funny to him.

They lifted every afternoon after classes were done, and they talked about the Bible together every day before bedtime. It was an unlikely friendship. Jeff was a loner who had never been in serious trouble, except for his drinking. Elvis was an extrovert who was always in trouble. He knew everybody and talked to everybody and made everybody laugh; he had been in and out of prison since he got out of high school. He hurt people. Jeff never hurt a soul.

The other guys could be raucous in class, asking questions that were designed to draw a laugh and that further demonstrated their ignorance. This was so particularly when they talked about sex or women. Elvis thought they were funny, but he admitted they were no help at all. Jeff could explain things to Elvis. When he talked things made more sense.

They talked a lot about the program. Some days they thought it was working; some days not. They both went up and down in their faith in its effectiveness. The house was at a low point just then. The mood was obvious just walking in to breakfast. You heard muttering and complaining and mumbled threats. Guys got into fights over nothing. Rumor would circulate that someone was on his way out, and then at dinner Elvis would see that one of the men was gone without explanation. Even if it was someone nobody liked, it always left a gap.

Everyone knew about the accusations against Jake in the newspaper, but for various reasons no one took them seriously. Many of the men had done jail time or prison; they had done worse things than what Jake was accused of. There was also the fact that many of them knew Kasha, and considered her a joke.

All the same, something had gone out of Jake. Ordinarily he radiated vigor, from his razor-gargling voice to his powerful torso. He was always preaching a sermon at them, which was generally okay because he had the right. They accepted that he was that kind of hard-charging guy, and they recognized he was utterly sincere. Something had changed, though it was hard to put your finger on exactly what. It was as though his colors had faded.

Every morning Elvis and Jeff went to morning devotions together, and then talked over breakfast. Between 9:00 and noon, they worked—Jeff in the kitchen, Elvis on guest services. After afternoon classes, after lifting, they ate dinner and, depending on which church was involved, attended the chapel service. (They were required to go to three per week.) They went to at least three AA or NA meetings a week, as the program required.

Elvis said to anyone and everyone that he needed tools, by which he meant strategies for slowing the vivid present and understanding what it was doing to him. He told Jeff he wasn't interested in being psychoanalyzed; he wanted practical skills to help him steer his way through wrecked cars spinning on the track.

The Twelve Steps study book gave lists of trigger points, offered self-check inventories, gave step-by-step descriptions of the path to relapse. Elvis studied those passages as though somewhere in the spaces between the letters he could find his own key. The analysis seemed convincing while he was reading it, but he found it very hard to apply later on.

Besides, he got tired of thinking. Jeff seemingly could go on explaining stuff all day, but for Elvis it took too much patience.

Ten months was a very long time. He inched forward, hoping that it would help him but uncertain how it could.

22

No Apologies

✧

By the beginning of July, when Kasha's lawyer Adam McLeod thought he had let the mission sweat long enough, he called Kent Spires at the office on Berger Street.

"I've got some good news for you, Kent. My client is willing to reach a settlement. It's not something I have recommended to her, but I am putting it to you because if I were in your shoes I would want to put this whole thing behind you."

Kent was the sort of man who could never act impolite, but he was very guarded in his response. "What kind of settlement are you suggesting?"

"We'd have to discuss that. In view of all that my client has been through, it would need to be substantial."

Kent suppressed his urge to mention all that the mission was going through. "Do you have an amount in mind?"

"I haven't discussed a number, just the general principle. Before I get into that I wanted to be sure that all parties were open to it."

"Of course we're open," Kent said. "But if you're talking about sums of money, we don't have it."

"It costs money to go to court," Adam reminded him.

Kent Spires called Jake to tell him about the conversation. Ordinarily this kind of business was out of Jake's orbit, but Kent knew that Krystle had gone to stay with her mother more than two weeks before, and he could imagine what Jake must be enduring. Kent had himself answered dozens of calls from pastors and donors and supporters. Some of them listened, but many of them were more interested in expressing their hysteria. Why were so many people so quick to believe the worst?

He had fully briefed the board and they were supportive. However, donations had plummeted. The mission survived on charitable gifts, hand to mouth, so the shortfall had an immediate impact. At the end of June they only barely met payroll. Kent had been calling their larger donors, and it had deepened his sense of alarm. A woman who had supported their women's work for a decade said she would never give to the Sonoma Gospel Mission again. She had met Kasha at a church women's meeting, and was so impressed by her understanding of the poor. Why, she wanted to know, was the perpetrator still at the mission?

Other donors had less dramatic outlooks, but said they couldn't help right now. Kent felt a trove of doubts hidden under their bland comments. He wasn't anxious to open that; he knew he could only take so many of these discussions.

"Kasha's lawyer called," he told Jake. "He said she wants to settle."

Jake took a few moments to respond. "What did you tell him?"

"I told him we don't have any money."

"What did he say?"

"He said he only wanted to make sure we were open to a discussion. Jake, I think they know they have nothing going for them in court."

"But if we don't have any money..."

"Maybe they will settle for something else."

Jake had anticipated something like this, and he had already made up his mind. "I'm not apologizing," Jake said. "I don't have anything to apologize for. As far as I am concerned they owe me an apology."

Kent had expected Jake to say something like that. All the same it did not make his situation any easier.

"Okay. We'll just have to see. Jake, partly I called because I wanted you to know that we really don't have any money. Anything you can do to cut expenses, please do immediately."

The mission often paid to help men get back on their feet. Sometimes it paid fines so they could get back a driving license. Sometimes it sent them to truck-driving school, or culinary school. Kent said Jake should put a hold on all that.

"Even if I've promised them?"

"Yes. Otherwise we aren't going to get paychecks this month. Donations have disappeared. I've called all our board members but I don't see any relief coming. We need to pray."

"It sounds like the best thing I could do is resign."

Kent sighed, and his voice grew softer. "No. That's not how we operate. We can trust God."

Afterwards, Jake brooded on the fact that Kent had not said no because he needed Jake, and could not do without him.

23

Sam and the Girl

✧

Sam found Lester at Taco Time, his gangly body dressed in a roomy yellow-and-red polyester outfit with a padded cap, looking surprisingly pert as he served customers. He got off at 9:00, so Sam waited in the air-conditioned plastic dining room. When a birthday party of nine-year-olds came in, the level of noise and commotion pushed him outside to sit on the parking lot curb. He felt better out there. The night air was cooling off, and the summer sounds washed through him: the guttural purr of cars starting up from the corner stoplight, the chatter of kids, a dog barking urgently from an unseen house on a parallel street. Sam felt a mixture of expectation and dread. He did not like to name what he was about to do, but he could not deny that he had come with only that in mind. He tried to put it out of his head.

"You Lester's friend?" Sam looked up to see a girl in a sleeveless t-shirt that was a little big on her; he could see her bra through the armhole. Her legs were nice, considering that she was short, and her flip-flops were gold with raised silver dolphins. She squatted down so close their hips almost touched, and introduced herself as Raylene. Sam said his name. He was never much of a talker, especially with girls.

"Did you go to Modesto?" she asked.

"Yeah. With Lester."

"I did too but I'm younger. Have I seen you?"

"I don't think so. I've been gone. I just came back."

"Where did you go?"

"Santa Rosa."

She said she had heard of it. She didn't ask him what he had been doing there, but seemed content just to sit with him. There was actually a slight breeze. When it faltered Sam could feel the heat radiating up from the parking lot asphalt. Heat was something real and undeniable. He could focus on the feelings of the heat and take his mind off other things.

Eventually he asked Raylene if she was waiting for Lester to get off. She said yes, and he said that he was too. "Are you his girl friend?" he asked, but she said no, Maddy was.

"Who's Maddy?" he asked, and she said he would see.

Lester got off exactly at 9:00 and wanted to go home immediately to get out of the yellow and red uniform. The three of them piled into his Tercel—Sam got into the back seat—and drove to Lester's house. Sam had forgotten where Lester lived, but as soon as he saw the street it all came back to him. It was lined with Modesto ash trees that had all been pushed into a slant by the prevailing west wind; the trees were fully grown and made you feel as though you were aslant, in a distorted universe. In middle school he and Lester had spent evenings—many evenings, it seemed to memory—lying on his parents' threadbare lawn and talking about the possibilities of alternative universes. When they began to smoke marijuana in seventh grade those fantasies expanded. They gave a name to their parallel planet, and laughed hilariously about it whenever they were stoned.

Lester left Sam and Raylene in the car while he changed, and Raylene came into the back seat. "Do you like my sandals?" she asked. "I just bought them."

"I thought those were flip-flops," he said.

"Whatever. Flip-flops are a kind of sandal, aren't they? It's a stupid name. My grandmother calls them zoris."

When Lester came out he didn't bother to get Raylene into the front seat. They roared off to pick up Maddy. "You don't know her," Lester said over his shoulder. "She's new. And she's hot. I'm lucky I got her."

Raylene put her hand on Sam's arm, as though it was the most natural thing in the world. He wasn't sure whether he was supposed to do something to respond, so he just waited. Probably it will become obvious, he thought.

They found Maddy at Starbucks. She was taller than Lester, and she wore a scooped black shirt with sequins that showed about an inch of cleavage. She got in and leaned over to kiss Lester. He put a hand on her thigh while he drove. It was several minutes before Maddy turned around to greet Raylene and Sam.

Lester drove out to a place he knew on the river. When he turned off the motor the sound of bullfrogs rose, as though amplified. In the dark Raylene put her hand into Sam's as they stumbled across mounds of gravel and found a place to sit on a sandy edge of the water. Pesky flies wanted to fly up their noses. The western sky was a deep purple shading into black as it turned to the east.

"It's hot," Raylene said.

"The sand is hot," Lester said. "The air is cooling off."

Lester and Maddy had put down a blanket some distance from where Raylene and Sam sat on the sand. Sam heard the scratch and flare of a match, and then smelled the sweet burnt skunk of dope. He expected Lester to say something, to offer him a toke, but no one said anything.

Raylene said it was too hot and she wanted to get her feet wet. She kicked off her flip-flops and waded in. It was too dark to see anything but a dim shape, but Sam could hear her splashing and making cooing noises. Then came a deep splash, and she cried out for help. Without thinking he jumped to his feet and stepped into the water, soaking his running shoes. Where was she? He could see nothing but a glimmer of reflection on the water. He could hear splashing and breathing.

"Where are you?" he cried out.

"Help!" she gurgled, sounding more annoyed than desperate, and he went toward her—the water only knee deep—until his searching hand found her sleeveless shirt. She was soaked through, and when he pulled her up she clung to him, wetting him too.

They staggered, arm in arm, out of the water. Back on the bank she said she could feel sand in her underwear. "It's awful," she said. "God knows what's in there."

"Why don't you take your panties off," Maddy suggested. "Nobody can see us."

Maddy and Lester had not moved in response to Raylene's emergency. They were sitting or lying close together, shadows in the darkness.

Sam began shivering—the water was cold. Raylene sat down close to him and said she was freezing too. "Put your arm around me, would you?" When he did he realized that she had taken off more than her panties.

"Tighter," she said.

It was hard for Sam to say whether he liked Raylene. She had little talk, nor did she make a pretense of being friendly or particularly nice, but she was clear and direct about what she wanted. That made it easy for him. Sam did not feel ready for a complicated relationship.

They generally met at Taco Time and drove with Lester and Maddy to the same place on the river, taking advantage of Lester's car. Occasionally, at Maddy's suggestion, they tried another location, and sometimes for no stated reason they stayed at Taco Time, hanging out in the parking lot or on the adjoining street. Most nights, though, they drifted back to the familiar riverbank. After that first night, when they ended up itchy and coated with sandy mud, Raylene told Sam to bring a blanket. He did, though he felt conspicuous carrying it on his bicycle.

Sometimes Lester offered to share a joint, but more often not. Considering that Sam had gone to Taco Time expecting to do drugs, he was surprised to find himself comparatively clean and sober. One time Raylene brought a quart of beer that she had found in her parents' refrigerator. That seemed relatively innocent. On the edges of Sam's consciousness, like a dust cloud no bigger than a man's hand, were the opiates that had never released their grip on his mind. He did not feel that he was unhooked, but only that the long monofilament line was slack for the time being. These drugs were the great looming possibility, and what he and Raylene did on the blanket mattered much less.

They followed the same procedure every time. With few preliminaries and little experimentation they lay down together, and afterward they put back on whatever clothes they had taken off and sat quietly, saying almost nothing to each other, until Lester was ready to go back to town. A few times Sam tried to ask Raylene about herself, to make conversation, but he was not very good at initiating questions, and she gave short answers. She asked him practically nothing. Sam could not say that he liked the way things went between them—he thought somehow male and female should interact in a more romantic way—and once or twice he considered staying home, not going to Taco Time. But in the end, almost every night, for lack of some good alternative he ended up with her.

When he thought of her he did not think of Raylene, the person, at all. He did not find himself terribly interested in her. But her body was intensely real, almost the only thing fixed and solid in a world of shadows. Each night he was all eagerness, focused to the point that his body sometimes trembled.

He continued working for his dad. He had no choice, since he had nowhere else to live but home, and nobody else would hire him with his drug record. By imagining Raylene and anticipating their meeting, Sam was able to abstract himself from his father's unpredictable rants and from his own hatred of the work. It helped him get through. Neither parent asked him where he went after work. He was usually home by midnight, and he got up to make his own lunch and get into his father's truck by 7:30.

After two weeks of this routine Raylene asked him, while sitting on the curb at Taco Time, whether he had any drugs. Sam did not know what to say so he said nothing.

"I heard that you are a doper," Raylene said. "You should share that stuff."

Sam wondered what she had heard. Did she know about his OD?

"I used to be," he said. "But I'm not any more."

Later on that night, Raylene asked Lester where to get drugs.

"You mean weed? I can get that for you."

"No. I want to try other stuff."

"Hard stuff?"

"Sure."

That was the only conversation Sam heard, but more must have followed because the next night Raylene brought out a pill bottle and rattled two blue pills into Sam's hand. "They say it makes it better," she said, and after watching him down his, she shook two into her own hand and swallowed them.

For a few minutes Sam wondered whether Raylene had been sold fake stuff. He had been cheated himself, a few times. It happened. But then the warmth of confidence began, a tiny dot in his brain and then a spreading sense of fullness and well-being. He felt very sexually charged and sure of pleasure.

Next morning when his alarm rang he nearly turned over to sleep in, feeling exhausted. It was a near thing; his father would have killed him. At work he felt raging irritability. He was fortunate that, hung over as he was, his words came so slowly. His dad was not going to put up with backchat; he could barely endure Sam when he was silent.

Raylene said nothing about the experience, whether she liked the drugs or not, but she brought four more pills the next night, and the following night too.

She knew that Sam spent his days as a plumber; it was one of the few pieces of information she had asked for and he had provided.

"Does your dad pay you?" she asked that third night, when they had finished. When he said yes, she asked him to do his share.

He said nothing. He did not really know what she meant.

"You bring some stuff too. It's not fair for me to do everything. I'm not rich."

"He doesn't pay me much," Sam said. "Not enough." That was true; his father threw a few dollars his way now and then but said he was charging him for training, not to mention room and board and transportation.

"You want me to talk to him?"

"No." He smiled helplessly at the thought of Raylene and his father making conversation.

"You could get smack," Lester volunteered from the front seat. "It's cheaper."

"Where?" Sam said after a long pause.

A week later his mother was waiting for him when he came in the door. Her face was strange, some blend of anger and fear that he didn't recognize. It was late; she was usually in bed.

"Have you got some in your pockets?" she asked, deadpan.

He couldn't say anything. She repeated herself, and then came across the kitchen with her palms out: give me.

"What?" he said.

"Empty your pockets."

Only after the equipment was on the counter did her face break. He felt a huge rush of shame, and would have wished for her to hold him like a baby. Instead she held herself, cradling her torso with her bare, sun-bronzed, well-used arms. He might have promised her anything at that moment, but as usual his words were missing, like a line left blank to be filled in by any user.

She began swearing at his father. He understood her reasoning, but at that juncture he did manage to say that his father was not at fault.

"Whose fault is it then?" she shouted.

It flashed through his mind: Raylene. If only he had never met her.

He said nothing.

"I found all your stuff," she said. "I went through your room. I knew something was wrong. You're going to kill yourself, aren't you? You must be trying to kill yourself. One time wasn't enough, you want to do it right this time, don't you?" Her face was stricken with a snarl; she looked like a wild dog on the animal channel.

"I'll tell you what." She actually grabbed the front of his shirt and tried to pull him to her face, but she couldn't move him. Small as he was, she was smaller. "I'll tell you what, you're not doing it here. Not in my house. I put up with your dad, I'm not putting up with you."

He would have given anything to comfort her. She was his mother, and he supposed he had a lifetime of lost memories stored up from when he was a baby, hours and hours of nursing and gurgling and smiling as babies did—all forgotten but not gone. And so did she, undoubtedly.

"I'll tell you what, you quit or you get out. You're not going out any more. You stay at home. You come home from work and eat dinner and what? You read books. You watch sports on TV. You don't go out. Who are you with? Who's doing this with you?"

He said nothing. That was his only defense, and one that had usually been effective.

"You don't leave this house, except for work. You hear me?"

He stayed home the rest of the week but by Saturday escape was all he could think of. Drugs and Raylene's body and summer night were all mixed together in his mind, one image on top of the other, a roaring combo. He knew his mother was right, that she wanted the best for him. That seemed to be irrelevant, however. He was operating by another logic.

When his mother went to the grocery story he watched her leave and then went through her dresser looking for money. He knew she kept a stash in her underwear, and he found more than he had expected: ten crisp twenties and a few singles. He stuck it all in his pocket and got on his bicycle. It was late afternoon, the hottest time of the day. He could see the air moving over the asphalt, like wavy dream sequences in old movies. To avoid his mother he cut off onto a back road, a narrow strip of asphalt that ran alongside an alfalfa field. Between the road and the heavy, saturated green of the alfalfa was a strip of dust, fine as talcum, the color of a clay pot. The sky overhead was dull blue, fading almost to white as it dropped to the horizon. The heat was a weight on his back and his head; his hair threatened to smolder. Sam felt so miserable inside he almost turned the bike around to go back home. As soon as he thought of how it would be to park his bike in the garage and go in the door to the kitchen, however, he knew he would be just as miserable there.

It was too hot to simply ride his bicycle, so he ended up going to Lester's house. Lester's car was gone. Laying the bike down in the gutter he stretched out in the shade, looking up at the slanted trees. Every time a car drove by he felt anxious. Irrationally he feared that his mother would come and find him—irrationally because she had no idea of Lester or where Lester lived.

He felt some comfort in the smell of the grass, the slight undulations of the leaves overhead, and the warmth of the air shielded from the blazing sky. He was hot but not unendurably so. He thought he could wait until Lester came home or something else happened. He thought he could wait all night, if he were left alone.

Again he told himself he could go home now. That was the right thing to do. Even if his mother had already come home, she would forgive him. He could make up a story. But even as he turned this over in his mind, he knew he was not going to do it. He was heading in another direction, and he seemed to lack the power to stop. He would play it out.

His sense of safety was interrupted when Lester's mother came home.

Sam must have fallen asleep, for he never heard her car. She appeared in his vision overhead, looking down on him. He hadn't seen her for years; she didn't recognize him, but asked sternly what he was doing.

"I'm looking for Lester," he said. "I'm a friend."

She studied him. She was tall and thin, like Lester, with an undershot jaw. She wore flip-flops and capris and a straw porkpie hat. The sun came from behind her head, and he could not make out her expression.

"Are you Sam?" she asked at length, in a voice that moved toward kindness. In middle school he had been one of her favorites. Sam wondered whether she knew about his OD.

"Lester's out with that girlfriend," she said. "I don't know when he'll be back."

"Do you know where he went?"

She paused to think. "Maybe a movie."

She added, gratuitously, "I don't know what he sees in that girl. She's about as friendly as a wall."

Sam thought, but did not say, "She's hot." He supposed that mothers did not see that.

Lester's mother did not tell him to leave, but neither did she invite him into the house. He would not have felt comfortable inside anyway, but given the circumstances he didn't feel comfortable staying on her lawn any longer. Lester's mother made herself busy watering some plants with the hose, waving at him casually as he took off on his bicycle.

There were still hours to go before the evening, and the temperature had not begun to relent. He could go to the Cineplex, and see whether Lester's car was there. If it was, what then? Would he go inside and try to find them? He did not want to spend $9 for nothing, and even if he found them, they might not be glad to see him there.

He had no idea where Raylene lived; they always dropped her off at a strip mall.

In his mind's eye he could see the paraphernalia he had laid out on the kitchen counter for his mother, the little envelopes and the spoon and the needles in their sealed plastic bags. They made him shiver because they were deadly, like a rattlesnake slithering over the dirt and into the shelter of a bush. And just the same, they promised an end to his anxiety, and the flush of inner confidence.

He shook off the vision.

Idly he rode his bicycle through random streets, quiet residential neighborhoods with tall trees and wide browning lawns fronting houses that sometimes needed paint. The thought of drugs came back to him. It was no good looking for Lester, who only smoked weed. Raylene was somewhere but could be anywhere. He should be looking for drugs.

He knew this was wrong. He did not want to kill himself. Fleetingly Sam pictured Jake at the SGM, a tower of strength—physical, spiritual, emotional—that had helped him stay sober for months. He tried hard to think of that, to make it immediate. But Jake was somewhere else; here he had nothing. It was going to happen and it might as well be now as later.

Remembering the old middle school, he rode there. The back of the lot, past the neglected Little League field, was as dry and deserted as it had ever been. It didn't look like anybody came there any more; there was no trash, and no bare spots to show where people had scuffled in the weeds along the cyclone fence. Sam didn't know how to get drugs any more. He had been too passive, depending on Raylene. He could look for people who were selling, but in the staring heat of the day nobody would be out.

He rode slowly to the Cineplex. It was on the north side of town and a distant ride; he had to follow a major street because of the railroad that split town. The Cineplex was at a mall that had sucked the life out of downtown, years ago; now in its turn it had been drained by big box stores on the freeway. Its vast acres of parking emphasized the desertions that had left many of the stores vacant. Only a few cars puddled around the entrances. Sam had to ride across these fields of asphalt all the way around to the back side. A handful of cars signaled attendance at the Cineplex's detached structure. One was Lester's blue Tercel. Seeing it brought a wave of relief to Sam, and then, in quick succession, anxiety, and then sadness. Part of him, he realized, had hoped to be stymied.

Lester was not completely pleased to find Sam waiting for him when he and Maddy left the Cineplex. Sam explained that he had gone to his house, looking for him, and his mother had suggested where to go. This strangely bothered Lester. He asked Sam repeatedly why he had gone to his house, and he wanted to know everything about what his mother had said and how she had said it. Sam told him what little there was to tell, except what she had said about Maddy.

Sam asked if they knew where Raylene lived. They didn't, but Maddy had her phone number. "What do you want her for?" she asked.

"I just want to see her."

"Can't wait, huh?" Maddy had on a string halter-top, and from the looks of it she didn't have a bra on. She had done something to her hair. She did look hot.

"He wants drugs," Lester said, guessing correctly.

"But not just drugs," Maddy said teasingly, perhaps the first time she had ever smiled in Sam's presence.

"I have some money," Sam said by way of explanation.

Raylene met them at the strip mall in front of a Vietnamese nail place. She wanted to see Sam's money and he showed her. "Okay, that should do it," she said, and took the money into the salon. While they waited in the parking lot, Maddy asked Sam if he was going to share.

"Sure," he said.

"Because you've never offered."

"I thought you guys just did weed."

They didn't say anything in response. When Raylene got in the car she patted the pocket on her cut-offs and said, "Got it."

They reached the river just at dusk. Sam had one time ridden his bicycle to see it in the full light of day, when he could see for himself how flat and dull it was. The water was murky and littered with sodden trash. No trees offered shade, and the bushes were gray and dry, as though completely unaffected by the nearness of water. It was a place without mystery.

Twilight transformed it, however. The color of the evening sky glinted pink and blue on the water, long shadows softened the shapes of the bushes, and color grew subtle and restrained.

Raylene was mad that he hadn't brought the blanket. They sat on a bank with their feet in the water, watching the darkness stealthily advance.

"How much did you get?" Sam asked.

"Enough."

Maddy and Lester had taken their usual spot well back from the water. Now Maddy walked down to the water's edge and asked if they were going to share.

"We don't have enough," Raylene said.

"I promised them some," Sam said.

"Easy for you. It's expensive stuff," Raylene said. "I only have enough for us."

Maddy said she hoped they enjoyed the walk home.

Sam apologized. "I thought that would buy plenty," he said. "I'm sorry. I'll make it up next time."

Maddy walked away. Soon they smelled dope.

"They don't need our stuff," Raylene said. She reached out and touched

Sam's chest, a gentle tap that seemed strikingly confidential. "We can make this a long night."

She took his hand and carefully placed two pills in the upturned palm. "We should have brought something to wash them down with," Raylene said. They waited for the darkness to grow deeper and for the drugs to spread their softness.

"You ready?" Raylene asked. Sam was not sure. The drugs seemed to be making him dizzy. Raylene tugged his hand and led him to a depression they had used before. As they began to touch she stopped and fumbled with something. "Here," she said, and found his hand with a baggy of pills. He could feel that there were more than a few of them. "Put them in your pocket."

Everything seemed to go very slowly, as though time dragged itself through mud up to its knees. Sam continued to feel dizzy. At one point he thought he was going to throw up. For all his lack of energy, Raylene seemed to have the opposite reaction: she talked. He could not really follow what she was saying, which was a complicated story about how she had found the people in the nail palace, who knew her best friend from high school, who was married to a cop. Sam didn't care. He tried to focus on what he was doing, which was difficult, because he didn't feel well.

"Raylene?" Sam asked quietly, but got no response. He seemed to be alone. He could not quite remember where he was. He was naked, and he could not find his clothes.

He could hear a whisper of water from the river.

He had a vague memory of somebody calling to him and shaking him. Perhaps it was a dream. He felt awful. From the taste in his mouth he knew he had vomited, and when he tried to stand up he staggered and fell to his knees. The sky full of stars would not stay still, but seemed to swing slowly through his vision as though attached to a pendulum. He began patting the dirt around him and found his shirt; he put it on. After sitting for a few minutes trying to make the stars stop moving, he began patting the dirt again and found his pants. His underwear were tucked inside and he put them on. Then, discovering that he had them on backwards, he laboriously took them off and put them on again. After another break he started on his pants. That was when he discovered the baggy of pills still in his pocket.

He pulled them out and ran his fingers over them through the plastic, feeling so many of them. Like beads. Like little jewels.

Something had gone wrong, he felt, or he would not have been left alone. He wished he could see in the dark. For all he could tell, Raylene or Maddy or Lester might be lying dead nearby.

No, that could not be. He told himself not to worry. But he was alone and he did not know where his shoes were.

He opened the baggy and took two more of the pills. He thought it would help. He sat waiting for the effect, the warming glow of capability that took away all his fear. Instead his head seemed to go into a vice grip, and he felt nauseous. He threw up into his mouth. It was so awful he began to panic. He pulled out the baggy of pills and took two more, then added an extra one. The situation was not good.

He fought his way to his feet and staggered forward. He had to find his shoes. If he had them, he could walk home. However, his directions were confused and he walked into the water instead of away. Surprised by the sudden step down and the resistance of the water, he fell forward. His body seemed tangled in itself; he could not figure out how to get up. He was about to vomit again. The water seemed to be rushing, a white water rapid, gleaming in the starlight. It was cool, almost cold. He could lie in it. He closed his eyes to make the sky stop moving. Instead the stars began to wink out. He watched each one as though he stood on the last day of the last world as the last observer to see the universe shrink into a cold ball. It was a sort of beautiful. His head spun. He felt nauseous again. Then everything was dark and he could hear a high-pitched music.

24

The Shadow of Death

✧

The news of Sam's death reached the mission a few days later, in the middle of the new week. It came first as a rumor, muttered from mouth to ear as men gathered in the chapel waiting for morning devotions. The official word, when Jake announced it at lunchtime, said Sam had accidentally drowned. Nobody believed that. All of them understood that addicts and alcoholics drowned, or suffered blood clots and heart attacks, or drove into a tree, because they were loaded.

The news bothered Elvis more than he would have expected. Sam wasn't the first of his friends to OD, and yet the loss seemed especially grievous. Elvis could picture that small and serious face, that frail body holding the flame of his stubborn, silent will. Sam reminded Elvis of his daughter Amber, also stubborn, also tending to plow straight ahead into trouble. Sam brought out the parent in him, and probably in other men, which helped explain why his death sobered the house so much. They had lost a son.

The mission had a good deal of turnover, so probably a third of the men had never met Sam. The way they took the news—lightly, as though nothing had happened—struck Elvis as obscene. Logically he couldn't blame them for chattering on, but it bothered him. It set him off with Tim, a candidate who had come into the program two weeks before with a dark and resentful expression and a nasty tongue. From the day he arrived he had been complaining to anyone who would listen that the mission was filthy and the food uneatable, that anybody who didn't fit the mission's fundamentalist Christian profile got pushed out, that the leaders were angry and domineering. When asked why he didn't leave—as several people did ask, the first time they heard his soliloquy—he snarled that he had nowhere to go and he wasn't going to let them shove him out the door.

Elvis sat down next to him at chapel, in the back of the room where the green plastic chairs were lined up against the wall. "Hey," he said at the first break between songs, "why don't you sing? It will do you good."

Tim glanced at him sideways but did not respond, so Elvis asked again. "Why don't you sing? Look at me, I can't carry a tune, but I'm singing. You'll enjoy this more if you don't act like you've got something stuck up your butt."

Tim looked at him as though he were a particularly loathsome discovery at the bottom of a dumpster. "Are you the one who killed the kid?" he asked.

"Excuse me?"

"The kid who drowned himself. Are you the one who talked him into going to North Dakota? Because I heard that was what did him in."

For once, Elvis was so taken aback that he had no quick comeback.

"The kid must have been pretty dumb. And come to think of it, that must apply to you too."

At any earlier time in his life, Elvis would have clocked him. Instead he turned away and walked to the other side of the room. The service went on without his conscious presence. All he could think of was Sam, and his face that day in San Francisco when they went looking for a free meal. Sam: new-moon pale, with an expression both simple and helpless.

After chapel, in the courtyard, he asked his friend Jeff about it. Did he think he had killed Sam?

"What?"

"He left the program with me. He wouldn't have gone back home if I had told him not to. Sam was just a kid."

"That wasn't your fault. He had a choice."

Jeff couldn't deny the primary wound, however: Sam was dead, in all his innocence. Death was the ordinary thing life led to. The sun rose every day only to set. They both knew that most addicts never reform. They spend their days roaming around the bottom of the cage: vowing to change, claiming they are fine, committing to reform, threatening to kill themselves, promising to become a new man, threatening to kill somebody else, and falling back into the trough. Who could be sure that this torment they put themselves through, this crowded, ugly program, was really worth anybody's time? Who was to say that Elvis and Jeff would be any different from Sam?

Twice the next day one of the program members scuffled with Tim, yelling at him that he was dead meat. Jake Dorner could have kicked them all out—violence or threats were part of the no-tolerance list—but he knew Tim was the root of the problem. He called him up to his office. Tim had a slight build and a black beard scraggling over his hollow cheeks; he seemed to leak through the door rather than walk. Every muscle fiber communicated his dislike and his resistance. He kept his eyes on the wall behind Jake's head.

"We're having a lot of fighting," Jake said, expanding his chest and his voice. "Most of it seems to involve you. Do you have any idea why?"

Tim wouldn't look at Jake. "It might have to do with people attacking me. I notice you haven't done anything to stop it."

"That's why I'm talking to you right now."

"You haven't called in the men who tried to hurt me. I assume that's because you want them to succeed. I know you want me out. This program doesn't put up with anybody who doesn't fit the diagram. You can only have one kind of person here, and that's not the kind of person I am and want to be."

Jake took a deep breath. He wanted to yell Tim into submission but he knew that wouldn't succeed. Besides, he felt so beaten down he did not have the energy he would need to dominate this punk.

"You seem to know more about this program than I do."

"So?"

"So I would have said, having been here for quite a few years, that this program will help anybody, as long as they want to be helped."

"Then why are you trying to freeze me out?"

"I'm not. I'm trying to get some peace and quiet so people can work the program and concentrate on sobriety. But I'm getting the impression you would just as soon stir people up. Including me."

The conversation went in circles. Every time Jake brought Tim around to taking responsibility he found a way to slip away. You couldn't pin him down. This didn't surprise Jake. Every addict did it, in one way or another. They diverted. Some did it by clowning. Some did it by rationalizing. Tim did it by attacking.

That it was a usual pattern didn't make it any less sickening. Jake already felt sorrow for Sam's death—for a kid that he and everybody liked. He did not join in any mournful discussions with program members, but he was noticeably distracted as he went about his work, rumbling through the hallways and hardly speaking to those who pressed up against the wall to let him by.

Kent Spires had called him repeatedly from the Berger office, wanting to know about expenses. Kent was never completely transparent about the state of SGM finances, but Jake knew that he was deeply worried. Even in good times Kent's secretary opened the mail every day with great interest. Things must be bad. Twice Jake offered to resign, but Kent brushed that aside. "We'll see what God has for us," was how he put it. "We don't need to make plans for God."

However, in his soft way Kent made Jake feel responsible. He commented that the place was leaking money. He asked Jake please to economize, as though Jake were not. He made passing comments about the state of the house, the bad vibe that seemed to be discouraging the men.

Kasha's lawsuit had disappeared from sight, buried somewhere in mysterious legal machinery. What remained, however, was the taint of accusation. Jake saw the frowns when people remembered. Even people he had known for years kept the subject at arm's length, not wanting—so he surmised—to be associated with whatever he had done, but equally not wanting to go into a messy discussion of his claims to innocence. They were perfectly willing to leave him for all time with a red letter—not a sharp and true red letter, but one you might see in the eye doctor's testing machine, fuzzy and bent but, with a squint, recognizably an A.

He went home to an empty house every night. He had begged Krystle to come back, but she said she couldn't do it. He had practically insisted, had even told her that he was dying without her and she was his wife. She wouldn't bend, she just wept. She became so terribly upset when he pushed that he backed off. They made do with skype calls every night at 8:00. In the hour before the call Jake would feel his anxiety amping up; and after the call he was low. Reggie was of an age that he couldn't sit still, and Krystle hardly looked at Jake, she was so preoccupied with Reggie. Most nights they barely started talking before Krystle said she had to go, and he couldn't really protest. You could see that Reggie wasn't going to give her any peace. Krystle's mom drifted through the picture, walking past in the background. She had always seemed dubious of Jake, wanting Krystle to come home to her real family whenever she could. Now she had her, and—so Jake thought—she didn't want to let her go.

Without Krystle, Jake drifted. Though he was the bruising and overpowering wide-body, and Krystle small and shy, she worked like a rudder on his life, keeping him aligned. Her absence became the most wounding of all his sorrows. He had been falsely accused, vilified as a sexual predator without any way to defend himself, and that was awful—but not so awful as her going away.

He had first seen Krystle at church, during that charmed time of his life after he had been grasped by the power of God, when new discoveries and ultimate possibilities poured in. He saw her across a room, waiting in line for coffee, in a huddle of chattering young women. By the rules of the program Jake was not allowed to fraternize with the opposite sex, so he kept his eyes averted and never said more than hello. Lots of men would have bent the rules, but he did not. He pretended not to notice her; he told himself that it would be wrong to let her see how she affected him. He was a strong man, and newly made clean, but compared to her he felt filthy and destructive. He would not tie her to his anchor. He would let her go free.

Krystle had straight dark hair almost to her waist and eyes that seemed destined to trust. Sweetness was written on her small face. Jake had known a few women in the years of roaming, but Krystle was different from any of them.

She came to the ceremony when he graduated from the program. He was so startled when he saw her that his mind slipped off his carefully memorized Bible verses. Due to her presence he needed numerous prompts to get through them, which was a humbling come-up for him since he had poured so much attention into the Bible these last few months. He had no idea who had invited her or why she was there, and he didn't go over to greet her afterwards even though, having graduated, he was now free from the rules about fraternization. Nor did he try to talk to her in the weeks that followed, when he moved into transitional housing and began working as Kent Spires' assistant in the house. He saw her at church, usually across the patio, but he avoided her. In his mind she had risen beyond the mere humanity of a girl; she epitomized all that was pure. The longer this continued the greater their differences seemed to be.

They finally made contact one Sunday in the fellowship hall, a room with indoor-outdoor carpeting and two basketball goals folded up overhead. He was not aware of her presence at all until suddenly he found her in front of him, darting a look upward into his eyes, then dropping them demurely.

"Hello, Krystle," he said.

"Hello, Jake."

He found that he was trembling, and he dared not open his mouth.

"You don't ever talk to me," she said, flitting another look at him.

It still moved Jake to think of that day, when the door swung open. He had no experience relating to someone like Krystle. He teased her, because he knew how to do that, but it nevertheless felt wrong to him. He knew he was embarrassing her, but he did not know how to do anything else.

Krystle's father had died of a heart attack when Krystle was still in high school. Within months her mother had moved them to Vallejo, from a rambling one-of-a-kind house a shout from the river to a tract home three blocks from the shopping mall. Krystle missed belonging to a place in the country, but her mother said that she didn't miss driving 20 minutes to get a can of beans.

Her brothers had already left home: one married, one working in Oakland, and one in college. Krystle was an only child now. She tried to keep up with her old friends from Eel River High School. She texted regularly, and sometimes called them, but the responses were few and far between. Her old friends were wrapped up in plans for prom and graduation, and Krystle simply wasn't part of those any more. In her new high school, she didn't know where to start in making friends. It was a big, urban school where nobody even noticed that she was new.

Her mother told her to stop moping. Once her mother started in with advice, she kept on repeating herself until Krystle wanted to cut herself. Then she could only retreat to her room, to weep or write poems in her journal. When Carol, a friend from Eel River, wrote that she was moving down to go to the junior college in Santa Rosa, Krystle made a snap decision. Her mother had been urging her to make a plan, to get a job, to do something. Going to school was something.

The apartment Krystle shared with Carol was a minimal two-bedroom on the second floor of a small complex surrounding a brick courtyard. The bricks, shaded by tall sycamores, had become dark with accumulations of dirt and mold. As to the building itself, generations of students had nicked the drywall corners while moving furniture, the ceiling was unredeemed sparkling popcorn, and the carpet a mustard shag. Access came from a narrow exterior walkway that Krystle appropriated for a balcony, moving a chair outside from their dining nook so she could read her textbooks while overlooking the courtyard. Carol had a boyfriend and was rarely seen, so Krystle cooked and ate alone. She made rice or noodles and ate from a bowl while sitting outside among the trees.

Her first weeks she reveled in the silence. She had been a compliant girl and for the first time she had no one telling her what to comply with. It elated her. She sat on her makeshift balcony marveling at her liberty.

This sense of freedom waned, however. She had never been on her own before. She had no experience meeting people, and barely put together face and name with her classmates. One Sunday morning it occurred to her that she ought to go to church. Her family had always attended, and she had never intended to stop. She simply had not thought.

She walked to a church she had seen in her neighborhood, a church that displayed a brief, weekly inspirational slogan on an illuminated sign. When she walked in, hesitantly, she felt immediately at home. People she had never met greeted her warmly. She already knew the songs they sang. She was invited to a women's Bible study that met on Thursday mornings. In short order, that church became the real center of her life.

Christian Community Church, or CCC, as it was known, was a recovery church. Her father's church on the river had its share of meth addicts and drunks, but that was just an accident of the place. Nobody had set out to reach them or help them especially. CCC offered itself as a church dedicated to people struggling with addictions. The pastor made frequent references to recovery programs, some of which met weekly at the church, and to special seminars dedicated to issues like pornography addiction or divorce recovery. He spoke of addiction without a hint of embarrassment.

Rather than shrinking into the corners like people ashamed of their skin, those in recovery were visible—in fact, loud, brash and boisterous. Circles of recovery people found each other on the patio each Sunday morning, and Krystle was drawn to them. Krystle found herself in conversations unlike any she had ever experienced, with people whose lives were nothing like hers.

She looked younger than she was: her dark hair drawn back in a braid, her face rounded and slightly pudgy, her chin undershot in a way that made her cute. She listened and smiled, standing unobtrusively on the edge. Nobody treated her like an alien. In time she knew everyone by name, and knew their stories, at least in fragments.

That is how she met Jake. She liked his size—her brothers were big men too—and she saw immediately that he was comfortable in the recovery world. Yet somehow his presence was larger. He was rowdy and exuberant but seemed more mature than the others. In some unspecifiable way he had authority. Months later Krystle learned that Jake led the New Life program at the mission. It made perfect sense to her.

She liked his brown brush of a beard; she liked his eyes. She did not dare speak to him, but she developed a poignant crush. Jake soon dominated her thoughts. She was not about to humiliate herself by telling Carol, or God forbid someone else at the church. She wanted to, however. The desire to share with someone was powerful. Once or twice, when her mother asked whether she was dating anyone, she perched on the verge of blurting out her wonderful infatuation.

Krystle knew perfectly well that girls go after guys, in both subtle ways and obvious, but it seemed more proper to her and certainly more romantic for the man to take initiative. She made no moves. She did not know how to flirt. Later, she marveled at the knowledge that while she was watching him, he was watching her. It seemed almost miraculous, how God drew them together. When Jake began to single her out for gentle teasing, she genuinely thought it meant nothing. When he asked her if they could meet for coffee, she grew flustered and did not sleep until the day came. When he got immediately to the point and asked whether she would be his girlfriend, she excused herself and ran out of Wolf Coffee. She found his attentions very hard to believe, and very hard to accept.

After they married, Jake realized that she was not made of chiffon, but of earth, and that for all her purity and grace she had her own kind of obstinate selfishness. Her family, too: at first he had wanted to become one of them completely. He hoped that no one would be able to tell him apart from her brothers. But that wore off: he found the family's endless board games boring. How could anybody care about this stuff? Whereas at the mission he dealt with life and death, addiction and suicide and hunger, these lives went from A to B and back again. They weren't curious about what he did, not at all. Their conversation was steeped in the mechanics of stuff. Jake wasn't a philosopher, but he did like to think about more than shopping and car maintenance.

Like her brothers Krystle was perfectly comfortable talking all day about good deals she had found—but it never bothered him in her. When Reggie was born her love of the mundane found its place, because while Jake had a short fuse on crying or diaper-changes, Krystle never lost patience. Jake found too, after they were married, and very much to his surprise, that she was a sensuous woman. Shy as she appeared to be, he had not guessed it at all.

He was a physical man. He missed her now in every way. It had been weeks since she left but it seemed like a hole in the regular progress of time: it blocked out everything else. If he had a car he would go and get her. Nobody could keep him away from her. He considered borrowing a car from someone, or taking the mission van. But either of those possibilities posed severe difficulties that he could not see his way through. Who did he know who had a car to lend? How would he explain himself? What if he got there and Krystle refused to come? So he only had her image on the computer, forcing him to sit and talk to a flat screen rather than to leap to her and hold her.

"Krystle," he told her on skype, his voice booming too loud, "I'm dying here! Can't you come home?"

She began to cry and said only that she couldn't, please don't make her.

"I'm not making you, I'm begging you. You don't know how miserable I am."

Those words seemed to scald his throat. He had never before told someone that he needed them. It was a terrible concession. But it seemed as though she stopped her ears from hearing. She wept, but she wouldn't listen. He wanted to shout at her, to use ear-shattering volume to make her hear.

Even if he had a car and went to get her, he was by no means sure that he could make her come home. He couldn't carry her off like a caveman. She had to want to come. Of everything, that was hardest to face: she didn't want to.

Jake found it difficult to sleep. His wretchedness brought him back to his days as an addict, when drugs were his medicine for agitation. They worked, of course. They had power. He got sufficiently lost in that memory to think of re-entering it, getting something to help him relax. Beer might do it, he thought. Then he thought, it would take something stronger. Then he realized what he was thinking and he stopped. He was not going there, no matter what. That was death. He had left that. He had gone from death into life. There was no returning.

He got up very early, sleep-deprived, to go to the mission. Men were waiting at the door for him when he arrived. Their faces jumped at him, distorted, urgent. They could not wait for him to attend to their needs or untangle their quarrels.

All day long needs pulled on him: conflicts, complaints, requests. One man wanted to know why he couldn't go to culinary school, and seemed unable to grasp that the mission depended on donations, which were few and far between at the moment. He was sure that Jake had rejected him personally, that Jake had it in for him, and he turned away with his face contorted in pain and fear. Another man came up to Jake's office shaking with rage and swearing that he would jump another man in his sleep, a man who had (he said) taken his favorite shirt out of his cubby and given it away. A group of three brought a complaint about a snorer who refused to wear a mouth guard. And so on, all day long, entitlement, self-pity and anger, wrapped up in the pettiness of men living too close together and lacking any insight into their own faults or any vision of a larger context. He was in charge and he was bigger and louder than they, but he could not solve their problems, he could only forestall them. By the afternoon he was bone weary. It was Friday, and at 2:00 came Phase and Praise.

It was his favorite activity of the week, because no homeless guests were invited, just the house and a handful of family members and church friends. By design they did no business at these meetings, gave no lectures and preached no sermons. The men moving up or graduating recited their Scriptures and read their essays; the rest of the time was given to encouragement and praise volunteered by the men themselves. Jake let the meeting flow without needing to take charge. He was part of a community where God had healed him and healed others. Almost every week it replenished him.

Four men were phasing up. They all said their Bible verses, and read their essays, and nobody failed. But today they seemed to have no heart for what they did. The same could be said of the time of encouragement. Words came by rote, using phrases that copied what somebody thought should be said. Jake felt that the flow of the Spirit was missing this week.

Jake thought of Sam. He had a weird thought that Sam was present, sitting somewhere behind him.

Sam's death made him wonder about the worth of the program. Whether any of these men had a chance was hard to say. When he tried to name those who had graduated and stayed clean and sober, he couldn't come up with names. A lot of them had fallen off. A lot of others were simply gone, moved, or disappeared, and who could say for sure what outcome for them? Undoubtedly, Sam was dead, the smallest and the youngest, whom he should have protected.

Suddenly he could see Sam in his mind's eye, as clear as a television picture, and it triggered a wave of remorse. All the tension that had accumulated for weeks crashed over him. He thought at first he could keep himself together. He stared down at the floor, holding on, while the weight of his head pulled him downward. He was exhausted. He lacked strength. Before he understood what he was doing, sobs were rippling through his chest.

The band had come to the end of a raucous praise song, and the room was deathly quiet. Jake should have stood to make some comments and close the meeting, but with him incapacitated nobody spoke. Everybody stared uncomfortably at Jake as he sobbed, but nobody moved.

25

Untangled Web

✧

Raquel Raise found herself immediately at home in Adam McLeod's office. The upholstered furniture seemed dated but neat. It made no attempt at impressing anybody, which impressed her favorably.

It had been more than a month since she first visited the Sonoma Gospel Mission, accidentally stumbling into the legal trouble they were in with Kasha. Raquel had seen it as an interesting tidbit, with no obvious importance to her, but afterwards she found herself unable to forget about it. She asked around about the mission, and inquired about Kasha. Raquel even looked up the lawsuit. It had been adequately summarized in the newspaper accounts, she found.

Still she remained curious, until she thought of visiting Adam, whose name she had learned in looking at the lawsuit. She was far from eager to do that, since it seemed eccentric to pursue information about a matter that didn't involve her in the least. In the end, though, she decided that she was retired now and had plenty of time to pursue anything she cared to. Call it eccentricity, call it entertainment, call it whatever you like, she made an appointment without revealing what it was about.

Adam's vaguely courtly manner, embroidered with a hint of self-mockery, set her immediately at ease. It was a style she had encountered many times in Washington among men who did not want to leave the impression they took themselves or their work too seriously.

Adam sized her up as an attractive woman of late middle age, with a striking head of heavy, auburn hair. She had made an appointment but had declined to state her business. He thought it was probably divorce. This was a game he played with himself: guessing the nature of people's trouble before they stated it.

This time, however, he guessed wrong. Raquel explained that she was a neighborhood volunteer with an interest in the Railroad Square district. On behalf of Ecology Action she was conducting a survey of residents to see what they thought about potential development in their neighborhood.

Even though this promised him no business, Adam remained engaged. He enjoyed the company of women, particularly though not exclusively women he found attractive. "I'd be interested in what you find," he said. "I have a client who is working on that."

"On what?"

"Developing that neighborhood. He's got very big plans."

"Would that be Buddy Grace?"

"Oh, you already know Buddy."

"Better to say I know of him."

"Whatever you've heard, it's probably only half true. But the half that is true, it's probably worse than you've heard." Adam smiled a dog-like grin, to show that he didn't mean it. "Buddy is a good friend." He lifted his eyebrows. "So how can I help you?"

"I'm just gathering data, to understand the state of play. I read about the lawsuit that you filed for Kasha Gold against the Sonoma Gospel Mission, and I hoped you could give me some background."

Raquel had actually rehearsed these lines while considering whether to come, an indication of how much she hesitated. The lawsuit had no obvious relevance to the neighborhood's development, and she could not fully explain, even to herself, what made it important to her. Jake Dorner's agitation, so obvious when she interviewed him, had drawn her as though to a hurt stray. Raquel found it difficult to imagine Jake doing what the lawsuit alleged. He was big enough, and rough enough, but not venal enough. Jake seemed almost fragile to her.

Who was the real victim? Raquel was no fool; she knew that her impressions of Jake could be mistaken. She came to Adam hoping to learn more, if only for her own satisfaction.

A pleasant but slightly satirical expression sat lightly on Adam's mouth. He was cautious about giving out information. "I'm not clear on what our lawsuit has to do with developing Railroad Square."

"Oh, probably nothing," she said. "The mission is a big presence in the neighborhood, and I'm trying to understand how it relates to everyone else. Ms. Gold seems to be quite well known as well. I'm confused about what happened between them. I read the police report and it's difficult to interpret. I'm sure you know that the police first arrested Ms. Gold, and then let her go."

"If you read police reports, you'll be confused all the time," Adam said. "Suffice it to say that Kasha was very badly abused. Not to blame the police, but when they come on a crime scene it's difficult for them to establish exactly what happened. We'll have plenty of witnesses to establish the truth."

"Do you expect to close down the Sonoma Gospel Mission?"

Adam frowned. "Why would I want to do that?"

Raquel smiled slightly, the first time Adam had seen an expression on her face. "I didn't mean you wanted to. But Mr...."

"Adam."

"Adam, you're suing them for $4 million. If they had to pay even, let's say, a million dollars, could they do it?" She lifted her eyebrows and smiled inquisitively.

"Miss Raise...."

She did not correct him.

"Are you a lawyer?"

She did not laugh. "No."

"Well, I've been practicing law for 35 years, and there are a few things that I've learned. One is never to assume you know somebody else's finances from looking at their appearance. I really have no idea about the Sonoma Gospel Mission and what they could survive. What I do know is that if they are violating women, they should be held responsible. Don't you agree?"

Raquel did not answer. She looked straight at him, her lips pressed together.

Adam shrugged his shoulders. "You don't have any relationship with the mission, do you?"

That drew a short, sharp chuckle. "No. No, Mr. McLeod, I do not have any relationship with an organization that has a neon 'Jesus Saves' sign over their door. I'm retired. I worked in government for many years. I'm volunteering with Ecology Action."

"That's a political organization. Progressive, I think?"

"I suppose some people would call us political, but we don't think of ourselves that way. We're certainly not partisan. We believe in helping neighborhoods identify the issues they care about and organize around them. In this case it's the question of how people around Railroad Square want to see development pursued. We're not actually advocating anything, at least not at this point."

He seemed to relax and deflate, slumping slightly in his chair. "Don't take me wrong. I feel strongly about my clients and their concerns. Kasha is a very interesting woman. I don't know what other people have told you about her. But she has a right to be treated as a human being. That's my concern."

"And you're also concerned to see Railroad Square developed by your client."

He sat up straight again. "If you mean Buddy Grace, I give him legal advice for his development plans. But there's no connection between that and Kasha Gold."

"Isn't there?"

"I'm not getting you," he said. His eyes were wide-awake now and his white goatee seemed to have grown white as snow.

"The connection is obvious, I think. Mr. Grace wants the mission to move. You are pushing a lawsuit that could bankrupt them. Understand, I don't personally care whether they go or stay."

Adam screwed up his face in a frown. "I'm still not quite getting you, then. If you don't care, what does it matter whether Kasha wins her suit or not?"

She looked like a schoolmarm, her lips pinched together and her back straight as a ruler. "I don't like coercion, Mr. McLeod. I am wondering whether this suit was cooked up just to force them out."

He lifted his palms in innocence. "You don't have to worry about that," he said. "The courts will sort it out. It's not going to affect anybody if they are innocent."

The next day, in the early evening, Adam was making ready to leave his office when Buddy's phone call caught him.

"You didn't tell me about this woman," Buddy said. "She's terrible."

"What woman?" Adam asked, though he had a sinking feeling that he knew.

"I don't remember her name. It's Mexican. She said she had seen you and you told her I was your client."

"Her name is Raise," Adam said, and spelled it. "I don't think she's Mexican. We were making small talk. She said she was interested in the Railroad Square neighborhood so I innocently mentioned your name. That was before I realized what she was up to. I owe you an apology."

"No kidding you owe me an apology. Adam, she's put it all together. She knows."

As far as Buddy was concerned, Raquel had arrived unannounced.

The truth was she had called and talked to his receptionist, who had shouted at Buddy through his open office door about seeing a woman who wanted to interview him. Buddy had said sure, any time after five, he would be out until then. He played golf with two of his contractor friends, and after the game they had a beer. He didn't get back to his office until 6:00, long after his red-headed receptionist had left. To his surprise he found a woman waiting in the reception. She was neatly though casually dressed, in turquoise capris and a white silk blouse, with perfect heavy hair and a ginger complexion. Buddy was immediately attentive.

"You've been waiting all this time?" he asked.

"It's fine," Raquel said. "You have quite an office." She appreciated the intricate carpets and the burnished copper lamps. She had been in lobbyists' offices that were similar in intent, though not so artfully done, she thought.

She did not like the stance she had taken with Adam McLeod. What was the point of pretending not to have any point of view? They sat on Buddy's low-slung leather sofas and she told him that he was using Kasha strictly to force the mission to move. It seemed wrong to her.

She managed to say this while not betraying the slightest emotion. She might have been explaining the Pythagorean theorem or observing the need for adequate parking.

"I love the mission!" he protested to her. "I wouldn't want to hurt them. I go to their fundraising banquet!"

"It's a strange way to show it," she said.

"Look, I'll explain it to you," he said. "Have you met Kasha? That woman is not going to court. We are just trying to nudge the mission to do what's actually in their interest. They need to move! They don't see it yet, but any objective analysis of their situation would show it. We have made them an extremely generous offer, but they keep balking. Have you ever heard the phrase, too heavenly minded for their own earthly good? That's the mission. They probably have to be that way to work with addicts and alkies, but they need to understand they're also in business. I've talked and talked to them but they don't hear me. That's why the lawsuit. I'm just hoping to get their attention."

She blinked but her expression did not change. "You have personally given money to them?"

"Yeah, my church supports the mission. They are good people."

"Then you should feel ashamed of yourself. Talk to Jake Dorner. Can you imagine what it must be like to be in the newspaper for sexually assaulting a woman? He's suffering. You can see it on his face. "

"Well, sure, it must be upsetting, but it's not going to last forever. People forget. You can't believe how quickly people forget."

They talked over and around it. Buddy found himself fascinated by this woman. He offered to take her out to dinner, to talk further, but she ruffled her feathers and turned him down.

"I'll think about what you've said," Buddy told her as she departed. "I promise you, I will." He asked for her card and instead got an Ecology Action brochure with her number written across the bottom. "But I want you to think about what I said too. The passenger train is coming, the neighborhood is changing, and the mission needs to move. That's a win for everybody. And I've made the mission an absolutely fantastic offer. How do I get them to listen to me?"

He fell back onto the sofa when she was gone. He was half alarmed and half enamored. Buddy loved women of substance. A girlfriend once accused him of looking for a mother replacement. That made him sound like a thumb-sucker and a mama's boy, which he was not. He found authority consistently attractive in a woman, however: he fell for those who knew their mind and told it to him. That was a mother too.

For several minutes Buddy meditated on Raquel and how he should approach her. He enjoyed thinking about their conversation, and the straight-laced lecture she had read him. This was a formidable woman.

At some point, however, his thoughts turned in another direction. He began to think about his plans for the neighborhood, and Howard Zenikov's refusal to consider a loan unless the mission was gone. Buddy was desperate for money, a subject that crept into his mind at undefended moments. That made him call Adam McLeod.

Adam asked him exactly what Raquel had said, but Buddy couldn't quite remember. He remembered her saying that Jake was suffering, and Buddy should be ashamed. But had she said anything about what she intended to do? He wasn't sure.

"Did she say anything about the newspaper? That reporter, what's her name?"

"Julie something."

"Yes, did she mention Julie?"

"I don't think so. Why?"

"She could go to the newspaper and you would be cooked."

"Well, we would just drop the suit, right?"

"And drop your development plans. You couldn't get a permit for a hot dog stand if this was in the newspaper."

"Then I'll call her before she does anything," Buddy said. "She gave me her number. I'll tell her I think she is right and I am dropping the suit. Nobody else needs to know. That will be the end of it."

"And still the end of your plans."

"Why?" Buddy was genuinely surprised.

"The mission doesn't move, Howard Zenikov doesn't give you a loan. Poof." The jovial tone that Adam used suggested he enjoyed giving the bad news.

"So what do we do? Adam, I have to get this project done."

Adam waited so long to answer that Buddy thought he had stopped breathing.

"I don't know. Let me think about it."

26

Night Duty

✧

Elvis Sebastiano was on night desk at the mission, working from 11 at night until 7 in the morning. Even though the doors were locked during those hours, and nobody could come in or go out, somebody needed to be awake in case of emergency. At 4:00 in the morning he would begin wakeup calls for men who wanted to shower in peace or take their time getting ready for the day. That meant finding their bunks in the dark and nudging them until they woke up. It was an eerie task, moving quietly among the breathing mummified shapes, guided only by a flashlight.

Until the wakeups, he sat in the cluttered office facing the front door, with a single floor lamp spotlighting the desk and only dimly illuminating the posted schedules and notices and calendars that papered the walls. Many nights somebody in the house was up and wandering, in which case Elvis often engaged in long conversation. He found it next to impossible to encounter another human being without finding something to talk about. The night solitude seemed rich and satisfying if he had company.

The night was also time for snacking, for he had free range of the pantry. He ate a lot of candy, particularly sour gummy worms.

When he had no company he read his Bible, and would write down questions to ask Jeff in the morning. There was a lot he did not understand. Elvis had never studied anything before—school had been wasted on him—but he felt he was slowly gaining traction, growing accustomed to the novel movements of his mind, shuffling phrases and ideas as though they were buses in the parking lot, learning to think. It touched on his hope to gain mastery over his life.

He was busy enough that he did not think of Angel very often. She didn't call him and he had limited phone access. His only really consistent out-of-mission contact was with his daughter Amber. He talked to her most nights, trying to nurse her along day by day. She was back living with his brother, which she hated. Angel had taken her there after she sent Elvis back to the mission.

His brother Tom had called just before dinner. Elvis had not yet qualified to have a cell phone, so he took the call in the office, where privacy was impossible.

Tom rarely bothered to say hello. He jumped right into whatever he wanted to say without a preamble. His voice trembling with anger, he informed Elvis that he had taken away Amber's cell phone. "And I told her she can only call you from here when I'm around. She talks to you and gets upset."

"What do you mean, she gets upset?"

"You want me to spell it for you? She starts crying and whining and we can't do anything with her. She's not doing her homework."

"How is it going to help if she can't talk to me?"

"You make her upset. I don't know what you tell her but she's a basket case every time. She's spending too much time on the phone anyway."

Caught off guard, Elvis had not reacted. During dinner and chapel and a meeting of Dogs on the Roof, the AA meeting that he attended on Fridays at the Journeys End Senior Center, he was too busy to think of it. But in the silence after midnight, he found himself steaming. What did his brother expect? Amber is 13 years old, her mother disappeared years ago, her father is a meth addict locked in a program, and she's living with a hard-ass-strict uncle and his Asperger's son. Let her cry a little, it won't kill anybody. Tell her to go to her room, but don't tell her she can't call her father any more.

Elvis's character was generous. He would stop to help stranded motorists, to check on drunks who fell down. If he thought you needed something, he would give it to you. Just as much, though, he was primed to fight. His instant response was to hit. As he boiled away over Amber he thought that if he had a chance he would grab his brother's throat and choke him, he would kick his balls. Let him get upset. "You wanna call somebody? You want to use the phone?" That was what he imagined asking Tom as he smashed him.

He wondered once again whether he was doing any good in this program. If his daughter went down the drain, what good was it? He didn't even know that he could stay on the right track when he got out of this joint; he could see himself beating somebody up—his brother Tom, for instance—and going straight to his dealer, like a squealer latching on to the mother pig.

Elvis remembered that he should be reading the Bible, instead of letting his mind go to these stormy places, but he just couldn't.

Somebody was buzzing the front door. It interrupted his train of thought like an angry wasp, but there was not much he could do with it. At one time there had been a working intercom between the front desk and the door; but it had been broken for months, maybe years, and nobody cared enough to fix it. What would be the point? The door was locked and the rule was absolute: nobody came or went.

Nevertheless the buzzing continued. "Shut up!" Elvis yelled to the invisible intruder. "Take two aspirin and come back in the morning!"

Whoever was out there did not want to give up. The buzzing touched up Elvis's agitation, until he got out of his chair and went into an adjacent office. By moving three sports bobbleheads off the windowsill, and putting his cheek against the glass, he was able to see the back of a dark figure leaning into the doorway. There was no light over the doorway—that was broken too—so he could not make out any details, not even whether it was a man or a woman.

Elvis rapped on the window. At first the figure did not respond, but as he continued rapping, the figure turned, faced in Elvis's direction, and walked slowly toward him. He thought it was a woman, wrapped in a trench coat with some kind of scarf or hood over her head. She stopped ten feet from him with her head swiveling. He rapped again, and she fixed on his location and walked right up to him.

"What's the problem?" he yelled. She seemed to talk back but he could not make out her words, only muffled sounds. "What do you need?" he yelled even louder, though he worried he would wake up the house.

He could not understand her, if it was a her. Elvis wondered whether he ought to unlock the door, but he discarded that idea quickly. She was just juiced, he thought. He was sorry that he had rapped on the window. No doubt he had raised her hopes, so she would stay around all the longer.

He went back to the desk. Re-entering the office he glimpsed a slick of gray scurry under a closet door so quickly it seemed to be a mirage. Elvis took his seat, but a minute later got up and walked into the pantry. He remembered some crackers there. He took a packet back to his chair and began setting a trail of cracker fragments, beginning at the closet door. Rats, mice, cockroaches, bedbugs: the mission had them all, horrifying some guests, but Elvis took a live-and-let-live policy.

The buzzer began again. After listening to it for a few minutes, Elvis went back to the window. This time he could see a second figure, just behind the bulky form in the doorway. For a few minutes he watched, not drawing attention to himself this time. What were they doing? The new figure seemed slender and tall, though the sidewalk was too dark to see much. There was a streetlight, but it was on the far side of the block and its light shone from behind the two figures. Were they talking? He thought he heard some sounds.

Without warning, the slender figure reached out a long arm and ripped the covering off the woman's head. She spun around out of the doorway and he shoved her back in. Something hit the door, and Elvis heard muffled high-pitched screaming.

He stood frozen for only a moment, then went to the phone and dialed 9-1-1. He told the dispatcher a woman was being attacked on the street and gave the mission's address. The dispatcher asked him to stay on the line.

He could hear squawking communication links. Elvis remembered that his instructions were to call 9-1-1 and then call Jake. He had Jake's cell phone number pinned to the bulletin board. He hung up on the dispatcher and dialed.

To Elvis's surprise, Jake answered immediately. The round, rough tones of his voice seemed to fill the phone. Elvis identified himself, then told Jake there was a fight outside.

"You called 9-1-1?"

Elvis affirmed that he had.

"Where is it?"

"It's right in the doorway. Some guy attacking a woman, I think. It's going on right now." He could hear something banging on the door. "I'm going out there."

"No, stay inside. I'll be there in a minute."

Jake hung up and Elvis held on to the receiver for a minute, listening to the continuing thumps on the door. He thought he made out groans and grunts. Elvis was not the type to wait around. The key was in the door, and he turned it quickly and wrenched the door open. Two bodies almost fell inside. They were locked together, a unit of furious energy, legs and arms and torsos intertwined. Elvis was shouting at them to quit, and trying to pry some body part away from the mass, but he wasn't getting anywhere. The two bodies suddenly tipped over on top of him, and he went down underneath. He had a grip on something, perhaps an arm heavily sheathed in a polyester coat, but he lacked any leverage and his head was crushed into the tile. Elvis was yelling at the top of his voice for them to get off him, but someone else was yelling too.

Elvis could not see how it happened, but suddenly he felt the burden lightened, and he was able to twist sideways on the floor and escape. He got on one knee and saw that Jake had a man wrapped in his arms, talking to him, calming him. The woman was on her feet shouting at the top of her lungs, periodically gasping for air and sobbing, making extraordinary noises. She was a remarkable sight, robed in a bright green overcoat much too big for her, with dreadlocks cascading in a profusion all around her head, her skin a beautiful coffee tone and her eyes like two fires.

A siren burped to a stop just outside the door, and Elvis realized he had been hearing the siren's call approaching for a minute or more, growing louder and more overbearing as it reached them. He only really heard it when it stopped. The woman's shouting stopped too. The night was still for just a moment, before they heard the slamming of car doors. A police officer appeared outside the door, standing in the dark, silhouetted by a searchlight. "Hands up!" he ordered. "Put your hands in the air! Now!"

Moving deliberately, Jake released his man and raised his hands. So did Elvis. The man, who was dressed in a black suit and a purple bow tie, followed suit, and lastly so did the woman. They all looked at each other and then at the cop. He had a hand on his gun, which was still in the holster. Behind him Elvis could just make out another cop, crouched behind their vehicle.

"That's good," the policeman said. "Don't move unless I tell you to. Now, do any of you live here?"

"I do," Elvis said. "I'm on the night desk. I heard this fight going on and I called 9-1-1. This man'—he pointed—"attacked this woman."

"Keep your hands up!" the police yelled.

The woman burst into tears, bending over at the waist as though someone had hit her in the solar plexus.

"And who are you?" the policeman asked Jake.

"I'm the program director of this house," he said. "Elvis called me, so I came over to break up the fight."

It took at least an hour for the police to search them all and take statements. Jake said they should do it in the office, in comfort, but the police preferred the street. They used the searchlight on their car to light the scene in a garish, sugary glare. Some of the men in the house came down to see about the commotion, and Jake had to tell them nothing had happened. He locked them inside with instructions to go back to bed.

The four of them sat on the curb waiting their turn, with one of the police watching them while leaning on his car. The other cop led each one of them a short distance away to get a statement. Neither Elvis nor Jake was able to get a clear picture of what had started the fight. The man, whose name was Bill Crumb, was terse and sullen when seated by them; the woman, named Julia something, sobbed and buried her head in her lap. She and Crumb seemed to know each other; it was not a random attack. The police handcuffed Crumb and put him in the back of their car. They asked Julia if she needed any help getting home, and she said no. After the police car drove away, Jake tried to ask her if she had anywhere to go, but she wouldn't answer. She walked off down the sidewalk, slowly and not quite straight, disappearing into the darkness. There were no streetlights at that end of the block. Dawn was still hours away.

When Jake unlocked the mission door to let Elvis and himself back inside, they found Joseph Berry sitting at the front desk reading a novel. Joseph was a talker, and he was dying to hear what had happened and to share his opinions about life on the street. Jake ordered him back to bed. "There's nothing to tell you," he said. "It was just a fight. Nobody got hurt. They were both too loaded. The cops came and arrested the guy. It's all over. I'm sure he'll be out in the morning, unless he has a record."

"Oh, that guy's got a record," Joseph said. "I can tell you, he's going back to prison."

"Great. Then we won't see him again. Now you get to bed, and don't wake anybody up while you're doing it. Tomorrow is another day and it's going to be here soon."

Jake himself, however, appeared to be in no rush to go. He loitered with Elvis.

"How did you get here so fast?" Elvis asked. "It felt like I had just called you. I opened the door and those two fell on top of me, and then before I knew it, you were pulling the guy off. How'd you get here so soon?"

"I was just down the block," Jake said. "Taking the night air."

That seemed strange to Elvis. "It's two o'clock in the morning. Don't you have a wife and kid?"

"I do, but they aren't here. My wife went to see her mother."

The tone of voice suggested there was more to the story, but Elvis wasn't sure he could ask for details.

"She's been there a month now," Jake volunteered. "It's killing me."

For Elvis, this was something new. Jake generally talked at you, not with you. Finally Elvis asked, "You go out at night a lot?"

"I can't sleep," Jake said. "I'm so upset."

Elvis noticed Jake's eyes. "Does walking help you to sleep?"

"No. Not at all. But at least I am doing something. Otherwise I just think."

Elvis understood that; he had felt that. He might not have dared to ask Jake more questions, but the office at night was his space, where he felt most able to gather himself. The very clutter was restful. The cone of light from the floor lamp seemed to create a concentrated, private space that belonged to him. Jake was sitting outside the cone, with his feet stretched out across the tiles, his face darkened and somber.

"Jeff and I thought when you yielded, at the Phase and Praise last week—you know when you were sobbing—we thought that was going to help you out."

Jake acted as though he had not heard. His face was turned down toward the ground, and his thoughts seemed far off.

"How did you feel tonight?" Elvis asked. "With the cops frisking you? Did it remind you of that day with Kasha?" Not that a visit from the police was so unusual at the mission, but the altercation with Kasha had become famous after the suit was filed.

"No, no, no," Jake answered. "I'm always glad when I have to do something. It's thinking that kills me."

They sat in peaceful silence until Elvis remembered Tim's accusation. "Jake, do you think I am to blame for Sam going off and killing himself?"

Before Jake could ask him what he was talking about, Elvis filled in. "You know how it is with addiction, you do stuff even when you have no earthly reason why. I knew that the fracking idea wasn't going to go anywhere. I went along because Santiago had some money and I thought, why not? I wasn't doing anything here. I ended up taking Sam along, because I liked him. I liked him so I led him into that crazy deal. And then I let him go home, and I knew that wasn't going to work. It never does. But I let him. Now I feel like I stood back and let him kill himself."

"Just careless," Jake said.

"Yes. Careless. That's it." The word seemed to pin a dart in Elvis's chest. It was not just Sam, it was also Amber and it was also Angel, and it was even his brother Tom. He lived carelessly. "And I don't know how to stop." That was the worst of it.

Jake seemed to be lost in his thoughts, silently brooding. His body was massive, completely covering the brown metal fold-up chair.

"No, Elvis," he finally said. "Just forget about it. Sam was an addict. Everybody loved Sam, everybody wanted to be his dad. Except his real dad. You want to take responsibility because he seemed like a kid. But he wasn't a kid. He was an addict. I don't know if they ever change. You can't take away Sam's power to kill himself. That was the way he was headed."

Elvis thought of Jake as a great source of wisdom, but at the moment he came off like one of the candidates when they first entered the program, spouting talk.

"Are you okay?" Elvis asked.

"Sure. Why?"

"You look like you might be getting sick. I bet you're tired. You definitely need sleep."

"No, I'm not sick," Jake said. "But you're right, I need sleep. I'm dead. And I just miss my wife."

"When does she come back?"

He shrugged his wide shoulders. "I don't know."

27

WITH KRYSTLE

Krystle had not intended to stay away so long. She had left Santa Rosa in a panic, running toward a shred of security, telling herself that she was protecting Reggie. That was not quite true. In her heart she felt she was the one endangered.

She could not decide whether she should be married. At first this had not come into her thoughts at all. Even though her life had grown isolated and depressed since Reggie was born, she still felt a tremendous physical attraction to Jake, a feeling wrapped up in his size and strength, which made her feel safe. She thought that she only needed a few days to regroup and regain her courage. In fact she felt terrible that she had abandoned Jake, who was obviously shattered. He needed her, and she had left him. This she had never imagined she was capable of doing. But it was only for a few days.

She would not tell her mother what had happened, but her mother was no fool. By the second day she had searched the Internet and found the newspaper article. That was more than Krystle had done. Her mother was at an advantage, using the facts she read to establish beyond a doubt that she had been right all along.

Her mother had hated the relationship from the beginning. Before she even met Jake she was acidly suspicious. He was an addict—did Krystle know what that meant? Did she want to go and have babies and then be left with a child to support and no education beyond high school? He was too old for her. At the very least she needed to finish college before getting mixed up with a man.

Now her mother pointed out that Krystle should have listened. Krystle would be a fool to take her baby back to that place until everything had been cleared up. If it ever could be cleared up.

She wore Krystle down, not to the point that she would admit that her mother was right, but to the point that she put off deciding anything. She was exhausted, the normal exhaustion that piles up from raising a small child, combined with the effects of weeping. She could not stop weeping. For Reggie's sake she tried to keep it out of sight and sound, but she failed repeatedly: and her mother used it as extra evidence. That man was killing her. She would be a fool to go back there.

In addition, she felt the seduction of a place where she could rest. Her mother gladly took Reggie off her hands, and cooked her meals, and did her laundry. The house was big enough to give her space; and Reggie loved to watch television, which he had never done. She went for walks, long walks—a luxury she had not had for years. It was all wrong, and of course it could not go on forever—she knew that perfectly well—but for the time being it appeared to be the only way.

It seemed to her that life had been constantly arduous since Reggie was born. He had come within a year of their wedding, which was exactly what she and Jake had hoped for, but the adjustment was difficult. Krystle made a fiercely attentive mother, to the point where she hardly left space for Jake. She could not explain why she bristled so when he tried to help or offered an opinion. Reggie took all her time and energy. She had, literally, no friends. She felt vaguely that she was failing as a wife and mother but that sense of failure impelled her to assert even tighter control over Reggie's life. And Jake was so busy, so preoccupied with the lives of his addicts, that it didn't seem to matter to him that she left him out.

Thoughts like those led her to wonder whether she was really fleeing her marriage. It went against all her principles, and everything she believed about herself.

It killed Krystle when she talked to Jake. He pleaded with her to return—pleaded, even at the cost of his dignity. She couldn't say no, but she couldn't say yes, either.

Those were times when all she could do was to weep; but there were other times when she had some strength and desperately wanted to talk to someone. She wracked her brain until it came to her: she should call the church. She could talk to the pastor.

But that was hard. She thought she knew what he would say: a wife should stand with her husband. He might ask her if Jake had hit her or abused her in any way. The answer was no. He had hit the wall, frightening her, but that was hardly a sin.

The potential of this conversation caused her to lose sleep, and exacerbated her feelings of misery. Krystle sat on it until her mother inadvertently suggested an alternative way.

"Why don't you ever call your old friends?" she asked.

"Who do you mean?" Krystle asked, thinking that her mother had an agenda.

"Any of the old gang. I never hear you mention them. Not even Carol. You lived with her for over a year, and it's like you don't even know who she is."

Krystle's co-residence with Carol at the junior college had been mostly theoretical, since Carol had slept at her boyfriend's apartment almost every night. She had used the apartment as a place to store her stuff and as a ploy to keep her parents from knowing the extent to which she was involved with her boyfriend. Her morals were different from Krystle's, but in some respects that added to her appeal as a listening ear. Carol would be objective. Krystle could get her perspective but not feel obliged to adopt it.

She still had Carol's number on her phone, though she had not spoken to her since shortly after her wedding. Before she could talk herself out of it, Krystle punched Carol's number and waited anxiously through five rings. Then Carol answered, her voice instantly familiar.

Carol, Krystle learned, had broken up with her college boyfriend and now was living with another man, a math teacher at the same high school where Carol taught Spanish. Carol had not heard about Reggie: Krystle loved telling her about his birth. Then Krystle swallowed and told Carol that she was living with her mom; her husband had been charged with sexual assault, and it was just toxic being around people who assumed he must be guilty. "He didn't do it," she said. "There's this crazy woman who accused him. Actually she assaulted him, and the police arrested her, but they let her off and she came up with this story. I don't understand why, but everybody believes it. It's been in the newspapers and you're guilty until proven innocent." She could hear her voice rising into a whine, and quit.

Carol was silent for a good half a minute. "You really believe he's innocent?" she asked.

"Yes. Absolutely."

"What's his background? I don't really know where you met him."

"I met him in church. I'm sure I told you." But Krystle went ahead to tell her the rest of Jake's story.

"What did he do?"

"What do you mean?"

"I mean what drugs? Ecstasy? Meth? Heroin? A lot of people are doing designer drugs now, you know."

"I think it was mostly meth. But I didn't know him when he was using drugs. He's totally changed. He's like a different person. He would never use drugs now."

Carol was quiet again, before saying, "Well, I wouldn't be too sure about that. Do you know many addicts?"

"No. Well, yes. Recovering addicts."

"I know a few." Carol kept her peace again, and so did Krystle, who was boiling with agitation.

"You didn't exactly ask for my advice," Carol said, "but if I were you I'd stay put. You don't know what somebody like that might do. He must be under a lot of pressure."

"And doesn't he need me? Doesn't a man need his wife to stand by him?"

"Well, sure. But you need to think about what you need. And your little boy. Imagine how you would feel if he got hurt. They are very sensitive when they are that age, you know. They hear everything and they remember everything."

28

Up the Ante

✧

Adam McLeod made a good living as a lawyer, but money was hardly his greatest interest. He was a connoisseur of human behavior. He knew everybody and everything in Santa Rosa, and he enjoyed seeing the oddities of their ambitions played out on a small space, like a game board. Though he had never read Dante—he read Ken Follett novels over and over again—he considered The Divine Comedy an inspired title. Like God, he enjoyed looking down on the creatures and laughing at their antics. His law practice gave him a front row seat.

Adam knew how to get things done, and people came to him less for legal advice than for that competence. If you wanted to make some problem go away, or gain a seat at a table, or win a bid, Adam was known as the best in the county. He liked to work behind the scenes, unheralded, but of course his reputation mattered to him.

If pressed, Adam would probably have admitted a great deal of skepticism about Buddy Grace's plans to turn the Railroad Square neighborhood upside down. Santa Rosa was at heart a small town, and small towns were conservative, the despair of rational planners and big-picture developers. Yet Buddy was his client, and Adam had practically promised him to get the mission to move. So the news that Raquel Raise had sussed out Buddy's scheme to move the Sonoma Gospel Mission disturbed him deeply. Raquel could blow them up in any number of ways. If she talked to the newspaper, his and Buddy's scheme would be exposed to all, and their reputations tarnished.

On the phone Buddy had suggested the most logical response: quit. If he dropped Kasha's suit, the entire affair would quickly disappear into the obscurity of the civil courts. But that would also mean Buddy's plans would be lost, because Howard Zenikov said there would be no money unless the homeless problem was solved. Howard, everybody knew, never bluffed.

Adam appreciated Buddy as an entertaining and talented player in the divine comedy, but Buddy, he felt, tended toward the herky-jerky. Buddy was panicking, to judge by his telephone call. Adam believed that nothing good was ever accomplished by rushing, and therefore it was natural that he tell Buddy to give him time to think. After their telephone call, he leaned back in his chair and sat unmoving. After ten minutes he sat up, pleased with the results of his reflections—quite self-admiring, in fact, when he took time to appreciate his plan.

He wanted to double down on their gamble. This was not exactly a bluff, it was a calculation that if they could create enough moral fervor it would become impossible to stop their momentum. Adam had seen this many times, especially in politics: positions reinforced repeatedly and held so fervently they became impervious to facts. If everybody knew that Kasha had been assaulted, and everybody felt the outrage of that, it would not ultimately matter if they learned that the lawsuit had been framed in order to get the mission to move.

What caused Adam to pause longest was the question of whether to include Buddy in his thinking. After some minutes sitting very still in his desk chair, he decided not. Buddy might become squeamish. And Buddy might talk.

Adam called the District Attorney's office and, after a little back-and-forth, was put through to the woman herself. Amy Bourgay had been Adam's colleague for two decades, first as a general practice lawyer like himself, then as a public defender, finally as a prosecuting attorney in the DA's office. It had been almost four years since she ran against her boss, charging the DA with insensitivity to women, a deteriorating atmosphere among staff, and a low level of convictions, particularly in cases involving domestic abuse. Amy had won a close election. She no sooner took office than she fired several top staff, which led to considerable office turmoil and several public complaints. The *Press Democrat* had run a he-says-she-says story about it. That trouble had disappeared from sight, but friends told Adam it was not forgotten. Meanwhile, equally hidden from sight, the conviction rate had actually gone down. Amy was up for re-election in the coming year, and it was a sure thing there would be a fight.

Amy's voice was rusty, like the covert smoker she was. It made her sound sultry, like a lounge singer. For Adam, the idea of a lounge singer in the DA's office was too delicious; he liked calling Amy just to hear her voice.

"Hello, Adam," she said. "Where have you been?"

"I've been avoiding you," Adam said.

"Why is that, darling?"

"My heart is weak."

"Oh, then I'll try not to excite you. What's on your mind?"

"There's a very troubling criminal case I've become aware of. Kasha Gold. I've brought a civil suit but it's really something your office should be involved with. You know about it?"

"I read the newspaper story."

"Stories, plural. The *PD* has shown a lot of interest."

"So?"

"I think there's widespread concern for women being abused in Sonoma County."

"And?"

"Somebody could get a lot of credit for taking a more careful look at this case. You know the police actually arrested Kasha, instead of the man she says sexually assaulted her."

"Why did they do that?"

"You'd have to ask them. I will say that Kasha can be a bit edgy. She's an advocate for the poor, and she speaks her mind. Of course you'll agree that's no reason she should be physically assaulted."

"You said sexual. Was it physical or sexual?"

"Both, according to her. There were quite a few witnesses. It happened in broad daylight."

She took a deep breath. "So, Adam, I know you didn't call just to hear my sexy voice. What are you wanting?"

"Sweetie, it's got nothing to do with me. Our civil suit is going to reward me for my time. I just thought you might profit from taking another look at this. You don't have to take my word for what happened. Just announce that you've heard an outpouring of concern for a woman who has been mistreated, and so you are going to re-open the investigation. You know, standing up for abused women, the rule of law against the old-boy network, blah, blah, no tolerance for even a hint of oppressive behavior. You know how to do that better than I do."

He could hear her thinking. Her breath rattled slightly.

"You think this might help my re-election campaign?" she asked.

"I suppose it can't hurt. Are you worried about that?"

She ignored him. "Tell me, Adam. If I investigate, am I going to find anything? Or are you just suckering me into some scheme of yours?"

"Amy, my darling, who can say? That's why I want you to investigate, my dear. Find out what happened. And if you don't find anything, there's no harm. The whole thing can be quietly dropped. Nobody is going to remember if you don't remind them. But I think you'll get some credit for caring about the plight of women, and holding the police accountable for the way they treat them. Don't you?"

29

Fallout

✧

On the first Wednesday in August, the Sonoma County District Attorney announced that she was opening an investigation of the events surrounding Kasha Gold's arrest on the premises of the Sonoma Gospel Mission. "Serious allegations have been made that our police force failed to respond appropriately when a woman was sexually assaulted and abused," the announcement read. "The District Attorney, Amy Bourgay, will personally oversee an investigation into these events. The District Attorney's office is committed to justice for all citizens of Sonoma County."

Though this statement was issued on the county website, and on the District Attorney's Twitter account, few people heard of it until the next day, Thursday, when the *Press Democrat* published a B1 story under the headline, "DA to Probe Gospel Mission Abuse." The news story not only noted the DA's announcement, but repeated what was known about the entire episode, including Kasha's lawsuit. Chief of the Santa Rosa police, Michael Ghiza, was quoted as saying his department would cooperate with the investigation.

Buddy did not get the newspaper delivered to his small, barely furnished apartment on the west side of town. His ritual was to stop at Starbucks on his way to the office, picking up a newspaper with his double latte. He liked to enjoy the paper at his desk, surrounded by beauty.

When he reached the office on this Thursday, he read the story through twice. His reaction was ambivalent. On one hand, he felt invigorated to learn that the DA was investigating. It was a seductive thought that Kasha's suit had merit and he might deserve some credit for launching it. On the other hand, Jake Dorner had been hung on the clothesline again. Buddy felt the sting of Raquel's accusations. He hadn't intended to hurt Jake in the first place, and he had hoped that when the mission agreed to move and they quietly dropped the suit everything would soon be forgotten. Here it was, leaping to life again.

He called Adam McLeod. "What is going on?" Buddy asked. He felt sure Adam had a part in this.

"You mean the DA?" He could hear Adam smiling over the telephone, his voice sunny. "I think Amy is running for re-election. And I think she's putting more pressure than ever on the mission. It could be a lucky break for you."

"I wish I'd never started this." It was uncharacteristic of Buddy to express regrets, but he was feeling deeply uneasy.

"Yeah, and then where would you look for work?"

The way Adam said it made Buddy even more suspicious. "Adam, are our hands clean on this?"

"Well, why not? What have we done? We've helped a woman take her complaint into the civil courts. Now the DA is looking into it as well. Kasha is getting her day. Will she win? I don't know. I don't know who's telling the truth. Do you? I assume we'll sort that out through the legal process."

For a moment Buddy was assuaged. He could see the point in what Adam said. Then, like a stab of lightning, another truth came to him.

"You put her up to it, didn't you?"

"Who, Kasha? You were the one who talked to her, remember?"

"Amy."

"Do you know Amy? She doesn't take directions from anybody. I talked to her about it. I thought she would be interested. I didn't 'put her up to it.'"

Buddy looked around him, swiveling in his chair to stare at the wall-sized abstract painting. It was a thing of love to him. He never pointed it out to his business clients, but he always felt sure that they stood in awe.

"Adam, don't do anything else unless we talk first."

"Of course. We'll just let this play out. With any luck the mission will move, you'll get your loan, and everything else will be forgotten."

When Kent Spires read the newspaper story, he almost ran to his Cortina and drove directly to the downtown mission. He parked on the street and, uncharacteristically, walked directly past the men hanging on the street, past the man on the desk—he did grunt hello—and up the stairs to Jake's office. He had brought his newspaper with him, and he slapped it down on Jake's desk harder than he intended. Kent was ordinarily so mild that he rarely showed anything more than a soft smile. But he had spent every waking minute over the course of weeks, it seemed to him, trying to overcome bad publicity. And now there was more.

"When will it end?" he said emphatically. "When. Will. It. End."

Having said it with such unusual forcefulness, he looked up to take in his surroundings and was startled by the deadness of Jake's eyes. Jake was a man brimming with energy, a volcano of vigor, and Kent had expected to find a match for his outrage. Instead, Jake looked at him as though he was ashamed and broken.

"Are you all right?" Kent asked.

"No."

"You read the paper."

Jake nodded yes. His face was a puddle of jowls.

Kent spoke more softly. "This has been hard on you, hasn't it?"

Still Jake said nothing.

"Hard on me, too," Kent said gently, and meant it. "I don't know whether we're going to make it. I'm doing my best, and I'm not sure it's enough. I keep expecting our donors to start giving again, but they don't."

"What do they say?" Jake asked in a low voice.

"They don't say. They just don't call back. Or they say they aren't sure about their family finances. It's like they're waiting for something, and I'm not sure what that would be."

"I should just quit," Jake said suddenly and emphatically.

"No, no." Kent said it, but to Jake it came across as less than wholehearted.

"I'm not helping," Jake said. "I can't get anything done. I'm useless. I'm miserable. I'm a distraction. If I were gone your troubles would be over."

Kent looked into Jake's face with a kind of wonder. "Is that what you're thinking? It's not what I'm thinking. That's not how we operate. When the men in the program encounter roadblocks, do we kick them out of the way? No, we don't. We don't abandon people when they get in trouble."

He paused to let that sink in. Then it occurred to him that he could be misunderstood. "Anyway, you aren't in trouble. You say you haven't done anything wrong, and I believe you."

Unfortunately, the "you say" in Kent's statement undermined his intent. Jake heard him saying that he had determined to believe in Jake against all evidence—"you say" as opposed to "it's obvious."

Jake didn't answer, leaving Kent puzzled as to how he might lift Jake's spirits. But Kent hardly possessed the mental space to delve too deeply into Jake's melancholy.

Jake tried to take heart in his work. Much of his day was preoccupied with sorting out personal problems that came from thirty men—all in recovery, most just off the streets, half in trouble with the law—living in cramped quarters. Cleanliness was a constant theme: personal habits, personal smells, showers or the lack of same, bedbugs, dirty clothes, mildewed towels, clogged toilets. Then there was gossip. You would think men who craved mercy for themselves would be generous with each other, but instead they passed on rumor and innuendo with gusto and apparently believed every word of it. Those rumors were sometimes true: it was not for nothing that every time they tested or inspected they found violations. Nevertheless Jake despised the meanness and the pettiness that came his way, repeated and repeated again.

He habitually preached at them in his rough, blunt way, telling them of a Higher Life that in the mercy of God they could attain. He had been like them, or worse. Jesus, he told them, could save them. And some, not all, believed him. A core of men listened to him as though he were their pastor.

Yet those men squabbled too. Jake held court on arguments whether the Catholic church was deliberately leading people away from God, what version of the Bible was acceptable, whether Mormons were going to hell, and so on. He had his own opinions, but it was wiser not to get caught in their arguments. Kent had taught him that such issues could distract men from their recovery.

Now without sleep, without personal peace, he found it exhausting to preside over these disputes, and to rein in harsh words and stubborn rejections. He sometimes sat in his office wishing that no one would knock—a wish that was seldom granted. He could hardly walk ten feet outside his office door before being stopped. Practical matters also surfaced: requests for weekend passes, questions about medical care, financial needs. These took time and energy, but Jake could handle that. It was the unkindness that undid him.

Only in the afternoon did he get some relief. Classes were in session, and he could walk through the building without encountering anyone. At least, that was the theory. Coming downstairs through the dining room he encountered Tim, the misanthrope, sitting at one of the cafeteria tables. Jake wanted to pass him by—he had experienced trouble upon trouble with Tim—but made himself sit down across from him.

"Whatcha writing?" he asked. Tim was writing in a notebook and had not raised his eyes when Jake sat down. Nor did he lift his eyes from the paper at Jake's question.

"Tim," Jake said, lowering his voice to just above a whisper, "I asked what you are writing. You're supposed to be in class."

"The teacher is an idiot," Tim said, still not looking up. "He's supposed to be teaching the 12 steps and he has never read the Big Book. I can't listen to that. It's a waste of my time. How do you expect anybody to get clean when you can't even get teachers who know the 12 steps?"

"I didn't ask your opinion of the teacher. You can register your thoughts on the evaluation we do every month. What I asked was, what are you writing?"

"Okay, if you must know, I'm working on the fourth step."

"So you're writing down the people you have offended. Must be a long list."

"You would know. Who is on your list? Have you got that woman you molested?"

Jake stood, majestically. He slowly reached a massive hand across the table. Tim did not move; he stared at Jake with the corner of his lips turned down, as though he had a bad taste in his mouth. Jake seized Tim's shirt by the buttons and pulled him across the table. His weight spilled forward and he slumped across the table, unable to get a grip to lift himself.

"If you think I molested a woman," Jake said softly, "you should be more careful with the way you talk to me."

Tim had stopped struggling. "Go ahead and hurt me," he said. "That's what you want to do. There's nobody here to see this time."

Jake let him go, and Tim slowly pulled himself back off the table. Jake pondered what devastating comment he could make, but he could think of nothing. He left the room. As soon as he turned the corner his mind was flooded with regret and self-recrimination.

That night Jake did not even try to sleep. He could tell by his restlessness that he would only lie down to toss around and wrap himself in the sheet like a mummy. Besides, he longed to be on the deserted night streets, to have solitude in motion. A piercing wind had come off the ocean, which guaranteed an even more profound quiet since no one likes to be out in such cold. Jake enjoyed walking up 4th Street when he had it completely to himself, after the bars and restaurants had closed.

He walked toward 4th on Humboldt, a residential street that cut through as a bicycle route. It had few streetlights, and those few were partially blocked by spreading trees. Shadows were so dark Jake almost stumbled into a man—he thought it was a man—standing on the sidewalk smoking a cigarette.

Perhaps his wife made him smoke outside. That made Jake smile to himself, and then to think of Krystle. He had skyped with her after her dinner. Those calls were never satisfactory, yet every day he chafed against time waiting for them. During the call, time scooted by. Something about the lighting was wrong so Krystle's face was darkened. He saw her mother better, walking past in the background and casting a skeptical glance toward the computer. Reggie popped in and out of the picture, curious but restless, shy and unwilling to speak to his disembodied father. Jake wanted to drink in Krystle's face. That was what he dreamed of while he waited for the computer to burr with its signal of an incoming call. To be still, to see clearly, to lock eyes. It didn't happen.

Often he was too distraught to say anything meaningful. He mumbled generalities, paying little attention to his words because his mind was all on the sight of his wife and his child. This picture, so unsatisfying in the moment, became something to hold in memory, to see through.

Jake stopped in his tracks on Humboldt, trying to gain the mental focus to remember that image of Krystle. She was a likeness of the sun, burned into his retina and quickly fading into a bright blur caught out of the corner of his eye.

It exhausted him, thinking like this. Without Krystle, without anything or anyone in his life to ease her absence, he knew one substance would do the trick to give him relief. He wanted drugs, Jake admitted.

The relief would be temporary, of course.

He shook it off. He had spent the last five years telling men that drugs were an illusion. Using would make him a liar, and would violate every inch of the life he had painstakingly constructed since the day God had rescued him from darkness. He was not going there. He would not even allow himself to think there.

But there it was. Drugs were a cubbyhole he could drag himself into, to lie out of sight, comfortably away from fear.

Yes, fear, Jake admitted to himself, as he waited for the light at College Avenue. The normally busy street was completely empty, but still the traffic signal cycled through its variations, as though people waited for their turn. That seemed to be a metaphor for his life. Everything Jake valued stood on the verge of collapse—the mission, his family, his life. He might be arrested. If the investigators chose to believe that Kasha had been molested, they might do anything to him. Jake knew plenty of stories to prove that justice was a whore. You couldn't be homeless without hearing those.

Just past College was an all-night market next to a gas station. Jake pushed the door open and tripped a loud electronic doorbell. He nodded toward the clerk, who was sequestered in a glass booth. Jake often stopped to get snacks here when he was out walking the night—a candy bar or cheese puffs, usually. Neither appealed tonight, but he was restless, he wanted something. Jake stared at the racks of garishly colored bags of snacks, trying to imagine each one's punch of fat and salt and spice. He could not decide. It was like trying to imagine his wife by staring at her picture, he thought. It didn't work.

The bags kept their secrets while he wandered around the store, examining the sacks of candy and the dog food, the car additives and magazines. The freezer on one wall contained ice cream bars, which he gave his attention to for a few minutes before deciding against it. Jake loved ice cream but he wanted salt, he decided. Perhaps Doritos chips. He wasn't sure.

Without thinking he found himself staring at a wall of beer that filled a standing refrigerator. Beer, he thought suddenly, was the flavor he wanted—a slight bitterness, a tang that would not cling to his mouth. Of course he did not drink any more. He was clean and sober. For several minutes, however, he found himself watching the beer, as though it might run away. He would not buy it. It was only a temporary attraction, nothing like that elemental longing for refuge he had felt just minutes before.

30

Raquel in Anger

✧

The Ecology Action office occupied a nondescript stucco building on East Sebastopol Road, possibly the least expensive rent in all of Santa Rosa. Inside was a cluttered mess. As far as Raquel Raise could tell, the director's office door never closed, and she was not completely sure that it could be closed, given the stacks of files on the floor. In order to sit down, she had to move a wad of papers off the extra chair.

It was purely serendipitous that as she sat down for her regular check-in, David Bruce, the director, offered her yesterday's paper. "Did you see this story? The DA is starting some kind of investigation."

Raquel grew quite angry as she read. Her first thought was that Buddy Grace and Adam McLeod had deliberately crossed her. She had called them on their scheme, and as soon as her back was turned, they took it further. Raquel possessed a strong distaste for injustice—it rankled her in an almost physical way. Even more, she had a strong sense of her dignity. These men had mistreated her.

She sat staring straight ahead while her mind crackled with dark energy. Should she contact the newspaper? She could talk to the reporter, Julie Kassebaum, and soon find out who was in on the game.

Raquel wanted to punish those men. She wanted to drive their noses into their own mess.

David Bruce had carried on writing while she read. He was a retired political science professor from Sonoma State University. He sported a white soul patch, a spreading paunch, and an easy, insidious laugh.

He glanced up from his desk and was surprised to see Raquel upset; ordinarily she was so calm. She made a terrific volunteer, reliable, organized. He had hopes to use her more. "What's up?" he asked gently.

Raquel was reluctant to tell him much before she thought through her own reaction. "There are two men," she said, "who I suspect are behind this. I think it's a deal to push the mission out of the neighborhood."

"And it makes you mad?"

"Of course it makes me mad. I don't think it's just."

"Well, maybe," David said, "but why should it worry you? They only get what's coming to them."

"What do you mean?" Raquel asked. "What does who have coming to them?"

"Oh, I mean the mission." He threw out a laugh. "They are quite censorious, you know. About sex, among other things. It sounds like they're getting some of their own medicine."

"The thing is," Raquel said carefully, "in this case, I don't think they did anything."

David did not want to push her on that. For all he knew, she might be a fundamentalist Christian herself. He didn't care, as long as she was a good volunteer. He switched gears. "So who do you think is behind this?"

She told him. He knew Adam McLeod; he had heard of Buddy Grace. "It fits," he said to Raquel. "Development types, full speed ahead." He stopped short. "And you're sure it's bogus? I mean, the DA is involved. It could be real."

"I don't think so." Raquel did not want to discuss it with him. She wanted to think, and that required being alone. "So let me tell you what I've found so far." She opened her satchel and pushed a one-page summary of her neighborhood survey across the desk.

Their discussion was brisk, and before David could go beyond her findings and begin to speculate about political action, she rose from her chair and asked if David wanted her to replace the papers she had moved from his chair. He said no.

"Are we done?" he asked as she made to leave the office. He wondered whether he had offended her.

She wasn't listening. When she got into her car she did not immediately start the engine, but sat with her hands on the steering wheel, thinking. It was a hazy day in early August, the sun barely beginning to pierce a high skim of clouds. Raquel did not see the sky or the street or anything else when her mind was so focused.

She realized that she couldn't expect anything from going to the newspaper. At best that might trigger a he-said, she-said story, full of charges and counter-charges. It would only make matters worse. When reputations were involved, it was not true that all publicity was good publicity—quite the opposite. Better to work behind the scenes, if you could.

Raquel started her car and began driving north on Santa Rosa Avenue. This was Santa Rosa's underbelly: tattoo parlors, carpet stores, Asian markets. She passed a Chinese restaurant that had been on the corner for 40 years, and looked it. Buddy Grace wanted to do away with this kind of development. He had a vision of clean, chic, and hip. Looking around she could see his point. But he was going about it in the wrong way. You can't bully people.

And Adam McLeod! He gave the impression of an old-fashioned, chivalrous country lawyer.

She drove immediately home. The sun had come out fully now, and the sky was a silvery blue. Raquel had planted two raised beds in front of her house, one with tomatoes and the other with basil and green beans. She took time to pick two tomatoes out of the deep, teeming foliage and carry them inside, placing them on her wood-block counter. This was out of character, to pick vegetables without a plan to use them. It jolted her a little when she realized what she had done; what was she thinking? Seating herself on her sage-green sofa she tried to study herself.

She was being drawn into defending an organization of evangelical Christians, with a "Jesus Saves" sign over their door. It was very abnormal.

After some time her thoughts wandered, slipping back into childhood memories of her sister: Cece, with her deep and penetrating voice, and her invincible attraction to men. Cece didn't like women, other than Raquel. She said whatever came into her head, without filtering. She was a funny girl, always embarrassing Raquel, never herself embarrassed.

Growing up, Raquel had tried to protect Cece from the meanness of other kids. It had never been necessary, as far as she could remember. The neighborhood kids treated Cece like just one more foot soldier in their games of touch football or war. But she, Raquel, had been continually on guard, expecting the worst.

She missed Cece, far more than she would have ever thought possible. And yet, she always remembered a knot in her stomach, a primal fear of failing her.

Raquel caught herself, realizing that she had lost her train of thought. She pulled her mind back to the mission. How nervous she had been going there, only to discover there was nothing to be nervous about. The mission seemed very artless to her. They obviously made do with very limited resources, even though they were running a fairly ambitious program. She admired that. And they didn't seem even faintly aware that they might expect to have more. They made do. They appeared to have no idea of better equipment or trained staff. Jake, for instance, how far had he gone in school?

On the edge of her thoughts was a linkage, and she strained to find it. The connection was obvious, once she recognized it. She was drawn to defend the vulnerable, and she owed that to her sister, lovably vulnerable to almost everything. The mission, like Cece, was simple, without self-awareness, and unable to defend itself. Raquel did not love it as she did Cece, but she fell into defending it.

31

Buddy's Agony

✧

Buddy Grace was a member of the Santa Rosa Links, the county's premier golf club. He played almost religiously twice a week, Tuesdays and Saturdays. Nothing he did made him happier; he basked in the camaraderie of his golfing buddies, who joked together like eighth-grade boys and occasionally spoke seriously about things that mattered to them. Buddy loved the game. He felt such freedom on the fairways, such power when he hit a towering drive. (He was a strong driver; his short game was his downfall.)

Today, a windblown, blue-sky day, he played with two of his regular partners: Joey, a construction manager of almost surreal optimism; and Franklin, the dark, brooding and caustic owner of an asphalt factory, who could be paralyzingly funny, usually at somebody's expense. It was on the third hole, while they were waiting for a very slow party just ahead of them, that Joey asked Buddy how his big project was going.

"It's going great," Buddy said. "We've got it all mapped out and we're going for it."

But when Joey asked when he would start turning over dirt, he admitted to a small hold-up.

"We're just putting a bow on the finances. It's all set but we're waiting on one sign-off, and it's taking forever."

"Who is it?" Joey asked as he stepped up to the tee, set his ball down and began to address it with his driver.

"Sonoma Gospel Mission," Buddy said.

"Who the hell?" Franklin asked.

Joey knew it. "It's that old place on McKinley," he said. "Where you always see the homeless. You know, when you drive by, there's always men standing around." He swung and launched his ball in the general direction of the pin. They paused to follow the tiny white orb as it arced through the sky, settling in one big bounce halfway down the fairway.

"You might as well throw the ball, Joey," Franklin said. "It would go farther." He turned toward Buddy. "I avoid the whole area. It's crawling with derelicts. I don't have any reason to go there."

"Starks is great," Buddy said.

"If you like steak. My wife won't go there, she says it's too dark."

"So what's holding them up?" Joey asked.

"They have to move," Buddy said. "We're offering them a boatload of money, it's a great deal for them, but they won't budge."

"Offer them more!" said Joey.

"Or pressure them," Franklin added. "You know any of their board members?"

"I've done both those things," Buddy said, feeling slightly annoyed, and also desperate to justify himself. "Ridiculous amounts of money, and I'm squeezing them like crazy. It doesn't do any good. They say that God has to give them written instructions, or something like that."

"How about a lightning bolt," Franklin said, scowling as he stepped up to drive. "I know people who can arrange that." His shot seemed to leap into the distance, almost disappearing as a tiny pale dot hanging in the pale sky near the horizon, but hooking at the last moment and bounding into a grove of trees. Franklin cursed, one vehement angry syllable. Joey laughed.

It was Buddy's turn. He always felt giddy and nervy when he stepped up to drive. It was the best part of his game, and he loved an audience, but he was no professional and inevitably some of his shots went wrong. This was a long hole with a wide fairway, nothing cute about it, and he knew as soon as he heard the ball click against his driver that his smooth and effortless swing had connected well. The ball went out, far out, and kept rising, seeming to float upwards like a helium balloon, defying gravity, until it stopped in the air and dropped, harmlessly, into the center of the far reaches of the fairway.

"Wow," Joey said. "Nice shot."

"Even a blind pig finds an acorn sometimes," Franklin said.

Buddy drove the cart and was alone in it after dropping Franklin to look for his ball. He took pleasure in his shot, but his mind also returned involuntarily to the questions about Railroad Square. What had he done wrong? It occurred to Buddy that something almost celestial stood against him.

Because it made no sense. He had a great plan. The numbers were terrific. The mission would be blessed by their move to a new, well-equipped building with enough money to run their programs and to spare.

He groaned, literally groaned out loud, a low, deflated moan. Buddy did not believe in luck; something was wrong.

Whatever it was did not apply to his golf game. He was on the green in two. He would have been happy to two-putt it, but instead he dropped a long, curving shot into the cup, then did a happy jig, circling to Joey to slap hands, then to Franklin who fell to his knees in mock surrender. They chafed him, he chafed them.

Moving to the next tee, Franklin began to complain about Petaluma environmentalists opposing his plant expansion. He was located on a derelict part of the river, flanked by an abandoned boat works and an empty grain elevator. "Where do they think asphalt comes from?" he asked rhetorically. "From the skies?"

"They know where it comes from," Buddy said. They had hit their tee shots and he and Franklin were in the cart, careening down the asphalt pathway. "It comes from the East Bay."

"Buy local, they say, but not asphalt," Franklin remarked.

"Or gravel," Joey added when they carried on the conversation at the next tee.

Apropos of nothing, Joey began to tell a story about a carpenter who had worked for him in Rohnert Park. "He was a good carpenter, but you know how some guys in the trades can be, he acted like he was worth a million dollars. He had a dog, a big German shepherd that he liked to bring to the job. I told him he needed to keep the dog in his truck, but then I would drive by and see the dog roaming around the property. Can't have that, you know, I'm liable if he bites somebody. But this carpenter, he always had some excuse. The dog has to go to bathroom, or he was feeding it, or something. You know me, I'm not a yeller. I told him nicely but he just didn't get it.

"So I called him in to my little office on the job site. I hardly ever used it but it was perfect for this. I had him sit down—there wasn't hardly room for two people in that trailer, let alone a chair—and I said, you know, we've had our little differences but you are a good carpenter and I want to keep you on the job. You do such a good job, and I would hate to lose you. So all I need to have you do is say, 'You're the king.'

"He looks at me like there is something he can't understand. What am I talking about? 'All you want me to do is say, "You're the king?"' I said yeah.

"He took a minute to figure it out. 'I don't think I'm gonna say that,' he said. 'Where do you think we are? This is America, and we don't have a king.'

"I said, you're right, and normally I would never ask you to say it, but we have been having these little differences of opinion, and I think this will help. I need you to say it, just to me, 'You're the king.'

"So he got a little uptight, and he said he didn't see why he had to say anything he didn't want to say. He said I wasn't his king and he wasn't going to say it. We went back and forth a bit and he got belligerent.

"Yeah, you're right, I said, and I wouldn't blame you if you just walked off this job today. You'd be within your rights to do that. Really, that might be the best solution. What am I into you for? About $18,000 I make it. Is that about right? Of course you are going to get that money. You are legally entitled to it. But then, it might take quite a while. By the time you took me to small claims court, and we went through that, you would get your money, sure, but it would be a lot of trouble for you. I notice you have a pretty new truck. You have a payment on that? I imagine that could be difficult for you. I don't know if you have any child support payments or things like that. I wouldn't blame you a bit for telling me to jump off a cliff and walking out of this office and never coming back, but hey, I think you'll realize if you think about it there's an easier way.

"He says, 'What's that?'

"You just say to me right now, 'You're the king,' and that will be the end of it."

They had arrived at the tee and Buddy and Franklin were standing, waiting to tee up, while Joey told his story. Now he left the last sentence hanging in air and they waited for a punch line. Finally Franklin bit.

"So what happened?"

"Oh, he saw it clearly. He told me, 'You're the king.' We got along really well after that."

Franklin liked the story. He chortled at it, and every time somebody made a putt on the next few holes he yelled, "You're the king!" and laughed. All three of them were doing it.

Buddy liked the story too, but a little ruefully. That was what he wanted to do with the mission. They should say, "You're the king!"

and sign. Part of him liked the mission, liked that they were trying to do good. But part of him wanted to grind their teeth into the curb.

He thought that he had to get to the bottom of it. He had to push harder to understand what was holding them back, because unless he could account for the obstacles, he had no chance of getting unstuck.

The slow party in front of them got tired of having Buddy and his friends run up their tails, so they let them play through. There was less talking as they moved ahead quickly through the next several holes, and Buddy had time to think more about his situation with the mission.

He also thought about Joey's "You're the king" story and chortled over it some more. Buddy loved stories, and he knew he would be repeating Joey's "King" story for a variety of audiences. Stories could affect people in surprising ways.

His father, who had died long ago, when Buddy's children were little, had loved stories. He put in his hours at a potato-chip factory, but unlike other fathers he did not spend his free time repairing the porch steps or installing new baseboard from scraps he had picked up from a demolition. He listened to the radio—gospel radio—and he told stories.

They were true stories—or anyway, purportedly true—warning of sin and judgment and the wide gate leading to destruction. There were miracle stories, family reconciliations, prodigal returns, seed sown for a harvest, and others, gleaned from a thousand sermons and a hundred thousand gospel radio presentations. Buddy's father remembered so many stories. He could have been a preacher himself, and would have been if he had been able to get the education. What would Buddy's father have thought of his dilemma? He would have been proud of Buddy—he always was. He would surely have come up with one of his stories.

Funny how they stuck to you. One in particular had a hold on Buddy's memory. It was about an engineer who designed a dam up the Los Angeles River. It stuck to Buddy's brain, maybe because it had to do with building things, which is not a common thread in gospel stories. Buddy had always been interested in building things.

Buddy's father claimed to have heard the story on Charles Fuller's Old Fashioned Revival Hour. When he told it, he adopted Fuller's California accent, losing his Oklahoma twang. That too stuck in Buddy's memory: his father talking strange.

In the story, the engineer designed a dam for water storage, relying on core samples done by a geological survey company. The dam was completed, the ribbons cut, the reservoir filled. Then the county manager resigned under a cloud, and the engineer heard of it. It prompted a hesitation in his mind. He had never liked the geologist who had done the core samplings, but the county manager had insisted on using him. On a whim one day he went to the county office and pulled the documentation. What he found chilled his soul. The documentation actually came from another site. The contractor had only pretended to do the testing.

The engineer had no reason to think that the dam had been built on a dangerous site. As far as he could see, the rock foundation was secure. However, since it had never been tested, he could not be sure.

He had to make a decision. He could expose the faulty testing. Or he could pretend that everything was fine. Nobody would know.

If he exposed the geological contractor, he did not know what might happen. He was professionally responsible for the dam, and he could be blamed for the oversight. Perhaps he would have to pay for new tests himself. If the dam was faulty, perhaps he would be held responsible to repair or replace it. He could be bankrupted. At any rate, the dam would be put under scrutiny. The engineer loved that dam. Irrationally, he did not want to have it brought into question. He decided to say nothing.

The dam was fine. Years passed, decades passed, and that dam was as solid as the rock of Gibraltar. The engineer forgot all about his concerns. He went on and built other dams. He had a full career of building things.

Then one day came a flood. The rain came down all over Los Angeles, and it poured down in the mountains above Los Angeles until it filled up that dam, right to the top, and came over the top through the spillway. Nobody thought about it. The dam had been designed to hold back the water in just those circumstances. But the engineer thought about it. It all came back to him. He was an old man, and he had time to think about the mistakes that he had made. He realized that if that dam gave out, it would wash down over the town where his son was living. He started worrying about it. What should he do? He decided to call his son and suggest that he get out of there until the water receded. He picked up the phone, but then he put it down. He did not want to have to explain to his son what he had done—or failed to do—so many years before. Everything would be fine, he thought. The dam had held these many years.

But the dam did not hold. Under the extra pressure of the downpour, it separated from its bedrock foundation. There was a terrible roar, like the coming of the Lord on judgment day, as a wall of water washed down the canyon. Some people were saved when the police chief of one of the small towns downriver got on his motorcycle and roared up the valley, telling people to get out. Most people, though, got no warning. The town where the engineer's son lived was carried away in the flood, with the engineer's son and his whole family drowned.

The engineer stood up in front of his church that Sunday and confessed what he had done. His pastor came up behind him and put a gentle hand on his shoulder, saying a few words urging the church to forgive him. Afterwards many people shook his hands and looked at him with tears in their eyes. The church forgave him, but he could not forgive himself. He went home, loaded a shotgun, and killed himself.

They reached the back nine. Buddy had continued to shoot well and tied his best score ever on the front nine. This might be the day when he set a new personal standard. Joey and Franklin were mired in inferior rounds and had stopped chirping that Buddy was having a lucky day. Instead they seemed to take actual pleasure in watching him play. He was good today; somehow his body knew just what to do, without him trying.

At the same time that his body was flowing so naturally, and his shots soaring, Buddy was living a parallel existence in his mind. He was remembering his father's story and wondering whether somehow it was an answer to his question of what had gone wrong. The story was intended as a morality tale, a story of sin and the need for confession. In Buddy's mind, however, it became the story of a practical decision. He was not much of a moralist; he thought in terms of plans and projects. Choices were hard; if you made the wrong choice you were doomed. But how did you know what was right? How could the engineer know whether or not the dam would fail? How did he know whether to make that telephone call?

Buddy decided that he should never have attempted this whole project. It was grandiose, full of hubris. He should have sensed that it was wrong when the money was not forthcoming, when Howard Zenikov turned him down. Forces were against it. Now he was in a terrible quandary.

He couldn't get that story out of his mind. Why was that? He hadn't thought of it for years.

It occurred to him that his mistake had been trying to force the mission to cooperate. He had used Kasha Gold. He had used Adam McLeod. Granted, they had been eager to be used, but from the beginning he, Buddy, had felt uneasy about it. He had shaken off those feelings. Like the engineer who picked up the phone only to put it down again.

He should give up the whole thing, he thought. He was out of money. It wasn't going to work.

Yet Buddy did not have it in him to give up. He could not bear the thought of losing in public, of seeing men at the golf club stare at him when he came in. Except he wouldn't even be at the golf club. He couldn't really afford to be there now. It was all credit card debt. Everything went on the card.

They finished the back nine. Buddy came close to breaking his personal record on the course; a birdie on the 18th hole would have done it, but he bogeyed it instead. His long putt missed the cup by inches and rolled ten feet beyond. Joey and Franklin eyed him as though expecting a tantrum, but he took it calmly. His mind was elsewhere. They went to the clubhouse and he treated them to a round. He was still operating on parallel circuits: he could joke with his buddies, but he was thinking all the time about what he should do.

When he got to the car he dialed the mission headquarters. A receptionist told him that Kent was out; would he like his voice mail? He said he would.

"Kent, this is Buddy Grace. Listen, you've been on my mind. I'm hoping that the Lord has spoken to you and you've seen your way clear to accepting our offer. This is a wonderful opportunity for the mission, and it's urgent that you let me know. I'm holding it open as long as I can, but there are a lot of other people who want to be part of this, and I can't keep them waiting. So could you call me?"

32

Two Women

Raquel went to see Kasha out of a sense of fairness and of caution. If she was going to be obsessed with this—and she recognized that she was treading on the verge of an obsession—she wanted to make sure she had the facts right. Before she did anything more, she needed to know what kind of woman Kasha was.

Raquel was pleased to see the vegetable garden in Kasha's front yard. The sight of this neat, thrifty practice encouraged her. So did the succulent plants growing in pots by the front door of Kasha's upstairs apartment.

For a long time she got no answer to her knock—so long that she backed off to double check the address. From her survey work, Raquel knew that people sometimes take an extraordinarily long time to get to the door. Even so, she was on the verge of giving up when the door opened on a short woman dressed in a fuchsia running suit. She said nothing, just stood blinking at the light. Her eyes looked smashed, with mascara rubbed all around them.

"I'm sorry to wake you," Raquel began.

"Who says I was asleep?" the woman croaked. "Who the hell are you?"

"My name is Raquel Raise. I'm a volunteer with Ecology Action. You're Kasha Gold?"

"What do you want?" the woman asked.

"It won't take long. I want to ask you about the Sonoma Gospel Mission."

Kasha looked at her fiercely and sleepily, reminding Raquel of an angry sheep, if there was such a thing. "God, everybody wants to know about the goddam mission. Come in," she said, and disappeared into the apartment. When Raquel followed her inside Kasha had stretched herself out prone on the sofa, which was of a Scandinavian-style design with foam cushions covered in blue flowers. She had her eyes closed, but she opened them to flail an arm in the direction of a chair. "You should get out of Ecological Action," she said. "Men talking down to women. Badly in need of consciousness."

"Where would I go?" Raquel asked. "I want to do something worthwhile for the community."

"They're bad," Kasha continued. "Nothing but men."

"You said that," Raquel said. "But they've been perfectly fine with me."

Kasha opened one eye to look at Raquel. "Better than the mission," she said. "That's all men. Not a single woman."

From her survey work Raquel had become accustomed to conversations that veered unpredictably off the road.

"That's true, but then it's a program for men. Can we talk about the mission? I know you've sued them, and now the District Attorney is investigating. I met your lawyer, Adam McLeod. And I also met this man, Buddy Grace, who has something to do with it. It all seems quite involved, and I wondered whether you could explain it from your point of view."

"All men again," Kasha said. "Nothing will come of it. How can it?"

"The DA is a woman."

"I haven't seen any DA."

"It was in the newspaper. She announced that she was investigating why you were arrested after you'd been assaulted."

"I was, too. Jake Dorner. He wouldn't give me an application."

"What were you applying for?"

Raquel did not get any answer. "What were you applying for?" she said again, and then recognized the soft buzzing sound of a woman who has fallen asleep.

Raquel wondered what had made Kasha so tired. She looked around the apartment as though it might tell her. It hardly seemed lived in, except for a table in the corner that had been turned into a kind of shrine, with a statue of the Buddha surrounded by a collage of feathers, shells and candles, and some Marian prayer cards balanced against it. The rest of the room looked like a cheap motel: beige, utilitarian, undecorated, uncluttered. It was neat, which was a positive. But it appeared depersonalized and almost institutional, which struck Raquel as odd. It surprised her that Kasha lived such an astringent life.

Kasha's breathing had grown huskier and louder, and Raquel thought to herself that nothing good would come of letting her drift more deeply into sleep. Raquel stood. She cleared her throat. Kasha continued her sleep.

She cleared her throat again, to no effect. Then she approached the sofa and gently touched Kasha's shoulder. Her breathing chopped short, then resumed its regularity. Raquel grasped Kasha's shoulder and waggled it. Kasha woke with a snort and sat bolt upright. "What are you doing!" she shouted. "Get your hands off me! What are you doing!?"

Raquel had backed away a few feet, and Kasha swung her feet to the floor and came toward her with her hands outstretched. Raquel retreated. Kasha waved her hands in front of her face, as though to scratch her. Raquel seized those hands and held them tightly. "I was trying to wake you," she said strongly. "You fell asleep."

"Don't ever touch me!" Kasha shouted, and threw her hands aside.

"All right, I won't. I only nudged you. You were sleeping."

"I was not." Kasha's face had turned bright red.

"Can we talk? I want to ask you about something."

"Don't ever touch me," Kasha said, and sat back down on the sofa, her legs splayed outward. She dropped her face into her hands and rubbed it, as though trying to scrub it of weariness.

"Why are you so tired?" Raquel asked. She felt anxious to be gone. But she felt purged of her reticence, too. She would ask Kasha exactly what she wanted to, and get this over with.

"I can't sleep," Kasha replied. "I have nightmares."

"Of abuse?" Raquel asked, on a hunch.

"Yes."

"How awful. Every night?"

"Lately, yes. And all night."

"You poor thing." And she meant it. Her impatience melted away, and she only thought how lucky she was, not to carry such burdens. "I'll keep this short. Here's what I understand. You were assaulted by Jake Dorner at the mission. I've met Jake and he's a giant of a man. It must have left you very frightened. No wonder you have nightmares. But the police didn't do anything to him. In fact they arrested you, and then let you go. That's what I've been told.

"But what I'd like to know is, when did you decide to take action and sue the mission? How did that come about?"

Kasha had been terrorized by something; the question became, for Raquel, whether the lawsuit was Kasha's desired remedy.

Kasha lay on her back with her eyes closed and her hands folded on her chest. She spoke slowly. "It was that developer," she said.

"Buddy."

"Yes. What a name for a grown man. Buddy. He asked me about what happened. He was very nice. He's quite a handsome man, I think. He wanted to know everything." She nodded to herself approvingly.

"When did you decide to sue?"

"Oh, that was his idea. He thought I should. He urged me to consider it. He said it would all be paid for, it would cost me nothing. He gave me his friend's name and number."

Kasha paused, drew in a deep breath, and then pushed it out again. "I signed some papers. I haven't heard anything since then. Is it still going?"

"I think so. You haven't heard anything?"

She scrunched up her mouth and shook her head. "No. Men don't tell you anything."

33

Temptation

An investigator from the county District Attorney's office visited Jake on Friday, arriving in the late afternoon after Phase and Praise. He was young, with a short, brilliantined haircut and a suit of a better cut than Jake expected in a county employee. His name was Rue Jimenez, and he tried to make small talk as they walked together down the dim corridor toward Jake's office. To Jake it seemed like telling jokes as you led the condemned prisoner to the gas chamber.

When he reached his office Jake looked at the totems on the wall and on his shelves—the Giants poster, the basketball trophy, some Christian novels—and saw them in the way they looked to others, which is to say, he saw them with a paranoid eye. Surely it looked like the office of an abuser.

"I don't use this office much," he said to the investigator. "I spend my time with the men in the program."

Rue took out his notebook and indicated no interest in what Jake did with his office. "You know what I'm here about," he said. "Tell me what you know about Kasha Gold."

That was uncomfortable ground for Jake. He didn't like Kasha and had never liked her, but that didn't indicate that he would molest her. In his response he kept to safe ground, merely saying that he had occasionally met her at meetings of social service providers, and that she sometimes ate a meal at the mission, so he would say hi to her while she waited in line.

"You never had any conflict with her?" Rue kept his head in his notebook, acting like he was thoroughly lacking in interest.

"Oh, yeah, we didn't necessarily see eye to eye. She didn't like the mission and she would tell us what we should do different. We had some disagreements, but they were always perfectly civil. It was no big deal."

Rue spent some minutes writing in his notebook, then looked up to ask Jake to describe what happened on the day in question. Jake told it exactly as he remembered it: Kasha shouting and cursing at Daniel, then attacking with a cane and breaking the glass, then finally breaking Daniel's arm.

"She broke his arm?" Rue interrupted to ask. "Do you have any medical records?"

"I don't," Jake said. "But he went to the ER. I'm sure they have a record."

Rue wrote down the hospital and Daniel's name, then asked Jake to describe what he had done to Kasha. He asked very pointed questions about how he had grappled with Kasha, where he had touched her, why he had touched her.

"Why didn't you leave her alone until the police came?" Rue asked. "You knew they were coming."

Jake felt frustration rise in his chest. His voice trembled when he spoke. "She had a metal stick," he said. "She was swinging it like a mad woman. She hurt Daniel and I thought she would hurt more people. And the police! They had already been there twice and didn't do a thing. I'm responsible for people's safety in the mission. I just wanted to grab her and make her stop hitting people."

"Now I understand you're on record as saying you touched her breasts."

Jake almost rose out of his seat in anguish. "I never said that. I threw my arms around her, and gave her a bear hug to get her to stop. I don't know if I touched her breasts or not but if I did it was just with my arms, incidentally."

Rue took half a minute to make notes on this. "And who saw this?"

"A lot of people saw it. There was a crowd watching. That's one reason I grabbed her. She could have hurt somebody else."

"Can I get the names of people who were there to witness?"

Jake could not think. He was too agitated, and when he tried to remember who would have been there he drew a blank. That lapse made him seem completely inauthentic, he knew, and his self-conscious embarrassment only made his memory worse. He could envision the crowd of faces like a blur, but in this state of mind he was not sure he could have retrieved Krystle's name. Finally he said he couldn't get it; could he think about it and call some names in?

"Oh, sure," Rue said. "Just leave a message for me at my desk." He put away his notebook and got up to go, offering a light handshake, just a touch.

Jake suddenly remembered Knox. "My assistant," he blurted out, as though he had discovered hidden treasure. "Knox. He was there, of course. We were doing drug testing."

"Who were you testing?"

"Everybody. The whole house."

"Including yourselves?"

"No, not us. We're staff. We tested the men in the program. We do that periodically."

"Mr. Dorner, is it true you've been in the program yourself?"

"Yes, I'm a graduate. Almost six years."

"So you are an addict."

A dark wave of shame washed through Jake's blood. "Yes. They say if you are once, you're always an addict. Yes, I am."

Rue nodded. "I've heard that. Once an addict, always an addict. Addicts lie, don't they?"

Jake flushed. "Some addicts do. It's not uncommon."

The way Jake remembered the interview, he had acted like a guilty man. Every word that came out of his mouth had seemed like a cardboard construction, which a clever man could easily poke holes in. He had come off stiff and unconvincing, a liar trying to smooth over his deception. A liar and an addict. The two were the same thing, according to the investigator, who had acted so neutral until the end when his true colors showed.

The reporter had been that way too. So many questions, and then you find that they already know just what happened and are merely trying to pin it on you.

Afterward Jake sat in his office with his basketball trophy in his hands, turning it mechanically. He didn't see the trophy. He couldn't think clearly. He knew that he should be writing down names of men who had witnessed his confrontation with Kasha, but when he tried to separate those faces in the crowd, to get them to resolve into individuals whose names he knew, he got nothing. He kept hearing his own words in the interview, wishing he had said something else, but not knowing what.

It occurred to him that he could step outside his office door to look at the house roster, to prompt his memory. But when he looked at the spreadsheet stapled to the bulletin board, the names had no meaning to him. He could not even read them; the letters were mere shapes. When he read the names out loud he was unable to make the connection to anyone he knew. His mind was not functioning. Had he ever been so bewildered? He did not think so, not even at the worst of his addiction.

He wanted to find oblivion. He could not think straight.

For the rest of the day he walked around the mission like a man in a trance. The kitchen crew was spread through the dining room, chopping and preparing, and several of them looked up and offered him a friendly greeting. He couldn't bear to look at them, let alone speak. It was the same with guests who came to chapel and to dinner. He circulated, but only because he had nowhere else to go. He found some protective cover in his role.

He walked home after dinner, and sat in his comfortable chair watching Comedy Central. He had turned on his laptop, and when he heard the mechanical burr of skype calling he walked over to peer at the screen. It was Krystle. He stared at her picture, rising and falling in its bubble. If he talked to Krystle he would have to tell about the interview. He let the skype call run out, and then listened to his phone ringing—eight rings before it stopped. He thought ignoring her was the worst thing he had ever done. But he could not talk to her.

Jake went to look at Krystle's photo on the refrigerator. In the picture she held Reggie when he was just a baby. His round baby head nested by hers, but what Jake saw were her eyes. He could look into them; they seemed alive. "I'm sorry," he said. "I'm trying, baby." Later on, when he looked at the photo again, he could not retrieve the same vision. It was just a photograph, with no life in it.

He could not have told you what he watched on television. The shows were just noise and color. He kept watching for the narcotic effect, numbing his mind. He wanted to go out, to walk, but he did not want to encounter anyone, so he stayed with the television racket. It came as a relief when, past 11:00, he could get out of his chair, put on a light jacket, and go out to walk. Nobody would be on the street now. He went through the junior college campus, which included old brick buildings with ivy growing up their walls, and curving paths under ancient oaks. Once upon a time he and Krystle had walked here, when she was a student and he would meet her after night classes.

She had quit school when Reggie was born and he never expected her to go back. He didn't care about money, he told her when she worried about their income. He had lived with nothing and slept by the creek, so if he slept by her side with a roof over his head he had more than he had ever hoped for. He wanted nothing more than to have her entirely to himself.

He mused over this as he walked. What if he was arrested and went to prison, how would she and Reggie live? He supposed that they would stay just where they were now, with her mother. Rather than finding relief in this thought, Jake felt his fear stoked. He was sure he would lose her. The humiliation of prison would be too much for her to take. She would never come back to him.

He had never been afraid. Not when homeless. Not in jail. Never. But in those days he had possessed nothing he cared for. Now he had a life to lose.

He could not imagine it. He could not imagine encountering people who had seen his picture in the newspaper. He could not imagine looking at Krystle while cuffed and shackled.

Jake's path took him through the neighborhoods to the 7-11. He had eaten no supper and was surprised to find himself hungry. That came as something of a relief: to realize that he still had an appetite. He was still alive, apparently.

The familiar layout of the store also comforted: he knew his choices here. There were no surprises in a convenience store. He found it a pleasure and a relief to browse the shelves and take his time.

He bought an It's-It ice cream bar, plus a bag of barbecue chips. As he carried them to the pay window he was surprised to see CJ as the cashier. CJ was a scrawny man with a pencil mustache and multi-colored tattoos up and down his arms. He had never come back to the mission after his episode as a fracker, except a week later as a guest for dinner, greeting all the men in the program with high-fives and fist bumps. He told them that he had a job at Goodyear Tires and had moved in with his girlfriend. So Jake heard; he had missed the visit. He had cautioned CJ's friends not to believe everything you hear.

CJ had been observing him as he shopped, and he already had a wide and knowing smile on his face.

"CJ," Jake said. "How long have you been here?"

"I just got on. Started today."

"That's great. What happened to Goodyear? That's where I thought you were working."

"Yeah, but the manager was an asshole. He was on my case all the time, so I decided this would be a better deal."

"Nobody to get along with here," Jake said. "What hours are you working?"

"Eleven to seven in the morning."

"Uh! What do you do with yourself all night?"

"I don't know. It's my first night. I guess I can watch television on my phone."

"Be careful not to burn up your data. I don't imagine you get wi-fi here."

"No, you're right. Hell, there's nobody here past midnight. I might just take a little nap. Smoke a little weed, take a little rest. That will make the time go fast."

Should he say anything? Jake felt neutralized, completely detached. He had buried himself so deeply in his own misery that he could hardly raise himself to consider someone else. CJ was a good example of the futility of his efforts: so clueless he was telling this to Jake. No way he would last at this job a month. He had spent months in the program, and he couldn't hold a job at a 7-11. He was unchanged. He was a druggie.

None of this seemed to matter very much, but it did underline the weightlessness Jake was experiencing, his sensation that he was a blimp untethered, smashing through houses and trees, blown by the wind.

He raised just enough energy to warn CJ. "You might want to think twice about that. I'm pretty sure they have cameras in these places. I bet they watch you."

A look of surprise raced across CJ's face. For a moment Jake could see the thoughts coursing through his brain. Then he leaned forward toward the glass, and Jake could hear his breath coming fast. No doubt his pulse had just shot up. "Thanks, man. Thanks for telling me. I didn't think of that."

Jake only nodded, but CJ was evidently seized by his thankfulness. "Just a minute," he said. "You saved me, man. I've got something for you."

He had a jacket thrown over a chair in the back of the booth, and he got up to retrieve something from it. He took a peek at whatever it was, while covering it with both hands, then slid it into the money slot. "Thanks, man. You are a great man. Even though I left the mission I always appreciated you. This is just a little present. Don't open it here. Just something small you might appreciate."

Without giving it any thought, Jake slid the brown paper bag into his pocket. It was folded over to the size of a 3 by 5 card. "Thanks," Jake said. "Don't forget my change."

"Oh, yeah, sorry. How much was it?"

Jake left with his purchases, breaking into the ice cream the moment he was outside, carrying the chips. He put his free hand into his pocket, trying to guess what CJ's gift might be. By the time he reached College Avenue he had to see. While waiting for the light, he unfolded the bag and found a plastic bag inside, filled with a dirty yellow powder.

It had an extraordinary effect on him. Unbidden, his heart speeded to a race clip, and his breathing increased in the same way. He felt his face contort, his nostrils swelling and his lips scowling. Quickly he shoved the packet back into his pocket, smashing it into a wad. Then just as quickly he removed the packet and straightened everything, placing the plastic bag carefully back into the paper bag, folding it neatly, and wedging it carefully into the pocket of his jeans.

He walked quickly, furtively. What was he going to do with this stuff? He had to get rid of it as quickly as possible. He could drop it in the gutter, and no one would know. Or throw it in the bushes.

But a kid might find it, and who could say what would happen then? That much heroin could kill someone.

He kept walking, thinking, sweating. It seemed an endless journey until—almost suddenly, like a pop-goes-the-weasel jack-in-the-box—he found himself at his door.

The safest thing was to flush it, he thought. Unlocking the front door and then immediately locking it behind him, he made his way through the dark living room and into the bathroom, where he closed the door first, then turned on a light. Shoving aside the plastic shower curtain, and taking a seat on the edge of the tub, he drew the bag out of his pocket again. In this light he could see that the stuff was the color of whole-grain mustard. He opened the Zip-loc bag. He smelled. Its scent was like a box of band-aids. This did something to him. It triggered memories.

He had meant to dump it in the toilet but now another process took precedence. No ritual was more fascinating for an addict than the first encounter with a new batch of drugs. Every sense must be enlisted: touch as you run it between your fingers; smell, taste. Jake licked an index finger, wiped it dry on his pants, and then dipped the tip in the heroin. It tasted faintly bitter when he applied it to his tongue. He smelled it again.

What was he doing? He stood on the edge of oblivion, about to step forward. It was not tempting fate, it was more deliberate than that. He felt surprisingly clear-headed. He knew where he was and what he was doing.

He should flush the drugs then and there, but he could not bring himself to that; he could not make such an absolute choice. One of his early drug counselors had talked, memorably, about "closing the door on drugs but spending all day looking through the keyhole." That was how temptation worked: you might say no today, but it would come knocking again tomorrow. And that was what he wanted, keeping the option open.

Actually it was more than that. He could use right now. When he thought of that he felt his pulse accelerate.

Looking around him in desperation, he saw the purple crocheted toilet paper holder that Krystle's mother had made to sit on top of the toilet. He thrust the drugs inside it, opened the cabinet under the sink, grabbed a roll of toilet paper, and shoved it on top of the plastic bag. His first impulse was to hide the crocheted bag under the sink, but he thought better of that and set it on the toilet. That was where it belonged.

No one would come to the house while Krystle was away, but before she came back he would have to be sure that the bag was gone.

He left the bathroom and turned on lights all through the house. He remained clear-headed, pondering his own mindset. It had changed so suddenly. He had accepted his fate: to be an addict, dedicated to hiding and pretending. The thought left him disgusted with himself, and yet simultaneously unmoved. Perhaps nothing had changed, it was only that the truth was being revealed. Perhaps he had always been doomed. Once an addict.

He kicked off his shoes and sat in his comfortable lounge chair, brown corduroy fabric with a retractable footstool. He flicked on the TV and surfed channels, restlessly seeking something to take his mind off the drugs. It occurred to him that he was already in their grip. He might as well use them now and be done with the agony of fighting against it. No, he told himself, he would not. As long as he had not given in he had a chance. Something might occur to save him. He would hold out as long as he could.

He tried a prayer but gave it up as imitation. He started the Lord's Prayer but quit on the third phrase. It was too phony, praying while you kept a packet of heroin at the ready.

He wished he had a beer. If only he could sleep.

After half an hour he got out of his chair, went into the bathroom, and pulled out the yellow brown powder. Would he inject it? He did not have a needle. The easiest would be to snort it, though he had always found that messy; he did not like anything in his nose. For at least five minutes he sat on the edge of the bathtub, staring at the substance in its plastic bag. This time he did not taste it or smell it. He found it mesmerizing just to look at it.

Then he nodded off, right on the edge of the tub, and caught himself before he toppled to the floor. It pleased him. Perhaps he could sleep now. He once again packed the drugs under the toilet paper in its purple container, then went to his bedroom, pulled back the cover, and crawled into bed fully clothed. He slept. For the first time in days, he really slept.

Jake awoke late, discovering that light had already flooded his bedroom. His first reaction was to roll over and marvel that he had slept. Wonderful sleep. His eyes played over the eggshell ceiling and the robin's-egg-blue walls, astonished by their color, which he had never noticed.

Then he remembered the heroin. He knew immediately that it was not a dream, that he did have drugs in his bathroom. But it felt like it should be a dream, for it had that dreadful inevitability of dreams.

What could have possessed CJ to make such a gift? Could it have been a set-up?

That struck Jake as plausible, considering all he had experienced in the last few weeks. Nothing bad was impossible. If it was a set-up, a raid was coming. He should flush the drugs now.

He felt the urgency and went into the bathroom to do it. Instead he found himself relieving his bladder and deciding that it was no set-up. If it were, they would have stopped him within a block of the 7-11.

Jake managed to leave the bathroom without looking at the heroin. It took will power even to do that. He wandered into the living room and took a seat in his comfortable chair. It was Saturday, a day off, full of empty hours. What would he do with himself? He doubted his ability to resist the appeal of the drugs.

If he stayed home, the drugs would overcome his resistance. In his mind's eye the crocheted purple holder seemed to swell to the size of a barrel. His only chance was to get away, putting distance between himself and that.

He was already dressed, since he had slept in his clothes. He did not shower; he put on his shoes and walked out the door. He followed the familiar route to work, through the old neighborhoods behind the high school, under the graffiti-streaked freeway overpass at Ninth, then straight down McKinley with its vacant warehouses and sad storefronts. He walked fast, feeling a little better. He knew how close he had come, but he had not cracked. One night of resistance and perhaps the tide of the battle had turned. Resist the devil and he will flee from you. Draw near to God and he will draw near to you.

At the mission he went into the kitchen to get a cup of coffee. Breakfast was long done and the kitchen crew was working on lunch prep. Jake said hello to them as a group but did not engage. He was too shaky. On the table he found a box of Dunkin' Donuts. He took one with pink frosting and sprinkles, and another glazed with chocolate. He would eat them in his office.

It felt almost like an ordinary day. He sat at his desk nibbling on the donuts and sipping coffee while he read through a batch of classroom evaluations. They were almost uniformly negative regarding Charley Owens' class on life skills. Should he talk to Charley? Or was it hopeless? Should he simply get someone else to teach? It was a difficult class to teach, since sexuality took up half the curriculum and the men were very out of step with a Christian view of sex. Jake sometimes thought it would be easier to explain the Christian view of sex to a Martian than to the men in the New Life program.

A knock at the door, and Michael Brooks stuck in his head. Michael was by far the oldest man in the program— he was at least sixty, perhaps even older. He had entered the program 20 months before, and was setting a new record for longevity. He could not memorize the Bible verses to move up to the next phase. He said his memory was shot; the words would not stick.

Michael's assignment was the laundry, washing, drying and folding sheets and towels for all the guests. You could always find him in the laundry room, methodically sorting and folding stacks of laundry. He didn't quarrel with the other men. He kept his nose clean. You couldn't evict him on the basis of not memorizing Bible verses. But going by the book, he couldn't phase up without reciting them. Jake was not sure what to do with Michael. But Michael was at the very bottom of his list of troubles.

"Excuse me," Michael said, leaning his receding hairline in the door without putting his feet inside. "There's some kind of fight with the cleaning crew."

"You want me to come?"

"I think you better."

He followed Michael down the stairs. As he got nearer the offices he heard the loud noise of thumping and cursing. He hurried. In the hallway behind Knox's office he found two men rolling over each other on the floor, one with a toilet plunger that he held smashed over the nose and mouth of the other. That man, in turn, had his thumbs in the neck of the plunger-wielder, and was violently choking him. It was a maelstrom of skin and limbs and clothes, like two cats going at it. Four or five other men, some with rags and spray bottles in their hands, watched and shouted, trying to edge close enough to pull the wrestlers off each other but unwilling to risk bodily harm to do it. They looked like line dancers, prancing up and back on the dance floor.

There was no dance in Jake's step. He fell forward on top of the two men, grabbing at anything, which turned out to be a crop of black hair on one man, and a collar on the other. At first he could not wrench them apart, but then he got a firm grip on the hair and its owner, with a shriek, came off. Jake held on to him, while eyeing the other who still held on to the stick of his plumber's helper. The corridor was filled with gabble, other men shouting and warning and explaining.

"Shut up!" Jake shouted, while breathing heavily. "You two come with me. The rest of you get back to work. I expect these bathrooms to be extra clean when I come back."

"I'm not talking to him," said the man with the plunger, whose name was Ron. He was a large, fleshy young man with improbably white skin. He had come into the program just a week or two before.

"No, you're talking to me," Jake said.

The other man was Abel: he was perhaps forty, with long, black hair tied in a ponytail. He was in second phase and had been placed in charge of the cleaning crew. It was the least favorite job in the house, cleaning toilets and showers and mopping floors. Men were constantly shirking it. When Jake got the two men to his office that came out: Abel believed Ron was slacking, leaving his responsibilities to others. Abel had been riding Ron mercilessly, until Ron attacked him with the plunger. Ron poured out his complaints. Abel stuck to his guns: he was the supervisor and Ron had to do what he said.

Jake asked them if they were ready to leave the program. They both looked at him, belligerent and surprised.

"Ron?" Jake asked. "You got a better place to go?"

Ron was still breathing heavily from the fight. It took him a minute of glaring to realize that a reply was expected. "No."

"Abel?"

Abel shook his head.

"You do realize that the rules of the house don't allow violence, or even the threat of violence, don't you? You broke that rule today, both of you, and you should be packing your bags right now."

Abel took exception to that. "He attacked me."

"I thought I saw your thumbs in his throat."

Ron said that he hated the cleaning crew. The bathrooms were filthy, with pee all over the floor and poop smears on the toilets. "The people who make the mess should clean up after themselves. Just because I'm here doesn't give him"—he indicated Abel with the jerk of his thumb—"the right to dehumanize me."

"So you want to go?" Jake asked him. "Just tell me."

Ron stayed silent, looking at the floor.

"I tell you what, guys, this is a Christian house. It's a Christ-centered program. So when you come in here, it's on the basis of following in Christ's footsteps. You have to surrender your life to him in order to find a new life. And Ron"—he turned to address Ron's large, reddened face—"that means taking orders and doing work you don't think suits your dignity. Think what Jesus did for you!

"Abel!"—Jake turned his whole body to look squarely at Abel's scrawnier shape—"that means when you are supervisor you are actually the servant. You are here to serve, not just give orders. That's how this program works, and it's how life works, if you want to be sober. You have to follow Jesus. That means becoming Ron's servant."

He meant what he said, but as he said it—familiar words he had used dozens of times, perhaps hundreds—he realized that he was a man guarding a packet of heroin in his house. That recognition ran through him like a hot charge of chemicals. He could not say another word; he escorted Ron and Abel out the door and soundlessly gestured for them to be gone. Confused, they looked at him. He pushed them down the corridor. If he opened his mouth, he knew he was bound to break.

As soon as he gathered himself, he made for the door. He deliberately left his phone, wanting no one to reach him. The hopelessness of his situation kept pounding at him. He could not stay at the mission as a hypocrite. For a brief time he had been on top. But now his wife was gone, his son was gone, he was soon to be arrested, he could go to prison, and he deserved his fate. He was an addict. He was going to use heroin and soon he would be back to the life he had made for himself.

He was walking toward home when he realized he did not have to go home. He could walk all day. He could sleep rough tonight. He had no strength to resist the drugs that he had brought into his own home, but he had strength to stay away, at least for today.

So he walked. He found the creek path where it began near the county complex, and he followed it out into the countryside, past vineyard and pasture where horses grazed. He moved slowly—he was not going anywhere, he did not have to hurry. He was passed by a handful of whizzing cyclists in bright spandex costumes. People were out walking their dogs. By the time he reached Sebastopol, seven miles down the trail, he was hot and weary and his feet had begun to hurt.

In town he lost his way temporarily. He cast about, looking for the trail, and eventually asked a man walking his poodle for direction. The man stared at him but pointed out a sign. Following the neatly asphalted trail north, Jake saw not a soul. He stopped under some oak trees to examine his feet, and found a tiny red blister on his right baby toe. There was nothing he could do about it, so he kept walking, though even more slowly. Out here he could see Mt. St. Helena far off to the east, looming on a purple horizon, and sometimes he caught a view of the plain opening up across miles of open fields. Jake had begun to feel hunger. He took the hunger pangs as a corrective punishment. He deserved whatever he got.

As the afternoon wore on, he could no longer keep thoughts at bay. They ricocheted wildly through his brain: fury, sadness, remorse. He was furious at Kasha, whose antics had triggered the troubles that had landed on top of him, setting off the sadness that permeated his bones. He was remorseful for the failing he anticipated, for he had no strength to resist temptation any longer. He lived in misery, which had a familiar medicine, heroin. He would take its solace. He could not resist it.

His pace grew slower, and thirst dragged at him. It was late afternoon when he reached Forestville, where the trail came to an end, spilling onto a country road. He knew he was badly dehydrated. Alongside the road was a stand-up chalkboard advertising eggplant parmigiana. Behind it a low-slung white building had roses climbing the walls. A sign said "Chellis." The middle-aged woman who met him just inside the door gaped in alarm, as though he were an exotic creature, but when he asked for water she said, "Just a minute," and disappeared into the kitchen. She emerged with a glass of water, which he downed while she watched. He asked if he could have more, and she took the glass out of his hand and went back into the kitchen again. This time she emerged with a 2-liter plastic bottle. "I just filled this," she said. "You can take it with you."

Jake sat on the front steps and sipped at the water until he was satiated. Across the street were vineyards, lit by the soft light of the lowering sun. It was lovely to look at, and the beauty triggered more sadness as he contemplated how much he would lose. He found himself paralyzed, utterly unable to move, until a car drove up and parked in front of him. Two graying couples got out, nicely dressed, and as they shut the car doors they saw him on the steps and hesitated. Jake stood up and walked away.

Now he did not know where to go. He was hungry but he had no money. He thought of hitchhiking back to Santa Rosa, but immediately discarded that idea. The thought of communicating with people in any way repelled him. He could not stand by the road waving his hand; he could not explain to strangers why he was there and where he wanted to go.

It came to him what he wanted. He wanted to go to church. The reaction was deep and visceral. He wanted the safety, the comfort, the humanity. He could rest there, rest from himself. As soon as he thought of it, that became his organizing cause.

In order to arrive at church on time Sunday morning, he would need to walk some of the distance tonight, he calculated. He thought that if he walked until dark, then slept in the fields, then started again at first light, he could be in time for the morning service. He would never enter his house, and falling into his addiction would be simply impossible for this one night, at least.

At dusk Jake left the trail and walked fifty yards into a vineyard. The grapes were swelling and he helped himself to as many as he could get down. They were sour and did not sit well on his stomach, but at least they took the edge off his hunger.

The cold, on the other hand, he could not help at all. When the sun dropped over the horizon, a wind came up from the west, trailing low wisps of cloud. His clothes were far too thin to withstand the temperature of that ocean air. He began to shiver before the moon came up, and he trembled violently as its silver light played slowly across the sky.

He could not sleep; he tried to pray. He asked God to help him, and to help his wife and child. Then he prayed for each one of the men in the New Life program. Some names he could not recall, and he circled back to them repeatedly until he retrieved them. Currently, there were 27 men in New Life: he counted them, going through each phase of the program until he had the names of all but two. Those he never got; and he must have dropped off to sleep sometime in the early hours because he had no warning of the gray dawn he woke to. It was just suddenly there.

He had no watch or phone, so no idea of the time. The vines were barely silhouetted against the sky, and he could make out no color, only shades. It might be six o'clock, and the service started at 10:00. He thought he could make it, if he walked steadily, but when he got to his feet he was so stiff he could barely stand. He swigged at his water bottle, relieved his bladder, and set out, slowly. The soft, uneven dirt of the row was hard going on his staggering legs. He was relieved when he reached the asphalt trail. There he stopped to pick grapes for his breakfast, but after he ate half the bunch he tossed the rest into the bushes. His stomach revolted against more sour grapes.

Soon a pearl sky appeared, and the sloping, shallow hills began to reveal themselves. Jake's body loosened and warmed as he went along, and soon he felt almost cheerful. On his way through Sebastopol he saw a public clock displayed in the window of a Volvo dealership. It was 7:15, and he thought that most likely he could arrive at church on time.

It was Krystle's church, too. She was very much loved there. He had arrived there before she did, but by now people knew him mainly as her husband. She was loveable; she had a child. At church Jake had grown quieter since his marriage. He stayed in the background as much as he could.

The church could do nothing to avert his self-destruction, and when they learned that he had fallen back into his addiction they would certainly be aggrieved. They would shake their heads. They would be profoundly disappointed. He did not want to think ahead to that. Today, they would take him in. Unlike anyone else in the world, the church would take him in.

Christian Community Church stood on a residential street east of the junior college. The assembly hall was an A-frame building, with tilt-up textured concrete walls and colored Plexiglas windows—utilitarian but endowed with some of the reverential qualities of a traditional church. Alongside the assembly hall was a multi-purpose room with basketball standards hanging from the ceiling—a gymnasium that was useful for all kinds of meetings. Behind both these buildings was a wide concrete patio, with tables and chairs and space to mingle. It was a very informal church. A rock band led most of the service. The pastors wore ties but practically no one else did.

Jake arrived limping just after 10:00, when the service had already begun. He was starving and light-headed, so he found it difficult to stand through four songs. He would have sat down, except that he was not anxious to draw attention to himself.

A pair of young women led the singing, bending and swaying and raising their hands with the music. Jake only listened, mute. He wanted to open his mouth but he could not sing. It made him deeply sad. He recognized how utterly their energy and vitality were missing in him. He had lost the Spirit.

Jake had always liked the pastor, Raymond Dull, who was warm and low-key and remarkably good at making spiritual truth sound like common sense. He got up to speak without notes, just a Bible in his hands. He had hair the color of carrots and an impish sense of humor. Nonetheless, Jake couldn't concentrate on what he said. His mind wandered off.

After the service ended, Jake shuffled out to the patio, where he lined up to get a muffin and a clear plastic glass of orange juice. They were gone in a moment and he stood awkwardly in the bright sunshine, wondering what he should do. Most of the faces were strange; and those he recognized did not seem to recognize him. Without Krystle, he had become invisible. Or unrecognizable. He wondered what he looked like. After all, he had spent the night in a field.

One couple did come up and ask him where Krystle was. They meant it in a friendly way, he was sure. "She's gone over to see her mother," he said. When the woman asked when she would be coming back, he didn't know what to say. He fumbled in obvious confusion before saying that he wasn't sure. Both the man and the woman looked at him with bright fascination, as though assessing in their heads what had gone wrong, but they only said to give Krystle their love when he talked to her.

He might have known such questions would come to him. He really had no standing here, except through Krystle. Jake opted for another pastry. By this time there was no line, but neither were there any more muffins. He settled for a Danish, which he found too sticky and sugary. He felt itchy, not at all what he had expected to feel as he anticipated church. He felt no warmth, no welcome, only the curious eyes of strangers.

Then laughter drew his eyes to Kasha. She was standing in a small group of churchgoers, but he could not see her clearly. Kasha was short, hidden behind others. When Jake moved to get a closer view he saw that she had on a purple tie-dyed pantsuit, and a matching headscarf wrapped turban-style around her head. He could not tell whether she was the one making others laugh, or whether she just joined in the merriment.

Jake had never seen Kasha at his church before. If she had been somber or sober, he might have walked away, but he could not endure her happiness. She acted like someone who belonged. It was like a stick in the throat.

When she looked up at him and recognized his face, she smiled at him. It was meant to be a welcoming smile.

"Jake," she said. "How are you?" Her tone was sympathetic, as though they were friends.

"I'm terrible," he said. "You've destroyed me, just like you intended."

"I don't know what you're talking about," she said, a little too loudly.

Jake wanted to shake her. "Lies come back to you, Kasha!"

"I don't know what you're talking about."

"Lies, lies, lies. LIES!"

He felt a hand on his elbow, and shook it off. The hand came back, more firmly, and he turned to look in the face of his pastor. His expression was firm, neutral, and impersonal. "Jake," he said.

34

The Confession of Fools

✧

The carpeted office where Raquel Raise waited to see Kent Spires might have been an insurance agency, complete with a gum-chewing secretary chatting on the phone. It was not what Raquel had envisioned, based on her experience at the downtown mission. That was elemental and impoverished; this was suburban.

The unexpected atmosphere knocked her off stride. She had come to tell Kent what she knew about Buddy Grace and Adam McLeod. After wrestling with herself whether to meddle in somebody else's business, in the end she concluded that it was a matter of fairness. It was only fair to expose what she knew about the lawsuit.

As she sat waiting for Kent, however, she realized that her reaction against injustice was tied in some complicated way to the esthetics of the downtrodden. She had imagined that everything the mission did had that sense of poverty and neglect. Encountering this normal, middle-class ambiance left her wondering what she was doing here.

Kent, when he came out of his office to get her, was also a different kind of character: smaller than Jake, he seemed to be made of a lighter substance. His hair did not bristle, it floated. He spoke cheerfully but hesitantly, as though unsure of himself, and welcomed her into his office like a man not certain how to do it, as though he had seldom done such a thing before.

Kent said nothing as Raquel explained what she had learned, nor did he take notes, but he picked up a pen, juggling it between his hands. When she finished he sat quite still, like a bird with its head cocked as it listens for the sound of worms underground.

"How do you know?" he asked. "How do you know that the lawsuit was Buddy Grace's idea?"

"They told me. Kasha told me he proposed it. Buddy himself didn't make any bones of it. He said he was doing you a favor, offering a great price for your building. He said the lawsuit was never going to go to court. It was just to push you into doing what was in your own interest."

Kent sat thinking of that. Finally he opened his mouth. "Maybe I was prideful. I was waiting for the Lord's permission to move. Maybe I should have seen that it was a fair offer."

"You don't have to second guess yourself," Raquel said drily. "Nobody is obligated to sell."

"But you see," Kent said, "it's practically ruined us. The bad publicity has nearly shut us down. I don't believe Jake did anything wrong, but as long as people believe he did, they won't contribute."

She had expected to provoke indignation, and instead Kent offered humility and sorrow. It made no sense to her. "What does that have to do with your pride?" she asked.

He blinked. "It could be a punishment," he said. "Pride cometh before the fall."

"What?"

"It's a proverb."

"You'll pardon me," Raquel said, "but I don't find the metaphysics very interesting. I'm just operating at a more practical level. You're being abused unfairly."

He actually smiled wanly at her. "So was our Lord. We don't want to suffer, but our concern is bigger. We want to do what is right before God. To be prideful has eternal consequences. Suffering is only for a moment."

It took Raquel a moment to get her bearings. "And what about Jake? Would he say that?"

"You're right, he's the one who suffers. If we go out of business, he won't have a job. And he has a wife and a child to support."

"Surely that matters too," Raquel said, groping for solid ground. "I'd like to help. If I can help you expose what's going on, I will."

"I don't know how to do that," he said.

"You could defend yourself. With what I've told you, you could stand up and fight."

He paused again to think. "I'd be assaulting their integrity."

"Yes," she said. "And rightfully so."

He shook his head slowly, as though his neck hurt. "But I can't do that. I have to turn the other cheek."

Raquel knew this phrase, "turn the other cheek," but it had never occurred to her to take it so practically. "You mean to say," she asked politely, "that you are willing to bankrupt your organization, and let Jake be slandered, because you can't take a public stand against men who have deliberately distorted the facts to do you harm?"

He let his shoulders rise in a brief and helpless shrug. "We can be slandered. Our Lord was. But we don't strike back."

"Even if it ruins you?"

He nodded, glumly.

"That's the worst thing," she started, angrily, and then hesitated. "You don't mind if I go out and defend you?"

"I would ask you not to. I don't think any good would come out of public acrimony. It's better for us to suffer. God will defend us." He tried to smile, though the effect was like a weak sun trying to break through the overcast.

"Miss Raise, I'm really grateful to you for your concern. But the only way ahead, I think, is for me to go directly to Buddy Grace and appeal to him."

She shook her head in disgust, a quick, sharp, "no," and began to explain that she had already done that. Before she got a word out, however, they heard talking in the outer office. Raquel lifted her head. She recognized the voice, or at least thought that she did.

"That's the man himself," she said. "I think he is out there."

After a moment Kent too lifted his head. "You think that's Buddy Grace? Really?"

He rose to his feet and went to open the office door. Raquel stayed where she was, but with the door open she could hear the voice quite clearly.

"Mr. Grace," Kent called out. "I'm here. Marci, it's all right, I was hoping to see him. Come in, come in."

Buddy did come in, tall and full of himself, well dressed in gray checked slacks and a golf sweater. He shook hands with Kent and then noticed Raquel. Just for an instant he hesitated, and then he was all graciousness again. "Miss Raise! I certainly didn't expect to see you here! What a kick!"

Kent got him seated in a molded plastic chair (Raquel had taken the only cushioned chair in the office) and said, "We were just talking about you."

"Were you?" Buddy's eyes jumped around, as though someone else might be in the room with them. "What a coincidence. Well, maybe it's not a coincidence, because I've been thinking about you, and the Sonoma Gospel Mission. Did you get my phone message?"

Kent said yes.

Buddy looked around the office with a charming smile on his face but deep foreboding within. He carried severe doubts as to whether he should be here at all. He felt just as he had on the golf course. He was doomed. He should have dropped this development when he didn't get the money.

He didn't know how to stop, however. He had built his life on smiling and moving forward, and it had become part of him.

After he called Kent from the golf course, pushing for a yes, he had spent the rest of Saturday and all day Sunday brooding over it. He didn't really expect to get a return call on the weekend. Part of him thought he should, however. Part of him kept thinking of the offer he had made to the mission, and how crazy it was that they couldn't respond positively.

He also couldn't get that damn story out of his mind, his father's story about the engineer who shot himself. Buddy could put himself in that man's place. Though he would never shoot himself. It wasn't in him to do himself harm. But the message in the story could be aimed at him.

Monday he went to his office at the usual time, to sit in a gray leather chair and brood over the state of his finances. Within minutes, his red-haired receptionist ran in, her hair and her blouse dripping wet, to tell him that the bathroom faucet had exploded. He followed her to find water spurting from the top of a broken handle, and the floor flooded. Buddy made no pretense of being a plumber, but he knew enough to open the cabinet and shut off the valve. He managed to soak his shirt, but fortunately he always kept a spare one in his office closet. He dried himself off and put that on, then told Vivien to wipe up the mess and call a plumber. He went back to brooding. Though Buddy did not consider himself superstitious, he had to wonder: was it a sign? Maybe the bathroom flood was to remind him of the engineer. Maybe it forcibly nudged him to pick up the phone and do what that engineer found impossible: call it off.

Yet once again, he could not do it. He did, in fact, just the opposite. He called Vivien into his office and dictated to her a memorandum of understanding. She was quick; she had it printed up minutes later. Buddy placed it reverently into his folder, as he had done so many times with other contracts. Then he got into his car to drive to the mission. Somehow he thought he would feel better if he could see Kent in person. Buddy had an almost invincible belief in his powers of persuasion, and he thought this was make-it-or-break-it time. He had to give Kent his all.

"What message?" Raquel asked. She had heard Buddy refer to leaving a message.

Buddy ignored her. He pulled his chair close to Kent's desk, which had the effect of putting Raquel slightly behind him, excluded from the conversation. "I'm so glad to see you. Face to face we can get something done. Look, I brought an agreement. It's a simple document of intent." He held a black leather folder in his left hand and drew out a typed sheet, which he handed to Kent. Kent took it reluctantly. "We'd need to have a much more detailed contract going forward," Buddy said, "but this states the principles we hold. It basically says that you intend to sell the downtown mission property, and it lays out a process for setting the price. It's what we talked about, basically. It's important for me so I can start moving forward on the financing."

Kent held the document as though it might be explosive. He showed no interest in reading it.

After a few moments of unnerving silence Buddy went on. "I'll tell you what it says. The process for setting payment would begin with an appraisal of the property. We commit to doubling that price. You end up able to buy or build something comparable or better to what's there now, and you have the same amount in cash going forward."

"How soon?" Kent asked.

"How soon what?"

"How soon do we get the cash?"

Buddy wagged his head. "That part we would have to work out. I'm assuming it would happen in stages."

"Would we get some immediately?"

Buddy nodded strongly. "Yes. On the day that the bank financing comes through, you get the first tranche. We could work that out.

Definitely."

"And when does the bank financing come through?" Raquel asked on Kent's behalf.

Buddy ignored her. "All you need to do now is read the agreement carefully and sign."

Kent still sat motionless. "I couldn't do that right now, Buddy. I'd have to talk to my board."

It looked to Raquel as though a tiny tic ran through Buddy's torso, though he kept his face smooth and unmoved. "Kent, we don't have that kind of time any more. We have to move ahead, or the financing just won't be there. Remember, this isn't the final deal. There is plenty that needs negotiating before we can sign a final agreement. This is just a statement of our intentions. You can back out of it later, if something isn't to your satisfaction."

Kent shook his head with the slightest motion. "Buddy, if I signed I would never back out of it. Let your yes be yes. We take these things very seriously. Our word is good."

"Fine," Buddy said. "In that case we can sign it now. I'm trying to communicate that I don't have any more leeway, Kent. I'm trying to help the mission but there's a limit to how long I can wait, and that limit is now."

Listening to this conversation Raquel found Kent's other-worldliness hard to bear. After what she had told him, he had to know that Buddy wasn't trustworthy.

"Listen, Buddy," she said, though it went against her nature to butt in. "I don't know what your hurry is, but I know for a fact it's not because you care about Kent or his organization. Kasha told me all about it. You put her up to suing the mission, and you set up the DA too."

He turned on her. "That's not true. I had nothing to do with the DA."

"Fine, your lawyer did it, because it fit your plans. You don't have to have your fingerprints on it to make it your own. Nobody in his right mind would sign a contract with you. You're a liar and a cheat and nothing you do can cover that up. Do you understand what you've done to Jake Dorner?"

She made this speech more for her own satisfaction than because she thought it would affect Buddy. Listening to him and Kent talk was like watching two dancers up to their ankles in mud. She was angry and longed for something clear and straight.

To her surprise, her words seemed to jolt Buddy. "What?" he asked. "What did I do to Jake?"

"I told you this before," she said coldly. "Imagine if you were the one accused of sexual assault. Imagine how you and your family would feel."

Buddy was not naturally empathetic. He had a mind that focused on his own happiness, but was vague on other people. "But he's fine. When I saw him he was fine. People don't remember. In a few months they won't even know what we are talking about. Jake is going to be just fine."

Since she did not actually know Jake's state, Raquel turned to Kent. "Kent, you tell him," she said.

Kent was looking back and forth between them. He swallowed before speaking. "It's true he's struggling, Buddy. His wife has left, and he's all alone. It's not easy for any of us, being accused of such things, with no way to defend ourselves."

"Why don't you defend yourselves?" Raquel asked. "It's ridiculous that you let them get away with such accusations."

She was beginning to realize that the Sonoma Gospel Mission was a very different case from her sister. These people made themselves vulnerable.

Kent swallowed again, and took a deep breath. "We would have to slander Kasha. She's not a bad woman; she isn't quite right but she doesn't deserve to be held up to ridicule. It would be cruel. We don't defend ourselves. We leave that to God."

To Raquel that seemed crazy. It seemed to permit anything.

"Maybe you won't defend the mission, but can't you defend Jake?"

Before Kent made an answer to that, Buddy interjected in a strangled voice. "I didn't mean to hurt him."

All day his sense of doom had been dueling with his habit of moving forward. Hearing of Jake's sorrows, the impasse broke and he poured himself into Jake. Jake was suffering like him. He would lose everything; Jake had lost everything. All Buddy's problems, his broken marriages and his failed development scheme, triggered a sensitivity to Jake. He felt sorry for Jake; he felt sorry for himself. Buddy was a man of passionate impulses. Jake's sufferings were a sign, a shadow thrown on the wall, in which he saw himself and felt for himself.

There was a long silence. Raquel was utterly thrown off. Evidently Buddy heard music that she was not singing.

"What can I do?" Buddy asked, his voice sounding as though someone had shoved a tennis ball down his throat. "I'll call the whole thing off."

"What good will that do him?" Raquel asked frostily.

"I'll publicly apologize. I'll admit there was nothing to it."

Kent's face screwed up into a grimace. "See, there's the trouble, Buddy. You can't defend Jake without smearing Kasha. That's what I've been facing all along." He turned to Raquel and held out his hands, as though begging pity. "Of course I want to defend Jake."

Raquel turned on Buddy. "At the least you can apologize to Jake."

She was completely surprised when Buddy nodded. "All right, I can apologize. What good will that do?"

"I doubt it will do any good at all. It's just the least you can do, if you've got a shred of decency."

Raquel couldn't see how to unravel the whole misguided affair, but she felt in her bones that Jake would welcome an apology. He would seize on it like a life preserver. She knew that apologies are just words. They don't change anything. But she was angry, and she felt for Jake, who was bereft and persecuted.

Buddy drove deliberately toward Railroad Square, afraid of an accident, because when Buddy was excited he was not a safe driver. His present emotions were a tornado, combining hatred for Raquel, that little bird who had dragged him into this; shame, for his part in hurting a man who had dedicated his life to serving God; fear, for his disintegrating business; and pride, for responding nobly. He was even excited by the unknown he would soon encounter. He was on his way to the mission to apologize. He had never witnessed an apology between two grown men, let alone made one.

He knew that his project was ruined. He felt the threat of humiliation, tied up with his own regrets. He wanted to do something, anything, to escape it.

Now he vacillated, however. Why should he be so concerned that the man's wife had left him? Charlotte had left him, and he never cried about it. You have to get up and go on.

Why such a fetish about apologies? The little redhead basically said it wouldn't change a thing.

Women left Buddy, Buddy left women. It happened. And yet Buddy could not deny that he had become overwhelmed thinking of Jake. With pity. With regret.

It made him proud, in a perverse way, that he was sensitive; it also made him angry. He was aware that Raquel was following him in her little Subaru, and he would have loved to back into her at a stoplight and smash her car. He did not need a mother. He resented that she had demanded he apologize. He wished that he had thought of it himself. It was, surely, the decent thing.

Suddenly, at a stoplight, he recognized the gravity of what he was doing—for effectively he was closing his business. A tidal wave of loss swept over him, most particularly the loss of his office and its wall-sized painting and gorgeous leather sofas. The extravagant desk. He could not save them.

Perhaps he had time still to change his mind! But when he tried to think of it, he realized that he had run out of time. He needed money from Howard Zenikov's bank, Howard insisted on the mission's agreement to move, and now that was impossible. Of course it still made sense, economically, for the mission. But he could see Kent Spires was not a man to sign. It would never happen. It was never meant to happen.

By the time he pulled up curbside to the mission, pity for Jake Dorner had again taken over Buddy's mind. Buddy, a most public man, would have dreaded Jake's fate above all: to become a public disgrace. Well, he too might be one, when he closed up his office and went begging for work.

35

The Fate of Jake Dorner

✧

After Jake screamed at Kasha and his pastor ushered him away into his office, he was unable to speak. He slumped in a chair, answering no queries. Pastor thought it was because Krystle was gone. He had a low, dry voice. Krystle would just need time, he said. Jake should be patient. He urged Jake to trust God through this wilderness time.

Pastor did not know that Jake had heroin in a purple crocheted container in his bathroom, under a roll of toilet paper. He did not imagine that Jake's misery was only partially related to Krystle. What a surprise it would be for Pastor when he learned that Jake was using again.

Jake finally gathered himself, thanked the pastor for his kindness, and left church carrying these bitter thoughts. He did not dare go home, but went instead to the mission, where he showered and got fresh ill-fitting clothes out of the second-hand-clothing room. He made a sandwich in the lunchroom and carried it to his office on a tray with a huge tranche of potato chips plus two Dr. Peppers. Since it was Sunday most of the men were gone; nobody bothered him.

After he ate, Jake fell asleep in his office chair and woke up hours later. His neck was stiff from sleeping awkwardly and he lay still for a long time, listening to the dim sounds of the house going about its business of living. He felt amazingly groggy, and for a time he could not remember how he had gotten to his office. Then he realized that he had nowhere to go and nothing particular that he had to do. So long as he stayed where he was, nothing could hurt him and no temptation could assail him.

So he did not move. The light in his office slowly faded out, from a murky second-hand sunlight to the ghostliness of twilight. Most likely nobody in the house knew that he was there, and he did not venture out, except to go to the bathroom. He tried to turn off his mind. Rummaging through a box of books that he had selected at the thrift store some weeks back, he located a Rex Stout novel. By his desk lamp, he read, even though he could not remember what the words said from page to page. His phone had run dry, and he did not recharge it. He did not need the world outside this office.

Late in the night, long after the house was quiet, Jake grabbed blankets from the storeroom and put them on the floor as padding. Miraculously, he slept most of the night, and felt the sweet healing of rest. Whether or not he dreamed of Krystle he could not say—he rarely remembered anything from his dreams—but somehow her kindness and her quiet penetrated his mind. He was not thinking about his future, or hers, but his thoughts reflected her silvery light. When he thought of her this way, he felt crude in comparison.

He was happy in Krystle until he felt his situation sink home again while he took a shower. His thoughts turned rapidly toward distress; what would happen to him?

He went to Monday morning devotions in the chapel. When he came in many of the men looked pleased and surprised, greeting him warmly. He rarely made it to devotions, as he had a family at home. But now he had no family.

Program members took seats against the wall, as far as possible from each other. They heard a short devotional pep talk from Tommy, who had joined the program just a month before and had an astonishing number of Bible verses committed to memory. Tommy's talk generated sound in Jake's ears but no meaning.

He remained in his seat after everyone else left. The chapel held special significance for Jake: here he had first been filled with the Holy Spirit, here he had witnessed dozens of men as they shook and cried out and sometimes sang while they encountered the power of God. The room was utterly utilitarian, its only religious symbol a large plywood cross hung on the wall above the stage. Battered plasterboard showed signs of warfare; the carpet looked diseased. It was a good fit for his life, Jake thought, as for all the desperate or dysfunctional lives that funneled through on a daily basis. He felt at peace here, more than anywhere. The chapel demanded nothing but attendance. You didn't have to sing the worship songs, you didn't have to bow for the prayers: all that was required was presence. Then you could get a meal and a bed.

His presence was all that Jake had to give.

Elvis had been watching Jake cautiously, nervously. Obviously something was very wrong, and though it never occurred to Elvis that he could help directly, he believed strongly that somebody should look out for Jake. He was carrying this worry when he happened to encounter Buddy at the front desk. Elvis had never seen him before, but he overheard Buddy asking for Jake and took note that Buddy was tall and well dressed. Immediately he stepped in and led Buddy to the chapel, threw open the door, and stood out of his way.

"Oh my God," Buddy said aloud. The chapel and its plywood cross looked like churches he had attended all over Oklahoma when he was young. It even smelled like them.

He recognized the slumping form in the back of the room. "Jake," he said in a loud and friendly voice. Jake lifted his head and turned to see him. His face seemed drained of life and hope. Without warning, Buddy found tears starting in his eyes, and when he tried to say Jake's name again only a croak came out.

He went to Jake and held out an imploring hand. "Jake, I did the wrong thing. I can't undo it, but I have come to say that I am sorry and to ask you to forgive me."

"Yes!" Elvis shouted. "Did you hear that?"

"I understand your wife has gone," Buddy said. "I take responsibility. I admit that I went too far. All I wanted was to push the mission to move to a new location. I didn't realize it would hurt you. I take responsibility. Where is your wife now?"

"She's at her mother's," Jake said, answering automatically because he was dazed. He still did not understand what was going on. "In Vallejo."

"Will she come home if she understands that it's my fault? That you did nothing wrong?"

Jake stared. He swallowed. He answered without understanding the question. "I don't know. She knows I didn't do anything. It's not that. She can't stand people saying terrible things to her."

"We can go together," Buddy said. "I'll tell her you didn't do anything wrong."

"She knows that," Jake said. "Everybody tells her."

"I can explain it to her," Buddy said with the invincible confidence of a salesman. "She doesn't have to worry."

In his confusion Jake saw a single ray of light. "Will you take me to her? Can you drive me there?"

"Of course!" Buddy said. "We can go right now!"

36

VALLEJO

✧

While he unlocked the door to his house Jake's heart weighed in his chest like a five pound hammer. The door swung open and he did not hesitate, but walked with resolution through the living room to the bathroom.

He wondered whether he was staunch to do the necessary. He shut the bathroom door carefully behind him, picked up the toilet paper holder, shook out the roll of paper, and claimed the plastic bag of powder. Yes, it was still there. He did not intend to even look at it, but he did: holding out his left hand he tipped a small fraction into his palm. It looked more brown than yellow now. It was ugly, really. Slowly, he tipped it out, letting it trail into the toilet. Then, more quickly, he lifted the bag over the toilet and let the powder flow out. It plunged through the surface of the water, a heavy substance disappearing like lead shot, with some of the lighter residue forming a scum riding on the surface. He flushed, and watched the whirlpool pull that scum into a vortex and carry it down. Jake threw the bag in after it, waited for the toilet to fill, then flushed that down.

He walked out of the house with a sense of lightness in his step, so vital and vibrant that he forgot to lock the door behind him. He remembered it just as he put a hand on the door handle to Buddy's car. "Just a minute," he yelled, and hustled back to lock up.

"You all right?" Buddy asked when he got back in the car. Jake seemed to have lost ten years in the house.

"Yeah. I'm good."

Buddy drove his black Mercedes south on 101. He felt he had already surrendered his beautiful office, but he mentally clung to the leather upholstery and the silent operation of the car; they seemed all the more precious to him. Buddy was not a man of irony, and he saw nothing strange in acting out his sense of sacrifice and suffering while driving a luxury car.

"You know how to get there?" he asked, and Jake, preoccupied, grunted yes. He had already moved on to thinking about what might lie ahead. What could he say to Krystle that he had not already said on skype? He wondered what he could endure, or what he might have to.

At least he had flushed the drugs. He was clean. Still.

With great deliberation he forced his thoughts toward Buddy. They were already out of Rohnert Park and gliding up the ridge, the geometric green of Gallo's vineyard on the right, a patchwork of dry tan grass and army-green oaks on their left. He felt slightly hallucinatory, not having been in a car for weeks.

"So you are not going to do it?" he asked Buddy. "All those buildings you talked about, the hotel, the condos.... I don't know what else. That won't happen?"

"Guess not," Buddy said, intending to sound chipper. "I guess somebody will do something like that at some point. But it won't be me."

He glanced sideways to Jake. "You wanted it, right? You were ready to move?"

"Yeah," Jake said, "I did. I'm so sick of that old building."

"It was Kent who held it up."

"Yeah, Kent is stubborn on certain things. For him that building is holy ground. I can't go against that. He sees some things that I don't, and he's been through a lot more than I have, too."

"It could have all been different if you were in charge," Buddy said mournfully. There was nothing Jake could say about that, so he let it lie.

"So what happens next?" Jake asked.

"For me? I'm working on that." Buddy grinned as though it were a matter of pure pleasure.

The freeway carried them down off the ridge and into broad farm fields, then through the small city of Petaluma. Buddy pointed to a sleek turquoise and silver six-story office building just off the freeway. "That one's mine," he said.

Jake was stunned. "You built that?" He had never known anybody who did such things; he would have been impressed just to meet somebody who helped to install the elevator.

They exited the freeway and followed a two-lane road running along the base of dry hills that slung their weight down to the San Francisco Bay. It was soft country, running beef cattle and milk cows and, in spots, growing grapes or alfalfa. Jake felt himself loosen and relax just at the sight of open country. He had, after all, grown up surrounded by vast farms.

He would like the calendar to stop right here, letting him ride forever in the car's luxurious interior, never arriving at Krystle's where he would meet his fate. He should think about what he would tell her. But the idea filled him with such a sense of dread that he shifted his attention back to Buddy.

"Tell me about your life," he said, which was the way he began with men who joined the program. "I can't believe you build things like that office."

The question turned Buddy on like a radio. He was happy to spin stories about his upbringing in Oklahoma, about the tricks of selling used cars, about the Baptist preachers who came for a week's revival. He had stories to tell about buildings, too, but he stayed off those.

"You don't sound like you grew up in Oklahoma," Jake said, interrupting as Buddy began to tell about high school. "What happened to your accent?"

Buddy laughed, a short bark. "Thank you very much. When I was a kid I started listening to the evening news and trying to sound like what I heard. By the time I was twelve I think I had got rid of the accent."

"Why?"

"Jake, my friend, you can't go anywhere with an Okie accent. People think you eat your peas with a knife. I figured that out by the time I was nine."

"Did somebody tell you?"

"I just watched. Maybe somebody said it to me. Come to think of it, it might have been one of those revivalists. I can remember talking to the youth evangelists about all kinds of things. They stayed at our house."

"So you went to church?" Jake asked. "Did you hear the gospel there?" That was the only important characteristic for him. He knew there were different kinds of churches, but many of them, he was told, produced a lot of religion but no gospel.

"Oh, man, I heard the gospel. That was like the only thing that was supposed to matter. I went to church four times a week and it was the same message every time."

"You didn't accept it?" Jake asked.

"Oh, sure I did. I'm a Christian. But it gets a little boring, don't you think, if that's the only subject? I always thought there was a lot more to life. I was itchy to get out of that town."

It was not in Jake's nature to let this pass. "I don't see how that contradicts. The gospel is the foundation to build on. It doesn't hold you down. It lifts you up."

"You ever tour a building and they want you to look at the foundation? All they wanted to do was talk about the blood of Jesus washing your sins away. It never excited me."

"Maybe you just didn't know what a burden you were carrying. I tell you, it still excites me."

"I imagine you've gone through some stuff I never did. Were you an addict?"

"I still am. Once an addict, always an addict." As he said it, the drugs he had flushed seemed to whiz by near his face. He had been so close to complete failure.

"Well, that's a whole different thing. I can understand how that would breed a certain amount of desperation. I've never been tempted like that."

Their road ran along the bay tidal lands. It was a narrow highway hemmed in by bodies of water and grassy wetlands on either side. Light glinted from water ripples like the silver sides of a fish. They crossed a high arching bridge and found their way into Vallejo, a working-class city. It looked flat and empty, as though the sun had bleached out the colors and everyone had fled. Perhaps they had.

Krystle's mother lived in the hills above the town, and Jake had to jog his memory to guide Buddy there. Several false turns took them in a long loop up and around. They pulled into the driveway of a modern beige stucco home, with dark painted beams in the eaves, and a tiny cutout oval of grass for a front yard. For Jake it was modernity, a vast improvement over the sagging, shaggy, makeshift homes of his upbringing in Taft. Buddy had a more negative reaction: he could easily place the building style as cheap subdivision, built from a plan without modifications. He had lived in similar places, but he had never built one, he was proud to say.

By the time Jake rang the doorbell his nerves were at a pitch. He had tried to think what he could say. He had nothing. All he knew was that he wanted Krystle to come home. It was like a dog that had clamped its jaws on his hand: he couldn't think of anything else, he didn't care about anything else than getting the dog off his hand, but its bite was so strong he couldn't shake it off. He wanted Krystle to come home with him more than he had ever wanted anything. But he didn't know if it would happen.

Reggie answered the door. Jake began to say something to him, but before he could get it out Reggie looked at them with his hard, serious eyes, and skedaddled away. Jake and Buddy waited before the closed screen for what seemed like minutes. "Should we ring again?" Buddy asked, but just at that moment Krystle's mother came to the door. She opened the screen and let them in without a word. From her expression it seemed that they were no surprise; nor was she delighted to see them. She led them into the living room, a cozy space dominated by a huge television that was tuned to a soundless shopping channel. "I'll get Krystle," she said.

Jake's eyes were drawn to the television, where sparkling jewels, pots and pans, juicers and area rugs appeared in the hands or under the feet of female models, who used slow, drawn-out gestures, like chameleons, to accentuate the features of each piece.

"This is nice," Buddy said. He meant the décor. The little room was painted in a deep, orangey pink, and a small throw rug picked up that color in a modern floral design. Chocolate leather furniture, not overstuffed but stretched on visible wooden frames, accentuated the colors.

Jake shrugged. He never could find furniture interesting. "My mother-in-law is a designer," he said.

"Good taste," Buddy said. Jake shrugged again.

Krystle came in silently, appearing in such a quiet way it seemed as though she had always been there. She was barefoot, and stood on one foot with the other sweeping the floor, toe out, unconsciously like a dancer. Her hair was down, and she did not smile.

Jake got up to give her an awkward and silent hug. He then introduced her to Buddy, who stood up to offer his hand. "Can I get you something to drink?" she asked. "Ice tea? Water?"

Buddy was taken aback by how delicate she was; he would never have thought to put her together with Jake. While she went to bring him ice tea he complimented her to Jake, who looked stricken and dumb.

Reggie poked his head around the corner from the kitchen, but disappeared when Jake called him.

There was a smell of cooking food in the air. Jake had not given any thought to the time of day, but when Krystle came back with two tall, beading glasses of brown liquid, he asked her whether they were breaking into lunch. She said yes, and asked whether they would like to join them. "We have plenty. It's a casserole that Mom made."

They sat around the kitchen table, eating a chicken noodle casserole from thick crockery dishes with a pattern of pansies that had worn thin on their raised surfaces. Of course the food was better than anything Jake had eaten in the past month. Krystle's mother had tight black curls on her head and a yellow smock covering most of her torso. She apologized for the meal but kept offering them more. "It's terrible, isn't it?" Krystle's mother asked as she shoveled more onto Buddy's plate. A bowl of carrot nubbins was the only vegetable.

"So Jake, how have you been?" she asked, as though he had been away on vacation, as though her daughter's separation was an ordinary event. Gloom had descended on Jake once again; Krystle seemed impossibly distant, and Reggie seemed not even to know him. On impulse, Jake decided to go with the truth. "It's been rough," he said.

"Well, of course," Jean said. "With such terrible reports."

Jake did not lift his eyes from his plate, but he gave his head a little shake. "Not so much that, Jean," he said. "More that I have missed Krystle terribly." And Reggie, he said to himself.

He lifted his eyes toward her, but she had her face turned away. Jake dropped his eyes and a silence followed.

"Reggie! Sit in your chair!" Jean said sharply. Throughout the meal Reggie had been out of his seat more than in it; he hid behind his mother and spied on his father. He would not come when Jake invited him, and when Jake smiled at him he hid his face.

Buddy tried to take up the slack in the conversation by talking about his own son, Junior. At Reggie's age Junior had been so shy, Buddy said, he would hide under his bed when guests came to visit. "Imagine! You can probably see I'm not the shy type. I had the hardest time understanding him." Buddy did not mention—in fact he rarely thought of it—that he did not know exactly how to get in contact with Junior. He believed Junior lived in Portland. They had disagreed over money.

"He watches too much TV," Jean said, as though Reggie were not there to hear. "If he spent more time with other children, he wouldn't act like this." She made a face at Reggie, who ducked behind his mother.

"You're the one who has the TV on all day, Mom," Krystle said, the first time she had opened her mouth since they sat down at the table.

Buddy tried to steer the talk back to Jake. Looking directly at Krystle, who kept her face buried, he leaned forward and told her that he had come to make an apology. "You can imagine it's hard for me to say this, but I have to take responsibility for the trouble your husband got in. I put Kasha Gold up to filing a suit. I paid her legal bills, even though I knew she wasn't trustworthy. No, scratch that, I didn't know whether she was or wasn't, and I didn't care. I just wanted the mission to move. I told Jake today I'm really sorry for what he's suffered, and I want to say the same to you, Krystle. It was my fault."

Little sparks of tears jumped into Krystle's eyes. "You did that?" she asked. "You're the one?"

"He was trying to push us out by causing bad publicity," Jake said. "You might remember when I told you that he wanted to buy the mission property."

"I also sent the health department," Buddy said.

"You did that?" Jake asked. He was caught short; he had never guessed at the conspiracy at work against him.

Krystle's emotions had taken over. She looked at Buddy with a furious scowl, her face twisted with rage and her mouth set in a sob.

"Should I take Reggie away?" Krystle's mother asked.

Frightened by his mother's emotions, Reggie tried to leap into her arms. "Reggie, you come with me," Jean said, trying to pull him away. Rather than helping her, Krystle seized Reggie and enfolded him. "You're a bad man," she told Buddy while she held Reggie tightly. "A very bad man."

"Krystle!" her mother said. "What a thing to say to your guest!"

"I don't deny it," Buddy said as contritely as he knew how. "I've come to tell you I'm truly sorry, and to ask your forgiveness. I've lost my business, you know. I was desperate to make this deal happen, and now I'm stuck holding the pieces."

Reggie had lost control of his emotions. He was writhing and kicking in his mother's arms, throwing a tantrum. Krystle was preoccupied with calming him, but the tighter she held him, the more upset he became.

"He watches too much TV," Jean said. "He's never learned to manage his feelings."

Jake got out of his seat and walked around the table to Krystle. He held out his arms for Reggie. At first he was ignored, but he remained by Krystle's side, hands extended. Reggie looked at him, hesitating, and then launched himself into Jake's arms.

Jake held the tight bundle in a squeeze. It felt unbelievably good to him, his warm son in his arms. Until that moment he had found the whole interaction sad and hopeless, but now it seemed entirely worthwhile, if he could just hold his son. He would never let go, never.

Krystle was wailing. Krystle, ordinarily so cautious and so contained, had lost control. Her face was on the table, and she flailed her hands on it like a spastic drummer. The rest of them watched, aghast and unsure if something could be done. All the emotions she had tied down over the past weeks, the doubts and the bad feelings, her anger and her fear, came loose. They seemed to her like wild dogs running through her, baying. They frightened her but she had no idea how to stop them.

None of the rest of them understood what had set her off. The truth was, it had gone through her head with a flash what Jake had suffered, and she saw quite clearly that it was not really Buddy's fault so much as hers. Jake would have been able to bear the accusations if she had not left him. He was a strong man and she had made him weak. She had never before seen herself this way, as an agent. She had never, ever, seen herself as holding power. Now she recognized it. She had done something terrible.

Watching her, Jake was consumed with love. Her stubbornness had angered him, but he now saw it for what it was. She was trying to get a grip on life. He knew how that worked. He had used drugs for the same reason. Instead of anger, he felt pity, and his compassion almost overwhelmed him. He knelt before her. Releasing Reggie with one hand he reached out and took hers out of the air. "Krystle," he said, "will you come back with me? I can't survive without you. It's just impossible."

Impulsively, quicker than thought, she was in his arms. He kissed her head while she sobbed, and Reggie complained that they were squeezing him.

"I guess that means yes," Jean said, her face disapproving.

"I don't know," Krystle said, squeezing her voice out. "How can I face people who think you have done such terrible things? How can Reggie face it?"

"Oh, people say things," Buddy interjected confidently. "But they forget pretty quick. The things I've heard people say about me, they would scald your ears, but the next week those people are inviting me out for a drink. People's brains aren't always connected to their mouths. You just have to make up your mind to do what you want to do, and try to ignore them. It will go away sooner than you can imagine."

It took forever for Krystle to get ready. Her stuff and Reggie's were all over the house, and once the decision was made to go home she reverted to type. She could not be rushed; she had to fold everything carefully and make sure that nothing got left.

Jean kept reminding her that Jake could stay the night and they could go home tomorrow. But for Jake that was an absolute impossibility. He was as patient as he could possibly be while he waited for Krystle's packing, but absolutely, and authoritatively, he told Jean no every time she raised the possibility of staying. He had to get Krystle and Reggie in the car and on the road. He said an awkward goodbye to Buddy—a firm handshake and a pat on the shoulder from Buddy—and then entertained Reggie while they waited. Jake did not sit down. He stayed near the door.

When finally they were in the car and on their way he was drained. He had nothing to say; he was utterly content with silence as they meandered toward home. Twice he forgot where he was and missed his turn, but he didn't snap as he usually would; he just turned the car around and went back. Krystle was equally silent. Jake didn't know what she was thinking, and she didn't say.

It was she who broke the silence, after they left the bay and were traversing the wide tawny spaces toward Petaluma. The sky was huge there. The car was a tiny bug traversing a vast open field.

"Do you think Buddy was really sorry?" she asked.

Jake thought about it. "No, I guess I would say no. I think he wanted to patch things up. I think it bothered him that I got hurt, and he wanted to do something to fix that. But I never got the sense that he was really sorry for what he'd done."

"You don't think he was sincere?"

He had to think again. "Yes, as far as it went. He really was sorry that I was hurt. That bothered him. But I'm not sure he really gets it that he did anything wrong."

She put out a hand to touch his arm. It was her first real physical expression of warmth since she had jumped into his arms, and what he felt was intense. It wasn't all healed between them, he knew. She was coming home but it would be weeks while they walked on eggshells.

He wanted her to say that she was sorry, but he didn't know whether she ever would.

The heroin came into his mind. Maybe he should tell her about it, but he wasn't ready for that. It was too frightening, for both of them.

Preoccupied as he was by his own introspection, he did not notice that Krystle was crying again, silently. Only when her breath was jerked by a sob did he look over at her and see. He reached his hand across to touch her, and she did not jerk away.

"It'll be all right," he said, though he had no idea what. "It's over."

"I'm so sorry," she said, her voice clouded.

"Sorry for what?" he asked, and regretted saying it as soon as the words came out, for there was an audible edge to them. He was angry, still. Far down inside his soul was an injured, sad person who thought it would never be all right. He didn't want to just patch it over, but he was afraid that was the best they could do.

"I'm sorry for leaving you, and staying away even when you asked me to come home."

"I begged you," he said.

"You begged me. And I wouldn't listen. I felt so stuck. I couldn't get out of my mom's orbit. She just held me in." She took a deep breath and let out a sigh. "I'm really not that weak. I acted weak, but I don't have to be like that."

Neither of them said anything for several minutes. Jake's mind was working furiously but nothing came out of it.

"I'm really sorry, Jake." She wept again, making small snuffling noises. "I never thought you did anything, but I was so afraid of being tormented. I left you there to take it."

"I didn't take it very well." He added, "I thought I was losing you."

"No."

"You say no, but all we had to do was keep going in the same direction, which is the easiest thing in the world. Funny that it took a man like Buddy to turn us around."

Jake kept looking over at her, as though he thought she might disappear. "So much happens because we bump into things," he continued. "I got into drugs because of a torn muscle. You met me because you had to get away from your mom. The guys who show up at the mission, they've been bumped a hundred times."

"I got bumped by Holly. At the park."

"And we both got bumped by a man who wanted everybody to be happy despite what he had done to them."

"That was a good bump," Krystle said. "A bump in the right direction."

37

Happy Hour

✧

Amy Bourgay bumped into Adam McLeod at the Chops happy hour. This was not by accident, Amy only contrived to make it seem like it. She had asked the sheriff if he knew where Adam went after hours, and the sheriff said that Adam often drank a beer at Chops after he left his office.

"Who is he with?" she asked.

"Nobody," the sheriff said. "He's a loner."

She reminded him that this was a private matter, and he said of course it was.

Amy walked into Chops at 5:30 and Adam was already there, at the bar, alone as predicted. That was how she wanted it.

"Hello," he said. "I don't think I've ever seen you here. I thought you worked late every night."

"This is work," she said. "I wanted to talk to you."

"Wonderful," he said. "Can I buy you a drink?"

"I don't drink when I'm working," she said.

"All right," he said. "How can I help you?"

"I heard that you dropped the suit," she said. "Why did you do that?"

He looked at her with a trace of amusement on his lips. "My client lost interest and didn't want to pay the bills."

"Who's your client? And don't say Kasha Gold, because I know she couldn't pay any bills."

"I can't divulge that information, as I'm sure you know, don't you Amy? Also, I would encourage you with one of my basic principles of the law: never assume you know whether or not people have money."

"I'm not assuming," she said.

He gave a small chortle. "All right. No it was not Kasha, it was somebody who was interested in Kasha's situation. He had an interest in justice being done, just like you."

"And now he doesn't?"

"Yes, of course, but his business situation changed and he couldn't continue."

"That's all you're going to tell me?"

Adam smiled. "What else do you want to know?"

Amy's face grew hard. She had strong smile lines around her mouth and eyes, which gave her a pleasant expression. When you looked closely at her face, however, you saw that the smile gave a mistaken impression. Nothing really moved. She was all business.

"What I really want to know is why you put me up to this. I went out on a limb. I announced an investigation."

"And?"

"You knew there wasn't anything there. Now I'm left holding an empty briefcase."

Adam pursed his lips and considered whether he ought to explain the situation clearly to the DA. He decided that he should. "Amy, there is nothing in the briefcase, you're right about that. But I can't see that it should matter to you. Surely you know how to tell the world that you did an investigation, that the details are private to protect the parties involved, but that you found no grounds for prosecution.

"Furthermore!" Adam raised one finger and smiled. "You may be holding an empty briefcase, but from the point of view of your loyal constituents it looks quite full. All they know is that you took the initiative to investigate whether the police had allowed a woman to be abused. You showed concern. You are on the side of angels, liberals and feminists. In this county, how could it be any better for you?"

Amy gave a scowl. She always felt that she and Adam understood each other, but she disliked his occasional grandstanding. "What about the woman?"

"You mean, will Kasha pursue this and make your life miserable? I don't think anybody can be completely sure what Kasha will do, but I don't believe you need to lie awake thinking of her. She has already moved on to other concerns. If you don't bring it up, I don't think she will. And if she does, she tends to undermine herself. I don't believe any complaint she might bring will go far."

Amy waved away the bartender, who had come to inquire whether she wanted anything. "What about Buddy Grace?" she asked.

"What about him?"

"You work with him, don't you?"

"I did. That's a matter of public record."

"What's happened to him?"

"Oh, Amy, you want to know too much. Buddy has gone to Arizona."

"Things didn't work out for him?"

"Not really. Not this time. But don't worry, Buddy always bounces back."

"I'm sure you're right," Amy said.

38

Graduation

✧

Elvis Sebastiano was extraordinarily nervous the morning of his graduation from the mission. The pieces of his life were due to come together, like the arms of a spiral galaxy finding their center. At least so he felt it, as we all do: that our lives are celestial and that at moments we see how grand.

The trouble was that he had no control. He felt like the impresario of a magnificent production who has his hands tied and his phone confiscated. He so wanted everything to shine, but had no power to make it so.

The significance of this graduation was a first for him. He had attended his high school ceremonies without any sense of genuine accomplishment, mainly because he had none. His tutors kept him playing football and baseball, doing whatever schoolwork got done under his name—homework and papers, not tests, which he regularly failed. The principal knew all about it but evidently decided it was enough. He wanted Elvis to finish and be gone. Elvis got rip-roaring drunk the night before the ceremony and almost killed himself driving home. He overslept the mandatory afternoon rehearsal and smoked dope just before the ceremony. His memories of that night were anything but triumphant.

This graduation was a different thing. He had come into the program a clown, doing his frantic best to misdirect people's attention from his incapacities. He never thought he would make it through to the end. He didn't, the first time. The second time he said the right things about his determination, but the ten months—and then eleven when he was penalized for missing church—hung over him like an avalanche about to come down. But one day passed and the rocks did not fall, and then another and another. Somehow he had made it to this day.

His daughter Amber was due to attend the ceremony, driving down from Fort Bragg with his brother and his 92-year-old grandma. At 11:00 his brother called to ask who else would be there. "Nobody," Elvis said, hoping it wasn't true. "You're the only family I've got."

His brother was not so easily fooled. "So no Angel?" he asked. He had quarreled with Angel over Amber's care months back, and nothing had been squared.

"Angel has to work," Elvis said, which was true as far as he knew. He had called to invite her, and she had been non-committal. He and Angel carried on in limbo, unsure of their ultimate destination. He wanted her to come, but he had lost any right to tell her so. Their relationship was bruised, needing air to heal, if it ever could.

"I'm not coming if Angel is coming," his brother said.

"I told you she has to work."

"Guaranteed?"

"Guaranteed."

His brother hung up and Elvis resisted the urge to call Angel. Instead he dialed up Rudy, his friend with the limo service. They had gone to high school together, and when Rudy started his business Elvis had urged him to get a stretch Humvee, something no other limo service offered. It had been good advice. Rudy now owned eight cars and had offered one of them for the graduation. Almost everybody who would attend lived at the mission, but half a dozen men would be working at the thrift store until just before the ceremony, and needed a ride over. Elvis envisioned them pulling up in a stretch Humvee.

Rudy didn't answer his phone. He had a complicated phone tree that raised Elvis's ire as he punched one for English, then (after listening to a substantial menu) five to leave a message. "Hey, Rudy, I hope you are listening to these messages today. This is Elvis. Press one if you remember that I'm graduating today. I'm just reminding you that you offered to send a stretch Humvee. If that offer is still good press 2 and call me back. There's a bunch of guys at the thrift store that need a ride down here, and it would be great if you could bring them. You'd need to pick them up at about 1:30, and I need to let them know if you are coming. So let me know, wouldja buddy? Thanks."

Then he had nothing else to do. He was standing on the sidewalk in front of the mission, his phone in his hand, wanting desperately to get on with it, to leap across the hours to the graduation. He wanted to commandeer all the participants, bring them all together to this place, and create a spirit of understanding between them. But he could do nothing. He could only wait. Elvis checked his rear pocket to see that he still had the piece of paper on which he had written his essay. He momentarily considered going over his Bible verses one more time, but discarded the idea. He knew them. He was ready. The day had come, and he could only wait and watch as the sun stealthily cut its way through the sky.

His phone rang, and he jumped on it. It was his brother.

"I'm not gonna make it," he said. "I just found out that the plumber is coming and I need to be here to let him in."

"Nobody else knows how to let him in?"

"Francine has plans in town. It's just me."

"What about Amber?"

"What about her?"

"Well, you were going to bring her. And Grams."

"You really think that's a good idea?"

"Well, yeah, why wouldn't it be?"

"Amber is in school. And it's a long drive for Grams."

"We talked that over a long time ago, and they wanted to come. They were depending on you to bring them."

"Well, sorry Elvis, it's not going to happen."

Elvis hung up before he said anything he would regret. He might have known. His brother could be such a jerk. He shouldn't have counted on him. He had imagined how it would be, his grandma and his daughter present to witness this day, his grams who had always believed in him even when she shouldn't, and Amber who wanted to believe in him and needed to believe in him because she had been shut out of so much else. He should have known.

Elvis never heard back from Rudy, so had to ask Jake to send the mission van to gather men from the thrift store. It was a disappointment, but only for Elvis. He'd mentioned the limo to a handful of men, and none of them had really believed him.

He did get his cousin Rafe to bring Amber and his grandmother from Fort Bragg, and he was especially pleased to hear that his uncle Noonan had tagged along. He had four family members, then. He called Angel to say that his brother was not coming, in case it made any difference, but she said she didn't think she was up to it.

Elvis was standing on the curb when Rafe pulled up, and for just a panicked moment he didn't see Amber. She got out of the back seat on the street side and stretched like a cat, a skinny, fresh kid with a wise-guy look on her face. "Hey you," he said, and went to gather her into his arms. He didn't say anything more because he couldn't; his throat was full of cotton. Amber shook off his arms as soon as she could.

"I couldn't stand another minute of that car," she said.

"Why? You weren't crowded, were you?"

She shook her head impatiently, so her hair flopped into her face. "The talking, Dad. Do you people even listen to yourselves?"

"Hey, that's your grandmother, your uncle and your cousin. You're lucky they let you ride with them at all."

But she wasn't listening to him; she had already fallen away into her private world. He didn't care, he was just happy. He went around to help his grandma get out. She was cross from the ride too. He told her thanks for coming, and she answered in her no-nonsense voice that it was a long trip and she didn't know if she could go such long distances any more.

"Come on inside," he said. "This is the mission. I've been living here for the last eleven months, can you believe that?"

"It looks like crap."

"Come inside," he said. "Rafe, Noonan, come on inside and I'll show you around."

That did not take long. He did not take them upstairs to the sleeping quarters; they toured through the kitchen and dining area, then through the yard to see the free weights and the bicycles, and finally the classroom stuffed with tables of aging donated computer equipment. He saw it with their eyes: depleted, exhausted, worn. They ended in the chapel, where he suggested they sit down. His grandma sank down in a plastic chair as though the tour had worn her out. She looked thin. Her skin had the texture of dried rose petals, no stronger than tissue paper. Amber took the seat next to her, with a face that dared him to say something positive.

It was still early, and the only people in the chapel were the musicians setting up. Their test notes hummed through the air. Elvis took a seat next to his family members and felt, again, an acute nervousness. He had to go through this ordeal. He could do nothing to hasten it, and waiting was torment. He got to his feet again. "I'm going to find Jeff," he said. "He's been my buddy all through this. He promised to come, and I want to introduce him to you."

Jeff Digitale had graduated a week before. Elvis would have liked to finish together but there was no way he could ask Jeff to put off his launch. Jeff had a room with a family from his church; he had a job in a body shop that promised to pay good money. Elvis thought of him every day, missing him. He himself was going to stay at the mission for at least a week before going into the transition house; his construction job paid minimum wage and he had been handing most of his paycheck to Angel, to help with her father's medical expenses. He had no money for a deposit and no prospect of finding a place, though he had put out word to his church. In practical ways his life was not going to change at graduation. He would still live in the mission, and eat at the mission.

He did a complete circuit of the building without finding Jeff. The program guys looked right through him, as though this were any other day, which for them, he realized, it was. He found Jeff on his second time through the dining room. He was happily slathering peanut butter on a bagel. His lank, dark hair fell into his eyes.

"That stuff will put the pounds on you," Elvis said. "When did you get here? C'mon, I want you to meet my grandma."

"Let me finish this," Jeff said. "Sit down. How are you? You ready?"

Elvis made himself slow down and take a chair. "Yeah, I'm ready. I just want to get it done."

Jeff had shoved the bagel toward his mouth and his teeth were mudded with peanut butter. "Yeah, I remember feeling that way, and then it's over and you feel like nothing ever happened. Are you going to go somewhere with your family?"

"I don't know. Maybe we'll go out to eat. You want to come?"

Jeff said he had to get back to work, because that was where his ride home would catch him. He didn't have a car yet. That would take a few weeks.

Jeff acted like a real gentleman with Elvis's family. He shook hands with everybody, even Amber who didn't know what to do but hung her hand out as though she were crippled. By now the guys were beginning to filter into the chapel, and Elvis signaled a couple of them over to meet his family. It was friendly, though there was not much to say beyond "Congratulations." Jake came over and met everybody. He told them he was proud of Elvis and he hoped they were too, because he would need their support.

After the singing died away and the musicians moved offstage, Jake called Elvis up. He stood in the center of the floor and launched into his Bible verses without introduction, rattling through them with minimal difficulties. Then he pulled his essay out of his rear pocket, carefully unfolding the lined school paper and raising his head to scan his audience. That was when he saw Santiago, sitting in the very back corner of the chapel. He had materialized like an apparition, his unlined face shining impassively, a Buddha. "Oh, man," Elvis said, and went to engulf him in a giant embrace. "Where have you been?" Elvis asked rhetorically, and then hugged him again.

Seeing Santiago rattled him, so he had difficulty refocusing when he got back to the center and held everyone's attention again. Santiago illuminated the moment, casting a ray of light from the past. Had that been his lowest moment, when he left here for the fracking?

Reading from his script, Elvis called out his family members and read his thanks to the program, to his mentor and his sponsor and his coach, to Jake and Knox and friends like Jeff who had cheered him on, and to Jesus Christ who had rescued him from darkness and given him a new life. Then he deviated from his paper to address the men still struggling through.

"Look, I know how you guys feel," Elvis said. "Because I've been sitting in your chair for how many months? Not just the ten months, but an extra month added on because I quit going to church, and then before that, four months the first time before I flunked out. I feel like I went to a million graduations and phase-ups, and I always looked at the guy moving on and thought, I'll never do that. I will never make it.

"You guys saw me hugging Santiago a minute ago? I guess hardly any of you know who Santiago is, because he left the program, what, a year ago? I left with him. We had a little bunch of guys who thought we had learned everything and we didn't need to go through the rest. We already had it down, you know? And being here is so hard, you want to believe that you're done. You talk yourself into it. We were so sure of ourselves, right Jake? You remember?"

Jake nodded.

"There was me and Santiago—I don't know what's happened to you, man—and there was CJ who last I heard was using again, and there was Sam, little Sam, who died."

He had not intended to mention Sam, his mouth had carried him there and without warning he found himself unable to say another word because Sam's face had come into his memory.

"He OD'd," Elvis managed to choke out when he was able. "He's gone. I'm not gonna forget him. He died, I'm alive."

He paused to gather himself, staring at his paper to get his bearings, but discovering that those written words made no sense to him.

"I'm here to testify that this place is hard but it's a good kind of hardness. When you think you can't stand another day, you can. You have to keep going. You can finish. If I can finish, you can finish. But you can't jump over anything. You have to go through it, one day at a time, with God's help."

Suddenly he knew he was done. It didn't matter what else he had written. He stopped and got down on one knee. Jeff came forward to pin him, just as he had pinned Jeff a week ago, and then he was surrounded by men laying hands on him, hands gripping his shoulder and his arm and even resting heavily on top of his head. There were prayers; he understood none of them.

When it was done he went to stand with his family members. They congratulated him and said it was a good service, they were glad they had come, but he could see from their eyes they didn't really understand. This isn't their world, Elvis thought. His grandma was tired and ready to go home. Noonan looked at his watch and asked if there were any plans for dinner. When Elvis looked blank he reckoned they would stop on their way home.

Jake appeared and they squeezed each other, then held back at arm's length to gaze. Something indefinable had changed in Jake, Elvis thought. He bristled with energy, an oversized porcupine. It was the way Jake had appeared to Elvis when he first joined the program. He was back to the way he was supposed to be.

"That was good," Jake said, nodding as he spoke. "What you said was good."

"It just came out. After I saw Santiago. He brought back all those memories, good and bad."

"You inspired me, man. You were preaching to me, too. I'm a graduate of this program too, you know. It never stops. You can't ever think you're done. That's not just when you're in the program, it's afterwards too. You inspired me."

Elvis could hardly believe that Jake was talking to him that way. He thought, I guess I really have graduated.

"Hey, where did Santiago come from?" Elvis asked. " He's not back in the program, is he?"

"No. He just showed up. I was as surprised to see him as you were. I tried to find him afterwards, but he had already vanished."

"Hope he's okay," Elvis said.

Acknowledgements

I rely heavily on friends to read my prose-in-progress and tell me where it needs improvement. I want to particularly thank Popie, my wife and best reader. My children, Katie, Chase and Silas, have also read very helpfully, as has my daughter-in-law Helen. My writing group, Robert Digitale, Paul Gullixson, and Dean Anderson, labored through early drafts, as did Dean's wife Mindy. They are all very helpful critics who have come to my aid many times. Philip Yancey, Fred Prudek, Mike and Joyce Fargo, Mandy Bankson, Harold Fickett, Scott Bolinder, and Janet Grant read through versions of *Those Who Hope* and offered many helpful suggestions—as well as much-needed encouragement.

Made in the USA
San Bernardino, CA
22 November 2017